saving forever

by jasinda wilder

*To Emma,
Believe in forever
♡ Jasinda Wilder*

SAVING FOREVER

ISBN: 978-1-941098-05-9
Copyright © 2014 by Jasinda Wilder

Cover art by Sarah Hansen of Okay Creations. Cover art © 2014 by Sarah Hansen.
Interior book design by Indie Author Services.

For Linda, who never woke up,
and for those who wait and watch and love.

part one

the girl on the beach

Carter

I dove into the water, slicing neatly into the cold blue. Four long frog-kick strokes under the surface, and then I came up and took a deep breath. My muscles immediately settled into a steady crawl stroke, carrying me toward the peninsula mainland. I had a small waterproof scuba diving bag on my back, holding the essentials: wallet, keys, phone, a T-shirt, flip-flops. I kept a steady pace until I felt my feet brush the sandy bottom, and then I stood up, flinging my hair back and smoothing it down. I trudged ashore, breathing hard, muscles trembling.

This early in the morning my beach was empty. It wasn't really technically *my beach,* since I didn't own it, but I thought of it as mine all the same. Very few people came here, not this far north on the peninsula. It was a secluded spot, a good twenty-plus miles away from the bustle of downtown Traverse City, and it was out of the way even for the constant flow of winery traffic on the peninsula itself. It suited me. I could stock my truck with a towel and a change of clothes, lock it, leave it parked nearby at the post office, and swim out to the island that was my home. I had a boat, of course, but I preferred to swim when the weather allowed.

I scrubbed my hand over my wet hair, sluicing water down my chest and back, and then stretched, yawning and squeezing my eyes closed, rolling the tension out of my shoulders. When I came out of the stretch, I saw her.

Five-eight. Long blonde hair with dark roots. A body that made my mouth go dry. Curvy, solid, luxurious expanses of flesh. She wore a pair of cut-off jean shorts and an orange bikini top. God in heaven, who *was* she? I'd never seen her before. There was no way on earth I could ever forget seeing this girl. She was, without a doubt, the most gorgeous creature I'd ever seen.

I stood, frozen, thigh deep in the water. Staring. Blatantly. I needed to know her name. I needed to hear the sound of her voice. She'd have a voice like music, to match the symphony that was her body. The need to move closer was an automatic response.

My feet carried me through the water, toward the girl.

She was sitting on the beach about thirty feet away from me. A towel was spread beneath her, and she had her nose buried in a book. I couldn't make out the title, but it didn't matter. My attention was on *her*. On the way her hair fell in a loose braid over her bare shoulder. On her arm, the way it flexed as she scratched her knee. She looked up from her book and saw me. Our eyes met for the briefest of instants. In that moment, something inside me shivered and burned. And then she looked back at her book. Almost too quickly. Too intently.

I walked straight past the girl. Why? Why couldn't I get myself to talk? I couldn't make my body stop. It had been almost a year now. I should be over what had happened. But I wasn't. Obviously. I couldn't even get a simple "hello" past my lips.

My feet carried me to my truck, and I didn't look back. I wanted to look back. I *needed* to. Her skin had been fair, flawless, looking satin-smooth and needing touch. My touch. I dug my keys from the dry-bag, unlocked my restored red-and-white two-tone 1968 Ford F-150. I toweled myself off and drove to the winery, thinking about her. About the expression on her face. It had been...tortured. Conflicted. As if the beach itself held as much pain as it did promise. That was a ridiculous, nonsensical thought. I couldn't possibly know that about her. But it was what I'd seen when I looked at her. And it made me want to know her even more. What could have caused her such pain? How could a beach cause such conflicted emotion?

I needed to push her from my thoughts while I got to work and tended to the grapes. I couldn't afford thoughts of a girl. Not now. This would be our best harvest yet, and we had to keep focused. My brothers and I had to get this winery turning a profit if we were going to make it up here.

Yet, as I worked in the vineyard, pruning and weeding and trimming and tying, my thoughts kept returning to the girl on the beach. To the heavy weight of her breasts held up by the orange fabric, which almost hadn't been equal to the task. She'd almost spilled out of the top, and that overflow of flesh kept cropping up in my brain. As did her long legs, shining with sunscreen and flexing with thick muscle. Her eyes, god, I'd only gotten a fragmentary glimpse of her eyes, but I thought they might be green. Deep jade green. Those eyes had held, in that momentary meeting, so many things. Curiosity, intelligence. Vibrancy. Pain. God, such pain.

I wondered if I'd see her again. I hoped I would, feared I would.

After a long day in the vineyard, I finally trudged slowly into the office. I hated the office and only went in when I had to. I twisted the knob to Kirk's office, pushed the door open, but it stuck, again. I kicked it free, and then swung it open and closed it a few times, realizing the door itself was warped and the frame was swollen. Unfortunately, my brother Kirk had several projects waiting for me.

"That damn door is a pain in my ass, Carter." Kirk spoke without looking away from the screen of the computer. "Think you can fix it for me?" He glanced at me, assessing my reaction. I nodded. "Good. That's project number one. Shouldn't be too hard. Ready for number two?" Kirk, like me, was tall, with black hair and pale blue eyes, but with more aquiline features. He was thicker through the chest than I was, and a few inches shorter.

I lifted an eyebrow at him as I took a seat facing his desk.

"I was in Arizona last week, right? I toured some vineyards in the Sedona area, just to see how they do things. And they had these tables in their tasting room made from old barrels. They just fixed some glass tops to the empty barrels, and that was it, but it looked cool as hell. We've got at least a dozen old unusable casks left over from when we bought this place, and I was thinking you could make us some tables for our tasting room. What do you think?"

I sat back and pictured what he was describing. Wine barrels were made from oak, and after a batch of wine was transferred out of a barrel, the sugars and the tannins left stains behind. Most wineries toast the inside of the barrel and reuse it. Some will do this several times, but eventually the barrel becomes unusable. At that point, the barrels can be sold off for reclamation and recycling. Wine barrel furniture was a huge fad, especially in areas where wineries and vineyards were common. I could easily make the tables he wanted in an afternoon or two, but I'd need the glass tops first.

Kirk, Max, Tom, and I had bought this vineyard three years ago, as well as two plots to the south. There had been a working winery here at one point, but it had gone bankrupt and we'd had to replant thirty acres of Riesling grapes, in addition to the additional forty acres we'd planted from scratch. The last three years had been spent cultivating the grapes to the point where they could be used to make wine, replacing the out-of-date vintner equipment, and building a brand-new tasting room. We were working out of the sixty-year-old building that had come with the land until the new premises were complete, but the building felt every single minute of its age. Every door was warped. The floors were either faded and cracked laminate or buckling, scratched hardwoods. The roof leaked, the windows were drafty, and the bathrooms and kitchen were hopelessly out of date. We'd considered trying to remodel the place, but had decided it was futile. In the meantime, I was splitting my time between taking care of the vines and keeping the old office building from falling down around our ears. I was managing the construction of the new place as well, and whatever other projects needed doing. So far, I'd replaced most of the doors, half of the window frames, three rooms' worth of flooring, and that was just what was needed to keep the place intact.

Of the four of us, I was the carpenter and handyman. I'd started out at fourteen working for my uncle's house-building company, and had gotten my finish carpenter certification by the time I was nineteen. I'd spent the next four years working my way up in the company until, at twenty-three, I was Uncle Mike's second-in-command. That was when Kirk and Max had come to me with their idea of buying a bank-owned winery. Max was the vintner in the family, and he'd learned the craft of wine-making in heart of wine country, Napa Valley.

Max was the oldest—four years my senior at thirty-one. Kirk, the second oldest, was the businessman and numbers guy. I was the builder and carpenter, third in line at twenty-seven. Tom was the youngest at twenty-five, and he didn't have a specific skill-set yet, but he was energetic and personable, and would probably end up being the face of the company, the spokesman and marketer.

Kirk cleared his throat, reminding me that I'd been spacing out. I gave him a thumbs up, and he slapped the desk. "Great. Those tables are no rush, obviously, since we won't have anywhere to pour wine for a few months yet, but make 'em look badass. The last thing is the bar. Max and I were thinking the bar itself should be the centerpiece of the whole tasting room. We want it to be sexy, right? Something big and masculine and handmade. You're the carpenter, so I'll leave the design to you, but I emailed you some ideas to start you off. Sound good?"

I nodded and stood up, pulling my phone from my pocket and bringing up Kirk's email.

"Hey, Carter, hold up." I stopped, hearing a curious note in my brother's voice. "It's less than month until August, and I was just…I know it's been a rough year for you. And I guess I wanted to know how you're doing. If you're…feeling better…about things."

I knew what he meant. And I knew how hard it was for my brother to come right out and ask me about it. But I didn't have an answer for him. I just met his gaze, trying for his sake to summon some words. Nothing came. Eventually I just sighed and shook my head, then turned and left.

I heard his voice ring out as I closed the door behind me. I turned back, watched him rub his forehead with a knuckle. "It's been a year, Carter. You gotta get better. We need you here, bro. We need you at a hundred percent." His voice was resigned, weary, concerned.

I wished I could tell him I was doing my best. I wished I could tell him anything. But I couldn't. I turned away without answering, hearing his sigh of frustration. I got my tools from my truck, measured the doorframe, made some notations, and then spent the next few hours in my workshop making a new door for Kirk's office. I ended up having to replace the frame as the well as the door itself, so it was after eight at night before I left the winery.

I took the long way home. I parked in my spot at the post office, locked my truck, shouldered my dry-bag, and circled the block on foot. I wasn't ready to go home. It was quiet, and empty. Lonely. Once I swam home to the island, there'd be nothing to do but kill time until I was tired enough to sleep.

So I walked around the block, hoping for a distraction. I was nearly back to the beach when I heard music. It came from one of the cottages facing the beach. That particular cottage had been empty for years. I knew that because I'd thought about buying it when I'd first moved up here and needed somewhere to live that wasn't the winery. It wasn't for sale, I'd been told. I ended up finding the island, which was perfect in so many ways.

Now there were lights on in the cottage, and the windows were open. The front door was ajar, with only the screen door in place. I slowed my steps as I got closer, and then came to a stop.

It was a cello, being played by a consummate professional. I recognized the skill because Britt had been a classical music freak. She'd dragged me to endless concerts, symphonies at the DSO, in San Francisco and Boston and New York. Her favorite was the London Philharmonic, and she'd brought me half a dozen times. I'd never understood it, really. There were no words—nothing concrete I could grasp onto. Just the music, and it never quite captured my imagination. The only time I'd really enjoyed a show was when we'd seen Yo-Yo Ma with…I couldn't remember which orchestra. I do remember being captivated by the way he'd played the cello. I'd kept wishing the stupid symphony would shut up so I could hear him play by himself.

What I was hearing right now sounded like that. A single cello, low notes wavering in the sunset glow. I edged closer to the screen door and peered in.

It was her. The girl from the beach. Facing me, the cello between her knees, her arm sliding back and forth, the bow shifting angles ever so slightly. Her fingers moved in a hypnotic rhythm on the strings, flying with dizzy speed and precision.

The music she played was…mournful. Aching. She played a soundtrack of pain and loneliness. Her eyes were closed. I was maybe six feet away from her, but she didn't see me, didn't hear me. I watched through the screen door, riveted. God, this close, she was even lovelier than I'd imagined. But the pain on her face…it was heartbreaking. The way she played, the way her expression shifted with each note, growing more and more twisted and near tears, it made my soul hurt for her. Just watching her made me want to throw the screen door open and wrap her up in my arms, making everything okay. I didn't dare breathe for fear of disrupting her. I knew I was being a creeper, watching her unbeknownst like this, but I couldn't move away. Not while she continued to play.

Jesus, the music. It was thick, almost liquid. I closed my eyes and listened, and I could almost see each note. The low notes, deep and strong and male, were like golden-brown ribbons of dark sunlit gold streaming past me. The middle tones were almost amber, like sap sliding down a pine trunk. The high notes were the color of dust motes caught in the rays of an afternoon sun. The notes and the colors twisted together, shifting, coruscating and tangling, and I saw them together, shades of sorrow melding.

She let the music fade, and I opened my eyes, watching her. She hung her head, the bow tip trailing on the carpet at her right foot. Her shoulders shook, and her loose and tangled hair wavered as she cried. God, I wanted to go to her. Comfort her.

But I couldn't. My feet were frozen and my voice was locked. As I watched, she visibly tensed, muscles straining, and she straightened; her shoulders lifted and her head rose and the quiet tears ceased. Her eyes were still closed, but her cheeks were tear-stained. They needed to be kissed clean, the tears wiped away. Such perfect porcelain shouldn't be tear-stained.

The way she pulled herself together was awe-inspiring. She was clearly fighting demons, and refused to give in. Refused to let them take hold. I pivoted away from the door as she took a deep breath and clutched her bow. I waited, my back to the wall beside the door, and then, with a falter, the strains of the cello began again, slow and sweet, speaking of better times to come.

I forced my feet to come uprooted, forced them to carry me past her door. To the beach. Into the water. I tugged my shirt off and stuffed it, along with my keys, phone, and wallet, into the dry bag, cinched it tight on my shoulders. Strode out into the cool, lapping water, kicking the moon-silvered waves until I was chest deep and then dove in. I set a punishing pace. I'd be exhausted by the time I got to my island, but that was what I wanted. I needed the tiredness, the brain-numbing limpness of exhaustion. It kept the memories from coming back. Let me almost sleep without nightmares. Almost.

I swam the two and a half miles in record time. I could barely drag myself onto the dock by the time I got there, but my mind was still racing a million miles a second. This time, thank god, it was with thoughts of the girl. The cellist. I kept seeing the sadness in her expression, the loneliness. The pain and the fear.

What was it, I wondered, that could bring that kind of searing pain to such a sweet and perfect beauty? I needed to know. But I might never find out if I couldn't get myself to talk to her.

Or to talk at all.

It had been eleven months since I'd spoken a single word. But for *her*, I might find the courage to simply say hello.

the sculpture

I didn't see her on the beach again for a few days. It'd be a lie to say I wasn't looking for her on the beach, but that itself was a cop-out, since I knew where she lived. But I couldn't tell *her* that. If I just showed up at her door, I'd seem like a stalker. Especially since I'd probably just end up standing there, flapping my mouth open and closed like a fish out of water, unable to speak. So I swam from island to shore in the morning and looked for her on the beach, and I swam from shore to island at night and looked for her on the beach. I never went by her house, refusing to let myself go around the block again. There was no point. No matter how much part of me might have liked the way she looked, there was no way I could handle actual interaction with her.

I'd never been particularly talkative. I'd always been far more comfortable with a tool in my hand and wood on the table than interacting with people. Britt had found a way through my shyness, but it had taken her months to do so. And even then, when she'd gotten me to ask her out and we'd started dating, I'd never been the kind to just blurt out whatever was in my head. She used to joke that most days she could count the number of words I spoke on the fingers of both hands, and that wasn't far from the truth.

I'd spent a long hot day spent in the workshop, roughing out the basic shape of the bar. Kirk and Max wanted something big and badass and hand-made, and that's what I would deliver. I'd hauled several huge lengths of oak into the shop, what amounted to thirty feet of solid oak. The idea I had was three separate sections making a U-shaped bar, each of the three sections hand-carved from a solid piece of oak. Each side would look different, but it would all tie together somehow. I didn't have any particular designs in mind, but that was just how I worked. I started with an idea and let the wood tell me what it needed to be. I was days away from any kind of actual design work yet, though. For now, I had to get the giant logs into some kind of shape that I could work with.

By the end of the day I was exhausted, covered in sawdust, dripping sweat, and looking forward to a slow and leisurely swim home. I parked my truck, stripped down to the swim shorts I wore under my jeans, stuffed my things in the bag. I was lost in thoughts of the bar, of what I'd have to do the next day, so I wasn't paying attention to the beach.

I nearly tripped over her. She was lying on her back, hands folded on her stomach, huge black sunglasses covering face, wearing a purple one-piece swimsuit. She had a book lying face-down next to her head on the beach blanket and a bottle of water on the other side. I froze as soon as I saw her, my bare foot scuffing, kicking sand onto her blanket and against her thigh.

She tipped up her sunglasses, and her jade gaze pinned me in place. I should apologize. I formed the words in my head, spoke them aloud in my mind. *I'm sorry.* But nothing came out. My mouth opened, but I couldn't make any sounds emerge. Stupidly, I just stared down at her, blinking, stunned by the vibrant shade of the green of her eyes. She seemed to be waiting, lying there staring up at me, sunglasses on her forehead, a faint frown pinching her brow and pale pink lips.

I clenched my fists, shook my head, and trotted into the water, diving in without hesitation. I stayed under as long as I could, kicking hard and pulling at the water, not surfacing until I was past Mr. Simmons' rarely used Sunfish sailboat, anchored a good hundred feet or more from shore. I cast one brief glance back at the shore, saw her standing at the water's edge, a hand shading her eyes. Looking for me?

Embarrassment at my caveman behavior shot through me, and I did a few crawl strokes, and then dove back under, gasping a deep breath and kicking beneath the surface until my lungs burned. I surfaced, ventilated, then oriented myself by looking for the arms of the peninsula and the mainland. Then I dove back under. The next time I surfaced, the beach was a faint line behind me and she was out of sight. I was panting and my arms shook, and I had to roll onto my back to catch my breath. I kept kicking, kept moving homeward, thinking of her. Those eyes. What had she been thinking? Her expression hadn't given anything away, except maybe curiosity. But how could she not be curious? I'd just stood there like a buffoon, after kicking sand on her. That swimsuit. God. It was a one-piece, but it was the kind that hugged tight in all the right places, cut high around her hips and low between her breasts, with little cut-outs at her sides.

I rolled over to my stomach and kicked into an easy crawl, pushing images of blonde hair and green eyes and fair skin out of my head. By the time I got home, I had to pull myself onto the dock, trembling and weak, and I nearly fell asleep there with the late-evening summer sun warming my skin.

I made myself get up and go inside. I showered off the lake water, then went out to my workshop. I didn't have the energy to work that night, but I made myself go out and look at it. The Sculpture. Her. Britt, in that last moment. I stood in front of it, staring at the lines, at her hands clutched into fists. I'd started there, with her hands. The way she'd held them in front of herself, the way they'd trembled. As if holding on, so desperately. On the sculpture, her face was blank. I couldn't bear to carve the expression that had been on her face that day. Not yet anyway. I could see it, though. I could feel the chisel scraping the wood shavings away from her eyes, from her mouth. I was nearly done. I had to finish her legs and feet, and then I'd have to start on her face. Maybe once I finished, I'd find the strength to speak again.

I left her there--—the carving of Britt. Even with her unfinished face, I could feel her staring up at me. The way she'd stared up at me that night. I turned off the light and closed the door to my shop, drank a beer and watched TV until I felt sleepy enough to go to bed.

A week later the girl was there, on the beach, just past dawn. This time, she was dressed in running gear, and even from fifty feet off shore I could tell she'd been running hard. She was bent over at the waist, hands on her knees, panting, ponytail hanging down by her face. I made my way slowly up to the beach, kicking the water louder than necessary so she'd know I was there. She heard me, straightened, hands on her hips.

Jesus, those hips. I brushed my hair back, stopped ten feet away from her, the water lapping at my calves. She was glistening with sweat, and each deep, gasping breath stretched the white material of her sports bra. I forced my eyes to hers, and again she kept her expression carefully neutral. But I could see the pain in her face. Not physical pain. Something deeper than that. The same pain that had informed the way she'd played the cello that night.

I moved past her, waving once, giving her a polite smile this time. It was something. It was communication. Almost.

Once I arrived at the winery, I helped the guys tend to the vines for a few hours, then went into the workshop and finished the rough shapes of the bar pieces. She was on my mind all that day as I worked, the careful neutrality of her expression, as if that vulnerability I'd seen the first time we'd met had been an accident, something she hadn't meant to let me see. I kept pushing her out of my mind, and she kept working her way back in. As I ran the hand-held planer across the oak, I wondered if she was waiting for me to speak, or did she think I was a mute, or just rude. I wondered what her story was, why she was here, appearing so suddenly. Maybe it was just vacation, a couple weeks in June spent alone on a remote beach.

Most of all, I wondered why I couldn't get her out of my head.

The next day was rainy, so I took the boat to the mainland instead of swimming. Work on the bar had progressed to hammer and chisel, working lines into the facade of the rough rectangle I'd made. I was seeing stylized grape vines for the front, carved in high relief so that the whole front—seen when visitors first walked into the tasting room—was a row of vines seen from close up, so each cluster and each grape was visible. It was slow, painstaking work, and I was antsy and restless by the time I'd made enough progress to call it a day. The skies had cleared to a flat lead-gray cloud cover, so I laced up a pair of running shoes and set off across the peninsula wearing nothing but the shorts and shoes, intending to follow the road north to the lighthouse park at the tip of the peninsula, and then cut down southward back to the winery, a path that would amount to a five-mile circuit. I was lost in a running trance and not seeing the road when I came up behind her. She was keeping a punishing pace just south of the lighthouse, her feet slapping lightly on the pavement, the West Arm waters rippling dull blue in the distance, her ponytail bobbing. She had a tiny iPod strapped to her left bicep, earbuds in her ears, wearing black skintight shorts and a green sports bra. I always ran in silence, using the rhythmic pound of my feet to hypnotize myself.

I moved abreast of her and she started, glancing sideways at me, and then turned her attention back to the road. She matched my pace, and we ran together without speaking. After maybe half a mile, she sniffed, wiped her wrist across her brow, ran a finger underneath her eyes. Was she crying? I sneaked a look, but all I saw was sweat. I blinked a trickle of salt out of my eye, and glanced at her again. She had her head down, and she was blinking hard, I could see the sharp angles of her clenched jaw. Hear the ragged rasp of her breath. She jerked herself upright, and her eyes were pained, wet, but no tears were falling.

She shot a look at me, dashed the heel of her palm against her eyes, and pushed herself even harder. I matched her, running beside her. I didn't have the words to ask her what was wrong. I didn't even know her name, but I could run beside her. I kept my eyes forward, breathing even, a good two or three feet between us. She glanced at me once, but I kept running.

Inhale…step, step; exhale…step, step; inhale… step, step. Don't think about the distance yet to run or the ache in my calves. I even found myself hoping she'd slow down a bit, because this pace was a killer. My lungs were burning already, and we still had almost two miles left in my circuit. I had no idea how far she was planning on running, of course, but with this kind of pace, it couldn't be too far. Either that, or she was in such good shape that I'd have to let myself fall behind.

I watched her foot hit a stone and slide out from underneath her. She stumbled, and my hand shot out, grabbing her arm just above the elbow. Her skin was soft and damp and sweat-slick. I righted her, made sure she had her balance and wasn't hurt before I let go.

"Thanks," she huffed. I just nodded. She ran a few more paces and then looked at me out of the corner of her eye. "You don't...talk much...do you?"

I shook my head.

"Can't, or don't?"

I just shrugged. She waited until it was clear the shrug was the only answer she'd get, and then she frowned at me, huffed, and put on a burst of speed to get away from me.

I didn't know how to answer her. Both? Neither? I was physically capable of speech. I just...couldn't. Dr. Brayer, the therapist I'd seen in the months following Britt's death, said my ongoing silence was a symptom of post-traumatic stress disorder. She claimed I'd eventually talk again—I just needed time to heal.

Sorry. The word bubbled up in my throat, and died. I let her run ahead of me, cursing myself.

After another mile or so she turned left, back toward the beach and her house. I kept running until I returned to the vineyard, collapsing against the railing of the porch, panting. When I caught my breath, I walked through the rows of vines, weaving my way up the hill overlooking the West Arm. I stopped there, watching the azure waters ripple and shift, thinking yet again of the girl. Of the tears she'd fought, of the way she'd powered through them and kept running. What had the power to make her cry that way? What secret sins or sorrow haunted her? I wanted to know, wanted to erase them for her. It was a stupid desire. I had my own secrets, my own ghosts rattling around the haunted bones in the closet of my past. I couldn't manage a simple hello, so how could I think to help her? Yet the strange urge remained.

"You're more broody than usual." My younger brother, Tom, spoke from behind me. I turned and lifted one eyebrow. He came up beside me, leaning on a post. "You only come out here and stare at the water when something is really eating at you. I mean, there's *always* something eating you, but when you come out here and stare…it's something new."

I scuffed at the close-cropped grass with the toe of my running shoe. Tom knew me all too well.

"It's been a year, bro. I miss the sound of your voice. I miss talking to you. Or rather, hearing you talk to me." Tom was the blunt one, the brother willing to just come out and say what was on his mind, in exactly so many words. "How 'bout you just… start simple. Something like, 'Whassup, Tom?' That's it. Two words. Or is it three? Two, I'd say. I think of 'whassup' as one word."

I shook my head at him, snorting at his rambling nonsense.

"No? Nothing? Say my name, then. One word. Three letters. T-O-M." I just glared at him. "Fine, then. Let's play twenty questions. Are you brooding about work?"

I shook my head.

"Are you brooding about what happened?"

Those two words—*what happened*—were code for Britt's death. I shook my head, turned away from him. I hated this game. He was always trying to get me to talk. Trying to joke me out of my silence, as if it was mere petulance on my part.

"Is it…someone new?" I didn't nod, but I didn't gesture in the negative, either. Tom seized on the lack of response. "It is! Holy shit, Carter! You met someone? For reals? Who is she?" Tom paused, frowning. "Wait a second. How does that work? Did you, like, use sign language?"

I tilted my head back and sighed in irritation, then gave Tom a long and scathing glare before starting forward, away from my obnoxious but well-meaning brother.

He caught up with me, moving around in front of me and stopping me with a playful shove. "That's it, isn't it? That's why you're brooding. There is some-one, but you don't know how to talk to her." He nodded sagely. "That makes sense. You always were the shyest, most introverted person I'd ever met, and then when...well, you know. When shit happened, you made shy and introverted into an art form."

It's not that simple, I wanted to say. *You don't get it.* How could he? Tom was the youngest, the baby. He was also a golden boy. Blessed. Everything came easy to him. He'd never experienced the kind of agony and guilt that can make a person's very soul go silent. The kind of pain and loneliness that can dry up your words, that can ruin you. Wreck who you are. Even Tom's breakups were mutual and painless. "We just went our separate ways," he'd say. "No big deal. We're still friends." How is that even possible? How much can you have invested in someone, in a relationship, if you break up and it's just...fine? How can you love someone and still be friends when the relationship ends? I didn't get it, but that was Tom. He made it work somehow.

He clapped me on the shoulder. "I know I make a lot of jokes, Carter. But seriously, you *have* to move on. I'm not saying forget. I'm not saying it'll be fine all of a sudden. I'm just saying, you have to *try*. Just... try. She'd want you to try."

That pissed me off. He barely knew Britt. He couldn't possibly know what she'd want. She was beyond wanting anything. Trite, pithy attributions of emotions to someone long dead held no comfort, only the mocking emptiness of wondering *what if.*

I walked away from Tom, from his well-meaning words and his easy-chair wisdom. *Lose part of your soul and then come talk to me,* I wanted to say. *Watch the woman you love die, and then come tell me about trying to move on,* I wanted to tell him.

Instead, I went home, the boat slicing though the low rolling waves, thunder growling overhead. I went to my workshop and stared at the sculpture of Britt.

Try.

I held the fine detail knife in my right hand, ran the fingertips of my left hand over the smooth cherrywood where her facial features would go. I closed my eyes, and I saw her. It was a memory I'd never be free of. She was in the bathtub, clad in a blood-soaked Stanford T-shirt, one hand limp on the edge of the tub, the other reaching for me. That's how she was in the sculpture. Her face was pressed against the side of the tub, her knees drawn up to her belly.

I'd been gone when it happened. She'd begged me to stay home with her. I'd gone out anyway, determined to put the finishing touches on the kitchen remodel I was doing across town. By the time I got home, several hours later, it was too late. I'd rushed her to the hospital, too late. Too late. She was gone by morning. The doctors had used terms like "missed miscarriage" and "sepsis." They'd intimated that if I'd gotten her help sooner, they could've saved her.

The carving knife dropped to the floor, clattering loudly, snapping the tip off the blade. I retrieved it, replaced the blade, clenched it in my fist until the trembling stopped. I let the memory wash over me, focusing on the expression on Britt's face. The pain in her eyes, the fear. Her slack lips. Her perfect nose. The tear tracks on her cheeks.

I touched the blade to the wood, slicing away a curling ribbon. Another. A third. Each movement of my knife brought up agony in me like rising bile. I kept carving. Flat wood became Britt's mouth, her cheeks, her chin. The dimples beside her mouth took shape. The lines of pain sliced into the bridge of her nose. I stopped before I got to her eyes. I nearly dropped the knife again. I stared at the place where her eyes would go, seeing Britt. With a deep breath, I summoned my courage and cut the wood away from her eyes. When I was finished, I stared down at the likeness of my dead wife, seeing her in the carved wood. I had to sand and polish and stain the wood yet, but it was done.

I had to look away. Her gaze was accusing somehow.

I stayed home the next two days, patiently scrubbing every inch with sandpaper until it was smooth, and then I polished, and then I stained. When the stain dried, I put on another coat. And again. Kirk and Max and Tom all emailed me, asking if I was sick. I lied and said I was. It wasn't entirely a lie, though. I was heartsick. Each moment I spent with the sculpture, I felt ill. Reminded. Seeing again. Feeling it all again. The hours of waiting in the hospital. The tight, pained expression on the doctor's face, the slight shake of his head. *I'm sorry, Mr. Haven. We did our best, but sometimes there's just nothing we can do. If we'd gotten her earlier, there may have been a chance.*

Finally, there was nothing left to do. I stood in the workshop, a white sheet in my hands, folded in a square.

I'm sorry, Britt. I wanted to say it out loud. I couldn't.

I'm sorry.

I covered the sculpture with the sheet, and Britt was gone. I wasn't healed, I wasn't fixed. I'd hoped finishing the piece would provide me with some kind of…release. But that had been a vain and foolish hope. A hunk of wood couldn't mend the damage to my soul.

first words

A month after our accidental running rendez-vous, and I hadn't seen the girl again. I'd thrown myself into finishing the bar. I'd completed the front piece, and was nearly done with the first side. The side I was working on now was going to be a row of wine bottles, with curling vines stretching between them. I had the bottles completed, and was a third of the way done with the vines.

It was a hot day on the peninsula, hitting upwards of ninety degrees, a clear, cloudless day, scorching, sti-fling, and humid. My workshop at the winery office wasn't air-conditioned, so I had the doors and win-dows open and a fan going. I was shirtless, wearing nothing but a pair of ripped, stained, and faded khaki cut-off shorts, the frayed hems hanging below my knees. I was barefoot, carving each individual tendril and vine in high relief and extreme detail. The only sound was the occasional rumble of a car passing in the distance, and the scratching of my carving knife.

And then I heard the sound of crunching on the gravel outside. I stood up, wiping my sweaty forehead on my wrist.

A hesitant rap on the front door. "Hello?" a female voice called from around front.

I was the only one at the winery today. Kirk and Max had gone shopping for more wine-making equipment, and Tom was working from his house, putting together a publicity package for the grand opening next spring. The hands were all at the farthest edge of the vineyard, weeding, way out of earshot.

I set my knife on the counter and scuffed through the sawdust and went outside, circling to the front porch. It was her. The cellist from the beach. God, I really had to learn her name. She was standing on the porch, in the act of knocking on the door again. An ancient ten-speed bicycle lay on its side near the foot of the stairs, the back tire still rotating. She was dressed in tiny blue running shorts, an orange tank top, and running shoes, and she was soaked in sweat.

What the hell was she doing on a bicycle this far from her cottage? It was nearly three miles from the beach and her house to the winery, and M-37 was hilly as hell. It'd be grueling in this extreme heat. I let my foot clomp down on the stair, and she spun around.

"You?" she asked, surprised. I shrugged. "Well, I'm glad someone is here. I need some water. I didn't realize how hot it really was when I left for my bike ride and—" She wobbled, swayed on her feet, and started to fall.

I lunged up the two remaining stairs, and my arm shot around her waist, holding her upright. A moment passed, her wildly green eyes on me. And then she blinked, wiped at her face with both hands, and struggled to regain herself.

"God, did I just pass out?" She rubbed her forehead. "I did. I can't believe I just fainted." She glanced at me. "Do you have some water?"

I jerked the screen door open, shoved the heavy interior door out of the way, and led her into the kitchen. I felt her eyes on me, felt her curiosity. I rummaged in the fridge, found a bottle of water and a bottle of Gatorade, and held them out to her. She took them both, setting the Gatorade on the counter and opening the water, chugging it without pausing for breath. Finished, she set the empty bottle down and opened the Gatorade, drinking it more slowly.

"So." She stuck out her hand. "I'm Eden Eliot." I took her hand, shook it, smiling. Reaching into my hip pocket, I retrieved a business card and handed it to her. She read it out loud. "'Carter Haven, Haven Brothers Winery.'"

I nodded.

"Okay, Carter. Are you mute?"

I shook my head negative.

"So you can talk."

I nodded.

"But you don't."

Another negative shake.

"Is it just me, or do you not talk in general?"

I frowned. This was awkward. Not exactly how I had envisioned things.

A step sounded on the stair, followed by the squeaking of the screen door, and then Tom arrived, a bottle of Fiji in one hand and a manila folder in the other. Tom looked like all four of us Haven brothers: tall, muscular, and dark-haired. He was thinner and more wiry than the rest of us, though, and his hair was more brown than black. He had the same pale blue eyes as well.

He extended his hand to Eden. "Thomas Haven. I see you met my brother, Carter."

"Yeah, we were just introducing ourselves," Eden said.

Tom looked at me in shock, and then back to her. "He introduced himself? Like, out loud?"

Eden held up my card. "Well, no. With this."

Tom nodded. "Ah. That would have been surprising."

Eden fixed her eyes back on me. "So what's your deal?"

I tried to summon an explanation, but nothing came.

Tom sighed. "That's kind of a complicated question to answer." He glanced at me, silently begging me. When I didn't break the silence, Tom rubbed the bridge of his nose with his thumb. "And I'm late for a meeting with Max and Kirk, so I'm gonna go. See you later. Good luck, Eden."

"Good luck with what?"

He jerked his thumb at me. "Him." And with that he was gone.

Wow, Tom. Very helpful, I thought, glaring at his retreating back.

A long silence and uncomfortable tension ensued, with me clenching and unclenching my hands in frustration. Eden sipped at her Gatorade.

After the silence had become intolerable, Eden pushed away from the counter, setting down the empty bottle beside the other one, and nodded. "Okay. Well. This has been awkward. Thank you for the drink. I'll just…be going. 'Bye."

She was out the door and on her bike before I could move. Not good. She'd just passed out on my porch. No way I should let her pedal home in this heat. I groaned. This was going to be difficult.

I grabbed my shirt from the workshop, fished my keys from my pocket, and took off in my truck after Eden. She'd gotten pretty far in a short period of time, and she didn't stop when I slowed to drive beside her. She glanced at me, though.

"Can I help you?" She sounded exasperated. Rightly so.

I jerked my thumb at the bed of my truck. She just frowned and kept pedaling, huffing and puffing, sweat pouring down her face. I sped up, jerked the truck to a halt in front of her, and jumped out. Eden skidded to a stop, wiping at her forehead.

"What gives, Carter? If you want something, say so."

I withdrew my cell phone, opened the Notes app, and typed a message: **Let me drive you home.**

Eden read it, then shook her head. "No. I'm fine. Thanks, though."

Please. Too hot. You'll pass out and get hurt.

"This is so weird," Eden said, handing me my phone back after reading the message. "We're passing notes back and forth like we're in third grade. I'll be fine." She stood on the pedal and pushed away, circling around my truck and working up the hill, struggling at the steep incline.

I watched her go. Felt panic. I couldn't just let her go. I couldn't. She shouldn't bike home in this heat, regardless of the grade of the hill. It was a douchey thing to let her do, for starters. And also…I just couldn't let her go. Something in my soul demanded that I catch up to her.

I gunned the engine, passed her, slid to a stop in the gravel of the shoulder in front of her. I jumped out of my truck, stood waiting. She squeezed the brakes and put her foot down, stopping a couple of feet away.

"What, Carter? What do you want? I said I'm fine. I am. For real. I'm tough, okay? I don't need your help." She was sweating profusely, red in the face, hair wisping free from the ponytail and sticking to her forehead and cheeks, panting for breath. "And to be honest, the whole not-talking thing? It's weird. A little creepy. No offense. Maybe you've got a reason for not talking. I don't know, some trauma or something. But I've got enough of my own trouble to deal with yours, too, okay? So…'bye."

She glanced behind her for traffic, and then stood on the pedal and started moving.

No. No. Wait. I thought it, heard it in my head. I sucked in a deep breath and focused. "Wait." My voice was raspy and hoarse and weak from disuse. She braked, hopping with the bike as it slowed to a stop, and then she turned to look back at me. I gestured at the truck. "Let me. Please." The most I could manage was a faint whisper, but she heard me.

She stared at me, as if weighing her options. Finally, she got off the bike and walked it to the back of my truck. "Fine." She started to lift the bike into the bed of the truck. I took it from her and set it in. I was impressed by how easily she'd lifted the bike, since it was a twenty-year-old rust-red ten-speed, and heavy as hell. This girl was strong.

"Thanks," she said as she crossed to the passenger side, glancing at me from across the bed of the truck. "I had it, but thanks."

I just shrugged and got in, turned the AC all the way up. Eden angled the louvers and closed her eyes as the cold air washed over her face. I watched her out of the corner of my eye. Eden. Such a perfect name for this girl. She said she had too much of her own trouble to deal with mine, and I wondered what that meant. What troubles did she have? I knew they existed—I had seen the pain and heartache in her eyes.

She sat back against the maroon leather seat and wiped her face with her palm, smoothing her way-ward hair away. "Thanks, Carter."

"Fine." My voice cracked, and I cleared my throat, tried again. "It's fine."

She glanced at me quizzically at the rough sound of my voice. "Were you sick?"

I shook my head. "No."

"Then what?"

"Long story."

"I've got time."

I let out a long breath. "It's…hard to tell."

"Painful?"

I shot a sideways look at her, a lifted eyebrow. "Yeah."

"How long have you been not talking?"

"A year."

"I got you to talk for the first time in a year?" She sounded pleased by this information.

"Yeah."

"Your brother is gonna love me for that."

"Or something." I turned onto the little dirt road that led to the beach, and her cabin. I loved this road. It was a narrow, tree-lined track, sunlight shifting through the leaves, dappling the ground in a chaotic chiaroscuro pattern.

I could sense her thinking. She was probably wondering what could make a man go completely silent for a year. I wasn't sure I'd ever be able to tell the story. My brothers knew what had happened, but only because they'd been around for it. They'd found me, collapsed on the bathroom floor beside the tub. I'd never told them what had happened, because I hadn't spoken a word since the moment I found Britt.

I drove past the post office, rounded the corner. The bay glittered brightly off to our right, homes lining the road on the left. I stopped in front of Eden's old yellow house.

I really looked at the old house for the first time. The yellow paint was almost completely faded, and the white trim paint was peeling. The porch was falling in, and the steps were rotting. The roof was ten years overdue for new shingles and probably leaked in a hard rain. The screens on the windows all had rips in them. I stared at the house, wondering how and why she lived here.

"How...how did you know where I live?" She sounded suspicious and, suddenly, a little afraid,.

"I—I saw you come out one day. From the beach."

She glared at me, eyes narrowed. "You're lying."

I pulled the manual transmission shifter into neutral and set the parking brake. "Fine. Sorry. I was running one day. Heard you playing your cello. Stopped to listen. Saw you through the open screen door. Didn't want to disturb you." God, it sounded like each word was painful, coming out staccato and harsh.

She didn't seem to notice, or if she did, she hid it well. "What was I playing?"

I shrugged. "Don't know classical music. You looked...lost, though. In the music."

"You're not stalking me or anything, are you?"

I gave her an amused grin. "Would I tell you if I was?"

She laughed. "Yeah, probably not. Now that you're actually talking, you don't give me the creeps, so I guess it's fine."

"I'm not stalking, promise." I shut off the engine and got out, retrieved her bicycle from the bed, and set it against the wall near the door. A VW Passat sat in the driveway, under the leaning carport. I grabbed the post of the carport and shook it; the whole structure wobbled. "This place is falling apart."

She shrugged. "Yeah. But it's mine, and it's all I've got."

"I'll fix it up for you."

Eden shook her head. "No. It's fine."

"It's what I do."

"Fix houses?"

"Build. I'm a carpenter." I gestured at her roof. "That's gonna leak."

Her expression told me that it already had. "Yeah." She fiddled with the strap of her orange tank top. "I discovered that the other day."

"Was it bad?"

"I had buckets."

"How many?"

She didn't answer right away. "Four?"

I lifted an eyebrow. "Let me fix it."

Eden sighed. "Fine. If you really want to. I can't pay you much, though."

I just snorted. "You're not paying me."

"Then no." She crossed her arms under her breasts, sounding adamant.

I made myself look away from the way her arms propped up the expanse of pale flesh barely contained by the tank top and sports bra. "Why?"

"Because I don't need help, and I don't need charity."

"Stubborn much?"

"Nope." She popped her lips on the last syllable.

I just laughed. "Right. So you'd rather have a leaky roof?" I pointed at the porch and stairs. "You're gonna put a foot through the wood at some point. Cut yourself open pretty bad, probably." I crossed the little yard and stuck my whole hand through a rip in a window screen. "Can't open the windows, or you'll have bugs fly in. But if you don't need help, that's your call."

"I'll be careful." I had nothing to say to that. She hesitated, and then sighed.. "You want to come in?"

I nodded, and she let herself into the house. I followed her, and discovered that the inside needed as much help as the outside. She'd done a lot of work already, scrubbing down what had to have been filthy walls and baseboards, replacing outdated furniture and appliances. But the ancient Formica counters were peeling, the kitchen floor sagged in places, and the hardwood floors in the living room and bedrooms needed a huge amount TLC, if not completely replacing. The wallpaper was hideous. And falling off the walls in places.

"Don't say it," Eden muttered, grabbing two bottles of water from the fridge. "I know. It was empty for a long time. I'm doing what I can, but it…." She trailed off.

"Needs some help," I finished.

"Yeah."

"I nearly offered to buy this place, a few years ago," I said. "But I opted for something a little more…remote."

She didn't ask where I lived. We both leaned against the counters and sipped at our water, neither of us talking.

"So why'd you move up here?" I asked.

"Why didn't you talk for a year?" she countered.

Neither of us answered the question, and eventually the awkward silence was too much. I finished my water and set it down. "Thanks for the drink."

"Thanks for the ride," she said.

I pushed through the screen door, letting it slam closed behind me. As I was opening my truck door, Eden called out my name. I turned and glanced at her.

"You really think you can stop my roof from leaking?"

"Yeah."

"Maybe…maybe I wouldn't mind a little help."

"I'll see you tomorrow morning, then."

"See you tomorrow."

I drove back to the winery and set to work on the bar once more, feeling strangely triumphant. I'd spoken. I'd had an entire conversation. The rest of the day flew by as I scraped and carved, going through in my mind the list of supplies I'd need to do Eden's roof, planning, thinking about Eden, wondering what her story was and how I could get her to tell it to me without having to share mine. Darkness fell, and I was lost in thought when Tom and Kirk wandered in, laughing and shoving each other. Max trailed behind, nose in his phone. They all stopped in the doorway, staring at the bar. It was after ten at night, I suddenly realized, and I'd finished the front piece and most of one side.

"Damn, dude," Kirk said. "That looks amazing." He came to examine the front piece with the carved vines, and then moved over to the one side I'd finished, tracing the contours of the wine bottles. "What's the other side gonna be? Grapes?"

Time to shock them. "Red wine glasses."

Max was tapping at his phone when he heard my voice. He actually dropped it on the floor, then cursed as he bent to retrieve it. Kirk and Tom just stared at me.

"Holy shit." Tom laughed, incredulous. "You spoke."

"Yep."

Kirk and Max exchanged looks. "Say something else," Kirk said.

"Fuck you." I grinned.

"That's Carter for you," Tom said. Then his gaze went narrow, sharp with suspicion. "Does the fact that you're talking have anything to do with that girl who was here earlier?"

I turned away instead of answering, picking up my tools and tossing them onto the worktable.

"It does!" Tom slapped my back. "Did you bang her? Is that what did it?"

I shoved at him. "Don't, Tom. It's not like that."

"Girl? What girl?" Max asked. Max, the oldest Haven brother, was the shortest of all four of us. He was built like a tank, hugely muscled, burly, biceps the size of my thighs and legs like tree trunks. He had the same black hair and blue eyes, but he kept his hair cropped close to the scalp and he wore a goatee. Kirk, Max, and I all tended to be taciturn, tight-lipped like our dad, whereas Tom was more like Mom, chattery, voluble, easily excited. Max, however, was the most reserved of all of us. He came across as grumpy to most people, but you had to know him to understand that he just didn't have much to say.

I glared at Tom. "Just someone I know. Not like Tom's thinking."

Tom laughed at my denial, then sobered. "If she got you to talk when no one else could for a solid year, she's something special, and I don't give a flying fuck what you say." He nudged me with his elbow. "Besides, she was hot as hell. You should make a play for her, if you haven't already."

"Back off, Tom," I warned, my voice a growl.

He held up his hands in surrender. "Hey, I'm just sayin'. If you won't, I will."

"The fuck you will." I turned and glared at him. The thought of Tom "making a play" on Eden made something in my gut churn. It felt an awful lot like jealousy. "Leave it alone. Leave *her* alone." My voice and my body language were all screaming *she's mine*, and my brothers sure as shit hadn't missed that fact.

"Carter, come on, I'm just messin' with you." Tom grabbed for my arm, but I shook him off.

"Well, it's not fucking funny."

"Lighten up, bro—" He stepped toward me, and I shoved him away, hard enough that he stumbled.

"You're gonna get decked, Tommy," Kirk warned. "Let him go. Joke's over."

Tom let me go, shoving his hands in his hip pockets. He'd pushed me past my boiling point frequently enough in our childhood to know it wasn't a smart plan. And really, only Tom could get me to that point, in the way only brothers can.

Max stopped me as I stalked out of the workshop. "Seriously. It's good to hear your voice, brother."

I clapped him on the shoulder, then left them all in the workshop admiring the bar.

The churn of emotions in me lasted all the way from the winery to the beach. Once I stood in my shorts on the cold sand with the black sky lit by a bright half-moon and a brilliant wash of silver stars, I felt the jealousy and the anger and the confusion ebb away. The water lapped at my ankles, silence stretching and sliding around me, calming me. I shouldn't have gotten so upset with Tom. He was just playing with me, and I knew it. He was a joker, and he didn't always know when to let the joke go. But something about what he'd said had gotten under my skin.

I had no claim on Eden. No reason to feel jealous. Except, for some reason, she *had* been the one to get me to break my silence. And she hadn't even really been trying.

I moved out to deeper water, wading until it was waist-deep, ducking under the rope marking the designated swim area. I was about to dive under when I heard the cello. It was faint, distant. Low, sad notes rolled across the water. I stood with the water chilling my skin, listening. The sorrow was palpable, thick and raw, even from this far away.

Something in the music made me want to wade back to shore, cross the road and barge into her falling-apart little house, wrap my arms around her and tell her it would be okay. Hold her until the sorrow went away. Take her sadness into myself. Even earlier today, when she'd been trying as hard as she could to pretend she was fine, to act like she didn't need help, keeping her emotions buried deep, I had felt it in her. She could pretend to herself all she wanted, but I knew she wasn't fine. I just didn't know why.

I dove in before my feet could betray me and carry me back to shore. The swim home was long, and hard, and cold. I crawled onto the deck, shivering and gasping for breath, dragged myself inside, grateful for the exhaustion.

The last thing I needed was to get involved with Eden, to get caught up in her drama. I had to focus on the winery. Get the bar finished. Get the new building finished. Make the tables and lay the floors, sand and polish everything, paint, hang artwork, make it perfect. Get the offices up and running, give Kirk and Max a beautiful place to do business. I couldn't afford time for a distraction. Not for a girl, not even one as gorgeous as Eden. Especially not one with such a visible burden of trouble.

Yet, as I fell asleep, I knew I'd be at her house bright and early with a truckload of shingles. And I knew I'd get involved. For better or worse, I was getting involved.

I was an idiot.

learning to live;
the importance of a kiss

Ever

I could make a fist, but I couldn't squeeze it. I could wiggle my fingers, but I couldn't grasp a glass. I could mumble a word or two, sometimes even three in a row, but I couldn't string a coherent sentence together. I could see and hear and smell and taste and feel. I could think. I was me. But…who I was had changed.

Eden had vanished. No one knew where she was. Caden said her phone was off, going straight to voicemail, and eventually her mailbox filled up. No one had heard from her in two weeks. She'd withdrawn from Cranbrook. Everything she owned was gone from her dorm. Her roommate said she hadn't left an address or a destination. Nothing.

I'd sensed the farewell in her last visit. I hadn't been able get out the words to demand she tell me where she was going, or why. I couldn't get out *any* words. Barely her name. I could sometimes repeat words like a parrot. I knew them, heard my thoughts in my mind, but my mouth wouldn't translate them.

I missed Eden. I needed her, and she was gone.

I couldn't make my hand hold onto a tennis ball, much less use a pen or paintbrush. I might never make art again. I might be trapped in this useless body for the rest of my life. I wanted to cry at that thought, but I refused to let myself. I had a routine. I only cried after Cade had gone home. I cried in my bed, alone. I never let Cade see my secret despair. He had to hope, because his hope was all I had getting me from day to day, getting me through each therapy session. Each grueling, agonizing hour of trying to merely grip a tennis ball in my fist. To wiggle my toes and straighten my leg on my own. To repeat single syllables: "Ball. Call. Wall. Fin. Tin. Bin. Much. Such. Touch." Over and over again until even my tongue was tired and my lips hurt from trying to make them form intelligible sounds.

All that pain and effort, sheer exhaustion from the simplest things, when inside, in my mind, I was me, I was Ever Eileen Monroe, the girl I'd always been. The woman I'd become, with Cade. But she was trapped in silence.

The one triumph I had, the one thing I'd managed, was to tell both Eden and Caden that I loved them. That was important.

I couldn't ask him what was wrong. I couldn't talk to him. That was probably the worst part of it all. He was in pain. I knew his Grams and Gramps had both died just before I'd come out of my coma. That had to have been the final blow for him, for my poor sweet man. He'd endured so much. So, so much hell.

But it was more than that. I knew it. There was something else eating at him. Something he wasn't telling me. There was *a lot* he wasn't saying. Maybe he was protecting me. Forcing me to keep focused on recovery. But there was a new darkness to him, my Caden. I hated it. More than anything I needed to banish it. To exorcise his demons, to kiss away the lines of worry and pain etched into his features. They hadn't been there, just yesterday.

Or, what felt to me like yesterday. It had been nearly two years, I'd been told. Christmas Eve, I was twenty years old. I remembered the screech of tires and weightlessness. Then darkness. I woke up, and I was twenty-two, almost twenty-three, and trapped in a useless, weak, skin-and-bones body. Atrophied muscles. Art gone. Speech gone. The cruelty of it was unbearable.

I couldn't even kiss Cade. He'd lean down, and his lips would touch mine, and I knew he was desperate to feel my lips respond to his, but I couldn't. I tried. So hard. I practiced when I was alone. I tried to purse my lips. Tried and tried to kiss the air so that when he showed up at seven the next morning, and every morning, I could kiss him back. That was my next goal. Using my hands again, talking, walking, those were all eventual goals. I'd achieve them. There was no other choice.

But before any of that, I had to simply kiss Caden.

Today was a good day. I'd slept through the night without nightmares of never walking again, never talking again, never kissing Cade or making love to him again. Those were the worst dreams, the nights I woke up alone, tears trickling down my face, sobs trapped in my chest. Sometimes I dreamed he got tired of me, sick of waiting for me to get better. In those dreams he'd leave me without a word. Or just not show up. Just vanish like Eden had and I'd be alone in life, and then I'd wake up with screams trapped in my gut, panic eating at me like a bird trapped in a house, banging against windows and walls.

Today, though, I woke knowing I'd slept without any of that. I felt hopeful. I practiced pursing my lips, imagined Cade's lips against mine and pictured myself kissing him. I could do it. I knew it. I felt it. Today would be the day.

I watched the local news while I waited for him. He always showed up at seven exactly. Today, he didn't arrive until almost seven-thirty. He looked haggard, exhausted. Bags under his eyes. Thinner than he'd ever been. Sad. Haunted. His eyes flitted around the room, taking in the walls, the bed, the side table, searching, and it seemed as if he was seeing something not physically there. It was as if he was seeing over and over again the heartache that had been in this room over the past year and a half. I could see the memories in his eyes, the pain…and that something else.

Guilt? Yes, that was what I saw in his gaze, in his posture, in the set of his mouth and the shifting of his eyes.

I pushed it away, the knowledge that he felt guilty. I couldn't take that. Couldn't handle it. He loved me, and he was here with me. That was all that mattered. He was here.

He perched on the edge of my bed, his thigh nudging mine, leaned down and wrapped his arms around me. I fought myself, strained, forced my arms up, up. Touched him. Hands on his biceps, trembling with the effort to keep them there. Something that should've been easy, but was anything but. I managed to hold on to his arms for almost thirty seconds before they dropped back down. He touched his forehead to mine, and I felt his breath on my face. He smelled so good, so familiar, and I pulled in his scent, drawing strength from him, from his nearness.

He pulled back and kissed my forehead. He sat back then, his hands on mine on my lap.

"Hey, babe." He leaned in again and kissed my cheek.

God, that was awful. A kiss on the cheek. It felt like an insult. Why not the lips? Did he not want me anymore? I was sick, I knew. I was all but useless. Skinny, pale, and weak. Unable to hold a conversation or do much of anything. But I was still his wife. He loved me. I knew he did. But did he still *want* me?

I focused, concentrated. Lifted one hand up, touched my fingers to his cheek. Traced the stubble on his upper lip. Ran my thumb along the crease of his lips. Stared at his mouth, at his lips, which had once kissed me so easily, so passionately. As if he couldn't get enough of me.

I needed that. Please, I wanted to scream. Kiss me! Love me! Hold me! Touch me! Remind me who I am to you.

I made the words come out, but they stuttered and stumbled, tripping. "K-ki—Kiss mmmm-me." I scrunched my brows with the effort needed to focus. "Please."

He held my palm against his cheek, kissed my thumb where it touched his lips. His gaze locked onto mine, wavered. I thought for a moment that he might cry. Slowly, slowly, he leaned in. My heart thudded crazily in my chest, and I wanted to weep with pure joy when his lips touched mine. I shifted my thumb away, felt the stubble at the corner of his mouth. He tasted like toothpaste and mouthwash and faintly of coffee. Like Cade.

His kiss felt so right, so beautiful, so warm and soft and delicious that I couldn't breathe for the ecstasy. It felt like a first kiss somehow. I remembered what I'd practiced, and made my lips shape against his. He breathed in sharply through his nose, a gasp of surprise. I wasn't breathing, but I was kissing him, and that was better than breathing. He moved his mouth against mine, and I felt his tongue slip gently against my teeth, and I opened to his tongue, felt him taste my teeth and gums and lips and tongue, and felt him kiss me like he had been dying as much as I.

An eternity passed in that kiss, and then he pulled away. He was shaking all over.

"Cade?" It was all I could manage, but he understood the question.

"I'm fine. I'm just…I needed to kiss you. I needed that, more than you could ever know. More than I think I even understood."

"Not as…much…as—" I had to pause and focus on forming the words, the letters, the sounds. "Me. Not as much as me."

Cade pulled me against his chest and held me. He had stopped shaking, but I felt the emotion radiating from him.

"Talk. To me." I was proud of how easily I'd gotten that out.

"About what?"

"You."

He let go of me, stood up, crossed the room in an anxious stride. "What about me?"

"What's…wrong." That was supposed to be a question, but it hadn't come out that way.

"Nothing. Everything." He stopped at the window, stared out of it at the beautiful summer day beyond. "I just…everything is so…*hard*. I love you. I missed you so much. I didn't know how to live, not without you. You were all I had, and you were gone."

"I'm here. Now."

"I know. I know." He turned back to me. "And you're getting better every day. You kissed me back! That's a huge improvement." I felt him pushing away the turmoil that had been boiling inside him, changing the subject.

I let him.

"Kiss me…again."

He stood over me, staring down at me. Brushed my cheekbone with his thumb, brushed my hair away. His eyes were on me, and I saw the need in him. He needed me. I had to fight my way back to normality. For him.

He leaned down and kissed me, ever so gently. I felt my lips twitch and respond, forming against his. It only lasted a second, and then he was sitting down beside me and holding me against his chest. His heartbeat was a steady drum against my cheek. I was elated, jubilant. I'd kissed him back. Barely, but he'd felt it. He knew exactly how big a deal that was for me. And I knew what a huge thing it was for him. I wanted to hold on to him. Wrap my arms around him like I used to. I couldn't, and that hurt. It was all about small, attainable goals. I knew that. But it didn't make it any easier to get so excited about something as simple and everyday as kissing my husband.

When he finally let me go, I looked up into his eyes, and I saw the turmoil there once more, layered and hidden beneath the love and the pride. I didn't understand it, what it meant, where it was coming from. It was more than watching me struggle every day. He was always proud of every little milestone I reached, praised my every tiny success. His smiles were genuine, his love real. But…there was something beneath it. Some pain and confusion whose source I couldn't fathom. It was guilt. I knew it. Couldn't avoid the truth of it. But over what, though? That's what I couldn't figure out. Was it guilt over the accident? Surely he knew it was just that, an accident? There was nothing he could have done any differently.

There was no way to know what he was feeling, and he wasn't telling. And if it was guilt I saw and felt in him, I wasn't sure I wanted to know where it was coming from just yet. I wasn't sure I could handle it.

I forced the thoughts away as he went with me to therapy. I couldn't afford any distractions while I was at therapy. It took all of my focus, all of my concentration, and every ounce of strength I had. He stood beside me, held my hand. Every time I felt discouraged or frustrated, I'd look at him and I'd know I could do it. I had to. For him. He needed me. Cade had always seemed so strong, so steady despite the hardships life had thrown at him. But now he seemed...almost fragile. As if one more blow, and he would crumple. I had to get better. I had to get my speech back, had to get my mobility back. I had to be able to comfort him, to love him the way he deserved. Right now, though, I needed *him*.

So I curled my fingers around the tennis ball, clutching it with all my strength, squeezing with every muscle in my arm, sweating and trembling from the exertion required to merely hold on to it. After maybe a minute, my fingers uncurled, and the ball rolled away across the table. I paused, panting, and then nodded to Darrel, my therapist, who put the ball back into my palm. I gripped it, focusing with everything I had.

Cade stayed with me for several hours, like he did every day. Around four-thirty, he left to go to work. He'd sometimes swing by after work, stinking like sweat and looking as rugged and handsome as ever. That evening, however, he didn't come back after work. I sat in my bed, watching *So You Think You Can Dance*. My night shift nurse, Lucy, came by with my dinner, helped me eat. In late middle age, Lucy was a sweet woman with graying brown hair and a hint of a southern accent. As she was cleaning up, she bumped the table at my bedside, and the bottom drawer slid open. I glanced down at it and saw what looked like a shoebox.

"What's…that?" I said, training my gaze on it.

Lucy followed my eyes and saw the box. "Oh, that? That's your letters."

I was puzzled. "Letters?"

She nodded. "From that wonderful boy of yours."

He'd brought our old letters to the home? "Old?"

She seemed confused by the question. "Old? No, honey, those are all from since you've been here. While you were in your coma, he'd come by every single day and read you a letter. A new one, sometimes two. There's almost two boxes full in there. He must've written you…oh, lord…hundreds of letters."

My eyes watered. He'd never said anything. Never told me. "Every…day? Letters?" God*dammit*. I hated not being able to speak clearly. I sounded like a three-year-old just learning to talk.

She nodded, bent over and lifted one shoebox out, and then opened the upper drawer and pulled out a second one. She set them on the bed by my leg. She lifted the top off both boxes, and the tears streamed down my face in earnest. There were, as Lucy had said, hundreds of letters. He had written to me while I was in a coma. Every day. Every single day.

"Read them?" I asked.

Lucy sighed, pulled up a chair, and sat down. "Yeah, sweetie. He'd come in here, usually in the afternoon, sometimes in the evening. He'd sit here, where I am. He closed the door most times, and he'd read to you. Sometimes he'd talk, but after a while I think…I think all he could do was read the letters."

"Read? To me."

Lucy lifted a bundle of envelopes from the box. That bundle in turn was divided into four smaller bundles, each containing three, four, or five enve-lopes. A few had more. "The boy's organized, I'll give him that." She slid the first envelope free—it hadn't been sealed. My name was written on the front in Cade's distinctive all-caps handwriting. "Looks like he has them done up by week, and then by month."

I recognized the system. He'd shown me the boxes containing my letters to him from our years of being pen pals, and that was how he'd bound these as well.

Lucy pulled the folded paper from within the envelope. She scanned the first few lines, and then shook her head. "I don't think I should read these to you, hon. They're…very personal." She thought for a few seconds, clearly trying to figure out a way that I could read them, given my inability to hold a tennis ball, much less a piece of paper. "How about I lay it on your lap so you can see it? When you're ready for me to turn it over, just look at me."

I frowned. "Patients?"

Lucy blinked, and then waved me off. "I'm caught up on my rounds for now. I can sit with you for a few minutes." She smoothed the letter out on my lap and then sat back.

It was an odd angle, and my instinct was to just pick it up. My brain wanted me to be normal, but my body simply wouldn't respond. I blew out a frustrated breath, and then focused on the words, despite the awkward angle.

Ever,

My love. It seems like it's been forever since I wrote you like this. Since I sat down with pen and paper and expressed my thoughts to you. So much has changed since then.

Everything has changed. I don't even know where to start. We met IRL (I didn't know what that phrase meant, way back when you first used it, you know), and we fell in love and we got married. God, all that seems like a lifetime ago. I don't know who that was, that Cade who was with you back then. I'm someone else now. This... hole in the world, man-shaped. Me-shaped. A vacancy.

I can't pretend like you're going to read this, like you're going to write back. I'm sorry, but I just can't. You're in a coma, and you might never wake up, and I'm alone. You promised, Ever. You promised you'd never leave me. I know you didn't want to, you didn't mean to. But you still did, and I'm back to being numb and floating through life, through every day.

Except now I don't even have you, just your letters to keep me tied to the earth.

I couldn't read anymore. My head flopped back against the wall, thumping painfully. Tears slid down my cheeks, a flood of grief for my poor husband. I felt a small hand wipe across my cheek. Lucy, literally wiping my tears away.

"He loves you something fierce, Caden does." Lucy wiped my other cheek. "I've worked in nursing homes for going on twenty-five years, Ever. I've seen a lot in those years. A lot of patients have come through these doors. They go, too. Nature of the business, and it never gets easier. But that boy of yours. God, he was so devoted to you. Your sister, too. She brought him every day until he could bring himself. You're lucky, Ever. You have the love of a good man. Not everyone finds that. He stuck by you."

Oh, I knew. I knew so well.

I turned my attention back to the letter.

It's been six months. It's summer, and it was the day before Christmas the last time I heard your voice. The last time I saw your smile and your eyes.

I have to make some decisions now. Finish school? Keep the condo? Do I pack your things away? Do I hang up the sweater you left draped over the kitchen chair? I haven't yet. Do I put away your shoes that are by the door? Do I put all of your stuff in a box like you've died?

I can't. I know I should. Seeing your stuff just like you left it on December 23rd, it hurts. Every day I see it all there, just like you left it. But I can't bear to act like you're never coming back. I have to hope that you will. Because you will, right? You'll wake up. You'll come back to me. You love me, and you're just...lost. Somewhere out there, trying to come back. Like Odysseus fighting to get back to Penelope.

I don't know how to live without you, but I have to try. Don't I? If you were to wake up and I've given up, just stopped living, you'd be so mad. You'd kick my ass. So I have to keep going. I have to pick myself up, and live. I don't know how I'll do it, but I will. For you. For US.

I love you, forever and always.

Cade

Tears sluiced down my face faster than Lucy could wipe them away. I sniffed, and Lucy dabbed at my face with a Kleenex. She slid the letter back in the envelope, and took out another one.

Ever,

Some days it's easier to write you like this than others. Some days, my thoughts just flow out like water, and I fill a page or two without trying. Other days, it's hard to get a single paragraph. Today is one of those days. The hard to write days. I don't know what to say. What to write. I don't even know what I think. Except I miss you. So much. So, so much.

I couldn't read anymore. I leaned my head back and tried to breathe through the tears. He'd suffered so much, my poor Caden.

"Enough. For now," I said.

Lucy nodded and put the letters away. She patted me on the shoulder. "You'll walk out of here on your own two feet, Ever. I know it. Won't be long."

I hoped so.

For my sake, but most of all, for Cade.

questions without answers

I had a new goal. Regain enough mobility and fine motor control to read the letters by myself. I wasn't sure how long I'd have to stay here in the nursing home, but I knew I'd need to be able to do things on my own when I did finally go home. Caden shouldn't have to babysit me, take care of me like I was an invalid. So, to that end, I worked harder than ever. Pushed myself harder and harder, longer and longer, until I was crying with pain and exhaustion. I mastered the tennis ball. I could hold it in my fist and not let go. The next goal was to isolate my fingers, touch the tennis ball with each finger. Just touch it. We take things for granted in life. Big things, like loved ones and kisses and the ability to hug. And little things, like being able to extend your index finger by itself.

Days passed. Turned to weeks.

Tests revealed, according to my team of doctors led by Dr. Overton, that my brain patterns were completely normal. It was kind of miraculous, they said. There was no lasting damage to my brain. I'd suffered a minor stroke apparently, which was common in cases like mine. Many brain injuries that resulted in a coma would see the patient left paralyzed on one side from the stroke. I'd come through mostly fine. The right side of my mouth drooped a tiny bit, but it was barely noticeable. My right hand was slightly weaker than my right, and it was a harder process to get my right hand to do what I wanted, but I would regain use of it in time, the doctors said. I was a very lucky woman, they said.

Caden continued to come see me every day, staying as long as he could. He'd kiss me hello and goodbye, but once again they were chaste, empty kisses. He was holding back. Holding out. As if he didn't want me anymore. I had to remind myself that he'd been through hell, and I had to tell myself that things would go back to normal eventually. He loved me. He wanted me. He was just…confused. And lost. Maybe he didn't want to push me.

Or maybe there was something else, something dark and horrible. Some secret that was eating away at him like a cancer. Day by day, I saw him withering and shrinking, even as I got stronger and stronger.

With every day that passed, I regained more and more ability to do things for myself. I could almost pull the letter from the envelope now. I could almost dress myself, as long as I was sitting down. Darrel had begun working with me on standing up, but I was still months away from being able to walk.

In the meantime, Dr. Overton had told Caden and I that I would be able to go home soon. My speech patterns were still off, but I could make myself understood now. Weeks of work had seen a huge amount of progress, but any pride or sense of accomplishment I might have felt was eclipsed by my worry for Cade. He seemed like a shadow of himself, a ghost of the man I'd known, and was unresponsive to my attempts to draw him out on the subject. He would say that my coma had been really hard on him, but that he was glad I was up and he was fine.

He wasn't fine.

I read his letters. Two or three at a time, then I'd take a break, and read more. The grief, sorrow, and despair were agonizing to read. The desperation he felt was palpable in each letter, worse in each one. The closer the dates of the letters got to the day I woke up, the more difficult they were to read.

When I read things like this, I would weep for hours:

I never understood how much I loved you. I didn't. You know how we talked about our love, how it was this thing that was EVERYTHING to us? It was everything to me, Ever, every last goddamned motherfucking thing, and it's gone. You're gone. And I needed it even more than I knew then, when I had you.

Will you know me if you wake up? Will you love me?

I was spiraling emotionally. Reading the letters made me cry, and watching Cade suffer made it only worse. I wasn't sure if he knew I knew about the letters.

Finally, one afternoon, I broached the subject. We were on the bed together, my head on his chest. It was a familiar, comforting embrace, but it wasn't what I wanted. I knew we had zero privacy in the nursing home, but I still wanted to feel as if he wanted me. I wanted him to try to touch me, to kiss me, to act as if he was drowning without my kisses, like he once had. Yet, always, he only ever held me platonically.

"Cade?" I asked.

"Hmmm?" His voice was a rumble against my head.

"I've been reading your letters." I still had to think about what I said, and work to make my speech sound normal. "I found them in the side table."

"Yeah?" He was trying to sound casual.

"Are you sure you're okay?" It felt like a lie, asking him that. I knew he wasn't. I could see it. No one could write what he'd written and be okay.

"Those letters were the only way I knew how to deal with how I felt."

"And now?"

"Now you're awake. And getting better."

"If there was something wrong, something bad, would you tell me?"

He hesitated. "You need to focus on getting better. That's all that matters."

Slowly, and with great effort, I pulled away from him, turned, met his eyes. His amber gaze was raw and conflicted. "Don't ever lie to me, Cade." I kept my eyes on him. "I'd rather know the truth, the hard, painful truth, than live with a lie."

"Ever—" He closed his eyes, squeezed them tight, and drew in a harsh breath.

"Do you love me?"

His eyes flew open, and for once his gaze blazed. "Yes! Of course I do. How could you ask me that?"

"Sometimes I just...I feel like you're not... telling me everything. Maybe not lying, but...hiding. Something." I reached out, touched his knee. "And...I need you. Like things were. I want our life back. I want *us* back. I want...I *need*...love. Our love. The way it was."

He sighed, and took my hand in his. I could see him thinking, making an effort. "Ever, babe. I know I'm—I know I've been...off lately, but...I'm trying."

"Trying what?"

He shifted as if the question made him uncomfortable. "Honest to god, I don't even know. I just don't know. I'm a mess, Ev. You're awake, you're getting better. I don't know what's wrong with me."

That sounded to me like an evasion. Maybe even a flat-out lie. Why would Cade lie to me?

I sighed, realizing I wasn't going to get anything else out of him. I felt lost dealing with this new and different Cade. It was like…like I didn't know him. Like I'd woken up and the Cade who visited me, hugged me, kissed me…that was a Cade I'd never met, a Cade who had taken the place of the one I'd known before the accident.

I felt the tear fall, and I didn't bother wiping it away. I didn't bother stopping the rest, either.

"Ev? What's wrong?"

How could he ask me that? "What's—what's wrong? God, Cade. *Everything*. You're not…I don't know you. You're not the same. I'm trying, Cade. I'm working as hard as I can to…to get better for you. To be the woman you knew. I'm sorry I'm not there yet, but I will be. I'll be there for you. I'm *here*. And I need you, but you're not…I feel like I can't reach you."

He choked and slid off the bed, crossed the room and pulled the door open, paused, turned to look at me. "I'm sorry, Ever. I'm—just…I'm sorry." And then he was gone.

I'd read all the letters. I'd stayed up all night, reading. Hoping for a clue as to what had happened to my Cade. The letters didn't provide any direct answers, but they hinted, in a very oblique sort of way, that *something* had happened to him, and now the Cade who used to be was gone. Ruined somehow. Wrecked. Maybe it had just been too much. Losing his mom, then his dad, then me, then his grandparents. It was too much for anyone to endure, yet it had happened to him, and how could he not lose himself? How could he not show the effects of such suffering?

It only reaffirmed how much I needed to get him home and be his wife, his best friend. His family. Support him. No matter how lost I felt myself, I had to be there for him. He *needed* me. I felt cold without him. Alone.

I missed Eden. I'd borrowed Cade's phone and called her. *The voice mailbox of the person you are trying to reach is full. Please try again later.* Where was she? What was she doing? Why had she left?

So many questions, and no answers.

The last line of the last letter Cade had written haunted me:

No matter what, I love you. I'll never stop loving you. I don't know if you'll love me when you wake up. If you'll be able to. But even if you don't, I'll love you. Forever, and after forever. Even if I don't deserve your love.

Why wouldn't he deserve my love? I didn't get it. Couldn't hope to understand. I loved him. Completely. I needed him. I trusted him. I wanted him. I wanted him to kiss me like he meant it. I wanted him to kiss me, and for his kisses to grow impatient, to become demanding. And yet, when he did kiss me, his lips barely touched mine, and then he moved away. A chaste, impossible brush of his lips, and then it was over. No heat, no passion.

What had I done to lose his desire? Was I no longer beautiful to him? Had the coma changed me in some way? I'd seen myself in the mirror. I looked pretty much the same. Thinner, yes. My boobs had shrunk with the rest of me, but as I got healthier that would change. My hips were slimmer, but that, too, would change. My eyes were the same shade of green. My skin was paler than usual, sure, but I could tan a little, if he wanted me to. My hair had been shaved for surgery, I'd been told, but it had grown back. It was brushing my shoulders already, and would get longer. It had dead ends that needed trimming, maybe, and it hadn't been getting the kind of regular brushing I usually gave it, so it wasn't quite as shiny or lustrous as usual, but that, too, would change with time.

Why didn't he want me?

Why didn't he think he deserved my love? I could only guess. Notions flitted through my head, but I forcefully dismissed them all before they could take hold. I couldn't bear to doubt him. I couldn't bear to doubt our love, because it was the only thing holding me together.

But my marriage to Caden seemed to be crumbling before my eyes.

After a year and a half in a coma, and two months of recovery and therapy in the nursing home, I was finally going home. Cade had brought me a pair of jeans and a T-shirt and a pair of sandals. I'd dressed myself, sitting on the hospital bed. I was going through the motions, but part of me didn't really believe that I was going home. I felt like I'd always been in the hospital. In terms of time elapsed, to me, I'd only been here for two months. But in reality, it had been almost two years. I'd lost *two years* of my life.

That was almost irrelevant, though. It felt like I'd lost Cade, and I had lost Eden. I didn't even know why. Why would Eden abandon me when I needed her the most? Now, in all my life, I needed her more than ever, and she'd vanished into thin air. Caden was wasting away, seemed to be literally dying before my eyes, and my connection to him, which had once seemed unbreakable and inviolable, was severed, fading, crumbling along with the man I'd known and loved.

Suddenly I was sobbing. Sitting on my hospital bed for the last time, I found myself bawling uncontrollably, shuddering and gasping and choking, unable to breathe or to slow the tears.

"Ev?" The door opened and Cade came in, sitting on the bed beside me.

I couldn't answer. I could only turn into him and bury my face against his chest and wish he was who I needed him to be. His arm went around me, holding me.

"What's wrong, babe?" His voice was soft, hesitant.

"Everything, Cade. Me. My life. Us. You. It's all… wrong. You're…different. Something happened while I was in a coma, and you're not the same anymore. It feels like…like you don't love me anymore. Not the way you did. You barely even kiss me. I know I've changed from being in the coma, but…I didn't think that would matter to you. I thought you'd—you'd want me. But you don't. And I don't know how to get that back. How to get—you. You back." The more upset I got, the harder it was to make sense, to get the words out in the right order. I'd worked my ass off to be able to speak normally, to use my hands normally. I was working my ass off to be able to walk normally. But sometimes, it was just too hard. "I'm sorry, Cade. I'm sorry."

"Jesus, Ev. There's nothing for you to be sorry for."

"Then what's *wrong* with you? I know you've been through hell. I know you've lost…everyone. But I'm here. I'm back. And I love you. I *need* you. Even when you're physically here with me, it feels like you're…a million miles away. I don't know what I did, or what happened. And I don't care. I just need you now, more than ever."

Cade had gone still as stone, and just as cold. "Ever…while you were in the coma, I—"

I put my hand over his mouth. "Don't. Just stop. I can't handle anything else. I don't care. Maybe I should. Maybe I will someday. But right now, I just need you. I need you to love me. I need you to tell me it's going to be okay. Lie to me if you have to, and tell me everything will be okay. I'm lost, Cade. And you're the only north I have."

Cade shook, shuddered. "Ever, god. *Fuck.* I've failed you. I'm falling apart, right when you need me most."

"So be there for me." I clung to his neck. I put my lips to the warm hollow behind his ear. "Pull it together, Cade. For me. Please."

"I'll try. I do love you. I never stopped loving

you. I just…got lost. For a while." He sounded as if he was trying to convince himself as much as me. "I'm here. I'm not going anywhere. I'll be what you need me to be. I promise I will."

I didn't let him go. I whispered in his ear, "I need to know…that you're still my husband. Not just my best friend, my supporter. Not just a caretaker. I need to know you're the man I married. I need to know… that you want me. I can't live without that."

He inhaled deeply, his chest swelling against me. He let out the breath and cupped my cheek with his big, rough hand. His eyes were liquid amber, damp with tears I didn't understand, tears he fought away. I watched him strengthen as he gazed at me. Watched the guilt and turmoil subside. Buried, perhaps, but gone for now.

And in that moment, I didn't care where those emotions went. I was being selfish, I knew that. But I needed him. I couldn't find myself in this new normal without him, and I'd take lies and denial if necessary. Someday I'd face the truth, whatever that might be. But I wasn't strong enough mentally, emotionally, or physically to take anything painful, or to endure any more suffering. Neither was Cade. For now, we had to cling to each other, bound together by time and by the ropes of agony, by the lies we were telling ourselves and each other.

He was hiding something from me. I knew that.

I wasn't fool enough to be able to ignore that. I was fool enough, however, to pretend it didn't matter. To pretend I didn't care.

His thumb brushed my cheekbone, the edge of my eyebrow. My temple. Down, touched my lips. He blinked, a long, slow shuttering of his eyelids, almost as if in slow motion. The war in his eyes faded further yet, buried deeper. I watched this happen, watched him summon reserves of strength I don't think he knew he had.

And then…he kissed me.

Truly, deeply, kissed me. His mouth was warm and wet, and he tasted like coffee, and his lips on mine were hesitant at first, then demanding, strong and devouring. My fingers curled around the back of his neck, clutching at him, and I kissed him back with all of me, drawing his breath into my lungs, sucking at his tongue with my mouth and tasting him, and we breathed together, held each other and kissed as we'd never kissed.

He pulled back first, let his forehead rest against mine with a soft bump. He was breathing hard, his fingers digging into my shoulders. "Ever…." It seemed like nothing so much as a prayer.

"Cade. It's you and me. It's always you and me."

"I know."

"Do you?"

He remained there, forehead to mine, as if unable

to move. "Ever, just…no matter what, I love you. I'll always love you. I'll always need you. I'll always be only yours. No matter what."

"No matter what."

"Don't ever forget that."

I heard the plea in his voice. "I won't," I said. "I promise."

As Cade drove me home, I wondered, deep in the shadowy, secret places of my heart, if I would be able to keep that promise.

closer

ays turned to weeks, and weeks to months. In some ways, it felt as if Cade and I were back at square one in our relationship, but a square one we'd never really had. We dated. Really, truly dated. He took me to therapy and encouraged me as I learned to walk and to write and to dress myself standing up and to do my hair, and helped me do my makeup and taught me to draw all over again. He was patient, and considerate. He went on walks with me, from the front door of our downtown Royal Oak condo building to the corner and back, shuffling slowly beside me, holding my hand, as if we were eighty years old together. He took me to dinner and to lunch and to breakfast. He left me for a few hours in the evenings to work, and I spent those times watching TV, walking from one wall of the condo to the other, slow and clumsy.

My art was gone. I had to relearn that, too. I could barely write my name. My mind knew what to do, but my body didn't. I couldn't even think of painting. It simply hurt too much. I refused to go near the studio. I felt like I was missing a piece of my soul, a fraction of my identity.

I spent many of the hours Cade was at work crying in frustration and loneliness. He was loving, attentive, sweet. He put my needs before his own. He helped me shower. Helped me dress. Helped me do everything and anything I had trouble with, and he never complained.

He kissed me sometimes. Slow and delicate kisses, soft feather-light touches of his lips to mine. His hands never wandered, though. His kisses never regained that passion I'd once known. He was trying, I knew. He did love me. That much was obvious. But if I tried to push the kiss further, he would back away, acting scared, or guilty, or confused. I wasn't sure which, or maybe it was all three. Something I didn't understand and couldn't fathom. He said it wasn't me; again and again he reassured me that he loved me, that nothing had changed.

He wanted to take it slow, he once said.

Three months after going home—three months of loneliness and self-doubt and emotional turmoil,

I finally lost my temper with him. We were sitting on our couch, watching DVRd episodes of *Game of Thrones*. His hand was on my leg, resting an inch or two above my knee. Touching bare skin, since I was wearing one of his old T-shirts—and nothing else. He surely knew I was bare beneath the shirt, but he made no move to touch me, to skate his fingers up my thigh. I needed it. I needed his touch.

I needed reassurance that he loved me, that I was his, that I was still beautiful. That I wasn't alone. Because even though he was taking perfect care of me, and was physically present in my life, he seemed out of reach, distant. Untouchable.

Over the last three months, my tolerance for his emotional frigidity waned, and my temper reached a boiling point.

I was confused, hurt, angry. And, besides all of that, I was just simply horny. I was a young woman, and I was regaining my health, and I had a husband to whom I was deliriously attracted, with whom I was madly in love. Yet he never took any of the hints, no matter how subtle or blatant. In the hospital, before we left, I thought I'd been clear about what I needed.

Now, with Daenerys and Sansa and Gregor and Robb playing out their drama on screen, I found myself boiling over. Silently seething. I couldn't take it anymore.

I grabbed the remote from Cade's lap and clicked the TV off.

"Hey!" Cade protested, turning to face me.

"I can't take this anymore, Cade." I tossed the remote aside, pivoting on the couch so one leg was dangling to the floor and the other was curled beneath my butt. "I'm going crazy."

"What are you talking about, Ev?" He frowned at me in confusion, but I could see fear beneath that.

"Us. You. I'm alone, Cade. I'm lonely."

"I'm here, Ev. I'm with you."

"NO! You're *not!*" I yelled. "Your body is here. You're going through the motions of being with me, but you're…who you are, who you were…it's gone. You're…cold. Closed off."

Cade tipped his head back and groaned, wiping his face with both hands. "God, Ever. I'm trying, okay? But what if…what if that guy you knew is just gone?"

"That's bullshit, Cade. You claim you love me. You claim you've never stopped loving me. But you haven't touched me since I woke up."

"You're still healing, Ev—" Cade started.

"I'm well enough to make love, Cade," I interrupted. "I need you. I need that. I need you to touch me like you want me. Do you? Do you want me?"

His answer was automatic, immediate. "Yes!"

"Then prove it." I stood up in front of him, clutched the hem of the T-shirt where it hung to mid-thigh.

"Ever, babe—" He shifted, and his knees fell open. His eyes flitted from mine down to my chest, to my legs, and back up.

"I never thought I'd have to beg you, Cade. But I am." I lifted the T-shirt up, up.

My crossed arms lifted my boobs, and then the shirt was free and my boobs bounced back down. I'd put on ten pounds or so, and I was nearly back to my pre-coma weight, a healthy one-twenty. I had my curves back, and I knew Cade had once loved my body. Once, he'd not been able to get enough of me. Now, his eyes roved over me. Starting at my face, searching my tumultuous gaze, then sliding down to my breasts. He licked his lips as he looked at me, and I watched his body shift. Watched his zipper tighten. His gaze went down to my legs, to the juncture of my thighs. I'd taken a bath earlier in the evening, and I'd taken extra care to shave myself for him. He liked me clean-shaven. Or he had, once. Now, I didn't know what he liked anymore.

I stepped forward, between his knees. His thighs brushed my hips, and my tits hung at eye-level. "Touch me, Cade. I'm yours. Take me. Show me I'm still what you want. Please. Please, Cade."

"Jesus, Ever." His face tipped forward and his mouth touched my belly, his lips grazing my ribs. "I'm sorry. I'm so sorry. I wish I could explain what's in my head, in my heart. But I just can't. You're so beautiful, Ev. So gorgeous. So strong, so brave."

I feathered my fingers into his long, black shaggy hair. He'd let it grow since the accident, and it was now curling around his neck and shoulders. He shaved, but didn't let his facial hair grow into a beard, so he was always scruffy and stubbled with several days' worth of growth. I liked the look, but I wanted my Cade back, the clean jawline and the messy but clean-cut hair.

"I don't need you to explain, Cade. Not now, at least. Yeah, I've got a million questions, and I just don't understand what's happened to you, but none of that matters. I know you need something I can't give or don't have, and I'm sorry. But right now, all I can think of is how badly I need this. I'm standing naked in front of you, Caden Connor Monroe, and I need you to make me feel something. You're my husband. Please, please, *please*…be my husband. Be my lover."

His hands ascended from his knees to my hips, and his fingers dug into the flesh just beneath my hipbones. His face tipped up, and he looked at me from between my cleavage. "You're perfect, Ev. You're everything."

I stared down at him, my fingers in his hair. "Then show me that." I pulled his face to my breasts, and his mouth met the hot flesh and his tongue licked out, laved the pale round expanse of my right breast, just beneath my nipple.

But I was watching him, and I saw the pain on his face, the inexplicable guilt and sorrow in his expression. I clamped my eyes shut and pushed away the wonder and the fear and the curiosity and the need to know what was causing that in him. I shut down my thoughts and focused on simply feeling. Focused on his touch, his mouth that was finally, *thankyougodfinally* taking my erect nipple into his mouth and flicking it with his tongue, focused on his hands that were clutching my hips and curling around to cup my ass.

If I thought too much, I would ask, and he would admit, and everything would be ruined. And I *needed* this first. I couldn't face the truth without feeling this at least once. It felt like I was stealing something from him. Dragging it out of him.

I was a fool, and I knew it.

Yet I didn't stop him, only encouraged him with little moans as his tongue darted out to flick my left nipple and his lips wrapped around my breast and his hands carved and possessed and roamed.

He groaned, and my nipple left his mouth with a *pop*, and he fell back against the couch, chest heaving. "Jesus, Ev."

I wasn't sure what the epithet meant, and I didn't care. I took his hands in mine and tugged at him. He stood up, looked down at me. "Say my name, Cade."

"Ever."

I slid my hands up underneath his thin white V-neck, pushed it off, and tossed it aside. Touched his chest, his abs. His shoulders. Found the button of his jeans, ripped it open, found the zipper tab and drew it down. Felt the springy hardness sheathed in black cotton boxer-briefs. His hands rested on the bell of my hips, and as I let his jeans drop, his fingers tightened. My eyes were locked on his, watching every shift in expression. I curled my fingers in the elastic waistband, paused, watching him, and then pulled the band away from his body and lowered the underwear past his erection. The boxers fell to the floor, and he was naked with me. His hands shook and his eyes hunted mine, moving back and forth, and his expression was unknowable, rife with a myriad of emotions.

Thank god, the most prevalent emotion was desire. He wanted me. But he was holding back, and I didn't dare examine why.

I lifted my chin, and he leaned down to kiss me. As it had been so often lately, the kiss was slow and gentle. Not what I wanted. I went up onto my toes and crushed my mouth against his, letting my sexual hunger have free rein. I put one hand to his face, holding his face to mine. My hand went between our bodies, my fingers wrapping around his erection. I just touched him at first. Felt the thick hot hardness in my hand, huge and straight, standing against his belly. A single slide down his length, and he groaned.

"Ever…"

"Cade." I pulled back and met his gaze.

"You don't know how good your hand feels on me."

"I belong to you, Cade." I whispered it against his chin. "I'm yours. Take all of me." Up, and back down his cock, sliding and slipping, reveling in the softness and the hardness and the heat of him.

He bent and kissed my throat, the hollow at the base, just above my breastbone. Between my tits. Knelt. His hands skated down the backs of my thighs, and I began to tremble in anticipation. I let my head fall back as his mouth found my hipbone, the dip where hip met thigh. The bare skin of my pubis. His hands clutched the back of my knees, and his lips kissed across my body, to the opposite hipbone. His hands tugged gently at my legs, and I slid my feet apart willingly.

This. Yes, please. This.

He breathed on my sensitive flesh, and I shook all over. Gasped. Threaded my hands in his hair and pulled his mouth to me.

"Please, Cade. Please." I would absolutely beg, because I remembered how good he could make me feel with only his mouth.

A questing flick of his tongue against my lower lips. I held my breath, and his mouth pressed to my opening and his tongue went into me, and I whimpered in sweet relief as rockets of raw pleasure shot through me. Within seconds, my knees were trembling and about to give out. He felt this, caught me up in his arms as he stood.

I was dizzy and disoriented. I knew only the strength in his arms, the tilt of the world as he laid me on our bed and hovered above me.

"Finish me, Cade." I didn't know what I was saying, didn't care.

He knelt between my legs and leaned over me, kissed my throat, palmed each of my boobs in his big rough hands, and I moaned. He ran his hands down my sides, cupped my hip, and then his fingers slid between my thighs and moved up, grazing the tender insides of my legs and touched me there, and I whimpered. He dipped one finger into me, and I gasped.

He curled his finger inside me, and I groaned loudly.

"Make me scream, Cade." I arched my back and kept my eyes closed, tangled my fingers in the pillow above my head.

He added a second finger and took my nipple into his mouth, and I was afloat, fire rippling in my veins. I knew I was making some kind of noise but couldn't hear anything except the rushing of blood in my ears, the pounding of my pulse.

This felt new somehow. Like my first time. Every molecule of my being was attuned to Cade's touch, which was the only familiar thing in my universe. It was all I needed.

His mouth descended to my clit, pressing soft wet kisses along the way, and he sucked the hard nub of nerves into his mouth and flicked it with his tongue, worked his fingers inside my slit. He did as I'd commanded, and made me scream.

I exploded, arching off the bed and letting my throat express the screams of release, and my belly shook and my head spun and my hands clawed at Cade.

Cade.

Cade.

My lover.

I clung to him, panting, pulled him up my body and clutched his neck with both arms, gasping his name over and over and over again. I felt his erection nudging my thigh. I opened my legs and wrapped my heels around his thighs. I was tight, and wet. In that moment, in the instant before he penetrated me, impaled me, I felt every single day of the year and a half that I'd been unconscious, felt every single second of his absence in my body. I felt every single fraction of time that I'd been without him, that he'd been without me.

With his cock poised against the opening of my pussy, I pressed my lips to his ear and whispered. "I love you. No matter what. Forever and Always." That was a mantra to me then. I knew, no matter what came in the months ahead, that those words would be my comfort and my strength. Forever and Always.

"You swear? You promise me? Forever and Always? No matter what?" He sounded so desperate, so afraid, that I buried my face in his neck and shifted my hips, buried his thick hard cock in my wet soft heat.

"Yes, Cade. I swear. I swore when I married you, and I meant it. Forever." My words were soft and quick and without hesitation.

He moved with me, and I thought I heard a stifled sob escape him, but it was gone just as quickly. "I love you, Ever. This…this is home. You. Me. This is my only home."

I felt him within me, filling me, completing me. Our bodies moved in perfect unison, as they always had, and time fell away. I was with him then, in every moment we'd spent together, bare flesh pressed to flesh, breathing in the living silence of our love, in the tender fierce fury of our mated bodies, I was there with him in the moment when we'd first made love, in my studio at Cranbrook. I was there with him in the studio of this very condo—a room which I'd not been brave enough to venture into yet—as he fucked me against the wall, bent over and grinding hard into me in the way I loved so much, watching us move together in the mirror. I was there with him in this bedroom, an endless parade of nights that was at once a lifetime of memories and not nearly enough time. I was there with him through the span of forever.

He planted a fist into the pillow beside my temple and stared down at me, his eyes intense and fiery amber, lit by the moonglow from the window, and he moved into me. I held onto him and let him move. I was still and searching his eyes, his soul through those beautiful orbs, and let him love me as I'd begged him to.

Then, when I could hold still no longer, I crushed my hips against his in a counter thrusting rhythm. I pressed my lips to the column of his throat and bit the muscle of his shoulder and clawed at his back.

When his rhythm faltered and his breath caught, I tangled my fingers in his wild black hair and met his mouth in a demanding kiss, and we found release together, him groaning and me screaming and both of us panting as it relinquished its grip on us and left us limp together in the sheets.

We rolled and found the position of afterglow bliss, my head in the crook of his arm, my breasts brushing his chest and my leg thrown across his thigh.

It was only as I drifted toward sleep that I thought of any kind of practicalities. "Cade…I'm not…I haven't—" My brain was muzzy and heavy with near-sleep fog. "Are we…protected?"

Cade sucked in a sharp breath, and his shoulders shook. "Fuck, Ever. *Fuck*."

I didn't understand the intensity of his reaction. "It'll be fine, Cade—"

"No, Ev. It's not." His voice was flat, the kind of emotionless tone that meant he was battling something painful and trying to hold on.

"Why not?" I dreaded his answer. "I mean, if I do get pregnant—"

"You won't." He sounded bizarrely sure.

"How do you know?"

He did sob then. "Don't make me say it." He wasn't talking to me, I didn't think. "I've spent the last two years refusing to even think about this."

"About what, Cade?" I sat up, not bothering to hold the sheet against my chest. "What aren't you telling me?"

"Before the accident, did you know…" He trailed off and swallowed hard. His eyes were closed, his expression pinched and pained. "Did you know you—you were…pregnant?" He could barely get the words out.

Shock hit me like a fist to the gut. "I was…
pregnant?"

He nodded. "Yeah. Eight or ten weeks."

I fell backward, and my skull thunked against the
headboard. I barely registered the pain, though. "I
was *pregnant?*" I couldn't breathe. "Was?"

Cade's hand curled into a fist and pressed against
the bridge of his nose. "Yeah. Was. You didn't know?"

"No, I didn't know!" I shot forward, dragging
my fingers through my hair, pulled at it so the roots
twinged. "I would've told you if I'd known."

Cade was shut down, every muscle tensed,
shoulders curled in toward his body, eyes closed, fists
clenched, brows furrowed. He looked like he was
suffering a beating, withstanding physical blows.

"The accident…I—I lost it? Lost the baby?" I
watched him with tear-blurred eyes, salt stinging,
chest tight and heart thudding.

Cade only nodded.

"I lost the baby. I didn't even know I was pregnant. How—how could that happen? I was on an
IUD."

"You'd just gotten a new one put in." Cade could
barely manage a hoarse whisper. "She said—she said
that's when there's risk of pregnancy. It's a small per-
centage that it happens to, but it does happen."

He still wouldn't look at me.

"There's more, isn't there?" I sat cross-legged on the sheets, watching Cade curl inward even further.

He nodded. I watched him, waiting. He sat up, breathing slowly through his nose. His eyes were agonized. "The accident...it caused you to miscarry. You were bleeding...so bad. There was blood everywhere. All over you. Me. The car. The snow. Fuck..." He covered his eyes with his hand, forced himself to keep going. "You were hemorrhaging really bad. They had—they had to do a hysterectomy to stop it."

"A—a hysterectomy?" I didn't understand what he was saying. I refused to understand. "What are you saying?"

"A hysterectomy, Ev. You know what that means. Please, fuck, please don't make me say it."

I clutched at him. "No. No. Cade, no." Everything was spinning.

The joy and the pleasure I'd felt only moments before wasn't even a memory. It was wiped out, erased. I didn't believe him.

"You're lying. They lied to you. It's a mistake." My hands were clawed over my belly. Over my womb.

Cade's head dropped, and his shoulders shook. "No, Ever. God, you think I wanted to tell you this? You think I'd lie about this?" He sounded as if razor blades were slicing his throat. "You can't conceive anymore, Ever."

My fingers dug into my belly, as if I could rip the horrible truth out of my body, change it by violent force of will. "No. *No*." I rocked back and forth. "Don't say that. Don't *say* that!"

I hadn't known, until that moment, what the ability to conceive really meant. I hadn't understood what it meant to me. I'd married Cade because I loved him, because we were perfect together. We belonged together, belonged to each other, and we always had, always would. I'd thought in vague terms of "having a family." Someday we'd have kid together, because that's what you did. We'd be ready for that step someday. That was what I'd thought. I remembered thinking it. I remembered the weeks before the accident, feeling nauseous at odd times. Being hungrier. Strange mood swings. But I'd not really thought about what it had meant. I hadn't known. I'd been pregnant, and I hadn't known. I'd been carrying Cade's baby inside me, and I hadn't known.

And now…now I'd never know. I'd never be a mother. I'd never have Cade's baby.

I'd noticed my lack of a period, but I'd simply dismissed it as a side effect of the accident and the trauma and the ensuing stress.

I lurched off the bed, stumbled into the bathroom, slammed the door closed with my foot. Fell against the wall and slid down to the floor, the tile cold against my butt and legs.

I'd sobbed in my life. I'd been a wreck. I'd cried until I couldn't cry anymore. But never in my life had I cried like I did on that bathroom floor. Naked and alone and cold, I wept for what I'd never have, for what I'd never be able to give Caden.

At some point, he came in and slumped to the floor beside me, wrapped me up and held me, unspeaking. He didn't reassure me, because it would never be okay, and he knew it.

Strangely, unfairly, I felt closer to Cade in that moment of utter heartbreak than ever before.

jumping off the dock

Eden

I sat down on the empty beach, glad of the solitude. I'd gone to the beach early, right after breakfast. Not even eight o'clock. It was already a warm day, promising to be hot. I had my well-worn copy of my favorite romance novel in hand, and a bottle of water. The cottage was only a short walk away, in case I got hot, or overwhelmed, or needed the solace of four walls and closed blinds.

As long as no one was around, I could leave my cover-up off and just soak up the sun. I was alone. I was okay, because there was no one else around to see the tears that fell when I remembered what I carried inside me, and the ruin it surely represented.

I got comfortable and opened my book. I became deeply immersed in re-reading my favorite scene. I'd read it at least half a dozen times, but I never got tired of it. It was a place of comfort for me.

I finished the chapter and looked up, surveying the lapping water of Grand Traverse Bay's east arm, the golden sand, the sun rising just above the horizon. Quiet, peaceful. And then I saw him. He'd come out of nowhere.

Thigh-deep in the water, six feet tall, lean and wiry, corded with muscles so defined they might as well have been cut into his body by a razor. His hair was black as a crow's wing, dripping wet, thick. I couldn't help watching as he stretched his body. Couldn't take my eyes off his long, hard biceps as they flexed, his abs as they hardened and shifted. He wasn't huge, wasn't a burly beast. But he was clearly in incredible shape. He was breathing hard, his chest swelling as he sucked in a deep breath and let it out, rolling his shoulders. He'd obviously swum from somewhere far away, but where? There were a few sailboats anchored off in the distance, but they'd been there for days, no one coming or going that I'd seen. There was a small island a couple of miles out, but surely he hadn't come from *that* far.

He'd literally just…*appeared*. A mouth-watering vision of male beauty. His face…god, his features were perfection, sculpted into a face that I couldn't look away from.

When our eyes met, I felt a jolt in my soul, an electric shock. I forced my eyes back down to my book, but I couldn't see the words on the page. They wavered and blurred as I tried to keep from looking up, from meeting his gaze. His eyes were a pale blue, so pale they were like sunlit chips of sky-blue ice. They held me in their thrall, even as I kept my attention on my book. Or, pretended to. In reality, I was watching him through my peripheral vision as he strode up out of the water and onto the sand.

He was, quite simply, a work of art from head to toe.

Fucking hell. How could I be thinking that way? What the hell was wrong with me?

I dug my fingernails into my thigh. I desperately wanted to look up, to see if he was watching me. What if he came up to me? What if he spoke to me?

On the drive up I'd stopped for gas at a Speedway. I'd gone in to buy some Gatorade and snacks, and the clerk had asked me, in a very bored and uninterested tone of voice, how I was doing. The way people do out of habit, as a greeting, rather than actually caring about your response.

"I'm pregnant," I'd blurted, my credit card held out in front of me.

The clerk had stared at me in confusion as he swiped the card. "Oooh...kay. Congratulations," he said, handing my card back.

I took my card, grabbed my things, and left, embarrassed. It had just popped out, an admission to a total stranger. The need to tell *some*one had been overwhelming. What I really should have said is, "No congratulations. W-T-F, you stupid whore, would be more like it." *That* was what I deserved.

What if this model-beautiful angel of a man approached me, and I blurted out the truth to him, too? I'd die. Just...die. So I gripped my thigh and my book, praying he wouldn't stop and talk to me, but also wishing, hoping desperately that he would. Because, *shit*, he was gorgeous.

His step faltered as he passed me, and I thought he might stop, but he didn't. He regained his equilibrium and kept walking, out of range of my peripheral vision.

A few minutes later, I heard—and felt—the stomach-shaking rumble of a throaty engine. Was it his? I wondered what kind of vehicle would make that kind of noise, and almost turned to look. But what if he was watching? He'd see me, and then maybe he'd stop to talk, and my wayward tongue would get me in trouble. I pictured a classic car, something low and sleek. Lean and powerful, like him. He'd moved with easy, predatory grace. He'd drive a car like that, something that would prowl, rumble.

I wondered what his voice was like. Would it be deep? Rough? Smooth? I leaned back on my elbows, staring up at the blue sky. Now that he was gone, I could relax. I'd picked a spot on the beach that was not visible from the road, so I rolled onto my stomach, untied the strap of my top, and let the sun bake my back. I'd slathered on a thick layer of sunscreen, of course. Maybe too much sun wasn't good. For me...or for the baby.

I wasn't even sure about what I was going to do. People talked blithely in books and TV shows and movies about "options." About "keeping it," or "getting rid of it." Those phrases weren't things to toss about so easily. Not for me. Keep it? Be a mother? Single, without a degree, without a family? I wouldn't, couldn't ask Cade for anything. He had Ever to take care of. There was no way to tell how she'd heal, how she'd recover. If she recovered. Dr. Overton had said she might not even recover completely. She could progress to a certain point, and then just... stop. Never recover all of her speech, or movement. There was just no way to tell. And if she did recover completely, it would be a long time before she was able to start any kind of life. It wasn't "resume life," really. It was more starting over. She'd have to relearn how to walk. How to use her hands. Re-develop her fine motor skills. How to write, how to draw, how to paint. Jesus, her painting. That was her life. How would she cope without that? Especially if she found out about Cade and me.

I knew that would happen someday. I'd turned off my cell phone when I left. It was still active, still connected in case I needed it, but I had it turned off. There was no one I wanted to talk to. I'd been gone for just less than a week. Five days, in fact. Cade would probably suspect something by now. I'd never missed a day with Ever. Not in the entire eighteen months of her coma. And now I'd just…disappeared?

It was cruel of me. To him, but to Ever most of all. Just vanishing, with no explanation? But I didn't know how else to handle it. Anything else would lead to the truth, and I just couldn't, wouldn't, lay that on Cade. But especially not on Ever. Not now.

And so I was here. Alone. On a beach.

I'd spent my first few days here cleaning the cottage. Tom—Mr. Callahan, the caretaker—had pulled the sheets off the furniture and turned on the water and utilities, but that was it. The whole place was coated in a layer of dust. There were decade-old canned goods in some of the cabinets. I emptied everything, dusted, vacuumed, scrubbed sinks and toilets and mirrors and counters. Mopped floors and cleaned windows. I bought a few cheap pieces of art in downtown Traverse City, just to make it homey. I replaced the twenty-year-old couch with something newer. Bought new bed sheets, towels, new dishes, cooking utensils, silverware. I stocked the cabinets with healthy food. No junk—except for a few treats, as a reward for eating healthier than usual—and no caffeine. That was hard. No soda, no coffee. Good thing I was alone, because right now I was a raging bitch without caffeine in the morning. No alcohol. That was the worst. Nothing to take the edge off. Nothing to help me forget. Just my own unrelenting thoughts…all the time.

I spent a lot time running. There was no gym here, not something close at least, so I ran. I started with two miles first thing in the morning. Finished it with pushups and crunches. I couldn't afford to let my weight go. Not now. I noticed I was hungrier, except midmorning, when the nausea would hit. I usually puked a few times around ten or eleven, and I'd eat some saltines—a tip learned from the Internet. The feeling would pass, and I'd be fine the rest of the day.

I also played Apollo. Ceaselessly. There was little else to do, now that I wasn't in school anymore. I worked on my solo. I played through the entirety of Bach's suites within the first three days. And then I started again. I hadn't dared bring Apollo to the beach yet, but I would. Someday. It was Mom's beach. Mom's cello. I had to play there, for her. For her memory.

I hadn't thought of Mom in a long time. I'd pur-posefully put her out of my mind—it was my way of healing. I'd bleached my hair to look like hers six months after she'd died, and I'd kept it that color ever since, out of habit. Out of memory. Besides, I liked not looking identical to Ever. She was already more beautiful than I was, skinnier, glossy black hair, slimmer hips, svelte waist, delicate shoulders. Over the years I'd become obsessed with keeping my weight down. I'd grown to need the gym. Need the rush of a killer workout. It wasn't about Mom, not anymore.

And now, here, at her family's cottage, I found myself thinking of her for the first time in years. Missing her. Needing her. Wondering what she'd say if she knew the mess I'd gotten myself into. Scold me? Yell? Scream? Refuse to talk to me? I didn't have any idea how she would have been as a parent to me in my later years. She'd been fairly even-tempered until the day she died. I got my temper from her, while Ever was more like Dad, inward-focused, quiet, slow to anger. Mom would get irritated with me and Ever. We'd get into trouble, and we'd play the twin-confu-sion card. She'd get fed up, and she'd yell. We always knew we'd pushed the game far enough when Mom got really mad. We knew we'd crossed the line when she stopped yelling and got scary-quiet. Now that I was an adult, would she sit me down and lecture me about my current situation? Or be a support? She would be disappointed. I knew that much.

After letting the sun roast me for a while, I retied my top, slid off my shorts, got up, and moved toward the water. I walked in, toes, ankles, knees, then up to my thighs. The water was thigh-deep for several more feet, and then I hit the rope marking the boundary of the swim area and ducked under. Now the water was up to my waist, and then my boobs went buoyant. Finally, I ducked under, swimming underwater in the cold depths.

Down, down, following the bottom until the pressure hurt my ears and the cold was too sharp. I let myself float upward, and I broke the surface. I saw in the distance a platform, bobbing gently in the little waves. The dock. It was still there. As a little girl, I remembered thinking it was so far out. Swimming out there had seemed so grown-up, so daring and adventurous. Now I realized it was maybe twenty feet from the roped-off section, if that far. The water was well over my head, though, and I felt an absurd moment of panic as I did a sloppy crawl stroke toward it. I'd swum in pools, of course, but I hadn't been in a lake in…years. Not since the last time I was here with Mom—well over ten years ago. How long? I calculated the time, distracting myself as I swam. She'd died when I was thirteen, almost fourteen. It had been…two years before her death that we'd come up here. I was twenty-two now. So, yeah, just about ten years.

By the time I'd figured that out I was at the dock, rounding it to find the ladder. I held on to the metal bar, kicking my feet in the dark water. Swimming in the open like this wasn't the same as in a pool. If you faltered in a pool, you could kick over to the edge and climb out. In a lake, there was no edge. If you swam out too far, there was no escape, no easy edge to save you. It wasn't actual fear of that happening that I felt; rather, it was more the potential, the knowledge of the possibility. I kicked and pulled myself up onto the dock, lay on my back, staring up at the sky. The morning air chilled my wet body, but the sun soon warmed me.

I had a memory of being here, on this dock, with Mom. Ever had been on the beach, tanning. She didn't like swimming as much as I did. So Mom swam out with me, held the ladder, and waited till I climbed up. Following behind me, she sat beside me on the rocking platform. The beach seemed so far away, miles distant. I was out of breath from the swim, elated, excited, a little scared. I was going to jump off. I'd been out here with Mom the day before, but I'd chickened out of jumping off.

Mom and I had lain, side by side, on the gently bobbing dock, watching the clouds shift overhead. We stayed until we were hot, and then Mom had climbed to her feet, slicked her hair back, and tugged on the elastic leg band of her swimsuit. I remember thinking, *She's so beautiful,* wishing and hoping I'd grow up to be as beautiful as she was, with her long blonde hair and green eyes and high cheekbones and easy, lovely smile. She'd glanced at me, smiling, winked, and then dove in, slicing perfectly. I'd stood, scared stiff, and watched the deep blue water shift and curl, imagining things lurking in the depths, imagining diving too deep and not being able to make it to the surface in time. Mom just treaded water and waited for me. I shuffled to the edge of the platform, peering over the edge.

"Stop thinking and *jump,* Edie!" Mom had laughed. "You're freaking yourself out. I'm right here, honey."

I was eleven. Way, *way* too old to be scared of jumping off some stupid dock. I'd closed my eyes and jumped. Feet first, arms flailing. I was immediately swallowed by darkness and achingly cold water. I'd fought the panic and kicked to the surface, felt the air on my face and sucked in a deep breath, spluttering, laughing. Mom had laughed with me, given me a high-five, and then we climbed back up and jumped off together, sending the dock rocking. Again and again we jumped off, laughing and making a game of who could jump farther.

Finally, drawn by our laughter, Ever had swum out to join us. She'd acted brave as she climbed up and peered off the edge, the way I'd done, but I'd seen the fear. I remember admiring her *so much* for how she just jumped off, no hesitation, despite her fear. That day, watching Ever do with seeming ease what I'd been scared of, I determined to never let fear get the best of me. I'd always been the first after that. The first to try something, no matter how scared I was. It may have turned into a slight case of impulsiveness, taking risks simply for the sake of not letting fear get the better of me.

Now I lay on the same dock, and I was gripped by fear. Every moment, I was scared. Terrified. I could barely breathe, I was so scared. I was scared of life. Of living. Of what would happen to me. I wasn't a teenager, sure. But I was *way* too young and unprepared to be a mother. A *mother*. Mommy. Me. Eden Irene Eliot, a single mother. I didn't know what I wanted for myself, much less what I wanted for a child. I didn't know how to be a parent.

And…I'd never even been in love.

I stood up, clenching my fists and forcing air into my lungs. Pushed away the rampant terror. I bent my legs and dove in, the way Mom and I had, so long ago.

By the time I reached the shore I was barely holding it together. I threw on my cover-up, toed my feet into my flip-flops, gathered my things, and hurried home. It *was* home, too. It felt like home. What if…what if it was the only home I ever knew? What if I had the baby here and raised him or her alone, here on the peninsula? What if I just never went back? Could I do that? Cut myself out of Ever's life? She was all that mattered, really. And Cade, of course, but he was a can of worms I couldn't deal with. Not yet. I had to push him out of my thoughts, out of my heart.

I sat on my couch, wet from the swim and sweating from running home, hyperventilating in an attempt to keep the wrenching sobs at bay. I couldn't lose it. Wouldn't. This was life now. Alone, in this cottage.

I hadn't loved Cade. Almost, though. I'd *almost* fallen in love with him. I'd seen it happening, felt my heart curling outward and trying to latch onto him. But he didn't love me, and never could and never would. Even if Ever hadn't woken up, everything we could've established would have been based on all the wrong foundations. I had refused to let that happen. I wanted better for myself.

His trip to Wyoming had come at the most perfect moment. That last tangle in the sheets had nearly been my undoing. But then he'd left and I pushed him away, knowing it would be the end. It *had* to be the end. We couldn't keep doing it to each other. It wasn't helping him, and it was only confusing me.

I'd teetered on the edge of a cliff, and then had stumbled back at the last moment. Tearing myself away, pushing him away. It had been wrenchingly painful. But far better than spending the rest of my life loving him and never being able to have him.

And then…and then I'd found out I was pregnant, and everything changed. Now I had no idea what was going to happen to me. I had no one. I'd cut Dad out of my life, although being the stubborn asshole he was, he'd continued to pay for my tuition and room and board. I didn't know why, and never would. He wouldn't visit us, wouldn't call us, wouldn't make any efforts to repair the damaged relationships, but he paid for school, and sent us a monthly allowance. I'd saved most of mine over the past few years. I had enough money put aside to live on a shoestring for maybe a year. I'd been saving it to buy a place when I graduated, only now that would never happen.

When Ever went into the coma, Dad had paid the hospital bills until she'd entered the Home, at which point she'd become a ward of the state. I think he had kick-ass insurance that had covered a huge portion of her bills, but it still must have cost him a staggering amount of money. I also think he paid Cade's hospital bills. I don't know if Cade even realized that.

But he wasn't a support system. I wouldn't ask him for money. I wouldn't call him. I wouldn't let him know what was going on.

I couldn't tell Ever or Cade, either. Mom was long dead, as were her parents and Dad's. So there was just me.

And I was paralyzed with fear. I had no plan, a limited amount of money, no job, no degree. No friends, no family.

I felt the tears begin again, and I lurched off the couch. I pulled Apollo from his case and sat down in the chair in the middle of the living room. I played, and played, and played. Until I broke through the calluses on my fingers and bled, until my wrist ached from holding the bow, until my teeth hurt from grinding them together. I didn't even know what I was playing, just that it was all that mattered, all I had to keep the fear at bay, to keep the brokenness from overwhelming me.

As I finally let the bow drop to the floor, a thought came to me: Each day, facing my fear and simply moving through the day, was akin to jumping off the dock as a little girl. Just waking up was facing my fear. Taking each breath was an act of will. Not breaking down in tears each moment was an effort. All I could do, every single day, was face my fear, jump off the dock, and hope I could swim to shore.

running from the truth

I was lying on the beach late one evening, a few hours before sunset. To the west, out over the water, the sun was an orange ball hanging above the horizon. I was glistening with a layer of sweat, ready to take a quick swim before heading home.

I heard the rumble of his car first. Heard the slam of the door in the distance, followed by a few minutes of silence. Then I heard his footsteps, kicking up the sand. I pretended to ignore him, keeping my eyes closed behind my sunglasses, my hands folded low over my belly, feet crossed at the ankles. I was glad I'd worn my one-piece swimsuit—I was starting to show, just a little.

I thought perhaps he hadn't seen me. His footsteps were passing right next to me. I felt a spray of warm sand hit my leg, and then a sharp intake of breath. I opened my eyes, and found it hard to think. He was standing above me, outlined by the sun. He was so close I could smell him. Sawdust and sweat. I tipped up my sunglasses to see him better. Sweat dripped from his nose and ran down his temple, coating his long, toned arms. He was shirtless, wearing a scuba diving bag on his shoulders. His washboard abs glistened, and the swim shorts he wore were tied low enough that I could see the top of his V-cut. I resisted the urge to lick my lips. Holy shit, he was gorgeous. And the smell of sawdust? Intoxicating. I could see it dappling his skin, sticking to the sweat on his chest and forearms. I wondered what he did to get so covered in sawdust. I wanted to watch him work. I had a vision of him bent over a worktable, scraping at a piece of wood with long, slow strokes, his back muscles rippling and his arms tensing and relaxing with each movement.

He just stared down at me, his pale blue eyes roving over me. Oh, yes, he saw me. And he liked what he saw. I could tell that much. His mouth opened, and I felt myself anticipating the sound of his voice. It would be a low, powerful rumble like the sound of an engine. He'd ask me to go swimming with him. Maybe. I'd learn where he lived. Maybe.

But then he shook his head, closed his mouth with an audible *click*, and headed toward the water.

His fists were clenched at his sides as he jogged toward the waterline. Now, what the hell was that? He'd been about to say something. I knew he had. And then he'd just...run off. Had I scared him off somehow? Although I couldn't imagine what I could have done to do that.

I watched him plow through the water until he was waist deep, and then he dove in and was gone. Just...gone. I kept watching, expecting to see him reappear a few feet farther away, near the dock maybe, or the boat. But he didn't. He dove in and was simply gone. I stood up and moved toward the shoreline, squinting at the bright reflection of the sun on the water, hunting the orange-diamond surface for a hint of him. Where could he have gone?

This was becoming a mystery. The man who never spoke, who appeared and disappeared on the beach. I couldn't think of any explanation for his behavior except perhaps he had some far-off destination to which he swam, somewhere out of sight. It really was strange, and it made him that much more of an enigma. Was he just shy? Did he want to talk to me, but was too nervous? But I dismissed that notion right away. He didn't seem like the shy type. His posture and his body language were that of a man who knew himself, who was comfortable in his own skin. He moved with powerful grace, athletic and in tune with his body. Yet he seemed unwilling or unable to speak to me. Maybe he was mute? But the way he'd opened his mouth just now made me think he *could* talk, but he just wouldn't. For whatever reason.

I waded into the water, dove under, and swam out to the dock, letting the blissfully cold water rinse the sweat off me and cool the heat from my skin. I tried to push away thoughts of the mystery man. It wasn't easy, though. The scent of him was in my nostrils, a seductive mix of sweat and sawdust, all man, sexy and drunk-making. Yet I had no business thinking about him. Even if he did get the courage to talk to me, it couldn't go anywhere. I could only hide my…condition…for so long, and then I'd be forced to tell the truth, and he'd be gone. No one would want to waste their time with someone like me. I'd be a single mom soon. And the story of how I'd come by my baby would be impossible to tell.

Where's the daddy? they'd ask. How was I supposed to tell them the father was my twin sister's husband? And that I'd conceived the baby while my sister was in a coma she wasn't expected to come out of.

God, that sounded more horrible every time I thought about it.

I dove off the dock and swam to shore, gathered my book and blanket and bottle of water. I jogged home, tripping on rocks and wincing as pebbles dug into my heels and arches. I barely made it home before the tears hit me.

What had I done? I couldn't imagine how to fix this. How could I ever face my sister and Caden again? Just show up at their condo one day with a black-haired and amber-eyed baby in my arms? *Hey, sis, meet your nephew. Oh, by the way, Cade's the daddy. How 'bout them Lions?*

It was better I was gone and out of their lives. Sure, they'd wonder where I'd gone. They might even come up here and look for me. Ever would think of this place eventually, and come looking.

I'd probably have to move away. Find a job and someone to watch the baby. Find an apartment. Maybe I could teach cello from home, and that way I wouldn't need to find a sitter.

Fuck me. I knew nothing about babies. I'd never even held one. I had no friends with children. No nieces or nephews or cousins. The closest I'd gotten to a baby was when my classical music history prof had had her baby and brought the strange pink, gurgling little thing to campus. I'd watched in horrified fascination as she held the baby, cooing and making bizarre noises and tickling its chin, making faces and talking in a high-pitched voice. I remembered seeing Professor Ennis with her huge belly. She had been barely able to totter and waddle from one end of the classroom to the other. She'd always been a pacer, Professor Ennis. She'd pace from one end of the room to the other, waving her hands and gesticulating wildly as she discoursed. By the end of her pregnancy, she'd had to lecture sitting down, her belly a massive thing almost big enough to topple her forward. And then she'd appeared after a month of leave to show us her baby, and everyone had oohed and ahhed, and one of the older students who had children asked a question about the birth and we'd all been privy to some truly horrifying details none of us had wanted to know.

That was going to be me, in a little over six months.

What was I going to do? How was I supposed to be a mother? I couldn't change a diaper. I didn't even know how to hold a baby. I was so unprepared.

I fumbled Apollo from his case and drew the bow across his strings, choking on my sobs of terror. The note was discordant and screeching, and I had to try again. This time, the note came out properly, and I focused on the sound, on the wavering golden tone. I drew another note. A third. I brought the bow across and tilted to hit the D string. Found myself playing the intro to my solo. Lost myself in it. The music dried my tears and buried the fear and the guilt beneath the weight of perfect notes. Music was the one thing I could do right. It was my only solace. I played the whole solo through, refusing to think about Ever and Cade even when I played the parts dedicated to them. It was just music, notes on a page, sounds in my heart.

Eventually I was calm enough to sleep, but when I did, I dreamed of an amber-eyed baby, and of Ever, her green eyes distraught with confused grief and betrayed hurt. I woke up crying, as I did so many nights after dreams like that.

The beach was my haven. I always ended up there somehow. Early in the morning, after my run, I'd stop at the beach and watch the sunrise. I'd put away Apollo late at night with aching fingers and turmoil in my mind, and I'd go to the beach with the stars shining like countless diamonds, clustered and scattered across a black felt cloth. The moon would be reflected in the rippling lake water and the waves would lap gently, and I'd find some measure of peace.

It was early morning, just past 6 a.m. Dawn was breaking on the water, and I'd already run three miles. I hated running, but it was all I had to keep fit, to distract myself. So I did it—three miles every morning. Maybe next week I'd try for four. I'd run until I was too pregnant to do so.

I was panting for breath, slimy with sweat, and my thoughts were starting to run wild with fear and panic. I straightened, gazed out at the water, and I saw him. The water god. He was suddenly there, just like last time. Waist deep in the bay, water sluicing down his lean, powerful body, hair wet and black as night and slicked back against his scalp. I stood watching him as he waded to shore and stopped about ten feet from me. I felt his gaze, felt his presence like some kind of electric force blazing in my blood. Blue like ice, like a clear winter sky, his eyes were inscrutable and piercing. I wished, stupidly, that I wasn't in my running gear, dripping sweat and gasping for breath. This stupid sports bra was too small, and I felt his eyes flick down to my cleavage, and then away. To my hips in my skin-tight shorts, and then away.

I felt a burst of something hot inside me at his gaze on my body. He liked what he saw, I knew that much. And Jesus, did I like what I saw. He was so, so beautiful. I didn't look away, expecting him to say "hi." To shake my hand or something. Anything. Make a move, even though I'd have to find a way to shoot him down, but not wanting to.

But he didn't. He just smiled at me, a small polite, not-quite warm smile. A nervous, forced thing. And then he moved past me, wiping drops from his face, and then making a fist. I turned to watch him go, and damn it if he didn't have the most amazing ass, outlined by the wet fabric of his shorts, round and firm-looking. I shook myself, forced those idiotic thoughts from my head. That was the kind of thing that I didn't have any time for, and had no place thinking.

But yet I couldn't help watching him go. He was striding quickly, as if angry.

Was he mad at me? It was a public beach, so I had every right to be there. I didn't get his reaction. He'd stared at me, acted like he was about to say something, and then he just took off. Maybe he was shy? But a guy that hot, with that kind of body? No way he was shy. Guys who looked like him were cocky, arrogant. Self-assured. Not…like he'd been. As if afraid to even say hello.

He rounded a corner, and then a moment later I heard the same throaty rumble I'd heard last time, and I watched the road leading out to M-37. A classic truck of some kind. Not a sports car like I'd thought. I didn't know anything about cars, classic or otherwise, but I knew his was sexy. Masculine, powerful, but not showy, not overdone. It suited him.

I went home and spent the day working on the house. It wasn't in good shape. There were things I just couldn't do, didn't have the tools or skills to fix, or the money to have them fixed. So I'd just have to live with it. Like the leaky roof, or the peeling paint on the outside. The floors that dipped in some places and bulged up in others. The screens that needed replacing. I could peel the wallpaper off, though, and I could probably manage to paint the walls. Maybe I could start on that. Or not.

The next day was rainy, so I spent it inside reading. I'd brought my box of favorite books with me, of course, and I'd also bought myself a Kindle and loaded it with about a hundred novels. It was summer, and I was determined to act like I was on vacation for as long as I could. I was trying to ignore the fact that this broken-down cabin on the beach on an isolated peninsula was my new home. It wasn't a vacation. Not really. It was life. I could pretend, though. Sit on the beach and read. Jog, swim, play the cello.

I was curled up on my couch with a steamy novel when I felt a drip on my head. And another. I looked up, and cursed. There was a huge dark spot on the ceiling. Another leak. Great. That made four. I tossed my book onto the coffee table, which was several years older than I was, and found an old plastic bowl in a cabinet, then set it on the couch beneath the leak. I already had a bucket on the kitchen table and one in the bathroom next to the toilet. I had another bucket in the second bedroom, near the closet.

God knows what would happen in the winter. The whole roof would cave in, probably. While I was sleeping, most likely. I'd be buried in snow and never wake up.

Maybe that would be the easiest way out.

I shook my head at the dark thought. I was no coward. Well, okay, so I was. I'd run away rather than deal with the fallout of my actions. But it wasn't just for me, I reasoned with myself. Maybe I'd go back someday. When Ever was stronger, physically and emotionally. When she wasn't so vulnerable.

By then, maybe, it'd be easier to tell the truth. Or maybe not.

The rain had stopped by late afternoon, so I changed into my running gear, needing to get away from my whirling thoughts. I put on my headphones, set the iPod to repeat my playlist—mostly electronic dance tunes with a fast beat and few words. It was humid and hot, the post-rain air thick with moisture.

I headed north, toward the lighthouse, setting myself a hellishly hard pace. After turning through the lighthouse parking lot at the tip of the peninsula, I headed south with the lake on my right, hidden here and there by a thin scrim of trees. I was panting and sweating, and I was sick of my playlist. I hit the "skip" button several times until a beat I didn't recognize came on. I had no recollection of downloading the song, but it was fast and lighthearted, a country song I'd heard once or twice before. I didn't usually like country, and rarely listened to it, so the appearance of Dierks Bentley's song "What Was I Thinkin'" on my iPod was a little strange. It was fun, though, and it helped me pick up my pace and kept my feet moving.

Why did I have this song? I just couldn't remember. None of the guys I'd ever dated had been too

much into country, so it wasn't that. Cade and I
hadn't ever shared music. Ever? She wasn't a country
music kind of girl, either. Where had the song come
from?

And why had I let myself think about Cade and
Ever again? I clenched my fists and swung my arms
to get my feet moving, to push my pace faster, to
get the burn and the ache to a roar loud enough
to distract me. It didn't work, though. My thoughts
returned to Cade. He seemed like a country music
type. He'd lived in Wyoming, after all. He'd been a
real-deal cowboy, living on a working horse ranch.
But he and I had never discussed musical tastes. I'd
played Apollo in front of him a few times, but that
was about it. I had no idea what kind of music he
liked. He watched James Bond movies because his
dad had liked them. I knew that. What else did I
know about Cade? Not much. His mom had died of
cancer. His dad had died of a broken heart, otherwise
known as a heart attack, caused by the burden of
grief. His grandparents had died of old age. He was
an artist.

I'd spent months with him, and that was all I
knew? I didn't know his favorite color. I didn't know
his favorite band. I was pregnant with his child, and I
knew nothing about him.

Fuck. I was an idiot. I'd gone running to escape
these thoughts, and now here I was wallowing in

them all over again. I fought the sting in my eyes, focused on the beat of the music pumping in my ears, a Three Days Grace song, "Misery Loves Company." It was a workout song, hard and fast, and it let me keep my feet grinding the miles away.

I couldn't outrun my thoughts, though.

The reality didn't always *feel* real. I had morning sickness still, and some strange hormonal mood swings, but that was about it. I was only showing a tiny bit, not enough to stop me from running in my usual shorts and sports bra. I didn't really feel pregnant. I was, though, and I knew it. I'd seen the tests, several of them, all showing positive. I hadn't had a period in months. So I *was* pregnant. It was real and unavoidable and undeniable. But it didn't always seem like a day-to-day reality. Maybe I could just take some Tums and the nausea would go away. I'd get my period. My moods would even out on their own. Maybe it was just stress.

But I couldn't do that.

I was really and truly pregnant with my brother-in-law's child.

At that moment and with that thought ringing in my mind, I felt something beside me. I glanced over and saw *him*, tall and toned and tan and iron-muscled, running next to me. Shirtless, as he always seemed to be. His chest muscles shifted and flexed as he swung his arms. He was running hard, covered in sweat. He wore nothing but a pair of blue shorts that matched his eyes, and a pair of battered New Balance running shoes. No iPod or earbuds, no evidence that he'd ever worn a shirt. He had no tan lines, only sun-darkened skin from forehead to hips.

Shit. Why was *he* here? I was fighting sobs as I ran, fighting terrified gasps as the reality of my situation rifled through me all over again. And here he was, this mysterious and sexy stranger who never spoke and always seemed to appear at the worst possible moments. I was out of breath and sweaty and about to cry, hair tangled and sticking to my cheeks and forehead and neck, my pale skin flushed. And he looked perfect. Lean and powerful, black hair thick and messy and artfully sweat-stained. As if he spent his life in a pair of shorts and nothing else, perpetually sweating and always pushing himself.

I looked away from him and tried to shove down the emotions, tried to pretend like I wasn't on the verge of stumbling to a stop and collapsing in tears on the side of M-37. I felt his gaze, though. As if he could see what I was trying to contain. I felt a single tear slip down my face, and I wiped at it. Another, and another, and then I was crying for real. I stifled a sob and poured on the speed, needing to get away from Beach God's too-knowing gaze. I was already running as fast as my conditioning would allow, but I needed to get away. I needed him to not see me like this. I needed to not be thinking about him. He had no place in my life. I belonged alone. I didn't deserve friendship, or company. I deserved the misery crushing me, and nothing else.

He kept pace, damn him. And he still said nothing. He didn't ask what was wrong, didn't offer any sympathy or understanding or anything. He just ran beside me, leaving space between us. He ran effortlessly, as if this insane pace wasn't destroying him the way it was me. I couldn't keep it up for much longer, yet I still had a couple of miles left. But still I kept running, no longer jogging but flat-out running, legs burning as they stretched to eat the road, lungs on fire as they strained to provide oxygen. And the tears remained. I had to wipe them away in a vain attempt to hide them from Beach God.

My foot hit a rock, pitching me off-balance. I felt myself going down, and I braced, knowing I'd hit painfully hard. Except the fall never came. A huge, strong, callused hand grabbed my left arm just above the elbow and held me upright as I stumbled a few steps and found my balance. My heart was pounding in my chest, adrenaline making my heartbeat loud in my ears.

I glanced at Beach God. "Thanks," I said, between breaths. He just nodded and kept running. I glanced at him out of the corner of my eye. "You don't...talk much, do you?" It was a lame conversation gambit, but it was all I could think of.

He just shook his head and kept running.

"Can't, or don't?" I asked, giving in to curiosity. He only shrugged noncommittally. I waited, thinking he might be trying to think of a good answer, or trying to catch his breath to speak, but he didn't. He just kept running.

I was irritated now. If he was mute, wouldn't he use sign language, find some way to communicate with me? He seemed interested in me—unfortunately for him—but if he was, he had a funny way of showing it. I couldn't figure him out, and there was no point in trying. As soon as he found out the truth about me, he'd be long gone.

I somehow found the strength to put on speed, leaving him behind. I ran, tensed, waiting for him to catch up and make an excuse, apologize, something, anything. But…no. He just let me run ahead, let the distance expand between us.

I couldn't deny the sense of disappointment I felt.

rusty

I altered my routine after that. I ran at night, late, usually. I avoided the beach at sunrise and sunset, which were the times when he seemed to be there the most. I didn't see him again for a month. During that month, I began to show for real. Just a bump, really, a slight protrusion, enough to seem like maybe I'd fallen off the diet and exercise wagon. I had to start wearing shirts that covered my belly when I worked out, though. I ran in tank tops, swam in my purple one-piece.

I wondered how long it would be before I was unable to run. Or if it was unwise to do so. I'd seen a doctor a few days after my arrival up here, of course, at the hospital in downtown Traverse City. He'd examined me, said things were "progressing apace," whatever the hell that meant. He gave me a prescription for some prenatal pills and told me to make sure I kept eating healthy and avoided caffeine and alcohol. Things I knew from TV, really.

I'd always been strict about what I ate, allowing myself a few treats here and there, a few indulgences. I let myself drink alcohol—or rather, I *had*, before—and to justify the caloric intake of booze, I didn't eat red meat and avoided cheese as much as I could. So cutting alcohol and caffeine out of my diet hadn't been as hard as for some women, I imagined. The alcohol I missed simply because I desperately wanted to seek the oblivion of forgetting, even if it was only temporary. Instead, I ran, and played Apollo. Which just wasn't the same.

And now, with my belly getting bigger, I knew my days of five-mile runs were numbered.

It was midsummer now, and the days were blazing hot. Too hot to run, even for me. I walked instead, just to get outside, away from the sagging roof and peeling wallpaper and rotting porch steps of my cabin. Away from my thoughts, which was never effective, but worth trying.

One day, a cloudy but stiflingly hot and humid afternoon, I passed a pile of junk heaped on the side of the road. Mostly trash, an ancient, boxy TV with rabbit-ears, a box of broken dishes and pitted, grease-stained pots and pans, an old broom and moldy-looking mop. An exercise bike missing a pedal, a black plastic garbage bag overflowing with stuffed animals and mismatched clothing. But what caught my attention was the bicycle, a ten-speed older than I was. It had once been red, I thought, but was now more rust-colored than anything. I pulled it free from the pile and pressed my thumb on the skinny, oversize tires, found them airtight. It had its chain and gears, the shifters, a scuffed but intact seat, brakes pads, levers, and handlebars. I noticed a stout woman wearing a floppy gardening hat kneeling in a bed of flowers beneath the porch of the house.

"Excuse me," I called out. She turned and looked at me. "Can I have this?" I gestured at the bike.

"All yours, sweetie," she responded with a wave.

"Thanks!"

I walked the bike home and gave it a more thorough examination. The brakes were loose, but usable, and the chain could use some oil, but other than that it was just old. Maybe this bike would buy me a few more weeks of exercise before I got too pregnant to get off my couch.

The next day was brilliantly sunny, the sky clear blue and the air hot. I was restless, antsy. Even Apollo couldn't quite push away the fear of motherhood, the panic my increasingly pregnant body inspired. What would I say when it was obvious to anyone who looked at me? I hadn't had to answer any questions yet. Of course, I rarely left the peninsula. I shopped at the cute little combination bar-and-grill/sandwich deli/gas station and grocery store that was about ten minutes south. It was the only place to eat or shop within a half-hour drive of the tip of the peninsula where I lived, and the lady who worked behind the counter most days seemed to know I didn't welcome chatter. She rang up my purchases, swiped my card, and let me leave without expressing any of the idle curiosity that was often so prevalent in small towns like this. Thank god for that at least.

I was due for an ultrasound at around eighteen weeks, which was in a little over two months. Until then, I was hoping to avoid going any farther south than the Peninsula Market. The mainland and downtown meant people, which meant curiosity and stares and questions. Oh, where's your husband? How far along are you? Is it a boy or girl? Do you have any names picked out? I couldn't answer any of that. Except how far along I was: almost eleven weeks. Nearly into my second trimester. I'd read What to Expect When You're Expecting, of course. So now I knew what to expect, more or less, but that didn't really help much. Knowing the morning sickness would pass by the second trimester was nice, but the talk of back pain and the ache of my boobs getting bigger and always having to pee…I wasn't looking forward to that.

I couldn't even begin thinking about actually giving birth. Or what I would do once I had. I knew I should be making plans, trying to adjust my life to my new reality, but I just couldn't. All I could do was try to survive emotionally and hope things would work out. That was stupid and foolish, and would only hurt me in the long run, but I was terrified, and alone, and confused, and wracked with guilt. And I just didn't know what to do.

Eventually, my chaotic thoughts drove me from the house. I got onto the old bike I'd rescued from the trash and pedaled toward M-37. It didn't seem so bad at first. Hot, but bearable. And then I got to M-37, and the shade from the trees disappeared and the real hills began, and the heat began to mount. My thought initially was to ride to the market, get some lunch at the deli, and then bike home. But I wasn't even halfway there when I realized I might have made a mistake in trying to ride today. The heat was intense, the sun a glaring ball above me. The hills rose and fell, each one more brutal than the last, especially heading south. I usually ran north to the tip of the peninsula and back, which was mostly flat. But going south the topography became ever more hilly, which was part of the reason vineyards were so popular. Hills were good for grapes, and so was the heat, but it wasn't so good for pregnant Eden. I hadn't brought a water bottle, since there was nowhere to put it. I was drenched in sweat from head to toe, and the pedals were getting harder and harder to push. The hills seemed endless. Each rotation of the pedals seemed like a minor victory.

I wiped my forehead with my wrist, gasping for breath, and glanced ahead. Another steep uphill grade. I was far enough away from home now that to turn around only meant more work. And I had to get something to drink. My mouth was dry, feeling like it was splitting apart. My head spun, my eyes felt heavy, and my legs were jelly. I had to find somewhere to stop. There was nothing, though. Only acre after acre of cherry trees, row after row of grapevines. An occasional dirt track leading through the vineyard or orchard, maybe a little shack used to house equipment. No houses, nothing.

I focused on the white line at the side of the road, focused on keeping my front tire on that line. Pedal, pedal, pedal. Don't think about the hill. Don't think about the ache in my legs, or the burn in my lungs, or the sweat stinging my eyes. Just pedal, and hope for someplace to rest and get a drink. Don't think about the miles to get back home.

This can't be good for the baby.

I pushed that thought away and kept pedaling. Finally, I saw an old white clapboard building with a deep porch, and beyond it the bones of new construction on a high knoll where it would overlook the eastern arm of Grand Traverse Bay, all surrounded by what had to be a couple hundred acres of grape-vines. A vineyard, and a real winery. Which meant people, and air conditioning. And water, hopefully. I turned off the road and let my bike carry me down the gravel driveway to the foot of the porch. I wob-bled to a stop, hopped off, and let the bike fall to the ground, the back tire *click-click-clicking* around slowly. I heard nothing except the whir of a fan from somewhere. I mounted the four steps to the porch, knocked on the door. No answer, no footsteps from within. If there wasn't anyone here, I might just cry. I didn't see any cars, didn't see anyone in the vineyard. I wasn't going to cry. It was just hormones. There'd probably be another winery in another mile or two. I could make that.

Hopefully.

"Hello?" I called out, loud enough that anyone inside should have been able to hear me.

I heard footsteps on the stairs behind me and whirled around in surprise. And then my mouth went dry. It was him, the Beach God. And again, he was shirtless and sweating, and this time he was cov-ered in sawdust, and little curled shavings of wood clung to his arms and chest and hair. He was barefoot, wearing tattered cut-off khaki shorts, long and loose, hanging off his trim waist. Damn him for being so sexy. He really needed to wear a shirt, just to keep me from ogling him, which I had no place doing. I mean, he was nice to look at, and looking never hurt anything. It wasn't like it could go anywhere, after all.

And of course, he was yet again seeing me in workout shorts and a tank top, sweaty and out of breath and about to pass out.

"You?" I asked. I heard myself making some idiotic excuses about a bike ride and the heat, and then the world wiggled and spun and tipped, and then I felt myself held aloft by something warm and slippery and strong. And he was above me, his blue eyes so pale as to be almost colorless, piercing me, but warm with concern. He was holding me. Jesus, he was strong. One arm around my shoulders, holding me easily. And he was fast. I hadn't even seen him move, and he'd been at the bottom of the stairs, several feet away. His cheekbones were just perfect. I was dizzy, and staring at his cheekbones. They were high and pronounced, and I wanted to run my fingers over them. I wanted to just stay like this, held by him, just for a minute.

I blinked the dizziness away and struggled to my feet, trying to wipe the stupid thoughts from my mind as I wiped the sweat from my face. There was absolutely no point in thinking about Beach God like that. Whoever he was, he didn't belong in my life. Once he got a whiff of the mile-long train of baggage that came with me, he'd be gone in a blink.

And good for him, because I wouldn't wish my troubles on anyone.

Embarrassment shot through me. "Did I just pass out? I did. I can't believe I just fainted." He edged away from me as I regained my composure. "Do you have any water?"

He didn't answer, which at this point didn't surprise me. Instead, he led me inside, into a kitchen that looked as if it hadn't changed since 1966. There were white lace curtains on the window, held up by a brass rod and sagging hooks. A green fridge the size of my Passat sat in the corner. An ancient two-slot pop-up toaster that might have come from *The Brave Little Toaster* was the only small appliance in sight.

Beach God offered me a bottle of water and a bottle of Gatorade. He probably meant for me to choose one, but I took both and slammed the water so fast my teeth ached and my head hurt. Then I cracked open the Gatorade and drank that at a more sedate pace. He sipped at blue Gatorade and watched me drink. Finally I couldn't take it anymore. I stuck my hand out and introduced myself. He shook my hand with a polite smile, and I thought for a split second that he might just break his code of silence and actually tell me his name, but he didn't. Instead, he produced a business card and handed that to me. It was plain white with black letters. I read it out loud. "Carter Haven, Haven Brothers Winery." There was an email address, the address of the winery, and the words "finish carpenter." No phone number, which made me think this not-talking thing was a long-term issue for him.

I felt a question bubbling on my lips, the kind that was taboo to come right out and ask a person. It came out anyway: "Okay, Carter. Are you mute?"

He shook his head, and didn't look as insulted as I'd expected him to.

"So you can talk?"

His eyes narrowed, and his lips tightened. He nodded.

"But you don't?"

This time, he shook his head. His expression was stone-hard, and when I asked if it was just me he didn't speak to, he didn't even have the decency to look chagrined. He did look upset, but whether it was my questioning that was upsetting him or the fact of his silence itself, I didn't know.

The door squeaked and the screen door slammed, and then a younger version of Carter walked in. This man lacked the power of Carter's frame, and his hair was lighter in shade, but they were clearly related.

"Thomas Haven," he said, shaking my hand. His voice was smooth, not too deep, and his smile was quick and genuine. "I see you met my brother, Carter."

I shook Thomas's hand, and wondered if Carter's voice would sound anything like this. "Yeah. We were just introducing ourselves."

Thomas looked so shocked I thought he might faint. Maybe even a little jealous. "He introduced himself? Like, out loud?"

So it wasn't just me. Carter looked panicked, or as panicked as his closed-off facial expressions would allow.

I gestured with the business card. "No, with this."

Thomas seemed almost relieved by this information. "Ah. That would've been surprising."

I wanted to ask why, but didn't. I looked at Carter, thinking maybe the presence of his brother would loosen his tongue. "So, what's your deal?"

Thomas and I both waited in expectation, but Carter held his silence. Thomas didn't seem surprised. "That's kind of a complicated question," he said, sighing. He left then, claiming to be late for a meeting, with two other men I assumed to be more brothers. As he was out the door, Thomas turned back to me and said, "Good luck."

"With what?" I asked.

He pointed at Carter with a thrust of this thumb. "Him." And then Thomas was gone, and Carter and I were alone again.

Carter's expression was even more shuttered than usual. He was pissed, though: his hands were opening and closing, fisting and relaxing, and his jaw was tensed, looking hard as a chunk of granite.

I finished my Gatorade and called it quits. "Okay. Well. This has been awkward." I moved toward the door, needing to get away from the mystery and intensity and beauty of Carter Haven. "I'll just…be going. 'Bye."

I fairly ran out the door, jumped on the ten-speed, and pedaled away as fast as I could. The heat hadn't lessened, but the rest and refreshment had restored some of my strength, so I pedaled hard. I made it maybe half a mile before I heard the distinctive leonine growl of his truck engine behind me. I didn't stop or slow.

As sexy and mysterious as he was, and as compelling as the question of his silence might have been, he had no place in my life, and there was absolutely no point in even bothering. It wouldn't be doing him any favors to involve him, and it would only provide temptation for me, teasing myself with something I'd never have. So I kept pedaling.

Only, he pulled up next to me.

"Can I help you?" I demanded. Carter jerked his thumb at the back of the truck. He wanted to drive me home, obviously. But this had gone on long enough. He was wasting his time on me, and I couldn't afford to let him think he had a chance. I pedaled onward, ignoring him. And then he zipped past me and skidded to a stop in front of me, raising cloud of dust. He got out and stood in front of me, arms crossed. He'd put on a shirt finally. It didn't help much, though, not with the way it clung to his damp abs and stretched around his biceps. If anything, the shirt only served to accentuate the power of his lean frame by hiding it. An interesting paradox.

He just stood there, though, and I lost my patience. "What gives, Carter?" I fiddled with the brake lever, not wanting him to leave me here, not wanting to have to ride home alone, but knowing it was best for both of us. "If you want something, say so."

He did the thing I least expected: he wrote me a note on his phone. **Let me drive you home.**

He had a cell phone? Why would he need one if he never spoke? Maybe he texted. He did have an email address on his business card.

I told him no, and he wrote another note.

I was exasperated by this time. How childish was this? If he wanted to talk to me, he should just talk. "This is so weird," I said. "We're passing notes back and forth like we're in third grade. I'll be fine." I stood up on the pedal to get the bike moving up the hill, back toward home.

And, yet again, he leapfrogged me in his truck, skidding to a stop in front of me, blocking my path. I was out of patience by this time. "What, Carter? What do you want? I said I'm fine. I am. For real.

I'm tough, okay? I don't need your help. And, to be honest, the whole not-talking thing? It's weird. A little creepy. No offense. Maybe you've got a reason for not talking." I pushed my sweat-damp hair away from my eyes. "I don't know, some trauma or something. But I've got enough of my own trouble to deal with yours, too, okay? So…'bye."

I didn't wait for him to not answer. I kicked the bike into motion, figuring my rude response would ensure that I'd never see him again.

Only, it didn't quite work that way.

"Wait." His voice. God. It was raw and rusty with disuse, and exactly as rugged and imperfectly perfect as the rest of him.

I was in so much trouble.

brushstrokes and ruins

Caden

Except for the months of pleasure I'd known with Ever before the accident, it seemed as if my entire life had been nothing but pain. I knew, intellectually, that wasn't true. Mom had died when I was fourteen, and life had been great up until then. Mom and Dad loved me. Grams and Gramps loved me. I spent summers at the ranch, and had my art at home. I'd had fourteen years of happiness. Now I was nearly twenty-three. That translated into not quite ten years of hell.

But never had pain felt like this. Ever needed me. She refused to face the truth I knew she saw in me. I knew she'd seen the guilt in me. I'd nearly told her the truth a few times. But I always chickened out. Justified it by telling myself Ever needed more time to heal, to recover, to regain herself, her life.

So months passed, and my guilt ate me alive. I loved her as fiercely as ever, but it was overshadowed by the lies, the guilt, the agony of knowing I'd betrayed her. I wasn't sleeping more than a few hours a night. I woke up tormented by nightmares, wracked with guilt. I woke up and stared at Ever, asleep in our bed next to me, clinging to me, her sweet soft arm across my chest, her breathing soughing in the darkness. I wanted to shake her awake and tell her to leave me, to find someone worthy of her perfection. I wanted to confess, so I could be free of the secret, rid of the weight of my silent sin. It festered within me, rotting and acidic, poisonous.

I couldn't eat. I worked, went to the gym, tried to chase my demons away. Tried, and failed.

I felt weak. I felt as if life was passing me by, and I was missing it. Ever was getting better every day. She was speaking normally, moving around on her own. Dressing herself, eating by herself. She wasn't an invalid anymore. I didn't have to take care of her, much. She needed me for things here and there, but overall she was making almost miraculous progress. Which meant the day I told her the truth was growing closer. And that meant I was that much closer to letting her go. I'd tell her the truth, and then I'd leave. She'd be heartbroken, but it was better than this web of falsehood I was caught up in.

She made love to me with wild abandon. Kissed me as if she was drowning and I was her air. I had been that once, but only I knew I couldn't be that person any longer. I kissed her back, because she needed me to, and I couldn't help but kiss her back. But I felt as if each kiss was tainting her with the venom of my guilt. As if she could taste the truth on my lips. As if she'd kiss me, touch me, hold me, make love to me, and look at me and know. Divine the truth of my sick sin and confront me before I could tell her myself.

It was my nightmare, waking me up every night. *Caden*, she would say. Her mouth wouldn't move, but I would hear her words tolling like bells in my skull, and her eyes would be sad and tearful and angry and confused and lost. *What did you do? Why? Why her? Why couldn't you wait for me? Why couldn't you have faith that I'd come back? WHY HER?* And I wouldn't have any answers. I could only offer apologies, and those were useless. They were as pointless as the condolences at a funeral. "I'm sorry for your loss," people always said, as if that had any power to soothe the grief.

Just the same, "I'm so sorry, Ever," couldn't possibly contain any salve for the ruin of her heart when she found out what I'd done.

Four months after she woke up, Ever came to me one day as I was making lunch for us. "I want to paint again," she said.

She hadn't so much as looked at her paintings since coming home. She hadn't gone into the studio, hadn't attempted to draw, hadn't even mentioned her art. It was too painful, I suspected. It was probably the hardest thing for her to have lost. Any other pain she could have faced, if only she had her art. But with that ability taken away, she had no way to cope. I didn't think she had the courage to face the studio, and to face the loss of the one thing that made her *her*.

I set the wooden spoon down on the stove and turned to look at her. She was holding on to the post at the entryway to the kitchen with one hand, the other fidgeting with the hem of her T-shirt. She was watching me intently for my reaction.

I stepped toward her, wrapped her up in my arms. Her hair smelled like coconut shampoo, a different scent than I was used to. She still used the vanilla lotion, though, and I could smell that on her. That smell, the vanilla sugar lotion, had the power to wreak havoc on me. I pressed my nose into her neck and inhaled, catching the scent of the lotion, and I was torn out of the present, thrown back two years to the moment when she opened her studio door and let me in, and I kissed her, smelling this same lotion on her skin, wafting from her in waves of seductive sweetness. And I was thrown back as well to the months of her coma. I'd stand at our dresser, holding the bottle of lotion. The cap would be open, and I'd squeeze the tube, just enough to let a current of the scent hit my nostrils, enough to torture me with missing her. And now I smelled it all over again, and it was really her, yet I'd destroyed us. She just didn't know it yet.

I inhaled again, seeking courage in the pain of her scent and her arms around me, so trusting and so innocent and so needy. "You're going to paint again?"

She nodded against me. "I have to try. I'm just warning you. I'll probably have a nervous break-down. So just...just be ready."

I took her face in my hands, brought her chin up, met her vivid, fear-fraught green gaze with mine. Tried to seem steady and strong and loving. Tried to hide the guilt, which was an every-moment-of-ev-ery-day labor. "If you have a breakdown, I'll be there to hold you."

"That's all I need." Her eyes shone with faith.

The horrible thing about this guilt was that I still needed her, still loved her, still wanted her just as much as I ever had. More, perhaps. I would take as much as she would give me until she knew. Her faith might have been misplaced, but I would do my best to be there for her, for as long as I could. Time was short. Soon, everything would change. I knew it, and I was pretty sure she knew it as well.

Ever lifted up on her toes to kiss me, and her lips were gentle on mine, yet still demanding. I kissed her back, because I couldn't do otherwise.

She backed away from me, and I followed her to the closed door of her studio. I wondered if she knew I'd seen her standing here, late at night, her hand on the knob, her shoulders shaking. I watched, and she never turned the knob. Never went in. So now, the scene was familiar. She stopped at the door, her hand on the knob. Her shoulders shook. I stood behind her, slid my arms around her waist. Kissed the back of her neck.

"What if it's gone forever, Cade?" Her voice wasn't even a whisper. It was…shreds of sound, ripped from somewhere deep within her.

"You've learned to walk again. You've learned to talk again. You can eat, dress, write. You can do this, Ever." I had to give her hope, had to give her everything I could, while I was still here to give it to her. Even the hard truths. "It will probably be hard as hell. You'll think about giving up. But you won't. You're too strong and too courageous to give up. Art is in your veins, Ev. It's who you are. And if you can't paint, by some strange fluke, you'll find some other way of making art."

"I'm scared." She leaned back against me, and I took all of her weight.

I crossed my arms over her chest and stomach, kissed behind her ear. "You can do it. Just go in, Ev."

"Baby steps?"

I chuckled. "Baby steps."

She twisted the knob and gave the door a gentle push. It swung open on silent hinges, bumped against the wall, and shivered to a stop. Everything was just as she'd left it. I hadn't dared touch a single thing in this room. An unfinished painting waited on the easel—a piece that reminded me of something Georgia O'Keefe might have painted. A gerbera daisy, seen from up close, an almost unlikely shade of violent orange, each petal seen in dramatic detail. The center of the flower dominated the piece, a ring of orange-red, each tiny fiber looking soft and real enough to touch. Only the edges of the painting remained to be finished, the outside of the petals. Ever stepped into the room, her eyes focused on the easel, on the painting. She walked to it as if in a trance, feet shuffling, one hand extending to touch the surface of the canvas. Her finger stroked the center of the painting, nail skritching on the dried oil paint.

"I remember painting this. I was trying to channel Georgia O'Keefe, but with my own touch on it."

"You got it perfect."

She remained completely still, her fingers splayed on the canvas as if in some silent farewell. After a long silence, she spoke in a hesitant, reverent whisper. "It's like me. Interrupted. Unfinished. Even if I could finish it, it wouldn't be the same as if I'd finished it then."

"Ever, you have to know—"

"I'm not that person anymore, Cade." She let her hand drop, curling her fingers into a fist.

"I loved the person you were then, and I love the person you are now." That, at least, was the pure, unvarnished truth.

"The problem is, I don't know who I am anymore. I lost something. Some part of myself, and I don't know what it is or how to get it back. And I know you love me." Ever turned in my arms, brushed my hair away from my face. "And I love you. But…it's not enough. You loving me doesn't fix what's wrong with me. And…*goddammit*—" She squeezed her eyes shut and sighed, stifling a faint sob. "You're not the same, either. You're broken, too, Cade. Everything… everything is broken."

I'd never seen this side of Ever, this raw and agonized despair. I didn't know how to make it better. "I know." It was all I could say. The only words that would come out. "I'm sorry. Fuck, Ever. I'm sorry."

"For what?"

For betraying you. "For being broken when you need me to be whole." I just couldn't get the words out; the truth was lodged in my chest. "For…for everything."

Her eyes searched me, and I saw the knowledge there. She knew. Not what, but that there was something to know, a truth hidden between us. A moment passed, and I met her gaze, unwavering. Pleading with her silently, begging her to demand the truth from me, to vilify me as I deserved. Instead, she clutched my face with shaking hands and drew my mouth down to hers and kissed me, and it seemed a vampiric kiss in a way, as if she was sucking strength from me, courage from me. I gave it willingly. She could take all of me, leave me limp and dead, if it would mean she was alive and happy.

Pulling away, breathless, she stepped back, searched the room for something. Found the age-soft and paint-splattered button-down white shirt, hanging on the back of a kitchen chair. Took it in her hands and stared at it. Memory showed in the bow of her shoulders. I stood, watching, waiting. Ever set the shirt on the chair back once more, reached down to the hem of the green V-neck she was wearing, pulled it off, folded it, and set it on the seat of the chair. She didn't spare me a glance. This wasn't about me anymore; I was merely a witness. Her fingers shook

as she unzipped and unbuttoned her jeans, put them
neatly atop her shirt. Standing in gray cotton panties and a green silk bra, she was more beautiful to
me than she'd ever been. Courage made her beautiful. Tenacity made her glow. To reclaim what was
stripped away so unfairly took more guts than I'd
ever have.

She had to pause for breath, pause to gather her
nerves. And then she reached up behind her back,
freed the clasps of her bra, and hung it from the corner of the chair back. She was facing away from me,
and I couldn't breathe for the sight of the curve of
her bare back. I stared, branding the image into my
mind. This moment, this vignette, it was now something sacred to me. She was physically exposed, emotionally vulnerable, braving her deepest fear, and she
was doing it alone. I didn't think she was even aware
of my presence any longer and, in a way, that was as
it should be. She'd have to learn to live without me.

She stepped out of her underwear, set them on
the chair. Ever stood naked in her art studio, her pale
skin pebbling from the chill in the air. I devoured her
naked form with my eyes, buried the memory of this
moment deep within me. I would need something to
hold on to, when it all fell apart.

At long last, she slid her arms into the sleeves of
the shirt, buttoned it with shaky fingers, smoothed
her hand down her front, over her hips, as if to press

the reality into her skin, as if to tell herself that she was truly doing this, and that she *could*. I stood with my back to the wall near the door, willing her onward.

She took a black Sharpie from the tray on the easel and signed her name carefully to the bottom right corner of the daisy painting, and then, beneath that, wrote: **"Interrupted."** Ever heaved a deep sigh, then lifted the four-by-six canvas from the easel, carried it across the room, and set it on the floor with a stack of other finished paintings.

She considered it finished, I realized, and I understood the symbolism in her choice.

Four-by-six was her favorite size of canvas to work with, and she had a stack of them pre-stretched. Ever chose a canvas, set it on the easel, added fresh paint to each primary color splotch on her palette. Chose a brush. Held the palette in one hand, her brush hanging at her side. Her chest rose and fell with heavy breaths, nervous and afraid to begin. I could almost hear her thoughts. *What if I can't do it? What if I forgot how?*

She stood still and silent for a long time, staring at the blank canvas. I was beginning to think she'd frozen. She nodded once, and then set her brush down and chose a different one, a thick, fat brush for broad strokes. She touched the tip to the black paint, and I could see her hand trembling as she drew the brush across the middle of the canvas. It was a thick, gloppy stroke, a harsh line of black on the clean white. Another long pause, and then she flattened the brush against the black paint and spread it around, added more, and more. With every stroke she grew more confident, and soon the whole canvas was black and she was filling in missed slices of white.

I couldn't even begin to wonder what she was doing, and I didn't dare ask. This was a private moment, one that belonged only to Ever, and I was privileged to watch. I crossed my arms over my chest and kept silent, making sure even my breathing was quiet.

Ever set the black-smeared brush on the tray and picked up the one she'd originally chosen, a medium-point brush. She dabbed at the white paint, brought it in an arc horizontally across the canvas, refreshed the paint on the brush and made a mirrored arc to match the first. Slowly then, she filled in the space between the arcs, merging the black and the white so that it seemed almost pixelated, as if the black was fading to white.

It wasn't until she stepped back that I understood what she'd painted: an eye, opening.

"The moment you woke up," I said. She only nodded. "You haven't forgotten."

Ever set her brush and palette down, turned in place to look at me, hesitated, and then ran and threw herself into my arms. She cried long and hard.

"I haven't forgotten." Relief filled her voice. "It's not the same, though. Even that is different. I don't— I'm not sure I can explain it. I don't see things the same. When I think about painting something, even the images in my head are different than I remember them being before."

Before.

Her life was split into *before* and *after*.

For me, it wasn't so simple. There was before, and there was after, and there was the unmitigated hell of in between. During. That time, the *during*, that was what had broken me. I'd survived the loss of my parents, my grandparents. I might have survived the loss of Ever, if she'd actually died. But she didn't. I'd lost her, but not completely. It wasn't the pain of her loss, the agony of limbo, or even the uncertainty of not knowing if she'd ever wake up that had done me in, though; it was the choices I'd made. The fact that I'd lost sight, lost hope, and betrayed her. And she'd woken up. I couldn't undo it, couldn't take it back. And even now, I wasn't sure if I could have done anything differently. But that didn't change the reality of my now. It didn't alter the fact that when Ever found out, it would gut her.

And that would crumble even the ruins of what remained of me.

art imitates life

In the weeks that followed, Ever rarely left her studio. She barely slept, barely ate. She painted. She filled canvas after canvas, and sent me out to buy more, since she wasn't up to stretching her own just yet. She painted, and painted and painted. And from what I saw, she was absolutely correct in her assessment: she had changed, artistically. She had almost totally regained her fine motor control, could use the finest-point brush to paint delicate strokes and pin-thin lines. It wasn't a change in skill, but rather, as she'd said, a matter of perception. She painted messily, with quick, harsh strokes. Dark colors, little white space. She'd had a light style before. Even when the subject matter was heavy or dark, she managed to make it seem bright and lively. She had a painting of a raven, one I'd seen when flipping through her old paintings while she slept. It was a week or two before the accident, and I was up early. The raven had been so lifelike that I'd almost expected it to step off the canvas. There were reflections in the raven's beady eyes, and the sun glinted off its feathers. The piece contained all the inherent creepiness of a raven, the hint of some ancient evil in the eyes, the omens and portents of darkness in the predatory shape and black feathers. Yet, for all that, the piece had been distinctly *Ever*, still infused with the beauty of her style.

Now, her paintings were…almost grim.

She painted a lamp, one that sat on our bedside table. It was an ordinary lamp, silver and straight and modern, with a pull chain and white trapezoidal shade. In the painting, the lamp was on, surrounded by shadows. The outline of a moth was silhouetted on the inside of the lampshade. The sense of entrapment was palpable. The moth seemed caught mid-motion, as if banging against the shade, drawn by the light but burned by the heat, unable to fly away and unable to resist.

She painted a still life of a bowl of fruit, but the apple was bruised, flattened on one side. It was true to life, an accurate representation of the fruit that sat in the bowl on our dining room table. Yet the painting seemed bleak. The sky in the window in the background was gray and overcast. The banana was flecked with black spots, looking soft to the touch.

She painted me from memory, and the look in my eyes was haunted. My face was shadowed with the stubble of a beard, and my forehead creased with worry lines. But my eyes…god. If the painting was any reflection of me, she could see my secrets, and saw that they were bearing down on me. I looked *old* in the painting. Tired.

I realized then that I hadn't touched a pencil or pen to draw since the day she woke up, if not long before. With Ever in her studio, warring with her demons and seeking herself in a thousand blank canvases, I brought out my sketchpad and pencil case and sat at the table with an empty page before me.

I drew Ever, in that moment of vulnerability, her back bare and curved slightly to the left, her shoulders bowed under the weight of her fear. I wondered, as I drew, if she had shed a tear. Private. Unseen.

My drawing did nothing to alleviate the torture within. I tried again, and I drew Ever once more. This time I drew her in profile. Yet, as the drawing progressed, I realized it was Ever in the hospital bed. Her eyes were closed, and her hands were still and thin on the sheets. I drew, and I could almost smell the antiseptic and sickness of the hospital.

Hours passed, and my hand cramped, and the pages of my sketchbook were filled, one after another, with drawings of Ever. In therapy, struggling with a pencil. Just her hand, clutching awkwardly at the pencil. Dozens of images, yet none of them quieted the ache inside me.

Finally, I drew Eden. Just her eyes and the tangle of hair by her cheekbone, a hint of her mouth. It was the moment I'd walked away from this very condo. The moment I'd known it was over, for better or worse. There was both relief and sadness in her eyes, and a huge amount of pain. There was no way to know it was Eden just by looking at it. Not unless you knew.

I closed the sketchbook and sat at the table, my head pounding, my eyes burning, my hand cramping. The condo was silent, and I wondered what Ever was painting.

I wondered where Eden was. Why she'd left.

I wondered why any of this had happened, and why my life seemed so cursed.

slide show

I found her asleep on the floor of her studio. She'd forgotten to wash her brushes, so I washed them, and put them away.

A painting sat finished and drying on the easel. Two doves, flying side by side. They were barely outlines on the canvas, dappled with hints of ivory. Wings were spread, faces turned upward, seeking the sunlight.

One of the doves cast a shadow on the ground below.

One did not.

She enrolled in classes at Cranbrook and began attending three days a week. She found a job answering phones at a physical therapist's office Monday through Friday.

She was establishing a new normal. I continued working at UPS, and found another job as a janitor at a local middle school. We both did our art, woke up and ate breakfast, had dinner together when our schedules allowed. We seemed, if seen from the outside, to be an average young married couple, making their way through life.

What you wouldn't see was the chasm growing between us. Was it me? Was it my guilt, pushing her away? Was it her knowledge of that guilt, combined with our mutual agreement to pretend it wasn't there? I didn't know.

The days passed almost as in a slide show.

We even made love, clinging to each other in the darkness of our bedroom, sweating together, skin sliding in a nearly silent susurrus. She told me she loved me, and I told her the same.

And we both meant it.

Yet that didn't banish the space between us.

Once I heard her crying in the bathroom, late at night.

Time congealed and stretched and slipped away, minutes becoming weeks, becoming hours, which became days...which became months.

And nothing changed. I withheld the truth, too cowardly to speak it, too afraid of hurting her worse.

And Ever? She painted dark and compelling images, passed her classes, and seemed to hold a part of herself removed from me, as if she was learning to be herself once more—or all over again—and asking if the person she was becoming included me.

I felt the end approaching.

part two

a story told; a story withheld

Carter

Eden was playing her cello when I arrived at seven-thirty the next morning. I parked my truck, hung my tool belt around my waist, and stood on the rotting porch, listening through the screen door. She was bent over her instrument, her hair in a blonde wave over one shoulder, swaying with the motion of her body. The piece she was playing was one of longing, slow and high, endless wavering notes that curled one after another. Her features were pinched, her eyes shut tight, her lips pressed flat together, lines of pain etched into her face and the corners of her eyes.

I wondered who or what had caused her such pain, and how I could take it from her. Then I shook the thought away. I couldn't do that, and I don't think she wanted me to try.

When she stopped playing and rested the bow on her knee, I cleared my throat.

She started violently, gasping. "Holy shit, Carter!" She pressed her hand to her chest and laughed. "You scared the hell out of me!"

"Who is it you miss?" I couldn't help asking.

Her expression shuttered closed, going carefully blank. "My sister."

I think she expected me to pry further, but I didn't. "You play beautifully."

"Thanks," she said.

She stood up, and I realized she was wearing nothing but a white T-shirt, "CRANBROOK, est. 1932" written in crimson on the front. It was sized to fit her, which meant everything from her waist down was on display for me. She had on a pair of red boy-short underwear, cut high across her butt. I'd seen her in a bikini, but this was somehow different. More intimate. Her legs were long, and thick with muscle, strong, sexy, and perfect. Her ass was a firm, perfect, round bubble, and her hips were generous, seductive curves. I hardened just looking at her, and had to forcibly rip my gaze away from her body. I focused on the wood planks at my feet, at the bottom of the screen door. Anywhere but on her, because she didn't deserve to be ogled and I was better than that.

"I…I'll just get started. On your roof." I turned away, down the top step.

"Want some coffee?"

I moved back up and turned toward her. Meeting her gaze was a challenge. She wasn't wearing a bra, either, and her nipples poked the thin white cotton of the shirt.

"Sure," I said, but didn't make any move to open the door.

She pushed the screen door open and let me in, and I couldn't help stealing a glance at her chest. She caught the look, and seemed shocked to realize she wasn't dressed. "Shit! Sorry, I—I wasn't expecting you. I know you said today, but—" She crossed her arms over her chest, clutching her biceps. "Give me a minute. I'll put on some clothes."

I stood in the kitchen, assessing what had to be done to the inside, and trying not to watch through the bedroom door, which she had mostly closed, but not all the way. Through the crack, I could see her step into a pair of yoga pants, and then pull her arms out of her shirt to put on her bra. She turned around after she'd tugged the shirt back into place, and her eyes caught mine through the partially open door. She knew I'd been watching her.

There was palpable tension between us as she entered the kitchen. She set a clean mug on the tray of her Keurig coffee maker, and put a fresh pod in to brew. In seconds, I had a mug of coffee, which I drank black and scalding. She made herself some as well, adding a ridiculous amount of hazelnut creamer, stirring until her coffee was nearly the color of her skin: pale white.

She saw me eyeing her coffee, and I must've been making a face, because she wrapped her hands around the mug defensively and frowned at me. "Shut up. I'm a girl. I like my coffee with a lot of creamer, okay?"

I gave a little snort of laughter. "You can drink your coffee however you want. Doesn't mean I'm not gonna laugh."

"Jerk." She was teasing, though, her eyes betraying her laughter.

"Sissy. That's not even coffee anymore. That's milk." I grinned at her over the top of the mug.

"Just because you can't float a horseshoe in my coffee doesn't mean I'm a sissy." She leaned against the counter beside me, and her elbow nudged mine.

I didn't move away, and neither did she. The silence between us as we drank our coffee was companionable, easy, the earlier tension having ebbed away.

"So, you're gonna put on a new roof?" she asked, glancing up at me. "Isn't that a lot of work for one guy?"

I shrugged. "It's fine. I don't mind." I swallowed the rest of the coffee and set the mug down. "It's not a big roof."

I'd already texted my brother's friend Jim, who owned a roofing company, and he arrived just then with a dumpster for the old shingles. Jim parked the dumpster in the driveway once Eden moved her car, and then we scrambled up the ladder, eyeing the roof.

"Want some help?" he asked. Jim was a few years older than me, bearded and stocky.

I shook my head. "It's fine. I'm doing this as a favor to a friend."

Jim nearly fell off the ladder. "Holy shit, dude, you're talking!"

I nodded, and Jim looked from me down to Eden, who had a vacuum beside her car and was cleaning out the back seat. She was leaning into the car, and his gaze lingered on her backside. Lingered a little too long, and I had to quell down the urge to call him out for it, if not just shove him off the ladder.

He looked back to me, and nodded, his eyes sharp and knowing. "A favor for a friend, huh?" He winked at me. "Well, my guys are all working on another job, so I can spare you a few hours."

"Don't have to."

He descended the ladder, saying, "No, but I don't mind. It's a beautiful day, and the scenery sure is nice."

And he wasn't just talking about the lake rippling in the distance.

He grabbed a heavy-duty shingle scraper from the bed of his truck and tromped back up the ladder. Once we got started, Jim and I worked in silence, broken occasionally by Jim's phone. With his help, the old shingles came off in a few hours, and he helped me take off most of the old felt paper underneath.

His phone rang again, and he listened to the other person talking with an increasingly upset expression. "Sorry, Carter. Gotta go. One of my new guys just fell off the fucking ladder."

"He okay?"

Jim shrugged. "Yeah, he'll be fine. Made a big fucking mess with the shingles he dropped, though. Goddamned new guys." He was gone in a cloud of dust and gravel-spitting tires.

I was honestly a little relieved he was gone. His help had been nice, as he'd cut the shingle-scraping time in half, but his gaze had wandered a little too frequently over to Eden, where she'd spent the morning detailing her car and washing it. I had no place being possessive or jealous, but I was.

When I slid down the ladder to clean up the bits of shingle that hadn't made it into the dumpster, Eden came out with two paper plates bearing sandwiches, and a pair of Cokes. We sat side by side with our feet hanging off the edge of the porch.

We ate in silence for a few minutes, and then Eden glanced at me. "So your friend was a little… ogle-y."

I winced. "Sorry. He's a roofer." As if that explained it.

She grinned at me. "Ah." She shot me a sly, sarcastic look. "And carpenters would never ogle, right?"

"Nope."

She laughed. "Uh-huh. Sure."

"For real, though. I'm sorry if he made you uncomfortable." I decided to go with honesty. "And me, for that matter. I should've been more respectful of your privacy." I folded the paper plate in wedge-shaped quarters, staring down between my feet.

Eden set her plate down and took mine from me, and our fingers brushed. She nudged me with her shoulder. "Hey, I was just teasing. It's fine. I didn't close my door all the way anyway."

I shook my head. "Should've been more of a gentleman. So…I'm sorry." I brushed the crumbs off my jeans and stood up. "Anyway, I should get back up there."

Eden stood up with me and stopped me with a gentle touch to my side. "Carter, look, I—" She cut herself off, as if reconsidering what she was about to say, and then started over. "You *are* a gentleman. And thanks for doing my roof."

I could only shrug, because she didn't know how much of a gentleman I wasn't. Just like Jim, I'd been sneaking glances at Eden all morning as she cleaned out her car, only I'd been more surreptitious about it. Jim was the type to stop working and just stare until he remembered himself. Unlike Jim, though, I'd been remembering the way Eden had looked that morning, in just a T-shirt and underwear. And thinking about what it might be like to wake up next to her like that, every morning.

I'd had to shake those thoughts away time and again.

So now I shimmied back up the ladder and attacked the remaining tar paper and underlying wood planking, until the framing two-by-sixes and insulation was exposed. The insulation need replacing, too, I discovered. I texted Jim, who sent his insulation guy, and we worked out a deal. By the end of the day, the roof was re-insulated and tarped over, ready to be covered the next day.

Eden was waiting for me again when I descended the ladder. "Insulation is expensive."

I nodded. "Yep. Ain't cheap."

"I told you I can't afford to—"

"Didn't ask you to."

"Carter. For real. How much will that insulation cost?"

I shrugged. "Couple grand." By "a couple," I meant almost five, but she didn't need to know that.

"Carter." Clearly, Eden could suss out a lie in me easily.

I left my ladder on the ground beside her house and threw my tools into the bed of my truck. "Eden. It's fine."

"I'm not a charity case."

"This isn't charity."

"Then what is it?"

"Friendliness."

She frowned at me, her jaw set and her eyes blazing. "Friendliness doesn't cover a several-thousand-dollar roofing job, Carter."

"Sure it does. And it's not that much anyway."

"Why are you doing this for me?" She'd followed me to my truck, and was standing right behind me. I could feel the emotions radiating off her.

"Why are you so angry about it?" I turned around, and was pinned in place by her fierce green eyes.

"Because...because I don't get it. Because you have no reason to help me like this. And I don't want to owe you anything."

I sighed. "You don't owe me anything. I'm helping you because you need help and I'm capable of doing it. And because I like you. You're interesting."

That shut her up for a moment, but she rallied quickly. "Carter, you don't even know me. You can't—you can't like me." There was conflict in her gaze, and pain.

I took a deep breath and let it out, going for broke. "You want to pay me for the roof? Go out with me."

She blinked at me. "Go out with you? Like, on a date? I—I—when?" Then she turned away quickly, as if stung, shaking her head in denial. "It doesn't matter. I can't."

"Can't? Got somewhere else to be?"

She shook her head, blonde hair bouncing in the sun. "No, I just…I shouldn't." She took a step away, her shoulders hunched as if to ward off a blow.

That was a confusing response. "Shouldn't? Why not?" She didn't answer, and I realized she was fighting some deep emotion, something she couldn't explain and didn't want me to see. "Look, it's just dinner. No strings. No expectations. Not a date. Just dinner between friends."

She turned back to me, her eyes dry but roiling with a chaotic welter of emotions. "Carter, I'm not—I mean…" She blinked hard, and met my gaze. "Are we? Friends, I mean?"

"You got me to talk. I'd say that makes us friends."

She nodded. "Okay. Friends." She held out her hand for a handshake.

I laughed and took her hand in mine. My palm engulfed hers. Her hands were soft and small, but as she squeezed my hand, I could feel the strength in her grip. "Come on. I'm hungry." I tugged her toward my truck.

She resisted. "Wait. I need my purse." I kept tugging, opened the passenger door, and guided her in. She complied as if trying to resist, but couldn't quite manage it.

"No, you don't," I said. "We're just going to the Grill, and I'm paying. You'll be fine."

She looked at me, still fighting with herself. "If you're paying, that makes it a date." That seemed to be a problem for her.

"Then make me dinner tomorrow to pay me back."

She frowned. "That's even worse. I suck at cooking."

I sighed. "Look, Eden. It's only a date if you want it to be. If you don't, it's not. I haven't said a word in a year, and I like talking to you. Quit making this a big deal."

She nodded, and I shut the door, but I heard her whisper to herself, "It is a big deal."

I'd shed my shirt sometime after ten that morning, and I grabbed it off the lawn, sniffed it. Grimaced at the stench. Fortunately, I always had a spare in my truck, along with deodorant. I opened the driver's side-door and snagged my bag off the floor, dug out the spare shirt and deodorant. As I made myself somewhat presentable, I felt Eden's curious gaze on me.

"What?" I asked.

"I've seen you with that bag. Coming and going from the beach. And I can't figure out where you go, or why."

I hopped in and started the truck. "There's an island three miles off shore. My house is on the island. I swim back and forth instead of taking a boat, when I can."

"You swim three miles one way, every day? Just for fun?"

I lifted a shoulder. "Yeah. It's good exercise, and I like swimming."

"Six miles a day. And you run?"

I laughed. "No. I only run when I can't swim. That'd be suicide."

"What do you do in the winter?"

"Run. Lift weights. I don't do polar bear swims, if that's what you're asking."

She laughed. "Good, that would just be weird."

She was always beautiful, but when she forgot to be closed up and tense, she was breathtaking.

Conversation drifted after that, from how crazy the yearly polar bear swim was, to what winter was like on the peninsula.

When we arrived at the Grill, Julie, the waitress, seated us and asked what we wanted to drink.

"Just water with lemon, please," Eden asked.

I hesitated. Julie was short and curvy, just past thirty with auburn hair. She'd worked at the Grill for years, and knew me before I went silent. If I spoke, it would be a big deal to her. There would be questions, and I didn't have any answers.

"Your usual, Carter?" Julie asked.

My usual was a pint of the local microbrew beer, but I'd planned on ordering wine, just to help Eden relax. I glanced at Eden. "Do you want some wine? Or a beer?"

Julie's mouth dropped open, and her eyes went wide.

Eden shook her head. "No, I—no. Thank you. Water is fine. You go ahead, though."

I turned to Julie. "Coke is fine."

"Carter." Her voice was incredulous. "You— you're talking."

I could only shrug, my response for everything lately, it seemed. "Yeah. Finally had something to say, I guess."

Julie nodded, knowing there was more to the story but too professional to come right out and ask, though. She eyed Eden thoughtfully, and then left to get our drinks.

"Not a drinker?" I asked.

She shook her head, fiddling with the strip of sticky paper binding the silverware in the napkin. "No. Not…not at the moment."

Another enigmatic answer that hinted at something. I ignored the urge to probe, and just nodded. "Ever eaten here?"

"No, just the deli. I shop at the market, though." She laughed. "I don't know what I'd do without the market, though. Having to go all the way downtown whenever I needed something would be a pain in the ass."

I nodded in agreement. "That's for damn sure."

"So, what's good?"

"Everything. I usually get the burger, though."

Julie came back with our drinks and took our orders, burgers for both of us. When she was gone, Eden took a deep breath and looked at me. "So, thanks for—"

"Stop thanking me," I interrupted. "It's getting annoying." I grinned, making it a joke. Even though it wasn't, entirely.

"You didn't let me finish. I was going to say thanks for…not prying."

"Prying?"

She unrolled the napkin and toyed with the knife and fork, fitting the knife between the tines of the fork and attempting to balance it. She didn't look at me. "Yeah. Prying. You've had a lot of opportunities to push for answers, I guess you could say. You don't. And I appreciate it."

"Oh. Well, we all have stories, I guess."

"Including you." It wasn't a question, more of a non sequitur.

"Yep." I sipped at my Coke.

A long silence extended between us, tense and awkward. I was pretty sure we were both thinking about our pasts, about the stories we kept so close to the vest.

"I was married," I blurted.

Eden dropped the silverware, shocked. "Was?" Her green eyes were rife with compassion and curiosity.

I swirled my straw through the ice, making it clink against the walls of the glass. "Yeah. Was." I felt the words tumbling out and couldn't stop them. I couldn't have said why I was revealing my deepest, darkest source of pain to this woman I barely knew. Yet I was. "We'd only been married a year. She was pregnant. Miscarried."

Eden's eyes searched mine, wavering. "Oh...god, Carter. I'm so sorry."

"I found her. In...in the bathtub." Jesus. Fuck. Why was I telling her this? My insides clenched, and my chest ached, and my eyes burned. I blinked and squeezed my hands into fists. "I was working. She'd told me she wasn't feeling good. Asked me if I could take the day off. I wanted to finish the project—it was this kitchen remodel for some rich guy. We were almost done, and I wanted it finished before she had the baby. There were a couple months of work left, and I was just…focused. On that. On finishing. I left for work that morning knowing I should've stayed home with Britt. But I didn't. I got home late. Past seven. Almost eight. The house was quiet. Too quiet. You know? You ever just suddenly *know* something is wrong?"

Eden ducked her head, nodding. "Yeah. I do." Her voice was thick.

"It was like that." I hesitated, licked my lips, and swallowed hard. "Brittany loved music. If she was awake, there was always music going somewhere. An iPod, the stereo, the car radio. The TV. Her, singing. So when I got home and it was just…dark and silent. I knew. I knew something was wrong. I called her name, and she didn't answer. But then I heard…I heard her. Whispering. For me. I ran upstairs, to our bathroom. She was in the bathtub. She…she was taking a bath. But she—she hemorrhaged. She'd been bleeding out, alone, for hours. So bad she couldn't get up. Couldn't call me. Couldn't call for help."

"Fucking hell, Carter." Eden's voice broke.

My hand was flat on the table, pressing down onto the wood as if to hold myself up. Eden reached out, put her small, strong hand on mine. My hand curled, tightened into a fist, and she fit her fingers between my knuckles. A simple, soothing, warm touch.

"Blood was…was everywhere. She'd been trying to climb out. Handprints on the walls. On the tub. She'd grabbed onto the towel rack and broke it trying to get out. And I…I wasn't there." My chest was heaving, dragging deep, harsh breaths in and out. I fought for composure.

Eden shook her head. "My god, Carter."

The guilt that had been eating me alive for the last year tumbled from my lips. My secret, my sin, my guilt. "If I'd been there…if I'd stayed home like she wanted me to…I could've…she'd still be here."

"You can't blame—"

"Yes, I *can*." I spoke over her, cutting her off with the quiet, hissing intensity of my voice. "The doctor told me as much. If I'd gotten her to the hospital sooner, they could've saved her. But I was gone. I was *working*."

"And you haven't spoken since?"

I shook my head. "Not until the other day." I scraped at a streak of dirt on my index finger. "I just…couldn't. I tried, god knows I did. I've never told anyone what happened. I don't even know why I told you."

"I'm glad you did. You had to get it out."

I scrubbed my hands through my hair. "God, what a downer, huh? Sorry."

Eden's hand was still on mine. "It's fine, Carter. I'm not exactly a barrel full of laughs myself."

Julie approached with our food, and we both fell silent. I was sure Julie could feel the intensity in the air, but she didn't say anything. Eden and I ate without talking, and this time the silence was companionable. After I'd finished, I excused myself and went to the bathroom. Our table was around the corner from the bathroom, so I overheard part of a conversation between Julie and Eden.

"It's kind of unbelievable, actually," Julie was saying.

"Why?"

"After what happened, he just stopped talking. Just…complete silence. He wouldn't say anything after Britt died, not to anyone, not for anything. He wouldn't even communicate for the first couple weeks. He was…gone. Eventually, he would at least respond when spoken to, even if it was nonverbal." Julie spun her tray on its axis, an idle habit of hers. "It was so tragic. He was one of the sweetest, kindest men I've ever known, and then Britt passed, and he just shut down. Went reclusive."

"He's still sweet and kind." Eden sounded oddly defensive.

"Well, sweetie, I don't know how you did it, but you worked a miracle in that man."

"I didn't do anything," Eden protested. "For real. I didn't."

I rounded the corner, scuffing my foot on the floor on purpose. Both women started and glanced back at me. I handed Julie enough cash to cover the bill and then some. Eden stood and waved at Julie, then accompanied me to my car.

"You heard us talking about you?" she said, once we were heading north.

I shrugged. "Yeah. People talk. It's fine."

Eden glanced at me, a worried expression on her face. "I didn't tell her anything. About what you said to me, I mean. She asked me how I'd gotten you to talk, and I just told her I didn't know."

"It's fine, Eden."

"I just didn't want you to think I'd talk about you."

"It's not a secret."

"But it is private." She tugged on the seatbelt, loosening it and letting it snap back into place.

"Yeah, guess so." I felt strangely exhausted, and couldn't offer up any more conversation. Eden seemed content to ride in silence, a quality I appreciated.

I pulled up in front of her house, left the truck idling, and walked her up to her door.

"Thanks for dinner," she said, not quite looking directly at me.

"No problem." I was tongue-tied now, as if telling Eden my story had sapped me of words. I was confused as to what it was about her that seemed to draw me out, pull things from me. And I was still reeling from the renewed onslaught of pain and guilt that the memory of Britt's death engendered.

I backed away, glancing at Eden as I went down the porch steps.

She stopped me with a touch to my elbow. "Are you okay?"

I shrugged. "As okay as ever."

She seemed to be struggling to find the right words. "Guilt sucks."

Not what I expected her to say. "Yeah, it does." I'd expected her to offer up the same old "it wasn't your fault" platitudes that people seemed to think I needed to hear.

It was my fault. I could've prevented it, could've saved her, if I'd only gone home earlier. Nothing could change that essential truth, and nothing could lessen the pain. Only the time would bring me any kind of healing.

I wanted to ask her what she knew about guilt, what had happened to put such pain in her eyes. But I didn't. Instead, I waved at her. "See you tomorrow."

She offered a small, tight smile and a little wave. She stood on her porch and watched me drive away. I wondered if I was imagining the regret I thought I saw in her eyes.

a pregnant pause

Despite everything, we settled into a pattern. I'd show up early in the morning, my truck bed full of supplies. I'd started taking the boat to the mainland, to save time and because the reno work was tiring, if satisfying. She'd be dressed, with coffee ready, and we'd sit on her porch talking and drinking coffee as the sun rose behind us. We never let the conversation get heavy, though. I never pried into her story, nor she into mine. We talked about music, about movies and books. Our favorite bands, favorite actors and actresses. Even with Britt, I hadn't been this open, this talkative, but something about Eden made it easy for me to just talk.

When I finished my coffee, I'd get to work. It took me three days to finish her roof, and then I started on her porch. I was qualified to do roofing work, but I disliked it. Building her a new porch, however, was different. I ripped the old rotten structure apart and had the basic frame of the new one built in one day. The next day I finished the build, then sanded and stained it.

After a day's work we'd eat dinner together, usually at the Grill. As the days turned into a week, I managed to get the complete exterior repainted, but Eden seemed more and more reticent to leave her house. She was closed off, hard to read, hard to gauge. Every moment she spent with me, she seemed to be at war with herself. It was as if she *wanted* to hang out with me, but kept trying to come up with some compelling reason not to. I couldn't figure it out, and I refused to pry. So I kept working also but kept asking myself why I was doing all this for someone I barely knew. It was a question Eden asked me frequently as well, but I didn't have any answers.

All I knew was, she never had visitors. Never took a phone call. Never got mail. Never left her house, unless it was with me, or to go to the beach, or on a run. She played cello, read books, and talked to me sporadically…and very little else. I don't think I ever saw her leave the peninsula, or go south of the Grill.

Something told me she was hiding, but from what? From whom?

I desperately wanted to know.

As the days passed, I also noticed changes in her, physically. Her clothing got progressively looser and more conservative. Gone were the spandex workout shorts and sports bra. Gone was the bikini. We'd gone swimming together the other day, and she'd worn a cover-up dress until she'd gone into the water and, even then, she'd faced away from me until the water hid her body. She seemed…ashamed of herself somehow. And I couldn't fathom why. Why would a woman as stunningly beautiful as Eden be self-conscious? And why so suddenly? It had been a noticeable transformation, to me at least.

Still, I never asked questions. She'd respected my privacy, and I would respect hers. I worried for her, though. She was vulnerable. She was clearly trying to project an aura of self-sufficiency, but it was a thin veneer at best.

Once the outside of Eden's house was taken care of, I turned my focus to the inside. Her floors needed redoing, badly. So I started in the bathroom and spare bedroom, ripping out dated, threadbare carpeting in the bedroom and the scuffed, peeling laminate in the bathroom. I left the old scratched and gouged hardwood floor in the bedrooms that lay beneath the carpeting and put down tile in the bathroom, one-inch squares in a complex pattern of slate gray and sky blue. Eden sat on her couch and read a book, a thick, dog-eared romance novel, what my mom would call a "bodice ripper," and watched me work.

"You're seriously crazy, Carter."

I looked up at her from the bathroom floor, where I was laying down caulk around the tub. "Why?"

"All this work. It's nuts. You really need to stop." She slid her index finger between pages to mark her place. "How much have you spent on materials?"

I went back to caulking, adding up mentally. "Not as much as you'd think. My brothers and I are building a tasting room for the winery, so a lot of the materials have come from there. I'm not worried."

"But I am. You keep brushing me off, saying it's fine, you're not worried. But you've spent hours and hours every day for almost two weeks, and I don't even know why. I can't...I can't repay you. And I can't be—I mean there can't—god. Between you and me. This can't be what you want."

I didn't answer until I'd finished caulking. I stood up, brushed off my knees and washed my hands in the sink, and then sat down next to Eden on the couch. I scratched at a ribbon of dried grout on the back of my hand. "Honestly, I don't really have an answer for why. It needs to be done. You can't live in a house that's falling apart and leaking. That roof would've given way with the first heavy snow. The insulation beneath it is molding. It's unhealthy and unsafe. The floors in here are just as bad. I think some of the paint on the walls is lead-based. Also super unhealthy." I glanced at her, took in her fearful, worried expression. "I mean, as long as you don't, like, *eat* the paint, it'll be fine. But it needs repainting." I sighed. "Look, I *enjoy* this kind of work. It's what I do. I'm a carpenter, a builder. It's what I've done my whole life. So it's not even really work for me. And I don't *want* you to repay me. Just spending time with me is payment enough."

"That's just it, Carter." Eden shifted, curling her legs beneath her butt. "I don't want you to get the wrong idea about…this." She gestured between herself and me. "It can't…I'm not—"

I held up my hand to stop her. "That's fine. You don't even have to say it."

"Aren't you going to ask why?"

I shrugged. "Nope. It's your business. If you're not interested in telling me, then you're not. Doesn't mean I'm gonna quit helping you midway through the remodel."

Eden groaned, letting her head thump back onto the couch. "God*dammit*, Carter. You can't fucking remodel my house just *because*. I'll be fine."

"You're not fine." I held her gaze and refused to look away. "I don't know who you're hiding from, or why, and it's none of my business. But you *are* hiding. You need help. This is the help I can give you, and the reasons why are my own."

"I'm not hiding," Eden protested.

I just laughed, a sarcastic bark. "I didn't take you for a liar."

She ducked her head, sniffed. "You should go."

I let out a long, frustrated sigh. "I'm sorry, Eden, I didn't mean—"

"I'm not mad. I'm just…tired. And not feeling well." She glanced up at me, wiped a finger beneath her eye. "I'm fine, Carter. I promise. I just need to rest. I haven't been sleeping well."

She looked pale, bags under her eyes. I stared at her, remembering Britt, remembering similar words. "Maybe I should stay for a while," I said.

Eden's eyes widened. "Oh, shit. No, it's not like that. I'm fine, I swear. I'm just tired. I'll make some tea and read in bed."

I stood up and went into her kitchen. I remembered seeing a box of chamomile tea in a cabinet. I put water on to boil and found a clean mug, a tea bag. "Go lie down," I told her.

"Carter, you don't have to—"

"Just go lie down. Please."

Eden hesitated, her expression torn between tender and terrified. After a moment, she disappeared into her bedroom. I heard the door close, then silence as she changed. The door opened again, and she reappeared wearing a pair of baggy sweatpants and a loose T-shirt. The water boiled, and I poured it over the teabag as she retrieved her book, then followed her into her bedroom with the scalding hot tea.

"Carter, you don't have to take care of me. I can take care of myself." She perched on the edge of the bed, one leg tucked beneath her thigh.

I set the mug on the bedside table. "I made you a cup of tea. That's hardly taking care of you." I stuck my hand in the hip pocket of my jeans. "Besides, everyone needs someone to take care of them."

"Who takes care of you?"

"My brothers, if I need something." I dismissed the topic with a wave, not wanting to talk about me.

"Well, thank you. For the tea, and for everything." She took the mug in her hands, watching me as she blew across the top.

"It's nothing. I'll see you tomorrow."

She frowned. "Why don't you take a day off? I'm sure you have other work to do."

"Tired of me already?" I teased.

"No!" she just about yelled in protest. She tried again more quietly. "No. I just—I need…space."

She wasn't tired of seeing me, but needed space. I couldn't even begin to try to figure that one out. I just nodded. "Okay, then." I felt hurt, a little, which was stupid. I shoved it away, then gave her a wave goodbye as I headed to the door. "I'll see you in a day or two, then."

Apparently I was being too casual, because she just sighed in resignation. "Wait, Carter. You've been really kind to me. Too kind. And it's confusing me. I know I don't make any sense, but there's just things I can't—I mean, my life is just—" She flopped back on the bed and groaned, her hand over her face. "I can't even make sense to myself. You must think I'm a lunatic."

"No," I said. "You can't explain, but part of you wants to. I get it. You don't have to explain anything to me."

"But you deserve answers, and I just can't give them." She stared at the ceiling as she spoke.

"I don't deserve anything. Don't worry about it. Just…know that if you ever do want to…talk, I'm here. I'll listen, and I won't judge."

"Don't make promises you can't keep, Carter." Her voice was hard, cold.

Another enigmatic response that I couldn't make any sense of. "I don't."

"You don't know me."

"I'd like to." I shouldn't have said it, but I did. "That's what all this is about, Eden."

"If you knew me, you wouldn't think that way." She turned away from me, but not before I caught a glimpse of her tortured expression.

I hesitated. She clearly wanted me to leave so she could cry alone, but for that exact reason, I didn't want to leave. I stood staring at her back, at the hunched, defensive curl of her shoulders, the wave of blonde hair with the two-inch-long dark roots. She looked tiny and hurting and so, so vulnerable. Lonely. Afraid.

I sat down on the edge of the bed, near her feet. "Eden. You're not alone."

"Yes. I am. And I should be."

"That's stupid. No one should be alone."

She was shaking from head to toe. "I should."

"Why?" There. I'd asked.

She only shook her head, a silent denial, a refusal. "Go away, Carter. You're wasting your time."

"It's my time to waste," I said. "I choose to waste it here."

I wasn't touching her in any way, but I wanted to. I wanted to rest my hand on her calf, or her foot, or her shoulder. An innocent touch of comfort. I couldn't walk away. I should. I knew I should. The girl had baggage, that much was clear. She had a world of hurt hidden away inside her, guilt and grief and torment.

I let my right hand drift out, settle on her ankle.

She flinched when my palm touched her skin, jerked away. "Don't, Carter. Just don't. You're torturing yourself, and hurting me. Just go. Please, just go. Don't come back."

"Eden—"

"Please, Carter." Desperation had never sounded so painful.

I stood up slowly. Walked out of her room, but turned back in the doorway. Her shoulders were shaking, and I could hear sobs coming from her. I squeezed my eyes closed, wishing I could erase the sound of her crying, but knowing I wouldn't, couldn't. I tried to walk away, but I simply couldn't.

She flinched visibly at each footstep as I re-crossed the tiny bedroom. She moved toward the wall as I sat down on the bed again, shifting away from me. Her knees curled up against her chest, and she trembled all over, trying to stifle her tears. In vain.

I sat by her hips, one knee up on the bed, the other foot on the floor, partially facing her. "I'm not leaving you like this. I can't, and I won't."

"You can't fix this."

"I'm not trying to."

"Then what do you want from me?" She was still fighting the tears.

"I don't want anything from you. I just want to be here for you."

"Why?" The single word question was a whispered, ragged plea.

"You're too beautiful to be this sad."

Eden didn't answer, only silently fought away the sobs. After a few minutes, she rolled toward me. Tucking one hand under her face, fixing her tormented jade eyes on me. "You're determined to make this hard for me, aren't you?" She smiled sadly at me.

"Make what hard?"

"I'm trying to push you away. For your own good." She closed her eyes, sighed deeply, then sat up. "Fuck it. You're going to find out eventually, so I might as well just tell you. Get it over with."

"Find out what?" I asked, but Eden just shook her head at me.

"Let me talk. Don't interrupt. Please." She crossed her arms over her stomach, hunched over, eyes downcast. "You were right. I am hiding."

A long, tense pause.

Her eyes turned up to mine. "I'm pregnant, Carter."

Shock rippled through me, quickly replaced by a dawning understanding. "You're—"

"Yeah. It's why I moved up here."

"You're pregnant. Where is—"

"That's the hard part." Eden fisted her hand into the sheets, her face contorted in pain. "Two years ago this Christmas Eve, my sister was in a car accident with her husband. It was really, really bad. She nearly died. She—she went into a coma. The doctors didn't think she'd ever come out of it." She paused, struggling for breath, for composure. "She's my *twin*. Did I mention that? Identical twin. God, I can't do this.

Shitshitshit." She sucked in a deep breath, let it out with a wracking shudder. "She was in a coma for a year and a half. They talked to Cade, her husband, about donating her organs. Letting her die. Cade, god, that man has been through hell. I wish I could tell you. He was injured in the accident, too. It took him months of therapy to even walk again. He—had no one. She was his only family. Parents, grandparents…he had no one. But her. And me."

I hated where this was going. Hated the devastation in her voice, the self-loathing in her eyes.

"Our dad, he's…he's not really a part of our lives, but our life story isn't important. There's no—no justification or explanation for what I did. What I let it happen. I was just…I'd lost my sister. My twin. She was my best friend, my only family, the only person who cared about me. She was…never coming back, but she wasn't dead. You can't imagine how that feels. And Cade…god, he was falling apart. We were both a mess. And it just—it just happened. Both of us tried to…to stop it from happening. But—fuck. It wasn't like I seduced him, I just—he was hurting, and so was I, and—"

"Cade is the father."

She nodded. "Yeah." Her voice was tiny, not even a whisper. Just an agonized breath of admission.

"Shit."

"Yeah," she agreed, with a bitter laugh.

"What happened?" I asked.

Eden was openly crying now, tears streaming silently down her face. She didn't try to wipe them away. Just sat cross-legged on the bed, fingers tangled together on her lap. "She woke up."

"Does she know?"

"No." Eden clawed at her face, scratching her nails down her skin so harshly I reached out and held her wrists so she couldn't hurt herself. "She woke up. She doesn't know. *He* doesn't know. How could I tell them? How could they deal with this? She may never recover, Carter. He's all she has, she's all he has. They have to have each other. I—fucked everything up, Carter. I slept with my twin sister's husband. While she was in a coma." She jerked her wrists away, curled over her legs, sobbing.

I didn't know what to say. How to react. What to even think. "But you're their family."

"Not anymore."

"So you just…left? Without telling anyone?"

"YES!" Eden screamed. "I *couldn't* tell them! I was afraid! I'm still afraid! I'm terrified, Carter. You don't even know the worst part."

Oh, god. There was more? "What's the worst part?"

"She was pregnant when she had the accident. She miscarried. It was part of why she was so close to death. She lost the baby, and to—to save her, to stop the bleeding, they had to remove her uterus. She'll never have kids. I'm carrying her husband's baby, and she'll never, ever have that herself." Eden fell apart, crying so hard she couldn't breathe.

I couldn't help reaching for her, grabbing her by the shoulders and pulling her against me. It was the only thing I could do.

She fought against my hold. "No. NO! I don't—I don't deserve this. You shouldn't be here. You should leave." Her sobs turned into hyperventilation.

I held her anyway, gently but firmly. "Eden. Breathe. Breathe." She sucked in a deep breath, and another. "Good. Look at me."

She turned her wet, reddened eyes up to mine. "Why are you still here?"

"I'm not leaving, Eden."

"Why?"

"Because I'm where I want to be."

She pulled away from me, slid off the bed. "I'm *pregnant*, Carter. What do you think could possibly happen between us?"

I didn't answer for a long time. "I'm your friend, Eden. I was your friend before this, and I'm your friend now. Maybe I thought…" I trailed off, shaking my head and began again. "No. Look, there're no ulterior motives. I'm here because you shouldn't have to go through this alone. No matter what happened, no matter what mistakes you may have made, it doesn't mean you should suffer alone."

"Yes, it does. I betrayed my twin sister. She's half of me. And I betrayed her. I'm a shitty, terrible, horrible person."

I stood up and faced her. "No. You're not."

Eden's eyes met mine. "How can you even look at me? How can you stand there and act like you're not disgusted?"

"I told you I wouldn't judge you, and I won't. I'm not." I turned away, hunting for the right words. "You want to know what I think? For real?" I pivoted back to face her. "It was a fucked-up, impossible situation. And I don't think anyone, least of all me, has any right to judge you for the choices you made. You want the truth? Here's a hard question for you: What if she hadn't woken up? Would it still have been a betrayal?"

She turned away from me, refusing to meet my gaze. "I don't know."

"Were you jealous? Did you do it out of some kind of…I don't know…manipulative rancor?"

"No!" Eden whirled on me. "I was confused! Alone! So was he! It was the only comfort either of us had." She deflated, her anger and outrage bleeding away, replaced once again by guilt. "But…there *was* jealousy. Not over Caden. Just…growing up, Ever was always better than me. Popular. Everyone liked

her. She made friends without trying. She was…
everything I wanted to be. Tried to be. She could eat
anything she wanted and stay skinny, and I've had to
diet and work out all my life to keep from getting fat.
I've just…I've always been jealous of her. In general.
And I didn't sleep with Cade because of jealousy.
I swear I didn't. But after I found out I was pregnant and she woke up, knowing I'd spent our entire
lives nursing that little seed of jealousy…it just made
everything worse. Made me question…everything. I
mean, *did* I do it to get back at her? But…I love Ever.
I do. I swear I do!"

"You don't have to convince me, Eden."

"I'm not going back. I can't. It's best this way."

"Listen, it might not be my place to say this
but…Cade or Caden or whoever he is does bear
some responsibility." I took a step toward her, hesitant.
Reached out and touched her arm.

She flinched away, pulled her arm out of reach.
"Don't, Carter. No matter what either of us might
feel, it's impossible. So just don't."

"What do you feel?"

"It doesn't matter. It won't ever matter."

I sighed, nodding. "Okay, well, be that as it may,
I'm here. I'm your friend. And I'm not going anywhere." I reached for her again, tentatively. "Friends
hug, right? Just a hug."

She sniffed, and then laughed. "That would be nice."

I chuckled and pulled her in. I was careful about how I held her, how I stood, where my hands went. She was my friend, and that was it. I wrapped my arms around her shoulders, turned my head to the side, away from her hair. She fit perfectly against me, her head tucked just beneath my chin. Her hair smelled like citrus shampoo, and I caught a whiff of body lotion. Cherries, or lavender. Something faint, but exotic. I resisted the urge to inhale her scent and just hold her. It was a hug, nothing more. There was space between our bodies, so she wouldn't mistake my intentions.

She let out a long breath, shaky, tremulous, and stepped away. "Thank you."

My hand reached out and brushed a lock of hair away from her eye. I hadn't meant to do that, but I couldn't take it back. She flinched from my touch, but she didn't pull away. I dropped my hand and shoved my fists in my pockets. "You're welcome."

"I mean, for…for listening. For not judging. For being my friend, even though I don't deserve it." She sounded as if she absolutely meant that last part.

"Eden. Everyone deserves friendship, and understanding. That's all I'm offering."

"You're sweet."

"So are you."

She shook her head. "No, I'm not, but let's just agree to disagree." She glanced past me at the darkness that had fallen. "You should get home. It's getting late. You're not swimming home, are you?"

I laughed. "Hell, no. I've got my boat. And I can always stay at the winery, if I have to."

"Good."

"I'm here, Eden. If you need anything, just ask."

She nodded. "I will. Now go. For real. I'm fine."

"'You keep using that word. I do not think it means what you think it means.'"

Eden laughed, a genuine, delighted laugh. "'Inconceivable!'" She said it with an exaggerated lisp, doing her best to sound like Vizzini.

I grinned at her. "If you hadn't gotten that quote, I might have had to rethink being friends with you."

"I'm glad I knew it, then."

"Me, too," I said.

And just like that, we were back to serious. Her eyes searched mine, and I wondered what she was thinking. Maybe I was better off not knowing.

The lock of hair fell across her eye again, and I was tempted to brush it away once more. I didn't. Instead, I hugged her again.

She fell against my chest with a laugh, hugging me back, her arms going around my waist, her hands on my shoulder blades. "You give good hugs."

"So do you."

She pushed me away. "Go."

I left and managed to drive away without looking back. I could feel her watching me from the doorway, though. I got all the way home before letting a brutal wave of exhaustion wash over me.

Eden was pregnant. It explained all the changes I'd seen in her, and it explained the back-and-forth of her emotions. There was something between us. She knew it, and I knew it. But like she'd said, it was impossible.

And just because I was talking again didn't mean I was totally over Britt, and what had happened there. If anything, telling Eden about it had brought it all back. I was doing my best to push it away, ignore it, keep it down and act like I was fine but, in truth, I wasn't. I missed her. Every day, I missed Britt. And, every day, I was sliced by pangs of guilt over having not been there for her. And now, with everything that was happening with Eden, I felt even more guilt about it. The seedling feelings I had for Eden were taking root all too easily. As if, somehow, I now wanted to replace Britt.

I went into my workshop and took the sheet off the sculpture of Britt. *I'm sorry,* I wanted to say. *I wish you were here,* I wanted to say. But I couldn't get the words out, not to a sculpture. It wasn't her.

I'd hoped maybe I'd find some answers out here with Britt's likeness, but all I got was silence, and misery. No matter what I felt for Eden, our situation was next to impossible. I could be her friend, because I'd made that promise to her. And I'd keep that promise. But, truthfully, I wanted more. I wanted her to feel for me what I felt for her. But she couldn't…or wouldn't. Even if she did feel as I did, acting on it was out of the question for her.

It all seemed so impossible. Yet I'd started the course, and I'd stay it, one way or another.

nameday

At the end of three weeks, Eden's house was finished. My brothers were bitching at my absence, but the bar was done, the tasting room was progressing, and the vines were in good shape. They'd survive a few weeks without me. Or so I told myself.

I'd redone the hardwoods completely, since what was there was too roughed up to be salvageable. I saved a bunch of the old wood, though, since I had a few ideas for ways to reuse it. In its place, I put down dark cherrywood, stained it until it was the color of thick brandy, coated it until it shone like glass. The walls all got stripped of wallpaper and old paint, and Eden chose ivory paint to go on the walls. She helped me paint, which I only allowed if the windows and doors were all open to vent the fumes.

The counters in the kitchen got polished slate to match the floors in the bathroom, with a backsplash using leftover tiles from the bathroom. The cabinets were in decent shape, so I sanded them down and repainted them a pale blue to match the tiles in the bathroom and backsplash. I pulled down the ceiling and re-plastered it, since most of it was ruined from the leaks. I even replaced the kitchen sink and vanity in the bathroom, as well as the toilet. By the time I finished, only the cabinets were original, and even those were unrecognizable.

The last project was replacing the screens on her windows and on the front door. The screens were easy enough, but as I pulled the old screen door off the front door, I realized the main door itself was as outdated and inefficient as the rest of the house had been, so I took Eden over to the Home Depot on South Airport Road and she picked out a new front door. I made her pick out a storm door as well, even though she protested it was an expense she didn't need.

On the way back from ordering the doors, Eden was quiet, lost in thought.

I glanced at her, turned the radio down. "Dollar for your thoughts?"

Eden snorted in laughter, shooting me an amused glance. "Isn't the phrase supposed be 'penny for your thoughts'?"

"I figure your thoughts are worth a bit more than a dollar."

"Oh, yeah? A whole ninety-nine cents more?"

I nodded. "At least. I could probably go a full two bucks." I turned left onto Garfield, which would take us to Center Road and up the peninsula once more. "For real, though. I can feel you thinking over there. What's up?"

She cranked the window open and closed her eyes as the wind tousled her hair. "Even if you're not charging me for labor, the parts alone of this remodel have to be costing you small fortune."

"Eden," I started, "I told you—"

"I'm not arguing. I'm just wondering how you can afford it. I'm sorry if this is nosey, but it just doesn't make any sense to me. I mean, if you were gonna flip this house, that'd be one thing. But I own the house with my sister. It was my parents' vacation cabin. So…obviously it's not a flip project for you. I told you up front I can't pay you, so you're not doing it as a contractor. I'm not even asking *why* anymore. I'm asking *how*."

I sighed. "My parents have money, and my brothers and I have all been earning our own money since we were teenagers. I started working for my uncle when I was fourteen. He's a builder, and he taught me everything I know. I built houses with him for eleven years, and I'm part owner of his company, on top of my quarter share in the winery."

"I don't know anything about wineries, obviously, but if you haven't finished your tasting room, how are you turning a profit?" she asked.

"We've been selling the grapes for the past three years, for one thing. They're not mature enough yet to make wine from, but they're still valuable produce, and we have a *lot* of vines. Plus, we've been buying wine grapes from other local vineyards and making wine from those and selling it. We don't have huge distribution yet, but you can buy Haven Brothers wine throughout most of Michigan, Ohio, and Indiana. Kirk is working on Illinois and Wisconsin as we speak, and we're hoping to get distribution on both coasts by the time we're harvesting grapes mature enough to make wine from, which will be this fall."

I pulled over onto the scenic turnout overlooking Chateau Grand Traverse's vineyard, and the rippling, sunlit East Arm Bay with the Leelenau Peninsula in the distance. It was a gorgeous spot, a favorite of tourists. During peak tourist season, this turnout would be packed with cars full of tourists snapping pictures with phones and cameras. "I also sell some sculptures here and there, but that's more for fun than anything."

"Sculptures?" Eden asked as she hopped out of the truck and leaned back against it, staring out at the bay.

"Yeah. Woodcarving."

"You must be pretty good, if you can sell them."

I shrugged. "I guess. There's an art gallery downtown that displays my work for me."

"So your point is, you're doing fine, financially."

I nodded. "Yeah, that's my point. And not only that, since I'm a contractor, I can get materials for cheap. I grew up on this peninsula, and I know just about everyone in the building business for a hundred miles in every direction. I get discounts all over the place, in return for help on various jobs. So please, stop worrying. I enjoy the work, I'm not hurting for money, and it means I get to hang out with a gorgeous, funny woman in the process. I can't lose." My smile faded when I saw the expression on Eden's face.

"I'm anything but gorgeous and funny, Carter." She scuffed at the dirt under foot.

"To me you are."

"We talked about this, Carter," she whispered.

"I know. I know. But that doesn't change my opinion of you. We're friends, and *just* friends. But that doesn't mean I don't see what's in front of me. You're talented, intelligent, and beautiful. And yeah, you might be a bit of a mess, and in a spot of trouble, but that doesn't define you. Or at least, it shouldn't."

"A spot of trouble?" Her voice was incredulous. "Is that what you call this?" She gestured at her belly, which was starting to pop, now.

I sighed. "Okay, yeah, it's a little fucked up. But it's not the end of your life. I know there's probably a lot more to the story, but it's not the be-all and end-all of who you are. You messed up. Everyone messes up." I pivoted and stood in front of her, looked her in the eyes so she could see my sincerity. "You're a good person, Eden. You have to stop vilifying yourself."

"I don't know how," she said, her voice faint, her eyes sliding away from mine and back to the bay, shining with unshed tears. "Every day that passes, the reminder of what I did gets more and more obvious. I don't know what I'm going to do, Carter. I don't know how to have a baby. How to be a mother."

"One day at a time, Eden. That's how. One decision at a time." I leaned against the truck, beside her but not too close.

She shook her head, a tear trickling unnoticed down her cheek. "Easy to say." She looked down, covering her face with both hands. "I couldn't... couldn't and wouldn't even think of having an abortion. It wasn't ever a choice. But...I don't even *want* to be a mother. Not yet. Maybe never. How horrible is that? I'm afraid I'll resent the baby. I know I will.

My whole life is thrown off-course because of this pregnancy. I was gonna graduate from Cranbrook and be a professional cellist. The DSO first. Like Mom. I already have an audition lined up. Or…I did." Her voice broke on the last word, and she had to suck in a deep breath and let it out to keep going. "Eventually, I wanted to play somewhere exotic. The Sydney Symphony Orchestra, maybe. Or London."

"Britt loved the London Philharmonic. She was a music teacher, eighth grade. She came from big money. Her dad owns a big tech company or something." Talking about Britt was hard. I had to force the words out. "She taught because she loved teaching. Music was her passion, though. She played the violin. She was good, really good, but she had major stage fright issues. Even a classroom was hard for her, but she managed it because she loved the students. A full orchestra, huge audiences…that was out of the question for her. God knows she tried, though. She just couldn't do it."

Eden smiled sadly at me. "She sounds like she was amazing."

I nodded, finding it hard to speak. "She—she was."

We'd somehow moved closer and closer as we talked, until our elbows touched. Eden leaned against me, resting her head on my arm. "Losing someone you love is the worst fucking thing ever," she said.

"You lost your mom?"

Eden nodded against my bicep. "Yeah. When I was thirteen. Car accident."

"I'm sorry."

"Me, too. She was incredible. She was a cellist like me, played with the Detroit Symphony Orchestra until she had Ever and me. She was a painter, too, like Ever. Beautiful. Fun."

"You miss her." It was a stupid, obvious thing to say, but I wasn't sure what else to say.

"Yeah. I mean, it's hard to remember her. I have specific memories, you know? From childhood. Going to the park with her. Family vacations up here. Things like that. She died so suddenly, you know? If I'd known I was gonna lose her, I'd have tried to remember more."

I choked. "God, I hate that feeling." I looked up at the sky, as if that could stop the burn in my eyes and the thickness in my throat. "I think that all the time. If only I'd known, I would've done things so much differently. I would've…appreciated her. The things she did, who she was."

"We always take things for granted until they're gone."

I could only nod in agreement.

A pair of RVs rumbled onto the turnout. Eden coughed at the diesel fumes, and I jerked my thumb at the road. "Let's head out." I opened the passenger door for Eden, and closed it behind her.

The ride back to her house was quiet, except for the wind blowing through the open window, and the radio turned down low, playing country. Neither of us was inclined to talk, lost in our memories of the past.

When I stopped in front of Eden's house, she kicked open her door, and then paused. "Thank you, Carter."

"Don't mention it."

I caught a familiar chorus, and turned up the radio. "One Day You Will" by Lady Antebellum. Eden sat with one foot dangling out of the truck, the other on the floorboard, listening. By the end of the song, Eden was sniffling and tapping her toe to the beat.

Her green eyes found mine. "Damn you, Carter. I'm sick of crying. It's all I seem to do lately." She slid across the bench seat, reaching around my neck with her arms.

I held her, resisting yet again the urge to inhale her scent. "Sorry," I said, "I just thought you could use the encouragement."

She let go after a moment, slid out of the truck, waved once she'd closed the door. "'Bye."

I watched her go in, wondering how I was going to find excuses to see her now that her house was done. In just a few short weeks her presence had become an integral part of my day.

I drove to the little marina on the opposite side of the peninsula, parked my truck with my tools locked in the cab. The boat ride home was a little over twenty minutes, if I went fast. Today I was loathing the silence of my empty house, so I took it slow. I docked at my pier, tied up, but didn't go inside. Instead, I sat on the bow of the boat and watched the sun go down, wondering yet again what I'd gotten myself into. Wondering if Britt would approve of Eden. It was a strange thing to wonder, since if Britt had been in any position to tell me, Eden wouldn't be part of my life. I wondered how long I could keep pretending to myself that I didn't have feelings for Eden that went past friendship, and how long Eden could pretend the same thing about me.

I knew I couldn't fix her situation, and I had no desire to become an instant father-figure to a child that wasn't mine. Losing Britt had been bad enough, but knowing I'd also lost my child had nearly been too much. It was something I didn't often think about, but I found myself doing exactly that as I sat on my boat, watching the sun set.

Britt had been sixteen weeks pregnant when she died. We'd been less than a week from the ultrasound that would have told us the gender of our baby.

We'd decided on Brett, if it was a boy. Irene, if it was a girl.

What if something was possible between Eden and me? Someday? When she had the emotional wherewithal to think about such things. She couldn't now, not yet. I knew that, and I respected it. But could she someday? And could I accept the things that would come with Eden, if such a time ever came? A child? The turmoil that would surely exist between Eden and her sister, not to mention the husband? I wasn't sure.

I had no way to answer any of those questions. Even allowing myself to consider the possibility was inviting heartbreak. Eden might not ever be willing or able to be with me. She might not *want* to. She might just be latching onto me as the only source of comfort in her life. She'd done it once, with Caden. Why not with me now?

I cursed myself for the judgmental nature of that last thought. But it was true, though.

I understood the way things had happened for her, with Caden. When Britt died, I'd been desperate for any kind of comfort. I'd drunk myself stupid for several weeks straight. And if Britt had had a twin sister—one who looked *exactly* like her—with similar mannerisms and personality traits, would I have felt the temptation to seek some kind of comfort in the familiar? I probably would have.

Unless you'd lost someone who was a huge, vital part of your life, you simply couldn't understand the agony, the desperation, the way that every day seemed impossible. Each breath hurt. Each second, each hour was an eternity of hurt. You'd do anything to stop the pain. To escape the torment, the ache inside, the gaping hole where that person should be. And if something or someone could offer some kind of comfort, even temporarily, you'd take it, just to find a single moment of peace. And if there was guilt involved, it was even worse.

So yeah, I got it.

But getting it, understanding how it had happened, and not judging her was one thing. But being able to weave the complications of her life into my own? That was something else. And I wasn't sure.

God, if I was this confused about things, what must Eden be going through?

I took a couple of days at home, cleaning up and finishing two sculptures I'd set aside. One was a life-size bust of an Arabian horse that needed a few coats of stain, and the other was a commissioned piece for one of Max's friends. It was a huge piece of driftwood that she had found while on vacation in Mexico. She had it shipped up here to me and had asked me to "do something with it." Basically, it was a case of making something pretty from the old hunk of wood. It was an interesting challenge, and I'd had fun with it. The piece of wood was almost eighteen feet long and four or five feet thick, twisted and gnarled, yet worn smooth as glass by the relentless movement of the ocean. I'd studied the wood for days before beginning to work, and even then it had been a process of discovery. Sometimes I started with an idea, and found a piece of wood to match the project I had in mind. Usually, though, I let the wood tell me what it wanted to be. This piece fell into the latter category. I worked a single stroke of the chisel at a time, scraping in one spot, carving in another, inch by inch, whittling away the wood slice by slice, always listening to what the grain of the wood and the twists and gnarls told me.

It was an abstract piece, sort of. It resembled a female body, in a way, but one that was reaching for the sky, spine twisting in dance, arms tangled and fingers twined. That was what I saw in it, at least. I knew Sharon, Max's friend, would love it, and would probably pay any price I asked.

I still had to finish the bar for the tasting room, and I had to check on the progress on the tasting room itself. But...I wasn't ready for any of that. If I went back to the winery, my brothers would want to ask me questions, talk to me. And inevitably, they'd ask about Eden, and I wasn't ready for that. I didn't have any answers. Even if I told the truth—"we're just friends"—they'd see the other part of the truth. That was the rough part of being thick as thieves with your brothers: they knew you inside and out, and could see past lies and omissions.

So, to fill the time, I began a new project. I took the pile of floorboards from Eden's house and went to work. The pieces were various lengths, and some were broken from being pulled up, and others were fully intact. I fit six of the widest pieces together edge to edge, and joined them together with some iron bands I had left over from another project. Then I puzzled the other pieces together, using intact pieces as well as broken ones, splitting other pieces to get fragments to fill holes, and bound the whole together with the same iron bands. This created a vertical side-wall which I joined to the bottom piece with a wedge and short wood screws. I repeated the process several times, until I had all four walls in place, and then once more for the lid of the chest. I found a pair of hinges in a box of metal parts, black iron to match the bands around each wall and the lid. The actual construction of the seaman's chest took most of one day, and that was the easy part. I planned to artificially age the wood, which wasn't a difficult process, only tedious. First, I bleached the wood until all the original stain was gone and the wood was almost blond, and then I used a ferrous sulfate stain to create a weathered, gray appearance. The wood itself was already scratched and pitted and gouged from years of use, so I only had to exaggerate the effect in some places and then add another coat of the graying stain.

When I was done, the chest looked like something that might have been rescued from a shipwreck. I was pleased with it, and hoped Eden would be, too. I hauled the chest from workshop to boat, and once I'd navigated over to the peninsula, I brought it to Eden's house.

It was mid-morning when I showed up, another clear, beautiful summer day in Traverse City. The sun was just starting to peek above the tree line in the east, shedding splintered shadows and spears of light on the beach. Eden was on the beach, with her cello. She'd set a blanket on the sand, and had brought one of her second-hand kitchen chairs out to sit on. I knew she heard me arrive, but she didn't pause in her playing.

I recognized the music this time. She'd played it before. The first time I'd heard it was the day I'd stood outside her door and listened, unbeknownst to her. I'd heard it again, one other time. She was facing the waters of the bay, her back hunched over the cello as she sawed the bow slowly across the strings, drawing a haunting, mournful tune from her instrument. I kicked off my boots and socks, rolled up the cuffs of my jeans, and joined her on the beach. I sat in the sand a few feet away, partly behind her so as not to distract her.

I knew enough about classical music to realize, after a few minutes, that she was playing some kind of solo suite, a collection of unified pieces, although I didn't recognize it. It was beautiful, but inherently sad. She paused between one movement and the next, taking a few deep breaths, then inhaling deeply, straightening her shoulders, and beginning once more. Her hair was loose, blonde waves shimmering in the sunlight around her shoulders, swaying as she moved. The roots were black, and I wondered, as I watched her, what she would look like if she let her hair go back to its natural color. Even more beautiful than she already was, I thought. The blonde was pretty, but her natural black would be... devastating.

I closed my eyes to listen, feeling the soul of the music weave magic around me. Wind soughed in the trees, the water of the bay lapped gently, the sun rose and warmed the air with golden light, and Eden played.

And then...she faltered. I heard the false note, the discordant scrape of the bow on the strings. I heard the gasp slip from her lips, and the choke of a stifled sob, and the sniff. I opened my eyes, and her shoulders were shaking, the bow tip trailing on the blanket, her cello resting against her shoulder.

I stood up, moved across the sand, and sat down close enough that she couldn't miss my presence. I touched her knee briefly, and kept silent. She cried for a moment and then dragged in a shuddering breath, making herself stop.

She glanced shyly at me, wiping her eyes. "Hi," she mumbled. "Sorry. I'm—"

"Don't apologize. I'll listen if you want to tell me."

She didn't respond right away. Instead, she closed her eyes, focused, centered, and began playing once more. This time, I recognized the piece as a well-known introduction to Bach, something I'd heard played by several soloists and orchestras. She played it masterfully, of course, but I saw a difference in the way she played it. This piece she played as if to withdraw emotionally, as if to calm herself, to push away whatever emotions had gripped her when she played the other solo. After the intro ended, she let the cello fall silent, waiting until the last note faded, and then she laid her instrument in the case, tucked away the bow, and clipped the case closed.

Only then did she look at me. "There's not a lot to say, really. I'm just—moody. Feeling everything, I guess." She put one palm to her belly, which was growing rounder every day. "I felt the baby kick this morning."

"First time you'd felt it?"

She nodded. "Yeah. It…it was weird. Scary. And…incredible. It really made it real. I'm really, really having a baby. There truly is an actual human being growing inside me."

I didn't know what to say, so I waited a moment and then asked, "What was the name of the first piece you were playing?"

She ducked her head. "A solo I composed. There are four parts to it, so far. One for my mom, one for my dad, one for Ever, and one for Caden."

"You wrote that?" I shouldn't have been surprised, but I was. "That was…so beautiful, Eden. It was really sad, though. Some parts were full of…I don't know. Longing? Tragedy?"

She nodded. "Thanks. Yeah, you heard me playing Ever and Caden's parts. I composed those while Ever was in the coma."

"Are you going to write any more?"

She shrugged. "Maybe someday." She put both hands on her belly. "For him, or her."

"When do you find out the gender?"

She hesitated. "In an hour."

"An hour? Downtown?"

She nodded. "Yeah.   Dr. Abernathy. On… Seventh, I think."

I stood up and extended my hand. "Well, we'd better get going, then."

She stood up but didn't let go of my hand right away, confusion on her features. "We?"

"Yeah. We."

She dropped my hand and pinched the bridge of her nose. "Carter. You're not coming with me to my ultrasound."

"You'd rather go alone? It's kind of a big deal, Eden."

A gust of wind tossed her hair across her eyes, and she brushed it away. "I know it's a big deal. I just—"

I leaned down and grabbed the handle of her cello case. She watched me nervously, following me as I carried the huge case across the road and into her house. "You should know I've never, ever let another person handle my cello."

I set the case down in the corner where I knew she kept it. "No? Is it old?"

"She nodded. Very. And…it was my mom's. It's the…the most special thing I own. No one touches it but me, no one carries it but me."

"I'm sorry, I didn't know. I just wanted to help."

She smiled at me. "And I let you. I trust you, Carter. At least, as much as I trust anyone. And if I let you carry it, I must trust you a lot. More than I should, maybe." She grabbed her purse off the kitchen counter. "Why do you want to go with me?"

"You don't have to go through this alone, Eden. That's why."

"But I can't—" She backed away from me as I stepped toward her.

"Just friends, something else, whatever. I don't care. I'm not asking for anything, Eden. I'm just… here. For you. I like you, and I want to be there. In whatever capacity you need me." She closed her eyes, going still as I stood inches away from her, brushing a wayward strand of hair from her face.

For the briefest instant, she nudged her cheek into my hand and then flinched, and turned away. "Don't, Carter. *Don't.* I *can't.*"

I stepped away, cursing myself. "Sorry."

"Yeah, sorry," She looked up at me, anger I wasn't expecting filling her eyes. "You're *sorry*. For me. That's all it is. I told you, I don't need charity and I don't want pity. This is my fucked-up mess and my fucked-up life, and I don't need anyone trying to fix it for me. And I keep telling you, I *can't* do what you want, be what you want. I can't have… that. You. This thing between us. You fixed my house. Spent weeks and thousands of dollars. You've done so much, and I don't have anything to give you. I might not ever have anything to give you. Yet you keep hanging around, and you say you're fine with just being friends. And, damn it, I'm lonely, so I accept it. But then you do *that*. Touch my hair. My face. And you look at me with those fucking gorgeous blue eyes of yours and all that stupid compassion, like I—like I *mean* something to you." She stopped for breath, but then barreled on. "I can't have that, Carter. I don't *deserve* that. I've told you that, more than once. Yet you keep…pushing. And now you're gonna go to my ultrasound with me? Playing the couple? You're gonna hold my hand, too, I bet. Let me tell you something, Carter: all you're doing is teasing me with what I can't have. You don't want this with me. You've been through your own hell, and you deserve hap—happiness." Her voice broke on the last word. "And you'll never find that in me. All you'll find is trouble."

"Your ultrasound is in forty minutes." I moved to the door, held it open, and extended my hand to her. "Are you coming?"

She gaped at me. "Did you not hear anything I just said?"

"I heard." I let the door close and my hand fall. "And if I choose to keep going, despite that, it's my business. If I want to tilt at windmills, that's my choice."

"Tilt at windmills?"

"*Don Quixote.* My mom is a literature professor." I shrugged. "It just means to do something idiotic over and over again. If there can't ever be anything but friendship between you and me, then so be it. If I feel something more, that's on me. I can't and won't just walk away from you. You need a friend, and I'm here. And guess what? I need a friend, too. And that's you."

"You've got brothers. You've got—everyone on this peninsula, probably."

I shrugged. "None of them are you."

"If you want a fucked-up hot mess like me for your friend, there's got to be something wrong with you."

I sighed. "Eden, just—come on." I walked toward my truck, not waiting to see if she followed.

She did, at a distance, with her purse hanging over one shoulder, her posture defeated, looking down at the ground. I was waiting at the passenger door, and opened it for her. She stepped up on the running board, and happened to glance back at the bed of the truck, where the chest I'd made for her sat forgotten.

"What's that?" Curiosity tinged her voice.

I followed her gaze. "Oh, shit! I forgot all about that! I made it for you." I left her door standing ajar and opened the tailgate, dragged the chest toward myself by the edges. "I used the wood from your old floors. It's just a chest. A seaman's chest, I guess. I thought you could put it at the foot of your bed."

She slid out of the cab and came over to stand beside me, tracing the roughened, weathered-look-ing wood. "It's beautiful. But how did you get it to look so...old?"

I shrugged. "There's lots of ways to age wood. I wouldn't be much of a carpenter if I didn't know a few of them."

She ran her hand along the side again, and then looked up at me. "It's so beautiful. You really made it for me?"

I ducked my head. "Sure. It's your wood—I just put it together again."

"Thank you. I love it."

I carried the chest into her house, with Eden holding the door open for me. I set it on the floor at the foot of her bed, and she immediately went to rummaging in her linen closet, and returned with what looked like a hand-knitted blanket made of pale blue wool. She folded it in a thin, long rectangle and draped it over the top of the chest.

"Perfect," I said. "Now come on. You're gonna be late."

She followed me back out to my truck, then paused with one foot on the running board and one on the ground. "Carter, you don't have to go with me. I'll be fine."

"I know. Now let's go." I pushed at her shoulder gently, and she stepped in and sat down.

I shot her an easy grin and slid behind the wheel, stepping on the gas pedal as the engine turned over, so it caught with a beefy roar.

Under normal driving conditions, it took twenty to twenty-five minutes to drive down the peninsula, and another ten or fifteen to get to the southern end of town where most of the non-tourist businesses were. Eden was quiet for the entire forty-minute drive. I could've made it in less time, but I drove more carefully than ever.

I was quiet, too, thinking of the first—and only—ultrasound Britt and I had gone to. It had been a day just like this, sunny and clear, warm but with a stiff westerly wind. She'd sat in the seat where Eden now sat, and Britt too had stared out the window at the bay and the vineyards, nerves showing, just like Eden. I'd been silent then as well, not knowing what to expect from an ultrasound. Britt had explained that it would just be a lot of measurements, to make sure the baby was healthy and developing normally. I'd still been nervous, and so had she.

Eden's hand rested on the red leather seat between us, and I was tempted to take it in mine but didn't. I was tempted to turn on the radio, but I didn't. I just drove, one hand on the wheel, the other fidgeting with the knob of the gearshift.

The OB/GYN office was like any other, a quiet, tastefully decorated waiting room, chairs lining the walls and a low coffee table in the center, scattered with motherhood and parenting magazines, and one old back issue of *Time*, and a copy of *US Weekly* from

the previous fall. Eden went to the sliding glass window and signed in with the receptionist, and then sat
down. I took a seat beside her, flipping through the
issue of *Time* while she filled out some paperwork.

A young woman sat by herself across the room,
nervously spinning her phone in her hands. Her belly
was huge, seeming entirely too big for her diminu-
tive frame. She glanced at Eden and then me, smiling.
"How far along are you?" she asked, her voice bright
and friendly.

Eden seemed startled that anyone would talk to
her. "Oh…um. Seventeen weeks. Eighteen tomorrow. You?"

"Thirty. I'm high-risk, so I've had ultrasounds
every other week since my first trimester. My first
baby had intra-uterine growth deficiency, so they're
monitoring this one a lot more closely. I'm here for
an amniocentesis."

Eden clearly didn't know how to take this flood
of information. "Oh. Um. I see. Well…I hope things
go okay."

"Oh, he's doing fine, so far," the woman said,
patting her watermelon-sized belly. "He's right on
target, but he's inverted still, so unless he flips on his
own, they'll have to do a C-section. Which, with as
hard as Nicky's birth was, I don't think I'd mind. My
girlfriend had one natural birth and the other was a
C-section, and she said the C-section was easier." She

leaned forward, whispering conspiratorially. "You don't have to wait six weeks afterward to do it, for one thing."

Eden blushed and stammered. "Oh, I—we're… oh. Yeah. That—it would be…nice. I guess."

The other woman finally saw Eden's hesitancy in her responses. "Is this your first?"

"Yeah."

"You're probably pretty nervous, huh? And here I am chattering on, probably making things worse."

You have no idea, I thought, but didn't say anything, and she babbled on, oblivious to everything. "It'll be fine. There's a lot of pain, of course, even with the epidural, but I promise you, it's totally worth it. You completely forget about how bad it hurt after you hold that little baby for the first time, I swear. And then…oh, nothing, just *nothing* can compare to that feeling. They're so tiny and perfect, and…oh, my god, it's just magical."

Eden's eyes got wider with every word, until she looked almost physically ill and ready to bolt. Her hand was clutching the armrest of her chair in a white-knuckled grip. I rested my hand on hers, and Eden glanced at me, then turned her hand over to grip mine, palm to palm, fingers closed and separate. She clutched my hand as hard as she had gripped the chair.

Babs the Babbler opened her mouth to fire off another salvo of terrifying over-sharing, but we were spared when the door opened and the nurse called Eden's name. "Good luck!" the young woman said instead.

"You, too," Eden said, and then, once the door was swinging closed behind us she muttered, "TMI, much? Jesus."

I laughed. "She was a little...exuberant."

Eden stared at me. "Exuberant? She was fucking ecstatic! How could anyone be that happy about shitting a watermelon out of her vagina? It's unnatural." She made her voice go high-pitched, mimicking the other woman. "'It's magical!' God. I'm so nervous I could puke, and now I'm worried about upside-down babies and C-sections."

The nurse patted Eden's arm. "Everything will be fine, you'll see. Just relax. Let me get you up on this scale first, okay?"

Eden stepped up on the scale, and then shooed me away with her hand. "Don't watch this part."

I snorted, but turned away. The nurse seemed perplexed. "You're not honestly concerned about him knowing your weight, are you?" She obviously assumed we were together, and that I was the father. "That's just silly."

"He's not—" Eden started, then stopped. "It's just a pet peeve."

I shoved my hands in my pockets, examining a poster on the wall until the nurse led Eden and me into an ultrasound room.

"Just lie down and sit tight, sweetie," the nurse said. "Lisa will be here to perform the ultrasound in just a moment."

"Do I—do I need to change or anything?"

The nurse shook her head. "Oh, no. This is a standard external ultrasound. She'll just roll your shirt up a bit and move the wand over your belly. Nothing to worry about." She was gone with a perky smile and a click of the door.

Eden let out a shaky breath, and then slid gingerly onto the exam table, smoothing her hands over her stomach. "It's just an ultrasound. Why am I so nervous?" She looked at me, her eyes wide and fearful.

I reached out and took her hand. "Why wouldn't you be nervous? It's normal. And I'm here. You'll be fine."

This time, Eden threaded our fingers together. "Thank you, Carter. I think I would've fainted if you hadn't been here."

I squeezed her hand and smiled. "I'm not going anywhere. I'll be here every step of the way."

Eden looked up to the ceiling and let out shaky breath. "God, why do you always make me cry? I swear to God I normally don't cry this much." She tried to smile at me but couldn't quite manage it.

"Just blame it on the pregnancy hormones, yeah?" I joked.

Eden laughed, sniffing. "It is that, to some degree. But it's also…everything else. Ever. Caden. The whole thing. I'm just a mess."

"Here's the thing about messes, Eden: they can be cleaned up."

"Not mine."

"Yes, even yours."

The ultrasound tech came in at that moment, a slim, middle-aged woman with brown hair going silver at the temples and a kind smile. "Eden, how are you? I'm Lisa."

"Hi, Lisa. I'm okay."

Lisa sat on the swiveling desk chair and rolled across the room to sit at the ultrasound machine, glancing at Eden. "Okay, huh? You look like you might be a little nervous. Am I right?" Eden just nodded. "Well, that's perfectly normal. We're just gonna take some measurements, make sure Baby is developing on track and all that, and, of course, we'll determine the gender, assuming he or she cooperates and gives me a good shot. Just hold onto Daddy's hand, and everything will be fine."

Eden didn't correct the assumption that I was the father, and neither did I. I understood why, too. Explanations were far harder than just going along with incorrect assumptions. It was simpler, and I didn't blame her.

Lisa squirted a bit of blue goo on the wand, and then touched it to Eden's belly and smeared it around. "It's a bit cold at first, but it'll warm up." She moved the wand around, wiggled it back and forth, swept it from one side of Eden's belly. "Let's see… a-ha. There's the baby. See?"

Eden and I both looked at the black and white images on the screen. Things were blotchy and distorted at first, but then shapes began to appear. I saw the curvature of the skull, a leg, an arm.

Lisa pushed a button and moved the wand around a bit, hunting for the right angle. "Looks good so far. Baby is head down already, which is good news. Ten fingers, ten toes. There's the heart, pumping steadily, but we'll look at that again later. Lungs. And…oh, come on, move for me, huh?" Lisa seemed to be talking partly to herself, partly to the screen, to the baby, and to us. She moved the wand up to the top of Eden's belly, angled it downward, and then shifted it incrementally one way and then another, altering the image on the screen slightly. Finally, she seemed to find the angle she was looking for. "A-ha! Gotcha!"

She tapped a couple of buttons, and a machine spat out pictures of the image on-screen.

"I've got a good potty-shot, here." She glanced from me to Eden and back. "So. You want to know the gender, or is it a surprise?"

Eden blinked a few times. "Tell me. Please." Her frightened green eyes met mine. "Us, I mean. Tell us."

Lisa didn't seem to notice the "me/us" gaffe. She pointed at the screen. "See that? It's a girl! Clear as day, no question." A few more taps, and another set of ultrasound pictures printed out.

Eden teared up. "A girl."

"Have any names picked out?" Lisa asked as she swiveled the wand around, tapping buttons and scrolling and turning the screen to shifting colors and back to black-and-white, measuring various things.

Eden hesitated for a long time. I'd never asked her if she'd thought of names. I somehow didn't think she had.

Her voice was barely a whisper. "No, I—no." Her hand squeezed mine so hard it hurt.

castaway

Ever

Christmas was fast approaching. I'd been out of my coma for over six months now, and things with Caden had reached a kind of plateau. They weren't getting any worse, but they weren't getting any better, either. He was distant, as if some part of him was wandering the earth, separated from his body. As if he was hiding behind a wall. I could see him and I could feel him, hold him, kiss him, love him, but there was a part of Caden that I simply couldn't reach, no matter how much I tried. And for my part, the constant effort to reach him, to get him to talk to me, to open up on his own was sapping me of strength—and worse, of my desire to even try anymore.

Things had to change, but I just didn't know how.

I'd been working at the office, answering phones and filing paperwork, which wasn't exactly taxing work, but it kept me busy. And it also left my mind free to wander. Aside from the question of Caden, the thing most on my mind was Eden. I called her phone once a week, and it always rang once, and then went to the full voicemail message. I tried her email, and never got a response. I went by her dorm room, talked to her old roommate. I talked to the college office, who only knew that she'd officially withdrawn, no reason given. I even called Dad, who didn't answer and didn't return my call. Asshole.

Everywhere I went, I found myself looking for her, as if she was somewhere close by, but was just avoiding me. I knew this wasn't the case. When she'd come by the Home, just after I woke up, she'd said goodbye. And to remember that she loved me. To never doubt that, no matter what.

I doubted. Why did she leave? Why? I needed her. I needed her to tell me what I was doing wrong in terms of Caden. I needed her to eat ice cream with me when I couldn't take Cade's morose silences anymore. I needed to hear her play her cello.

God, what was the name of her cello? Some Greek god. Apollo? That was it.

I twisted the problem around and around in my head, worrying at it, trying to think of various reasons why she might have run away from me. Maybe she was terminally sick, and didn't want me to know. She was a lesbian. She was pregnant. She'd eloped with some guy. None of them fit. None of them made any sense. She had to know I'd never judge her, no matter what. She was my twin. She was as much a part of me as my arms and legs and lungs. Yet she'd run away.

There was only one place I could think of that she might have gone. The cabin, up north. The problem was, there was no phone there, and I couldn't find the address book that had the address written down. We hadn't been up there since we were… what, eleven? A couple of years before Mom died. I knew it had been in Mom's name, and after her death Dad had gotten a caretaker for it, and had registered it in Eden's and my name. He hadn't been able to stomach going there, I think. He and Mom had spent a lot of time there before Eden and I were born, and once she was gone, he couldn't take the reminder. I hadn't really thought much about the cabin in the intervening years.

I thought of going up there, but I wasn't sure I had the courage. What if she wasn't there? What if she'd gone somewhere else, somewhere I'd never be able to find her? What if the reason she'd left had something to do with me? Some reason I couldn't fathom, a reason that would have driven her away from me?

A niggling seed of an idea germinated in the deep, dark pit of my belly, but I denied it, pushed it away. Refused to let it bloom into a full-fledged question. There had to be some explanation, some reason for it all.

After Christmas, I'd go. I'd drive up there, and just see if she was there. Christmas was the two-year anniversary of the accident. And the closer December 24th got, the more tense and silent Caden became. He'd sit at the kitchen table, sketching. Page after page. Obsessively. The same thing, again and again. My eyes. Various expressions, but always my eyes.

He gave me monosyllabic answers if I asked him a question. He'd sit beside me and watch if I turned on the TV, but he never asked to change the channel, never commented. Just sat in silence, watching until the program was over.

He'd respond if I touched him, but it seemed automatic, rather than from desire. And when we did make love, it was in silence. Gone were the grunts of need, the gasps of pleasure, the impassioned pleas for more. The sighs and the whispered protestations of love were a thing of the past.

By Christmas, sex was almost a memory.

On the anniversary of the accident, Christmas Eve, Caden didn't get out of bed. At noon, I finally went in and sat on the edge of the bed, near his feet.

He was awake, staring at the wall. He didn't even look at me when I sat down.

"Caden?" He slowly shifted his gaze to mine, and when he did, the pain and despair in his eyes was enough to make me want to cry. "Talk to me. Please."

He shook his head and looked away.

"Cade. Baby. I'm here. Look at me. Talk to me. I'm scared, Cade. What's wrong with you?"

He closed his eyes, squeezed them shut, and shook his head. And then I watched as he gathered himself, wormed his way to a sitting position. "Sorry, Ev. I'm just…I keep seeing the accident. In my head, over and over."

I took his hands, slid closer to him. "I'm here now. I'm okay. I'm better." I bent my head to hide my tears. "Come back to me."

He moved his knees apart and pulled me against his chest. I lay back against him, and felt his breath on my hair. "I'm trying. God, I'm sorry, Ever. You need better. Deserve better. And I'm sorry."

"I just don't get it. Where are you? What's going on with you? Talk to me, Cade. Please, talk to me." I grabbed his hands where they were crossed over my breastbone. "I need you. And I—I feel like I can't find you."

"I don't know."

"I'm here. I'm awake. It's Christmas. Shouldn't we both be happy? Celebrating?"

"I am happy you're back. More than you know. More than I can express."

"It sure as hell doesn't feel that way," I whispered. "It feels like...like you resent me." I almost asked him what he was hiding from me. Why he seemed so consumed with guilt.

Before I could, he heaved a deep breath in and let it out. "Let's go celebrate. Right now. Have a fancy dinner. Maybe see a movie." He'd clearly made a herculean effort to banish the nightmares and the guilt. He sounded almost happy, almost genuine. I knew, though, if I turned to search his gaze, his amber eyes would still hold hidden pain and deeply buried torment.

Instead of pushing it, I took what he was offering. "Sure. I'd like that."

"Me, too."

We both showered—separately—and dressed, and ended up at Andiamo, sipping on expensive red wine and sharing an appetizer as we waited for our entrees. Conversation stayed light, and I could tell Cade was trying as hard as he could to keep the darkness inside him at bay. I was grateful. As dinner progressed, I almost managed to forget everything. He was as close to his old self as I'd seen him since I woke up. I almost felt happy, a little. I almost felt hope that we could truly find peace in each other once more.

Almost. Nearly. But his eyes betrayed him, though. The slight stoop to his shoulders, the way his knee bounced and his gaze shifted from place to place, rather than ever really settling on mine. As if he was afraid of meeting my eyes, afraid that I'd look too deeply and see the truth.

I *wanted* to tell him I didn't want the truth. I wanted happiness. I wanted to be able to feel like I had a new lease on life. I'd nearly died, and had been comatose for a year and a half. I shouldn't be here. But I was, and that should be a source of joy. Yet it wasn't. Without Cade as my center, I was adrift, castaway. I couldn't find the earth beneath me, couldn't find the sky. Couldn't find up, or down. I could only slip from one day to the next, wake up and go to school and go to work. I was playing at life. Pretending at adulthood.

It was all empty. I was empty.

Cade sensed my mood as we picked at dessert. "Ever...don't—don't give up on me, okay? I know I've been a mess lately, and I'm sorry. I love you. So much." He set his fork down and wiped the corners of his mouth with his napkin, sat back and finally, for the first time all night, met my eyes. "Don't give up on me. Please. I'll—get better. I'll do better."

"I just want us, Cade." I searched his eyes and saw what I knew I'd see--—the guilt and pain and torture--—but I also saw hope, and love. "I want you.

I want you to…I don't even know. I just want us back."

"Me, too." He ducked his head, twisting the cloth napkin into a tight spiral. Fighting emotions.

Tell me what's wrong. The thought skittered through my head, but it wouldn't come out. I was terrified of hearing the answer. Scared shitless of the truth. So instead I reached across the table and took both of his hands in mine. Felt the familiar comfort of the strength in his grip, the rough calluses.

"I'll never give up on you, Cade. I swear. I promise. Forever and always, right?"

"Forever and always."

But why did he sound as if the three words were choking him?

promises and portraits

For Christmas Cade gave me a framed drawing he'd done. It was full color, and huge, a life-size portrait of me…and Eden. I was on the left, smiling, hair down, loose, caught by a breeze. Eden was on the right, her hair pulled back, a more serious expression on her features. He'd captured our eyes perfectly, as well as the subtle differences in our faces, which he'd merged at the centerline. He'd even given Eden dark roots near her scalp.

I teared up when I ripped open the gift and saw Eden looking back at me, joined with me on paper as we were in life, body, mind, heart, and soul.

Or should have been, if she hadn't run away.

"I know you miss her," Cade said as I stared at the portrait.

I could only nod. When I found my voice, it was
quiet and tremulous. "Yeah. I just don't get it. Where
did she go? Why did she leave?"

Cade didn't answer right away. "I don't understand, either." Yet there was a lie in his eyes.

I handed him his gift from me. It was a self-por-
trait. In it, I was nude, sitting upright with one knee
crossed over the other, using my hands to cover my
breasts. It was an intimate, provocative pose. I'd used
my camera and tripod and a timer to take the picture,
and then had painted the portrait from the photograph. As I'd posed, I'd thought of Cade as he had
been. The Cade I missed, not carefree exactly, but
present and passionate, and I'd thought of the way
we used to be together, and how badly I wanted that
again. I'd tried to communicate all that in my expression. My desire for him, the way I missed him. The
way I loved him.

Cade stared at the portrait for a very long time, his
features shifting from one emotion to another, from
desire and love to guilt and sadness and back again.
Finally, he looked up. "God, Ever. It's…amazing."

I'd worked on it for weeks. Nothing had ever
been so hard as that portrait. I didn't feel beautiful. I didn't feel desirable. Even alone in my studio,
with the blinds drawn and the door closed, I'd felt
awkward and vulnerable and gawky, posing naked
like that. And even the process of painting had been

different. The way I formed my brushstrokes had been different—shorter, choppier, less smooth than before the accident. I had to focus intently on each individual stroke, and I'd messed up a hundred times, had to retouch and fix again and again. When doing my eyes, I'd messed up so badly I almost had to start over. And when I'd finally finished, I knew it was good, but not as good as it would have been *before*. But it was the best I could do.

"Turn it around," I said.

Cade glanced at me in confusion, and then flipped the frame around. I'd printed out the original photograph and tucked it between the canvas and the frame. He slid it free, held it in both hands, staring at it.

"You are...so gorgeous."

I closed my eyes. I wondered if he had any idea how badly I'd needed to hear that. "I don't feel like it."

His face constricted, contorted into a mask of pain. "I'm failing you. You need love. You need me... and I just...I'm not giving you what you need."

I tangled my fingers in his hair. "I just need *you*, Cade." I leaned in and pressed a kiss to his cheekbone, to the corner of his mouth. "When I married you, I promised to love you, *no matter what*. I promised to love you in sickness and in health. For richer or poorer. I promised to love the good and the bad. And I do. I always, *always* will."

Cade buried his face in the crook of my neck, and his hand fisted in my hair. He turned his body toward mine, breathing me in, shaking and shuddering. "What if—what if I mess up?"

"I'll forgive you." My heart was hammering, pounding, pouring fear-spiked adrenaline throughout my body. My pulse was thundering in my ears, and my fingers trembled as I clutched the back of his head. "Anything. I *love* you, Cade. I'll always love you."

He just held onto me, fingers gripping my hair near the roots in a death-grip, almost painful. His breath scraped past his teeth, and he swallowed so hard I could feel it, hear it. "Always."

"I swear it." Could I say that? A sliver of me doubted. "Just be mine."

"I am. Only yours." He tugged my hair gently, pulling my face away from his long enough to look into my eyes.

I saw love, determination, and need. Fear, too. Hurt and guilt. But all that was subsumed by the need.

I flattened my body against his, crushed my lips to his. Inside, I was pleading for him to give me the passion I so desperately wanted, the soul-baring fervor my dried-up and starving heart needed.

His mouth responded to mine, hesitant at first, and then with growing strength. His fist released my hair and slid down my neck, palmed my shoulder, caressed my spine. Rested on the bell of my hip. His kiss took on heat, and I breathed a whimper of needy relief when his mouth left mine and touched my neck. I tilted my head back to bare my throat, my hands clasping his head against me. His lips touched my breastbone above the buttons of my blouse. His teeth nipped, his tongue flicked.

His fingers curled into the flesh of my hip.

"Ever. God, Ever." He brought his free hand up to my face, brushed my wayward hair aside. "How could you not know you're beautiful? You are. You're perfect. Inside and out. You're too good for me. Too much, too incredible. I don't deserve all that you are." His mouth slanted across mine, sipping at my breath.

"Because you…you're what makes me feel beautiful. This. Us."

He shook his head. "No, Ev. You're beautiful in every moment. With me, without me. You have to know that."

"I don't. I can't." I slid my hands around his waist and under his shirt to glide my palms up his strong back. "You have to show me." I wouldn't push it. This had to come from him, not me.

He searched my eyes with his and, as always, I saw the mountain of tangled emotions in his gaze. But as

I stared, I watched him push all that away, focusing instead on my mouth, my lips. Down, to the swell of my breasts and the hint of cleavage. He breathed in, and lifted both hands to the top button of my shirt. His brow furrowed, and his hands shook with nerves or desire as he slid the button through the gap. I breathed deeply, swelling my chest, straining against the remaining buttons. Hints of black lace showed, a sliver of the cup of my bra and my pale skin. I was still, sitting beside him, my body facing him, my knee pressed into his, thighs touching.

He leaned in, kissed the hollow at the base of my throat, and his hands circled my waist. Tugged me toward him. I brought my leg over his thighs and sat astride him on the couch, looking down at him now. My calf-length skirt caught, stretched tight, and tangled, and I lifted up on my knees to free it, then sat back down. Lips slid across my skin, descended between the valley of my breasts. Cade's fingers fumbled at the buttons, freeing them one by one, and then his palms carved over my shoulders to push my blouse off, letting it tumble to the floor. He reared back, gazing at me, eyes dark and hooded with desire as I straddled him, each deep breath swelling my chest.

Still I didn't move. I let my hands rest on his shoulders, watching him.

He glanced up at me and then touched my bare

shoulders, palms skating down my arms, back up. Around to my shoulder blades, pulling my body to his mouth. He pressed soft kisses down the swell of one boob, stopping at the edge of the cup and crossing over to kiss the other slope of flesh. His hands fluttered up my spine, teasing and tickling, and then he ran a finger inside the strap of my bra. Another kiss, this time nudging the cup down with his chin to nip at the darker circle of my areola. I sighed, curling one arm around his neck, fingers tracing the shell of his ear, the shaggy hair at his temples.

A brief fumble of his fingers, and then my bra fell away. He leaned back, pulling the undergarment free from one of my arms, and then the other, and then he tossed it to the floor near my discarded shirt.

"God, Ev. So fucking gorgeous." He dipped in, flicking my nipple with his tongue. "What would I do without you? What beauty would there be in this life without you?"

I cupped his head with both hands, moaned as he scraped his teeth over my nipple. "Don't—don't ever find out."

Cade buried his face between my tits and inhaled, then cupped each heavy globe in his hands and pressed them together, took both of my erect nipples in his mouth and tongued them. I moaned again, and the sound shifted into a drawn-out sigh as he slid his palms over my back, scratching and smoothing, caressing and touching. Tender, gentle, insistent.

"Take me to our bed, Cade."

He stood up with me, supporting my weight with his hands under my ass, and I crossed my feet at the ankles behind his back, pressed my nose to his neck and tasted the salt of his skin. I felt hope burgeon inside me, hope that he'd find his way back to me, hope that I'd been imagining things, inventing the guilt in his eyes.

Cade set me carefully onto our bed, holding onto my thighs as they gripped his waist. He kneaded the muscle of my legs, gazing with open desire at my bare upper torso. He leaned forward, traced around the waist of my skirt, searching for the zipper. I angled one hip up, and he found the pull-tab at the center of my spine, tugged it down. Curled the fingers of both hands into the waistband of the skirt and the elastic of my panties, black to match my erstwhile bra. I'd dressed for this, hoping, praying, wishing for this. I'd shaved my legs and crotch, shaved myself bare for him.

He pulled the skirt and underwear down, tossing them aside, and I curled my legs around his waist once more. His eyes roved over me, from face to boobs to belly and core, and then he faltered and stopped at the scar tissue where the surgeons had done the hysterectomy. Cade reached out and touched the scar, tracing the ridged line of tissue where it ran from one side of my torso to the other, low, just above my pubis.

I tensed at the touch. We'd made love before now, and he'd obviously seen me naked, so surely he'd seen the scar. Yet he acted as if he hadn't. His fingers paused on the scar, and his mouth opened as if to speak.

I put my hand over his, pushed his touch lower. "No. Don't talk about it. Not now." He hesitated still. I brought his touch to the apex of my thighs, lifted my hips. "Please."

I wouldn't say it again. I'd begged him once. I wouldn't again. I shouldn't have to.

He nodded and then bent over me, kissed my diaphragm, my ribs on the left side, down to the crease of my hip. Kissed across the scar, inch by inch, kiss by kiss. The inside of my thigh. Slid his hands under my backside, lifting my hips and kneeling down at the foot of the bed. My legs hung over his shoulders now, my thighs framing his head. His stubble scratched the tender skin on the inside of my thighs, and I couldn't quite catch my breath as the heat of his mouth warmed my core. He knew how much I loved it when he did this, when his tongue slid into me. God, yes, just like that, bringing me to the rocking, fiery, roiling edge of pleasure. His tongue and lips, his hands splayed under my ass, supporting me as I hung partially off the bed, my knees bent over his shoulders, heel hooked over his ankle, toes curling with each laving lick of his tongue into my wet aching heat.

He always knew when I was on the edge, and this time, he kept me there, letting me come away from the edge before falling over.

I opened my eyes to meet his. "What...?" I couldn't breathe; the ache in my core and the need rifling through me was stealing my words. "I need... Cade...more—"

He helped me slide up onto the bed, and I leaned back on my hands, shaking, watching him as he peeled his shirt off. I edged forward and planted my feet on the floor, twisted the button of his jeans free, jerked the zipper down. He stilled, letting me finish undressing him. I stared up at him as I tugged his pants down, his eyes blazing with need. I didn't look away as I pulled the elastic of his underwear away from his erection, slid them down past his hips. I didn't look away as I lowered my face to him, keeping my eyes on his until the last second. Cade gasped and then grunted as I wrapped my lips around him, gliding my fist around his steel thickness, caressing his soft skin stretched so tight around him.

He moaned my name and tangled his fingers in my hair as I slid my mouth down his length, tasting the moisture leaking from him. I worked my fingers gently around him at the root, slid my hand up as I let him fall from my mouth, spreading my saliva over the broad head of his cock with my palm. His knees buckled as I twisted my hand around his tip, dragged my thumb across the head and then licked the drips of pre-come as they leaked out.

I brought Cade to the edge, as he had me, and then I released him. I sat on the edge of the bed, one hand wrapped around his cock and the other clutching the firm globe of his ass. He was breathing hard, staring down at me, eyes hooded, muscles tense. He grabbed me by the forearm, tugging me upward. I stood slowly, my body sliding against his.

We stood naked together, face to face, body to body, his erection an iron length between us, hard against my belly. I reached up with one hand, dragged the back of my hand across his jaw, then my palm across the opposite side, cupped his cheekbone and leaned in to kiss him. As our mouths met, he pressed into me, leaning down, his arm supporting me at my waist, a hand at my nape, laying me down.

He knelt over me, staring into my eyes. I smiled up at him, clawed my fingers into the muscle of his buttocks, pulled at him. And then I had an idea.

I scooted up the bed, wiggling out from underneath him, ignoring the confusion on his face. The look cleared and turned to heat and burning desire as I rolled to my stomach and brought my knees up beneath me. Lifted my hips to him. For him. "You used to love this."

He growled in his chest. "I still do."

I craned my neck to watch him lift onto his knees and slide up behind me, fitting his cock between my buttocks, taking my hips in his hands. I felt my body tensing in preparation. He held his erection in his fist and guided himself into me, into my tight wet waiting cleft. I moaned and rocked forward as he entered me, biting my lip at the delicious feeling of fullness.

I fisted my hands in the sheets, letting all my weight rest on my forearms. He slid deep, groaning, and then pulled back, paused. Palmed my ass cheeks, smoothing his hands over them, then gripped my hips and drove deep. Whispered my name. Pulled back, almost out, and impaled me once more. I gave full voice to my pleasure, to the perfection of his body puzzle-made to fit into mine. I rocked back into his thrusts, moaned and groaned and grunted deep in my throat as he set a rhythm, slow but pounding hard.

A thick balloon of tension welled up inside me, burgeoning tighter and filled with explosive heat, intensified with each grinding clash of our bodies. His voice met mine in the late morning air of our bedroom, his deep rumble of pleasure winding around my higher whimpers. We moved together, finding true union at last.

One of his hands slid up my spine and the other tugged me by the crease of my hip against him, moving faster and faster now, encouraged by the needy, mewling shrieks of my impending orgasm.

"Yes, Cade, yes…don't stop…god, yes, fuck me hard, Cade—" I heard my voice grating and gasping, distinctly feral growls as detonation neared, white-hot lightning spearing through my core. "Now, harder, please—yes, yes—oh, fuck, Cade, yes!"

I slammed back into him, breathless and shaking as I was seized by a wrenching, spasming, dizzying climax.

And then he pulled out of me completely, leaving me empty and clenching and moaning with confusion and need. He nudged at me, pushed me over onto my back, and I grasped at him, pulled at him, found his slick hard cock with my hands and fisted his length desperately, guided him into me, frantic for his body to complete mine yet more.

"I need to see you," he whispered, "I need to see your eyes when I come inside you."

I locked my legs around his waist and clawed at his shoulders, needing to feel his skin against mine, his weight and his heat and his flesh. I rocked my hips against his, keeping my eyes open and fixed on his.

He pulled back and slid deep, breathing hard, holding back, tensed and flexed. Again, and then again, he drove into me. I accepted his thrusts and met them with my own, and each slide of his cock inside me sent lances of ecstasy through me as he stimulated my sensitive nerves. I held on to him, pulling him against me with my legs, lifted up and kissed him, sucked his tongue into my mouth and bit his lip.

And then he couldn't hold the kiss, could only slump over me, pressing his mouth to my chest, and gliding hard and fast into me as his own orgasm gripped him, made him frenzied and wild. He grunted against my skin, gasped my name, wrapped his arms under my neck and held me tight. I lifted up, arched my back and held him to my breasts, grinding my hips against his, clenching with my inner muscles as he thickened within me.

He came with a shout, squeezing his eyes shut and then forcing them open, meeting my gaze as he emptied himself inside me. I held him, caressed his back, his hips and his ass and his thighs and his face, everywhere I could reach.

"I love you, Ever. God, I love you."

"Forever, and after forever, Cade. Always. I love you, no matter what. No matter what. I promise."

He let his weight cover me for me a few minutes, a few short perfect moments of complete bliss.

I held onto those moments of afterglow, cradling Cade's head on my breast, hoarding the joy I felt, the completion and love. I'd need them, something told me.

All too soon, he rolled off me and tucked me into the nook of his shoulder, and we drifted off to sleep together.

northward

I woke up alone in bed. His side was cold. Pale yellow sunlight streamed in through the open window, the weak remnants of a late winter's afternoon. Without sitting up, I glanced through the open doorway, catching a glimpse of Cade. He was at the kitchen table yet again, wearing a pair of gym shorts, his sketchpad open in front of him, pencil case to one side, a bottle of Jameson and a tumbler on the other. The glass was empty, and the bottle was a third gone. It had been full the day before, brand new, a gift to him from his supervisor at UPS.

He was leaning forward, his elbows on the table, head in his hands. Fists clenched in his hair. His posture was one of utter agony, pure defeat. His breathing was slow, as if he had to convince himself to drag in each breath.

I hurt for him. I wanted to take away his pain. I wanted to share it with him.

But cowardly me…I was afraid of the pain, afraid that it meant pain for me, too. I could endure pain if it meant helping the man I loved. I could endure pain if it meant he and I were together. But if the pain was sourced in a wedge between us, then I wasn't sure I could withstand it.

I watched him from my place in our bed. I watched, and I worried.

Long minutes passed, and he didn't move except to breathe. He wasn't a heavy drinker, my Cade. But this man, the broken ghost who sat in my kitchen, poured another half-glass of golden whiskey, liquid the color of his eyes swirling in the glass, and he knocked it back, hissed, finished it, and slammed the glass down on the table. Then did it again.

Unable to take it anymore, I slid out of bed, padded still naked into the living room. I didn't speak, didn't ask him what was wrong. I stood beside him, leaned against him, waited until he reached for the bottle once more. He poured, and I grabbed the glass from him. Swallowed the contents in three burning gulps. Coughed, my wrist to my mouth. His arm snaked around my hips and held me. I held the glass out to him, and he went to take it from me, but I shook my head. "Again," I rasped, my throat still raw from the first shot.

He hesitated, then poured once more, while I held the tumbler. I sipped it more slowly this time, exploring the burn, the smoky fire of it, the way it made my throat convulse and shudder as I swallowed.

"If I asked, would you tell me?" I said to him, setting the glass down.

His fingers scratched at my hip, dug into the crease where leg met hip. "I don't know."

"Do I want to know?"

He shook his head. "No. You don't." Cade reached for the bottle but missed, and his hand flopped to the table. "Fuck, I'm drunk."

I put the cap on the bottle, pushed it away from him. "Even though I promised you I'd love you forever, no matter what?"

"Yeah."

I turned to face him, and even drunk his gaze was tormented. "I have midterms coming up soon. We're going to go on vacation, and you're going to tell me then." I put my hands on his cheeks, my thumbs brushing his temples. "I love you, Cade."

"Okay." He slumped forward, his face resting just beneath my boobs. "I love you too, Ev. Don't ever doubt that."

I choked, hearing Eden's words, all those months
ago. Just before she left me. I blinked away tears.
"Don't say that. Eden said that, and now she's gone."

"I won't leave." The way he said it made it seem
like someone would be leaving, but it wouldn't be
him. "And we'll find Eden. She'll come back. She
loves you too much to have left forever."

"If she loved me, why did she leave?" It was
a question that had plagued me since the day she
walked out of my room at the nursing home.

Cade just shook his head, shrugged one shoulder.
"Dunno."

I stepped away from him. "Go take a shower, and
then watch a movie with me." I pushed at his shoulder, trying desperately to regain the happiness I'd felt
only hours before. "It's Christmas Day. We have to
watch *Christmas Vacation.*"

He nodded sloppily, and shuffled into the bathroom. I put on one of his T-shirts while he showered
and then got the movie cued up, curling in the corner of the couch while I waited for him. He emerged
a little clearer-eyed half an hour later, his hair mussed
and shaggy and way too long, wearing a pair of clean
gym shorts and nothing else.

He laughed with me at the movie, even though
we'd both seen it countless times. Eden and I used
to watch it every year on Christmas Day. We'd drink
eggnog and eat a shitload of cookies, and quote our

favorite lines along with the actors. Cade had told me once that his mom had loved it, too, so it held significance for him as well.

When it was over, I eyed the shelf of movies beside the TV. "How about James Bond?" I knew those movies reminded him of his dad.

Cade's expression shuttered closed, and he shook his head. "No. Not Bond." I was puzzled by the strength and immediacy of his reaction, but didn't push it.

We ended up watching the entire Riddick trilogy, and didn't go to bed until after two in the morning.

Merry Christmas.

With the knowledge that midterms were approaching, and with it the conversation both Cade and I knew was coming, time slipped past all too quickly. Yet not fast enough. I dreaded the conversation, yet craved the closure I knew would accompany it, for good or ill. It meant an end to the wondering, an end to the questions and the fear. But it meant pain. I knew that much as clearly as I knew my own name.

Cade was easier to be with, strangely. I didn't question it, though, only tried to enjoy the casual conversations he'd engage me in, the way he held me tight at night. The way he'd wake me up early in the morning and make love to me with silent fervor.

They were wild, those morning tumbles. Intense. Not so much passionate as…desperate. Frantic. As if he was afraid he was going lose me.

I always held him, and told him I loved him, and he returned it, but his eyes held a distance, a sadness, a resignation.

January wound down, and spring break approached. I took my tests, turned in papers, and fought the feeling of impending doom. Some days, it felt as if I couldn't breathe, as if a weight was sitting on my chest.

Prompted by I didn't know what, I put in my notice at the office where I worked part time.

Cade requested two week's vacation from both jobs, and ended up quitting the janitorial job when they'd only grant him one week.

The last day of midterms was a bright and sunny Friday. I only had one exam, mid-morning, a low-level math class I had to take to finish out my requirements. I hated math but was pretty sure I'd at least passed the test, which was all I cared about.

I turned it in, put on my coat, shouldered my purse, and sent Cade a quick text that I was on the way home. When I arrived, he had a bag packed for us. We were going to the cabin. I'd managed to find the address and had printed out directions.

Cade drove. We were both quiet, tense.

"Think she'll be there?" Cade asked.

I'd wondered the same thing myself, over and over again. I'd written a letter, put it in an envelope, and put a stamp on it, but hadn't been able to send it. I couldn't bear the waiting, the not knowing if I'd get a response from her, or a yellow "return to sender" sticker, or simply nothing at all.

"I don't know," I said. "It's the only place I can think of that she might have gone."

"Are we planning on staying there?"

I shook my head. "Probably not. If she is there, she's been living there for almost nine months, and we couldn't crash in on her like that. And if she isn't there, the cabin probably isn't in any condition to stay in."

He just nodded, and silence descended between us once more, and lasted the rest of the way up to Traverse City. We ate at Red Ginger, a sushi place downtown, and walked the sidewalks together, hand in hand, stopping into shops here and there, browsing through the trinkets and baubles and artwork. We spent over an hour in an art gallery on Front Street, admiring the work of local artists. There was a series of landscapes which were fairly underwhelming, some abstract pieces that had Cade and I both nodding in appreciation, and, along one entire wall, hand-carved wood sculptures by someone named Carter Haven. They were fascinating pieces, all of them. They were varied in style, ranging from life-size squirrels and birds to topographical maps of the Traverse City area, to abstract twists of wood fused with straps of black iron.

I had put off the trip up the Old Mission Peninsula, and I knew Cade was putting off the conversation. *The Conversation*. It deserved the capital letter.

But I knew we couldn't put it off any longer. I stood with Cade at the corner of Front Street and Union, cars passing and flurries of late winter snow swirling around us. I took his hands in mine, looked up at him. "We should head up."

He nodded. "Okay." A glance down at me, to assess my mood. "You ready?"

I shook my head and shrugged. "Not really. But I have to know if she's here."

I'd booked a room at a hotel on the tourist strip, so we didn't have to worry about finding somewhere to stay once we'd visited the cabin.

With evening falling around us, Cade pointed the Jeep north on M–37 and, with every passing mile, my heart pounded harder.

She was here. I could feel her. I could sense her.

unlikely wisdom

Eden

Summer faded into fall, and my belly went from bump to protruding round bulge. With the cabin remodel finished, time spent with Carter was hit or miss. He was busy all the time, I discovered. He was heading up the construction of the tasting room for the Haven Brothers Winery. He supervised the day-to-day care of the vines, and he also ran a handyman service on the side, mostly for friends on the peninsula. If you needed your cabinets repainted, you hired Carter. If you needed help with a brake job on your car, you called Carter. If your sink leaked and the plumber couldn't come soon enough, you called Carter. He could do a little of everything, and was willing to help anyone, even if they couldn't pay him. On top of all this, he also sold his hand-carved wood sculptures out of the gallery downtown, and he'd mentioned that he would occasionally do pieces on commission.

But despite how busy he was, he always found time to stop by the cabin every day, even if just to check on me. As fall progressed and my belly got bigger, it got harder and harder for me to move around. That in itself was a hardship I hadn't anticipated. I was a fit girl. It was who I was. Being insecure about my weight and body image, I was fanatical about exercise, obsessed, even. I *had* to work out every day, regardless of the weather or my mood or anything else. And now, suddenly, I could barely get up off the couch.

By the time the first snow hit in late November, I was so hugely pregnant I felt like a walrus. I waddled. Actually *waddled*, with one hand pressed to my back. I'd seen pregnant women, of course, and I'd always shuddered in sympathy for them. I couldn't imagine being so slow and ponderous, carrying around this whole other person.

Nothing could have prepared me for how hard the reality of pregnancy was. As my belly got bigger and bigger, my back hurt more and more. And I peed all the time. I was hungry all the time, and craved bizarre things. According to the reading I'd done, I was under the impression that cravings were a first-trimester thing, and should fade away as the pregnancy progressed. I hadn't had any weird cravings at all in the first trimester. No pickles and ice cream, or sushi at three in the morning, or peanut butter and olive sandwiches. If anything, food made me nauseous. It wasn't really all that bad, but enough that I only ate when I was actually hungry enough for a meal.

And then I hit my third trimester, and I was hungry *all the time*. I wanted Triscuits and Irish cheddar cheese, literally every moment of every day. I had to have Greek yogurt twice a day: peach in the morning, black cherry at night. With granola. Real granola, not the fake bullshit with the sticky clumps of oats.

And decaf coffee. That was one of the hardest things. Giving up caffeine was like trying to rip my arm off. I tried cutting out coffee entirely for about two weeks, and then gave in, allowing myself one cup of actual real coffee in the morning, and then I had to switch to decaf. The idea was to psych myself out with the fake crap, but it never worked. I knew it was decaf, and it wasn't the same. But it was something.

The one thing I wished the pregnancy books had mentioned was that I'd pee my pants. That would have been nice to know. If I had to pee really bad— which was every hour or so—I'd find myself *leaking*.

Like…seepage. I took to wearing maxi pads all the time.

Carter usually stopped by around lunchtime, and he always brought me something to eat, most frequently a burger from the Peninsula Grill, or the parmesan-crusted whitefish, my other favorite menu item. He'd sit in my kitchen with me, and we'd eat and talk for a while, and then he'd leave.

I didn't dare examine why exactly my heart would start going pitter-patter as the noon hour approached. Or why it would start hammering when I heard his truck crunch to a stop on the gravel of my driveway. I'd have to stop myself from scurrying around the house, picking up before he came in. I had to stop myself from sighing every time I saw him, too. God, he was gorgeous. And the smell of sawdust and sweat that was wrapped up in his iden-tity sent my pulse racing and made my mouth dry and made me quiver, just a little. Not as quivery as his eyes made me, though. He'd cast a glance at me with those ridiculously beautiful blues, and I'd have to blink hard and force my knees to stay locked. His eyes were so pale, so piercing, so knowing.

I couldn't think about why I reacted to him so strongly, and there was no point in thinking about it. I knew he liked me. I knew he was attracted to me. And he was *there* for me. But…for how long? He had his own life. Mine was a whole train wreck of baggage, and I wouldn't wish it on anyone.

And, oh, yeah, I was *pregnant.* Very, very pregnant.

Which, maybe, just meant the attraction I had to Carter was just due to hormones. Some chemical inside me creating a false sense of need.

I couldn't afford to hope that he'd stick around for much longer. He'd get tired of hanging out with a guilt-stricken pregnant woman, one who was prickly and moody and complicated. And…I got exhausted just thinking about what it must have been like for him, being around me.

Why would he want to? He owed me nothing. He hadn't knocked me up; he had no responsibility to me. And I'd told him, numerous times, that there couldn't be anything between us. Not now, while I was pregnant, and not later, because I'd be busy trying to figure out how to be a single mother with no job and no degree. My only real talent or ability was playing the cello, and that was kind of hard to turn into a career when you had a newborn and no support system.

He wasn't a support system. I couldn't rely on him. Refused to. He was a friend. An acquaintance, even.

But…he found ways to support me and help me without ever being asked. He'd swing by with his mower and mow my grass. He came by three times over the fall to rake up my leaves and cart them away to burn at the vineyard. He replaced the garbage disposal when it quit on me. He took me grocery shopping a couple of times every week.

And those trips, the ones to the real supermarkets down the peninsula, they were the hardest for me. He was so attentive to me, always pushing the cart and opening the car door, grabbing the heavier items and loading and unloading. People always assumed we were a couple, which embarrassed me and made my heart ache a little, but Carter seemed to take it in stride. We didn't usually bother to correct the misconceptions. I'd answer their questions vaguely, wait through the awkward exclamations of how big my belly was and questions about when was I due, and were we having a girl or a boy, and oh, I bet the baby would have Daddy's eyes. Carter would just smile and wait patiently.

Basically, Carter was doing all the work of acting like my husband or boyfriend, just without any of the benefits. Especially since my company wasn't all that stimulating or fun most of the time.

The closer to my due date I got, the more the panic and guilt and worry consumed me.

By Christmas—a little more than two months from my due date—I was so afraid and worried and stressed out that I couldn't get out of bed, as it was often simply too arduous a process to even bother.

The only times I'd go through the effort of shifting my whale-sized body out of bed was to pee and to get something else to eat while I read my thousandth book.

Playing the cello was nearly impossible. Getting my bow arm around my belly and my cello required an act of contortion that was physically painful.

I was bored.

I was scared.

And, through it all, Carter was himself, calm, quiet, supportive. Attentive, occasionally more physically affectionate than I could tolerate.

Not because I didn't want him to touch me, but because I did. So much. I lived for the moments when he'd accidentally reach out and brush my hair away from my eyes. Once, when crossing the parking lot on the way into Meijer, I slipped on a patch of ice, and he caught me in his arms. And, as if the feel of his arm around my waist wasn't enough, he held my hand the rest of the way. I felt like a teenager as we walked across the parking lot, hand in hand. That tiny, innocent gesture made my heart hammer so hard I felt it in my ears. His hand was warm, despite the bite in the air. Rough, and strong. Like him.

Ever since Mom's death, Christmas had been a strained, difficult holiday. It had been her favorite time of year, and like everything else Mom had loved while alive, Dad hated it after she died. By the time college rolled around, Dad was simply a check in the mail, and Christmas was just Ever and me, usually at her place. We'd watch *Christmas Vacation* and stuff ourselves sick with eggnog and cookies and pie, and then on Christmas Day we'd exchange gifts and spend the day on a movie marathon.

This was the first time I'd ever been truly alone for the holidays, and maybe it was just the hormones, but the idea of spending Christmas Eve alone made me cry. I actually had to sit down on the couch and cry, and try to catch my breath. I missed Ever. I wanted to call her. I wanted to see her breeze through my door with a tin of green- and red-sprinkled sugar cookies and a bottle of rum. I wanted to hug her and have her tell me it would be okay. Tell me I was being an idiot and to woman up.

But she wouldn't. How could I just call her now? *Oh, hey, sis. How are you? I'm good. Just thirty weeks pregnant and carrying a beach ball around in my stomach. Who's the daddy? Your husband. Sorry I didn't tell you sooner—I've just been busy being a coward.*

I'd run away, and now it was too late to take it back. I couldn't figure out what I could've done any differently, but that didn't make it any easier to deal with my own cowardice. I'd have to face them someday. But when? It would never be easy. There would always be the questions and the heart-wrenching answers. The marriage-ruining answers. The home-wrecking answers.

I was lost in a downward spiral of self-loathing and self-pity when Carter showed up. It was eleven in the morning, Christmas Eve. He was dressed in a pair of tight, faded blue jeans and a terrifyingly ugly Christmas sweater. It was glaring red and had Frosty the Snowman embroidered on it. That wouldn't have been so bad, except that Frosty was wearing a red and green scarf. An actual, physical scarf sewn across the sweater. It was horrible, but yet I couldn't look away.

He rapped on the door as he let himself in, as usual. I looked up at him from my place on the couch, eyes red from crying and my nose running, and I saw him.

"What—what the fuck are you wearing, Carter?" I couldn't help laughing. Except laughing made a little pee squirt out, so the laugh turned into a moan of frustration.

"It's my Ugly Christmas Sweater," he said, and something in the tone of his voice lent the capital letters to the title. "What's the matter?"

I sniffed and wiped at my eyes. "Well, for one thing, I just peed." I'd already explained the pregnancy-pee scenario to him. "And aside from that... everything."

Carter sat down beside me, and put his arm around my shoulders. I couldn't help nuzzling into him, burying my face in the wool of his sweater and inhaling his clean scent. He smelled like shampoo and faint cologne and, of course, sawdust.

"Everything?" he asked.

I nodded. "Everything. I'm due in two months, and I don't know what I'm going to do. I'm almost through my savings already. I should've been working over the summer, but I just…couldn't. I didn't know anyone up here except you, and by the time I knew people I was too pregnant to be able to do anything. Besides, I'd have to quit before I had the baby anyway, so there wasn't a point." I felt the tears start all over again, and tried to stop them. It seemed all I did was cry anymore. "God, I'm sick of crying. You have to be sick of it, too, I imagine."

Carter just shrugged. "It's fine." He leaned away from me, looking at me. "There's something else, isn't there?"

I sighed. "It's Christmas. I miss my sister. She's the only family I really have, and I can't just call her. I can't spring this on her now. Not at Christmas."

"There'll never be a good time," he said, his voice quiet.

He thought I should just bite the bullet and tell them, get it over with. He was right, but it was easy to say, and hard to do. I'd nearly called her once, had my phone in my hand. Ever's number was on the screen, my finger on the "call" button. But I just couldn't do it. I'd turned the phone off and buried it in my sock drawer.

"I know," I said. "I'm a coward. I don't know how you can stand me."

Carter sighed, and when he spoke, irritation tinged his voice. "Eden. Being afraid to tell them this is perfectly understandable. It doesn't make you a coward. It makes you human. And I'm just saying, the longer you wait, the harder it'll get. She's your family. She'll understand."

I shook my head. "How could *anyone* understand what I did? I betrayed her in the worst possible way."

Carter hesitated a moment. "Look, I know it was his wife—your sister—that was in the coma, and I know he'd been through a lot, but…. This Cade guy has to bear at least *some* of the responsibility, doesn't he? He made the choice just as much as you did. You can't take all the blame yourself, Eden."

"I know, and I appreciate what you're saying," I said, pulling away from him. "But knowing Cade is partially responsible doesn't make my part of the blame any easier to bear. It doesn't change the fact that I'm about to have his baby, and that Ever will never have that choice."

Carter had no answer for that, because there was none to give. He stood up, turned to face me, and extended his hands to me. "Come on, we're gonna be late."

I took his hands, and he pulled me up to my feet. "Late for what? Where are we going?"

He traced his middle finger across my forehead, over my temple, and behind my ear, his touch gentle and tender and tempting. "Christmas lunch, of course."

"With who? You and me?"

"You and me…and my brothers, and my mom and dad. A few other close family members. Nothing huge."

Ice flooded my veins. "Oh, *hell* no. Thanks for thinking of me, but no."

He frowned. "Oh, hell *yes*. You're coming. There's no way I'm letting you sit here alone on Christmas Eve. I already told Mom you were coming, so she's expecting you. She set a place at the table and everything."

My hands shook. "Who did you say you were bringing? Your single, pregnant pity-friend?" Carter's expression shuttered. I'd hurt him with that one.

"I'm not your friend out of *pity*, Eden." He turned away, scrubbing his hands through his hair, which he'd taken the time to actually comb and style. "I'd hoped you thought more of me than that."

I moved closer to him, resisting the urge to smooth his hair down. "I'm sorry, Carter. I just—I'm not—"

"We're not having the what-we-aren't conversation right now. I can't deal with it. Just tell me if you're coming or not."

"You really want me at your family's house for Christmas? Won't that be…awkward?"

He pivoted to look at me. "Yes, Eden. I wouldn't have invited you if I didn't want you there. And, no, it won't be awkward. Kirk's bringing his fiancée, and my half-sister will be there with her boyfriend. So you won't be the only non-family member."

"Half-sister?" He'd never mentioned a half-sister.

"Yeah. My mom was married before she met my dad, and she had a kid. Lucy lives in San Antonio, so I don't see her much, but she comes up for the holidays. She's cool. She's two years older than Max."

"Did you tell them I was pregnant? I mean, how are we going to explain it?"

"We don't have to explain anything to anyone. It's your business. You aren't the first unwed pregnant woman in history, you know." He gave me a reassuring smile. "It'll be fine. No one's going to judge you."

Yes, they would, if they knew. But like he'd said, they didn't have to know any details. I was tempted to go. I really didn't want to be here alone. But…it *would* be awkward. They'd be wondering if we were together, and how that worked if I was pregnant with *not* his baby.

"Come with me, Eden. No one should have to spend Christmas alone."

"Okay. Okay. I'll go." I tried to lighten the mood. "I don't have any ugly sweaters, though."

"It's fine, the Ugly Christmas Sweater competition is more between the guys anyway."

"It's a competition?" I asked.

He grinned. "Oh, yeah. Every year my brothers, my dad, and I try to find the ugliest sweater possible, and the girls vote on whose is the ugliest. We all pitch in on a bottle of Oban, and the winner gets the bottle. I've won the past three years in a row."

I laughed. "You must have a lot of ugly sweaters, then."

He snorted. "You have *no* idea. I've got, like, four huge storage bins full of them. It's kind of a problem, actually, 'cause there's not much you can do with a collection of ugly Christmas sweaters. You can't wear them again, because every year you have to have a new one to compete with, but how do you get rid of it? Just throw it away?"

I nodded, keeping my expression serious. "That is a problem. Whatever are you gonna do?"

He gave me a fake glare. "You're mocking me, aren't you?"

I held my fingers an inch apart. "Just a bit."

"Not nice." He tugged me toward the door. "Now, let's *go*. They'll eat without us, and then there won't be any of Mom's sweet potato pie left. And I *can't* miss out on that—it's my favorite part of Christmas lunch."

I laughed at him. "You're funny. Okay, let me just change real quick. I can't wear this to meet your family."

I was in my preggo uniform: yoga pants, a tank top, and a zip-up hoodie. It was comfortable, and the tank top/hoodie combo let me adjust to the hot and cold flashes that hit me without warning. It was a far cry from flattering, however.

"Why do you have to change?" He looked me up and down. "You look fine. It's just family hanging out. Dad will probably be in sweats, and I don't think I've ever seen Lucy wear anything but pants just like the ones you're wearing."

"Carter. I've worn these clothes for two days straight, for one thing. And you just don't do that. You don't meet someone's family for the first time wearing *this*." I gestured at my outfit. "I'll be quick, I promise. Give me five minutes."

"Hurry."

I tore through my closet, hunting for something remotely acceptable that would still fit. What did you wear to something like this? I'd never dated anyone seriously enough to meet his family, especially not for Christmas. Except I wasn't dating Carter, so it didn't count. But I was still meeting his family.

I couldn't find anything, and started to feel as if I was going to hyperventilate. I rifled through the closet again, and finally found a stretchy cotton skirt, plain black and calf-length. It was nice, but comfortable, and it would stretch to fit under my watermelon-sized belly. I had a fairly nice gray T-shirt that would work, and a plum-colored cardigan. I threw the clothes on, slipped my bare feet into my Toms, which were my new favorite footwear. Easy on and easy off, comfortable, and went with everything.

My hair was tangled and felt like straw, but I didn't have time do anything with it, and I certainly didn't have time for makeup. So I tossed a brush and ponytail holder in my purse, and met Carter at the door in less than five minutes.

He grinned at me. "Now, that's a quick change. You look amazing, Eden. For real."

I shook my head at him. "Amazingly huge, but thanks." Putting on fifty pounds of pregnancy weight was wreaking havoc on my already fragile self-esteem. I donned my oversize winter parka, which wouldn't zipper all the way, but was the only winter coat I owned.

Carter closed my front door behind us, and then moved ahead to open the passenger door of his truck for me, handing me up. I was pretty sure I'd never actually opened a door on my own if Carter was with me. He was the most downright chivalrous man I'd ever known, and it was playing merry hell on my ability to remember that we'd never be anything but friends, no matter how gorgeous or gentlemanly he was.

The radio played traditional Christmas songs, and I found myself singing along to them under my breath, humming when I didn't know the words. Carter watched me out of the corner of his eye as he drove, a small smile gracing his lips.

I cocked an eyebrow at him. "What?"

He shook his head and shrugged. "Nothing."

"You're smirking."

"I do not smirk."

"You were, too. You were smirking at me."

He chuckled. "It wasn't meant to be a smirk, how about that?"

"What was it about?" I asked.

"Nothing. Just…you look so beautiful, sitting there with the snow behind you, singing along to Christmas music. You have a pretty voice."

I felt myself blushing. "Thanks. I don't really sing much. But I love all these old songs. They make me think of my mom. She had a *terrible* voice, but she would crank the radio and sing along, and singing while she cooked just made her so happy that none of us cared how bad she sounded."

"You don't talk about your mom much," he said. It was a tactful way of encouraging me to talk about her if I wanted, but gave me an out if I didn't.

"She was amazing. I don't know what else to say. She loved the cello—she was so passionate about playing. And painting, too. But that was more for her own enjoyment. She never sold any of her paintings, but she could've. She was beautiful, and always took time to make Ever and me feel special. That's hard, with twins. She never treated us like the same person, which so many people do."

"She died?" Carter asked.

I nodded. "Yeah. Car accident, when I was twelve."

"Are you close to your dad?" Carter swung the truck off Center Road and onto a side street heading toward the East Arm of the bay—on the opposite side of the peninsula from my cabin, and several miles south.

"No." I bit out the word. "He fell apart after Mom died. I haven't seen him in…god, almost two years. I saw him a few weeks after Ever's accident, but he just couldn't handle it. Some people just don't handle grief well, I guess. He shut us both out, spent all his time at work. He paid for college and gave us both money to live on, and he paid for Ever's medical bills, but…we never wanted his money. We wanted *him*."

"He doesn't know you're here?"

"No one does." I stared out the window at the snow, watching the thick, fat flakes drift down lazily.

"Are you gonna tell him?"

I shook my head. "No. Dad's not part of my life, and he hasn't been since Mom died. I don't even think about him anymore."

Carter shook his head, whether in disbelief or sadness, I wasn't sure. "You're amazingly strong, Eden. You've gone through this all alone."

I ran my thumb along the seam of the leather seat. "I'm anything but strong. I was lucky that I had enough money saved to be able to stay up here without working. I was lucky to have the cabin to go to. But I'm a mess. I'm terrified. And…I don't—I don't know how to be a mother. I'm giving birth to this baby in two months. *Two months.* And I don't know how to…what to do. I feel her kicking sometimes, at night when I'm trying to sleep usually, and I don't feel—I don't know…*connected*. Like, I'm carrying this baby, but I can't fathom being a mother. A person depending on me for everything. Calling me *Mommy*." I choked. "That's not me, Carter. I didn't *want* this. And I feel terrible about it because sometimes—sometimes I resent it, the baby, I mean, for messing up everything. If I hadn't gotten pregnant, things would've been tricky, but not impossible like they are now."

Carter took the wheel with his left hand and threaded the fingers of his right hand through mine. "You'll figure it out. One day at a time, okay? And you're not going through it alone. I'll be there."

"What would I do without you, Carter? You've literally saved my life. I can't even begin to thank you for everything you've done."

He squeezed my hand and smiled at me, but said nothing. I forced away the doubts and the thoughts and the fears, trying to bring myself to a more positive frame of mind. I couldn't go into his parents' house a hot mess like this.

A couple turns, and then we were on a dirt road running parallel to the bay, the water rippling steel-blue through a bank of trees. He pulled up to a beautiful, rambling ranch. It sat high on a hill overlooking the bay, a rolling hill falling down to the waterline, with a long dock stretching into the lake.

"It's amazing," I said.

"It sure is." He slid out of the truck and opened my door, not letting go of my hand when I hit the ground. He touched my chin, and I looked up at him. It would be all too easy to lose myself in his blue eyes, but I couldn't. "Just be you, okay? Have fun. Don't worry about anything. And if you're ready to go home, just let me know and I'll take you, okay?"

I nodded, and had to rip my gaze from his before tempting thoughts flooded my mind. "Thanks for bringing me here, Carter."

He pulled me in for a hug. "Don't worry about it. No one should be alone on Christmas, especially not you."

I had to push away all too soon. He smelled too good, felt too good. Too comforting, too familiar. "Let's go in before I lose my nerve."

He didn't let go of my hand until we got to the front door. "Ready?" he asked me, his hand on the knob.

I nodded. "Nope. Not even remotely."

Carter laughed. "Quit worrying, Edie. You'll be fine." I froze at his use of the nickname used by no one but Ever. He noticed my reaction. "You don't like that nickname?"

I could barely whisper. "Ever calls me that some-times. Or she used to."

"I shouldn't have done that," he said. "I'm sorry."

I shook my head. "No, it's fine. It just took me off guard."

He squeezed my hand once more, then pushed the door open and led the way in. A wall of noise hit me: music, laughter, voices, pots and pans clanging, a dog barking, a TV going. I'd never seen so much activity in one place in all my life, and it overwhelmed me. There were at least a dozen conversations happening, and there were at least ten people here that Carter hadn't told me about. Cousins, aunts, and uncles? I didn't know. A family this size was an anomaly to me. There was a little boy running around, clutching a toy sword and shouting something indecipherable, and, as I watched, he whacked someone at random across the knee with his sword with an ear-piercing "HI-*YAH!*"

As soon as the door opened, all the conversations stopped, and every eye turned to Carter, and to me.

"Hey, everybody!" Carter called out as he kicked off his boots. I shrank back against the door, feeling the weight of at least twenty pairs of eyes on me, assessing, wondering, judging. He pulled me forward gently. "This is my friend, Eden." He emphasized the word *friend* ever so slightly.

A chorus of hellos hit me, and a woman who looked exactly like Carter bustled over to me, smiling brightly, wearing a Pepto Bismol–pink apron that was spattered with sweet potato, pie crust, flour, cranberry sauce, and who knew what else. She was tall, with ink-black hair tied up in a messy bun. "Eden, welcome. I'm so excited you're here!" She leaned in and hugged me, keeping her messy hands and apron away from my clothes.

Why? I wanted to ask. "Thanks," was what I said. "You have a beautiful home." I sniffed the air, smelling the various dishes she was preparing. "It all smells delicious."

"Thank you." She turned to glare at Carter. "I'm Karen. My son seems to have regained his powers of speech lately, but obviously not his manners."

"Sorry, Mom." Carter cleared his throat and shuffled uncomfortably. "Eden Eliot, this is my mother, Karen Haven. Mom, this is my friend Eden."

I wondered if maybe he was overdoing it a bit with the emphasis on our friendship status. But, then again, that might have just been my subconscious wishing vainly that I could have been meeting his family under other, less platonic circumstances.

Carter gestured at a tall, slim, athletic man with gray at the temples of his auburn hair. "Dad, this is Eden. Eden, my dad, Richard Haven."

I shook his hand. "Nice to meet you, Mr. Haven."

This earned me a snort, the same sound Carter so frequently made. "Richard, please. It's wonderful to have you here, Eden."

Karen whacked Carter across the arm, smearing sweet potato on his sleeve. "Now you're just being an idiot. This isn't the court of King Henry the Eighth, son. Such formality is entirely unnecessary."

I had to hide my smirk as Carter wiped at the smear of goo on his sweater. Seeing him put in his place by his mom was both funny and heartwarming. "It's nice to meet you, Karen."

Karen curtsied, spreading her apron in lieu of skirts. "Likewise, I'm sure."

I snorted, and matched her curtsey as well as I could, at least. "Milady."

Carter's glare shifted from his mom to me. "You're not supposed to encourage her, Eden. Whose friend are you, anyway?"

Karen took me by the arm and pulled me toward the kitchen. "Mine, now. Go say hello to your cousins, Carter. You can have her back later."

I followed Karen into the spacious kitchen. There was a huge island in the center of the room, clearly the focal point of the space. It was comprised of an enormous butcher's block, a slab of wood several inches thick. The rest of the counters were dark marble, and the cabinets were stained the same shade as the butcher's block. At the moment, every available inch of counter space was cluttered with bowls and utensils and covered plates, foil-covered casserole dishes, spice bottles, the weapons of a culinary war. There was a giant bottle of wine sitting on the island, opened, with a cluster of wine glasses surrounding it. I stared longingly at the wine, wishing I could have some.

Karen followed my gaze, and laughed. "Honestly, that was the hardest part of all five of my pregnancies. No wine for nine months?" She faked an exaggerated shudder. "Shoot me now."

I laughed, feeling at ease around this woman after not even five minutes. "It's pretty tough," I agreed. "And *five* times? How did you do it without going crazy?"

"This is your first, I assume?" Karen tipped a couple of inches of wine into a glass, and handed it to me. "You're allowed one half glass, I think."

I hesitated, then took the goblet, swirling the ruby-red liquid in the glass. "Are you sure? I don't want to hurt the baby."

Karen smiled gently. "Oh, I'm sure. A few sips of wine, once, isn't going to do any harm." She gestured at the living room, where the Haven brothers were rough-housing and laughing. "Richard had a knack for knocking me up in time for the holidays, so I could never drink with everyone else. I'd allow myself one glass, for Christmas Eve lunch. They all turned out just fine, I think."

I eyed the four men. They were all tall, dark, and handsome, each different than the other, but all four were gorgeous. None of them were quite as incredible as Carter to me, though. "I'd say so," I deadpanned.

Karen snorted, swallowing a mouthful of wine. She had to cover her mouth to keep from spraying me. "They're quite a collection, aren't they?"

I took a tentative sip of the wine. My eyes slid closed, and I moaned in appreciation as the dry, velvety liquid hit my palate. "God, that's good. You don't know how bad I've wanted this."

Karen chuckled. "I think I do. Five times, remember? Try being pregnant with three boys under seven running around."

I paled at the thought, watching the toddler as he tirelessly sprinted from one corner of the house to the other, leaping off the back of the couch, rolling across an ottoman, slicing at the air with his sword all the while. "Were they all like that?" I gestured at the little boy, who I thought might be three or four, but wasn't sure.

Karen nodded, peeking into one of two stacked ovens. "Oh, yeah. Danny there is a handful, but there's only one of him. All of my boys were wild little hellions. And they'd team up. Kirk was the brains, always coming up with devious plans, and Max and Carter would carry the plan out."

"What about Tom?"

"Oh, Tommy was the distraction. I'm telling you, they were *tactical*." She closed the oven, and turned back to me. "I remember once…Max was nine, which means Kirk was seven, Carter five, and Tommy three. Max wanted cookies. I'd just baked a tray of chocolate chip cookies, and I'd told him he couldn't have any until after dinner. So Max, he convinces Kirk and Carter to help him get some anyway. Poor little Tommy, he was too young to know any better, and he idolized his older brothers, Carter in particular. He'd do anything they asked. So they wait until Tommy was playing with his favorite toy, and then they snatch it from him. He goes haywire, of course. Which was what they wanted. I go to see what's wrong with Tommy, and while I'm in here trying to translate screaming toddler, the three older ones are in the kitchen, sneaking handfuls of cookies."

"Did they give Tommy any?"

Karen laughed. "Of course they did! They waited until I'd calmed Tom down, and then gave him a cookie. I didn't figure out what they'd done until Tommy comes into the kitchen, smeared with chocolate, asking for more cookie, more cookie."

I laughed. "Sounds like you were busy."

"Busy is one word for it. It was chaos, complete and utter chaos. The house was always a disaster, the sink was always full of dishes, the garbage overflowing. Toilets were nasty, showers needed cleaning. But...it was worth every minute."

Carter came in at that moment and poured himself a glass of wine. "Are you telling embarrassing stories, Mom?"

"Yep. I was just getting to the part where you ran around the neighborhood buck-ass naked until you were three."

I laughed, choking on my mouthful of wine. "He did?"

Karen nodded. "Oh, yes. I couldn't keep clothes on the boy. I'd get him dressed and he'd be naked as the day he was born within an hour. And he'd run away. I'd have to chase him down the beach, his skinny little behind waggling."

Carter shook his head, glaring at his mom. "Seriously? Are you gonna bust out pictures next? God, Mom."

With a devious laugh, Karen pulled out her phone. "Well, now that you remind me…. Richard scanned all of our family photographs in the computer last spring, and I have a few favorites on here." She tapped and scrolled through her photo album, and then handed me the phone. "Swipe right. Lots of good ones of the boys. And yes, there's the obligatory naked Carter in the bath pictures."

I giggled as I swiped through the images of Carter's childhood. He was an adorable little boy and, judging from the pictures, fearless. She had shots of him at all ages, from infancy to adulthood, and in many of them he was climbing trees, riding dirt bikes and horses, racing four-wheelers. And, as Karen had promised, there was a photo of Carter at age two or three in the bathtub. It wasn't a tastefully posed one, either. All of his little-boy bits were on display. In one of the bathtub pics, he was actually playing with himself. I could almost hear him, tiny little voice saying "boing…boing…boing…."

Carter glanced over my shoulder, and then started coughing and hacking. He snatched the phone out of my hands and held it up out of my reach. "MOM! Are you fucking serious? You're actually showing her bathtub pictures? Who even takes those?"

Karen just laughed. "When you have kids, you'll understand. It's cute! And, in your case, always good for a laugh." She glanced at me. "Did you see the one where he was—"

I snorted, reenacting what Carter had been doing in the photo. "Boing! Boing! Boing!"

Carter glared at us both, and Karen laughed so hard she doubled over.

A little hand grabbed a fistful of Carter's sweater and tugged. "You said a potty talk, Uncle Carter."

Carter looked down at the toddler. "I sure did, Danny. And I'm your cousin, not your uncle."

Danny frowned. "You shouldn't say potty talk. Can I call you Uncle anyway?"

"Sure you can. And no. I probably shouldn't say bad words around you, should I? I'm sorry, Danny. How about we make a deal? I won't say bad words if you won't." Carter knelt down and held out his hand to shake.

Danny crossed his arms. "How 'bout you pay me a dollar? Sometimes Daddy says bad words when he's watching feetsball. Mommy gets mad at him, and he has to give me a dollar every time he says one."

"You must have a lot of dollars, huh?" Carter asked, shooting an amused glance at the cousin who I assumed was Danny's dad, a burly, auburn-haired man with a long beard.

"He's got more money than he knows what to do with," the man said, not looking away from the game on the TV.

"Nuh-uh," Danny said. "I spended it."

This caught the father's attention. "On what?

"The ice cream truck."

"The ice cream truck? You spent *all* of it at the ice cream truck?"

Danny shrugged, looking down at the floor. He was realizing he might've said something he shouldn't have. "Not all of it. I got few dollars left."

"There was more than twenty dollars there!" The father glanced from Danny to a pretty woman with white-blonde hair and a lip piercing. "Where was your mother while you were buying ice cream?"

Danny glanced from his mother to his father. "Looking at her people books. I asked if I could play outside and she said yes, and the ice cream truck always comes right up to the fence and I don't even gotta go in the street or nothing!"

"On people books," the father said, lifting an eyebrow at his wife in accusation.

"I knew where he was, Alex," the woman said. "I just didn't know he was smuggling money outside."

"And you didn't notice he—oh, I don't know—had *ice cream?*" Alex demanded. "Maybe that's why he never wanted to eat his dinner all summer long!"

Karen stepped in at that point. "Marie, Alex. It's just ice cream. Relax."

Marie cast a grateful glance at Karen. Alex turned back to the TV, grumbling something under his breath about "social media time-sucks."

I'd watched the exchange with curiosity. Alex and Marie had basically argued in public, about what seemed to me to be a fairly serious parenting issue. Although, with the exception of myself, everyone in the house was family, so maybe to them it wasn't public. I couldn't fathom having that kind of conversation in such a public setting. But then, I couldn't fathom much of anything about how this family operated. It was just so *big*. There were at least ten different conversations happening all at once, with everyone trying to talk louder than everyone else. The result was that everyone was basically shouting at each other about golf scores and stock exchange tips and recipes and gossip about extended family members I assumed weren't present.

Case in point was Carter, standing next to me in the kitchen, munching on pita chips dipped in a bowl of what looked like homemade hummus. He conducted an entire conversation with someone clear across the house at a volume loud enough to be heard across a football stadium. The Carter I was seeing in this home, around his family, was almost a different person from the one I knew. He was completely relaxed, talkative, wandering around the room restlessly, easily moving from conversation to conversation. Around me, he was quieter, not exactly taciturn, but not chatty, either. He was given to stillness, whereas here he seemed almost physically unable to stay in the same place for more than a few minutes.

Yet, I noticed no matter where in the room he was, no matter who he was talking to or how deep in conversation he seemed to be, Carter was always aware of me. I'd feel his eyes on me, watching, checking. And as the day progressed, he made a point of always returning to where I was camped out in the kitchen.

Karen had pulled me into the kitchen when we first arrived, and I hadn't left it. I hadn't even crossed the threshold into the living room, which seemed to be the domain of the men, for the most part. The women, who were seriously outnumbered in this company, congregated in the kitchen around Karen, or at the dining room table. I'd offered to help her cook, but she waved me off, saying she enjoyed it, and there wasn't much left to do anyway. Yet, for all that, she was always busy, chopping or stirring or spooning out.

The other thing I didn't understand was what time we would be sitting down to dinner. Carter had rushed me out the door as if we would be sitting down to eat the moment we arrived. By all appearances, Karen was preparing a huge amount of food, and yet it was nearing three o'clock in the afternoon and the appetizers were still going strong. The table was littered with bowls of chips and dip, plates of cheese, trays of celery and carrots and peppers, a shrimp cocktail setup, sandwich rolls sliced into inch-thick snack-sized pieces, dishes of candy and unwrapped Reese's Miniatures...more snacks and appetizers than I'd ever seen in one place in my life.

The other thing in abundance was plenty was booze. The wine was almost gone, and the men drifted into the kitchen several times to grab a bottle of beer from the fridge. I'd sipped my half-glass as slowly as I could, and managed to make it last for almost an hour, which I felt had to be some kind of record for what amounted to a few sips. Even Carter had knocked back at least three beers that I'd seen, which seemed like a lot for him, from what I knew about him.

I snagged his arm as he passed by me to get a new bottle of beer. "I thought you said we had to hurry to get here before the sweet potato pie was gone?" I lifted an eyebrow at him. "It's past three. What happened to lunch?"

Carter chuckled. "Well, for one thing, the hur-ry-up bit may have been a ploy to get you here. I knew if I gave you time to think about it, you'd chicken out. I got you out the door as fast as I could, so you wouldn't flake on me. But, yes, Christmas 'lunch,'" he made air quotes around the last word, "is kind of a misnomer, I guess. We probably won't eat for another hour or so, and then we'll all eat until we can't eat any more... and then we'll keep snacking all night."

"All night? How is everyone getting home? Several people here seem three sheets to wind already and it's not even four."

Carter laughed. "Oh, god, no one actually leaves, babe. There are four bedrooms upstairs, two pull-out couches, a bedroom in the basement, plus a guest cottage down the beach a ways. My folks own almost forty acres, and over five hundred feet of that is waterfront."

Babe. He called me "babe." I shouldn't have liked that as much as I did. He'd mentioned his parents had money, but I'd forgotten. The house itself seemed modest, to my eyes. I'd grown up in a seven-thou-sand-square-foot mansion in Bloomfield Hills, sur-rounded by auto industry executives who liked to throw around their money. This family wasn't like that, clearly. If they had money, they didn't show it the way I was used to seeing. This house wasn't small, but it was gorgeous, and tasteful. The appliances were upper-end, but not luxury-brand, and the furniture was the same, nice, comfortable, but not showy. It felt like a home, well-loved and lived in.

I'd spent most of the afternoon talking to Karen, but I'd also met a few cousins, one of Carter's aunts, both of his uncles, and few others I couldn't remember. Everyone was easy to talk to, intelligent and willing to listen. And none of them asked me any awkward questions about my obvious pregnancy. Either Carter had asked them not to, or they were simply being tactful.

Two single-dollar bills filled my vision. "Two bucks for your thoughts?" Carter asked.

I smiled at him, and then shrugged. "Just...your family is amazing. They're all so kind...and there's so *many* of them. They've all made me feel welcome. I was kind of overwhelmed at first, but...it's nice. Loud, and crazy and chaotic, but fun. And did I mention that there's just so *many* of them?"

Carter laughed. "So there's a lot of them? Eden, babe. This is...*maybe* half of just my mom's side. She has five siblings, and they all have kids. Dad is one of five, and *they* all have multiple kids. On his side, there's an actual metric shit-ton of little kids. The people on that side are all horny bastards. There's a dozen first cousins between Uncle Mike, Uncle Derek, Aunt Julie, and Uncle Brad. And all those dozen first cousins have at least one kid each—most of them have two or three."

That made me dizzy. "How…how many cousins and aunts and uncles do you have?"

Carter leaned back, crossing his arms over his chest with his beer resting on his forearm. "Hmmm. I've never done an actual count. I don't think we've ever had all of them in one place before. I've got nine aunts and uncles, and…god, like thirty first cousins? I don't know. A lot. A *lot*."

"And you know them all?" I had to actually hold onto the counter.

Carter nodded. "Well, sure. They're family. One of Mom's brothers is kind of a hermit, so I've only met him once. He lives in Alaska, I think. Somewhere far and cold." He shouted across the room at his mother, who was perched on the arm of the couch with her fingers idly tracing through her husband's hair. "Hey, Mom! Where does Uncle Rich live?"

She didn't even turn around to respond. "Nome!" she shouted.

He turned back to me. "He lives in Nome, Alaska," he said, as if I hadn't heard.

"Yeah. Got that," I said, deadpan.

He seemed oblivious to my sarcasm. "But, yeah, we have them over for holidays all the time. Mom's family usually comes over for Christmas lunch, Dad's family comes over for Thanksgiving, and we usually have a huge Fourth bash in the summer, and whoever can make it comes." He looked at me inquisitively. "Your family's pretty small, huh?"

I shrugged. "Yeah. Mom and Dad were both only children, and Mom's parents died when I was really little, and Dad's parents died not long after. It was just the four of us growing up, and then when Mom died Dad basically shut down. Then it was mainly Ever and me for the holidays." I gestured with my head at the gathering of family. "So *this* is…just amazing to me."

Carter's dad, Richard, came over just then, and the conversation shifted to other things, but I only partially participated. I was taking it all in, watching everyone interact, wondering what it would be like to belong to such a huge family. It would be incredible, I decided. I'd give anything to be part of this family. That was probably an idle wish, I realized with a pang of sadness. This escape to Traverse City was destined to be a temporary solution to a permanent problem. I just had no idea what would happen after the birth of the baby.

I pushed those thoughts away as, seemingly without any kind of prompting, the huge dining room table was cleared off and places were set. Innumerable dishes were lined up down the middle of the table. People took seats where they wanted, and within minutes lunch was on, although four o'clock seemed awfully late to call it lunch.

If the chaotic nature of conversation earlier in the day had overwhelmed me, then dinner was downright lunacy. Dishes were passed back and forth, shouts to pass this dish or that crossed the table constantly, conversations took place end to end, willy-nilly. Everyone talked to everyone, all at once. Jokes were told, ranging from idiotically funny puns to dirty and cringe-worthy, yet no one ever got offended, no one got angry, no one insulted anyone or, if they did, it was in fun and returned in kind. Carter and his brothers, in particular, shared good-natured ribbing back and forth nonstop, and at one point they even started hurling dinner rolls at each other, which wasn't stopped until Tom started flinging mashed potatoes with his fork. Sitting next to Carter in the middle of the table, with Carter's oldest brother Max on the other side of me, gave me a ringside seat for all the action.

Midway through the meal, Max glanced at me with a curious expression on his face. "So, Eden. You gotta tell me how you did it."

"Did what?" I asked, biting into a biscuit.

"Get Carter to start talking again."

Conversation stopped dead, going in an instant from full-roar to so silent you could hear a pin drop.

The biscuit suddenly tasted like ashes. "I—I don't know. I didn't do anything." I stared at my plate, barely able to manage a shrug. "I didn't know he hadn't spoken in so long. I just thought he was either an arrogant asshole, or painfully shy." Everyone laughed at that, including Carter. "I didn't try to do anything. Sorry I can't make it more dramatic—I just…he just started talking to me."

Carter, despite laughing at my jibe, seemed equally as uncomfortable with the topic as I was. "So, did you hear the one about the priest and the nun?" he asked. As a topic-shift tactic, it was kind of lame.

"Shut up, Carter. You suck at telling jokes," Tom said. "You can't change the subject."

"Yes, I can. I can also break your ugly face."

"Boys," Karen cut in, her voice quiet, but they both silenced immediately. "You're making Eden uncomfortable. Carter started talking because he was ready to, and now that's enough of that. It isn't appropriate conversation for the dinner table." This from the woman who'd just laughed at a bawdy joke told by her own husband. Yet I was intensely grateful to her for taking the spotlight off me.

Carter's eyes met mine, pale blue and concerned. I smiled at him, trying to reassure him that I was fine.

Conversation hadn't really started up again, so I tried to break the tension. "I think it didn't really have a lot to do with me, anyway. I think he was just sick of taking shit from you guys." I gestured to each of his brothers with my fork. "He's always telling me how mean you are to him."

The three brothers laughed, while Carter gave me a wounded expression, as if I'd betrayed him. I could see the gratitude and humor twinkling in his eyes, though. "You bitch! You sold me out!"

There was a chorus of *oooohs* at that. I smacked his arm with the back of my hand. "You did not just call me a bitch. I know you didn't."

"I think I did," he said, arching an eyebrow.

I glanced at Tom, who gave me a meaningful nod as he swirled his fork through his mashed potatoes. I hesitated, then summoned my courage and scooped a heap of potatoes onto my spoon, brought it toward my face as if about to eat it, and then flung it at Carter at the last second, getting him in the face. Everyone at the table cracked up, except Karen, who tried in vain to stop the food fight that ensued. It was only when Kirk threatened to dump the contents of the gravy boat onto Max that Richard cut through the uproar with a calm but firm, "Enough."

Everyone pitched in to clean up, and then a shoot-'em-up movie marathon was proposed, which brought the majority of the group downstairs, leaving Karen and me alone in the kitchen, with a few people in the living room playing a card game.

I sensed a talk coming on when Karen poured herself a big glass of wine and pulled up a stool next to me. "I know you say you didn't do anything, but I just…I just wanted to say thank you. I wasn't sure Carter would ever really come back to us, and ever since he met you…he's been his old self again, and then some."

I ducked my head. "I really didn't do anything, Karen."

"Well, then, you being you was enough. And for that, I thank you. You've given me my son back, and I can't ever express how much that means to me."

"Carter is amazing. He's been there for me in ways I can't ever repay." I knew then as I looked into Karen's eyes and saw the glimmer of hope that I had given her some element of the truth. "He told me what happened. To Britt. He deserves happiness. And, Karen, I'm just not sure that I'll ever be able to offer him that." I rested one hand on my enormous belly as supporting evidence.

Karen nodded, sighing. "I get what you're saying. And although I am curious, that's your business and your story. But let me offer you a piece of wisdom. You haven't asked, but I'm a mother, and it's our job to hand out unsolicited advice."

I laughed. "Okay, let's hear it.'

"Life is never simple. Never." Karen ran her index finger around the rim of her glass. "I was a

single mother when I met Richard. I had an eigh-
teen-month-old daughter and a messy divorce that
wouldn't be finalized for another six months. It was
complicated as all hell. I liked him, a lot, but I didn't
think anyone would ever be able to understand my
life. Or that I'd ever find happiness again. Especially
considering the circumstances that led to my divorce.
I was so young, you know. Twenty-one, with a daughter and a divorce and a broken heart." She glanced up
at me, as if weighing how much to tell me. "My boys
don't know this, because I just…I just never knew
how to tell them, but…my first husband was abusive.
Mentally, emotionally, and physically. So on top of
the baggage of my life, I had distrust and trauma and
all this other bullshit. I decided I was too much for
anyone—even someone as amazing as Richard. So I
pushed him away. I did everything I could think of
to make him leave me alone. To hurt him. Because
I knew he'd hurt me eventually, and I didn't think I
could survive that."

"You had four kids together, so obviously
Richard didn't listen to you. What happened? How
did you end up together?"

Karen smiled, a small, private smile of reminis-
cence. "There's one problem, sweetie. We didn't *end
up* together. We made choices. Richard told me
something I've never forgotten: 'You think I don't
know you have a messed-up past, Karen? Of course

you do. Yours may be more complicated than mine, and you may be afraid.'" Her voice took on a tone that told me she was quoting words she'd had memorized for thirty years. "'But the choice to love you is *mine*. Not yours. You don't get to make that choice for me. You can choose to not *let* me love you, but you can't tell me what's too much for me to handle. That's for me to decide.'"

I sniffed away the tears that trickled past my nose. "God, Karen. And you let him, huh?"

Karen stared at me incredulously. "Have you *seen* my husband? Of course I did! He's a fox!"

I laughed. I had met her husband and, for a man thirty years my senior, I *knew* he was attractive. I could see where the boys got their looks. Richard Haven, even at fifty or sixty or however old he was, was tall and well-built, with wavy auburn hair just starting to go silver at the temples. His sharp features and ice-blue eyes were passed on to his sons.

Karen sobered. "Seriously, though. How could I deny what he'd said? I wasn't pushing him away because I didn't *want* him, but because I was afraid my baggage was too heavy for him. And he was *right*, Eden. We can't make choices for other people."

I sat perfectly still, barely daring to breathe, holding back all the things I wanted to say and trying to prevent the gush of yet more tears. "You know what I hate the most about being pregnant? Being so emotional. Literally *everything* makes me cry."

Karen laughed at that. "Sure, blame it on the hormones. That's a classic pregnant lady line: 'I'm not usually so emotional, it's just these damn hormones!'"

I gave a mock-glare. "Well, in my case it's *true*. I went the first twenty-plus years of my life rarely crying. A really bad breakup here and there, maybe. But suddenly, all I do I cry, and I'm sick of it, but I can't seem to stop it!"

"Oh, honey. I understand more than you know."

I doubted that. She couldn't possibly understand the tangled web I was caught up in. No one could. I nearly snorted out loud at that, realizing I was doing the exact thing that Karen was warning me against.

She must've seen the skeptical expression on my face. "All I'm saying is, try to keep an open mind. You never what's possible until you try. Such an old cliché, but it's true. Things always seem impossible when you're on the wrong side of fear."

"The wrong side of fear?"

"Well, sure." Karen drained her glass. "Fear can either make you cautious and keep you from making stupid mistakes, or it can blind you and paralyze you. *That's* the wrong side."

I nodded, understanding. "I'll try."

"One more thing. I'm saying all this because you obviously need to hear it, but I have more selfish and ulterior motives. I like you. And I like who my son is when he's around you. I've seen him change a lot, and for the better, and you can deny it all you want, but it's due in part because of you. So, yeah, I want you for my son. Plus, there're never enough women around here! I'm always outnumbered two to one… at least."

I sniffed while laughing. "You have a beautiful, amazing family, Karen. And, honestly, spending Christmas Eve with you guys has been the happiest I've been in—oh, god, *years*."

"We've all enjoyed having you here."

I blinked against the burn. "But I just can't—can't promise—" I bit my lip until the pain pushed away the turmoil of emotion. "You don't *know*, Karen. You just—you don't know." I'd only known her for a few hours, but I already felt close to this woman. I wanted to tell her everything, but I just couldn't. The words wouldn't come out.

She seemed to understand that there was nothing else to be said. Karen rose to her feet, extended both hands to me, and helped me stand up. "Come on. There's something to be said for movies that feature a bunch of shirtless men blowing things up."

I laughed and joined her in the basement, finding a spot saved for me on the huge L-shaped leather sectional. Carter was beside me, his long legs stretched out, one arm resting on the back of the couch. I didn't mean to sit so close to him, but the couch sucked me in, and his arm found its way around me, and somehow my eyes grew heavy. A heavily muscled man wearing a ripped white T-shirt wielded a machine gun with one hand, firing it with unlikely accuracy, holding on to a skinny blonde with absurdly huge tits with the other. Things blew up, including jet fighters and entire buildings.

Carter was far too comfortable for his own good. I fought it, blinked, and tried to shift away from him, but it was useless.

I fell asleep surrounded by his family, my head lolling against his shoulder. I missed the judging of the Ugly Sweater competition. It happened between parts two and three of the movie marathon, which meant I slept through an entire two-hour movie. When I woke up, all the guys were drinking Scotch and ribbing Carter about where he finds his sweaters, so I assumed he'd now won the title four years in a row.

It was well past midnight when I realized I was staying overnight at the Havens' home. Carter was tipsy, which made him the least drunk of anyone, yet for all that no one was obnoxious or rude, which had been my general experience with drunk people at parties. They were often just a little too loud, prone to slurring and making fun of each other for slurring and laughing at jokes that weren't funny to me, but which they found uproarious.

I watched Carter and his brothers as they got incrementally louder and more competitive playing Rock 'Em Sock 'Em Robots. They were playing the actual kid's game, and were taking it very seriously, it seemed. I even saw a couple of cousins put money on the outcome of the individual matches. When the competition got a little *too* fierce, Karen stepped in with a quiet but firm command to stop acting like barbarians, or to take it outside.

So Max and Carter did indeed take it outside, spinning and wrestling each other near the basement walk-out door. Tom, ever helpful, went ahead of them and opened the door so they could throw each other through it and into the piled-up drift of snow. I watched from my place on the couch, a little concerned and not a little shocked as the tussle turned serious. They were rolling around in the snow, and I thought I saw actual punches being thrown. Richard was at the opposite end of the couch from me, watching as well.

"Shouldn't someone stop them?" I asked.

Richard just waved a hand. "Those two do this every year. They're boys. They won't actually hurt each other."

"But they're rolling around in a four-foot-deep snow drift!"

He laughed. "They're both drunk. They don't even feel the cold." He smiled at me. "Carter can hold his own. Trust me on that, my dear."

Max was *huge*. He was three or four inches shorter than Carter, but outweighed him by twenty or thirty pounds—all of it solid muscle. Yet, as I watched, I realized Richard was right. Carter was consistently on top as they rolled around, and I saw him get in a few hard hits to Max's body. I cringed when Max returned them, but since no one else seemed concerned, I could only watch and hope no one ended up at the hospital.

Eventually, Max and Carter went still, lying side by side in the snow, laughing and panting. Carter stood up first, then helped his brother to his feet, only to plant a fistful of snow into Max's face, laughing and ducking as Max swung blindly. That was the end of the fight, though, both boys tromping in, soaking wet and breathing hard.

Carter peeled off his sweater and T-shirt, and I had to bite my lip to keep from moaning in appreciation. He scrubbed his hand through his hair as he stood by the sink in the basement kitchenette, picking clumps of snow from his hair and tossing them in the sink. He had a fat lip and the shadow of a bruise on his jaw, and I saw more red spots on his ribs that would turn into bruises.

I couldn't help brushing my fingers over the worst bruise on his ribs. "Are you okay?"

He snorted at me, smiling with amusement. "I'm fine. Not even bleeding."

"You guys fight like that often?"

He shrugged. "When we drink, yeah. Usually someone ends up putting somebody else in a head-lock, and then suddenly it's a wrestling match."

"Usually you don't punch each other in wrestling matches." I touched his lip, plucked a dripping clump of snow from above his ear. "But what do I know? I'm just a girl."

Carter's eyes darkened at my touch. "You gotta get in a few sucker punches."

"You're so different here. Around your family."

"Good different or bad different?" He accepted a bag of ice from Max and touched it to his lip.

I had to cross my arms to keep my hands from roaming his face, soothing his bruises. "Good different. You seem more like yourself. Relaxed."

"You've had a good time?"

I nodded. "Yeah. It's been amazing. I'm kind of sleepy, though." I couldn't bear to tell him what I really felt, how badly I wanted this family to be mine.

"You've got the room down here. I'll be on the couch over there." He pointed at a small couch tucked into a far corner near the pool table. "You fit in, you know. With us."

I smiled weakly. "Yeah." It was all I could manage.

He sensed my emotions, though. "What is it?"

I shook my head. "Just tired."

He frowned at my avoidance. "You slept through a movie and a half."

"I've gotta sleep for two, you know."

"A likely excuse." He grinned to make it a joke. "Come on, I'll show you the room."

It was a small room, just a bed and a closet and a chest of drawers, but it was somewhere to sleep. And Carter would be on the other side of the door. My skirt and T-shirt were comfortable enough to sleep in, so I kicked off my shoes, set my cardigan on top of the bureau, pulled my hair from its ponytail, and slid under the covers. Carter watched, his hand on the knob.

"Good night, Eden. Thanks for coming."

"Good night, Carter. Thank you for bringing me. It was a lot of fun."

He hesitated, as if he wanted to say something else. I hoped he didn't, because I knew my frazzled emotions couldn't take another serious conversation. In the end, he shut off the light and closed the door, leaving me in darkness except for a tiny nightlight in a plug near the floor. I felt like I was a kid again, on a sleepover at a friend's house, trying to fall asleep in an unfamiliar room. Except for the tiny foot kicking me from the inside, and the fact that I had to pee.

I felt myself falling asleep, but my bladder screamed at me, so I groaned in frustration and heaved myself out of bed. I wasn't sure if anyone was sleeping in the basement, so I twisted the doorknob as silently as I could, cracking the door open to peek through. Carter and Tom were both lounging on the sectional, glasses of Scotch in hand, feet kicked up, another shoot-'em-up movie playing on near-mute. "I don't think she thinks she deserves happiness," Carter was saying.

I knew I should close the bedroom door or make my presence known, but I couldn't do either.

"I wish I knew how to convince her."

Tom didn't answer right away, swirling the dark amber liquid in his glass. "You can't. She has to know it for herself. You can't give someone else a sense of self-worth, bro. Trust me on that one."

Carter glanced at his younger brother. "When did you learn that lesson?"

"Emily. She was a chronic self-hater. Anorexic." Tom shrugged. "I tried for almost a year to convince her that she was beautiful, but she just never believed me. Couldn't, I don't think."

"It's not like that with Eden," Carter said.

"Then what's it like?"

Carter sighed, and didn't answer for a long time. "That's not something I can get into, Tommy. Just... it's complicated, obviously."

"Yeah. A baby is a fairly big complication, I'd say."

"It's not even that, really. There's other shit. She just doesn't seem to see that I'd be willing to work past it, if she was." He scrubbed his face with one hand.

"So what are you gonna do?" Tom asked, glancing sideways at Carter.

"Bide my time," Carter said with his characteristic one-shoulder shrug. "Be there as her friend. She's worth the wait."

I backed away from the door, eyes swimming, heart pounding. I tripped over my foot and fell onto my backside against the bed, fighting for breath.

Bide my time. Worth the wait. Work past it. Could he really mean all that? Surely not.

I heard Karen's voice in my head. We can't make choices for other people.

I felt more lost than ever, more confused and mixed up than I'd ever been. Being around Carter's huge, boisterous, playful, loving family had given me a glimpse of what I'd have if I could be with Carter. It had given me hope. Made me want things I didn't know were even possible.

But they weren't possible. Were they? Could I really just…let Carter love me, fucked-up situation and all? It couldn't be that simple.

But what if it was?

The thoughts went round and round in my head until my bladder reminded me why I'd gotten up in the first place. I made sure the doorknob snapped loud enough to announce my presence. I gave the boys a shy glance and awkward wave on the way to the bathroom. When I returned to the bedroom, Carter poked his head in.

"Can I come in?"

I nodded, and patted the bed beside me. "Sure." I couldn't quite look at him.

He perched partially on the bed, facing me. "Something tells me you overheard Tom and me."

I nodded. "I didn't mean to eavesdrop."

"What'd you hear?"

"You think I don't think I deserve happiness, and you don't know how to convince me. I'm complicated, but you'd be willing to bide your time and work past it." My voice lowered to a whisper. "I'd be worth waiting for."

"So you heard all the good stuff, then." He did the Carter thing, reaching out with the middle finger of his right hand to brush the hair away from my face. "No matter what happens or doesn't happen, I'm your friend, Eden. Please remember that."

I couldn't stop a sarcastic laugh from escaping. "If you were trying to stick to the just-friends agreement, you kinda fucked that up a bit."

He didn't seem insulted. "I *am* trying. I'm just not succeeding, apparently."

"Apparently." I debated how much to say. "This has been…an incredible day. One I'll always remember."

Carter's face clouded. "Why does this feel like the beginning of a rejection?"

I picked at a loose plastic thread on the somewhat dated floral print comforter. "It's not. It's just… I'm messed up. In my own head. And I'm not sure if I'll ever get straight. If I did, and if I ever got to a place where I felt I could take on something like a relationship, you'd be my first and only choice. But I…can't. Not now. My life is so up in the air, and I feel like sooner or later Ever's gonna come looking for me and then the shit's really gonna hit the fan. I don't know what my life's gonna look like in two months, let alone two years. And I don't know how much of…of my heart I have to give." I made myself look him in the eyes. "I'm sorry. I'm just trying to give you honesty."

"So you like me."

I gave a bark of disbelieving laughter. "You missed the entire point of that whole speech, didn't you?" I shook my head. "God, Carter. Yes. I like you." That was an understatement.

"I was just being funny." He sighed, ran his hands through his hair. "Knowing where I stand is huge.

You're not leaving me in limbo or leading me on. So, for that alone, I have a lot of respect for you. And even though there's no guarantee of anything in the future, if it's all the same to you, I think I'll stick around for a while."

"Carter—"

"If I'm walking into heartbreak, that's my own choice, Eden." He stood up, backing away. "I'll be there for you, no matter what. Whether you can give me what I want in return or not, I'll be there for you." He left then, and I was bathed in darkness once more.

mistletoe reminders

Christmas Day at the Havens' was even more delightful than the day before. Breakfast was pancakes and bacon and scrambled eggs and waffles from a real waffle iron, toast and buckets of coffee (they even had decaf, miraculously) and orange juice and muffins and…more food than I knew what to do with.

Watching the family exchange gifts was…heartwarming. That was the only word for it. They had all clearly put thought and effort into buying or making a gift that suited the recipient. I loved giving gifts and I wished I'd been able to bring something for everyone, but it was nearly made up for by just watching everyone else get excited and rip open their presents. All the joyful energy of a Christmas morning.

Everyone had opened their presents, the wrapping paper was cleaned up, and then Karen reached beside her chair and handed me a slim, small package wrapped in glittery purple paper. She reached across the space between us, handing it to me.

I took it, stared at it, then looked up to Karen. "I—what? I didn't even know I was coming until Carter brought me here. I don't have—I can't…"

"You can," Karen said. "It's nothing much. Something I had that I thought you could use."

I hesitated, but everyone was staring at me and I couldn't very well refuse. So I opened it. Inside the wrapping was a thin black case, the kind of thing a necklace or bracelet would have been in. *Jared's* was written across the top.

"Don't worry, I didn't go to Jared's," Karen joked. "It was just what I had to wrap it in."

I opened the case, and inhaled sharply. Inside was a silver chain with a heart-shaped pendant. *Courage* was inscribed on one side of the heart, *Trust* on the other.

"It was a gift from Carter, actually. For Mother's Day. He was thirteen. He'd spent the winter shoveling snow to earn money, and he bought that for me himself. It was very sweet, but—"

"Completely random," Carter said. "I didn't know what to get you, and that's all the jewelry store had that I could afford."

I lifted the pendant. Courage and trust. Two things I didn't have. Two things Karen Haven seemed to instinctively know I desperately needed. "Th-thank you. So much." It was a fifteen year-old necklace that she'd probably never worn, yet it meant something to me. "I wish I'd known, I'd have—"

"Actually," Carter said, standing up, "you do have something you could give all of us."

"I do?"

He nodded, and then went to the closet by the front door and retrieved my cello case. "I went and got it early this morning. I know we'd all love to hear you play."

I closed my eyes and tried to breathe. "I don't know, I haven't prepared anything—" That was a copout, though, and I knew it. I could play fifty different pieces from memory. "Sure, I could play for a few minutes." There was a chorus of encouragement from the gathered family, Carter's voice the loudest. "I need a chair from the kitchen, though. One without armrests."

Carter brought the chair, set it in front of the fireplace facing the room. I opened Apollo's case, lifted him out, spent a moment wiping him down with the soft cloth I kept in the case. Plucked, strummed, tuned. I tried not to look at the faces watching me eagerly, expectantly. I wasn't typically nervous in front of crowds, especially once I started playing, but this was different. I settled Apollo between my knees, having to tip him back farther than normal to take into account my huge belly. I started with a piece I knew backward and forward, the intro to Bach's cello suite. It was like a warm-up for me, a familiar friend. Within a dozen strokes of my bow, I was lost to the music. God, Carter knew me so well. He knew this calmed me, knew I needed to play.

I went through the first suite in its entirety, and then paused. Part of me wanted to play my solo, but I knew I'd be emotional if I did. I was always a wreck after I played that. I glanced at Carter, found courage in his eyes.

"So…I thought I'd play something kind of special. I've been composing a suite of solos over the past few years. I've written pieces for those closest to me. My mother who passed away, my dad, my twin sister. Her husband—" My voice caught, and I forced myself to keep going, to cover over it. "Well, over the fall, I wrote a piece for someone else who has come to mean a lot to me. Carter, this is for you. It's…it's my Christmas present to you."

I closed my eyes, pushed away all thoughts and all emotions. I opened my eyes and focused on Carter, seeing only him. My bow drew across the A string, sending a high quavering note into the air. I held the note for a beat, drawing the bow back across the string, and then cut loose, my fingers flying across the fingerboard, the bow slanting and diving wildly. It was a fast, hard-driving intro-- —crazy like the crazy way we'd met. The pace slowed, turned melancholy and deep, no less complex for the slower pace. There was longing in the notes, places where the shifting of the tune seemed almost discordant, reflecting my inner turmoil over Carter. It was the longest piece I'd composed, oddly, considering I'd only known Carter for seven months. But in that short span of time, he'd managed to infiltrate my life, bringing a chaotic and turbulent mix of emotions into my life, disrupting my intentional isolation with his quiet strength and con-sistent presence. As I thought about Carter while I played, my hands had a mind of their own. They took over the cello and seemed to go haywire, flooding my normally smooth and precise style with intensity and frenetic speed and an edge of abandonment.

When the piece was finished, the room was silent for a tense heartbeat. Karen had tears in her eyes. "My god, Eden. That was…breathtaking. Thank you for sharing that with us."

I ducked my head. "Thank you for sharing your Christmas celebration with me. It's been…magical. You don't even know how much it's meant to me."

An hour later, Carter took me home. I paused at the front door of the Haven home, turned to wave goodbye to everyone. I got hugged a good twenty times, twice by Karen. "We'll see you again, right?" she asked as she stepped away from me.

I nodded. "I hope so."

Fifteen minutes later, Carter pulled up into my driveway and helped me into the house. He carried my cello for me, and I could tell he was nervous to do so by the way he held it and by how gingerly he set the case down. I hung up my coat, and turned to find Carter standing at the front door, watching me, staring at me intently.

"Thank you," he said.

"For what?"

"Everything? For coming over. For playing such beautiful music for my family. For the piece you wrote for me." He paused, licked his lips. "For being you."

I resorted to sarcasm in an effort to conceal how deeply his words touched me. "That's a stupid thing to be thankful for. Who else would I be? Michael Jordan?"

Carter gave me a disgusted look. "Eden—"

I held up my hands in surrender. "Sorry. Defense mechanism. You're welcome. And thank *you*. I didn't realize how much I was dreading Christmas alone until you showed up."

He held out his hand, and I took it, let him draw me to his chest. "I have a gift for you, too." He gestured at the far corner of the living room where a sculpture stood.

I stepped toward it, my breath stolen by the beauty of the piece. It was nearly as tall as I was and, at first glance, it seemed to be nothing more than two lengths of wood woven together. But as I got closer, details came into view. It was part of a tree, or carved to look like one, two trunks split at the root and twining together, wrapping around each other, tangled until they formed a single entity. Each trunk was entirely covered with an intricate array of Celtic knot work. The amount of work that he'd put into the knot work was simply mind-boggling. It was extraordinary, each knot threaded into the next, every available inch of wood turned into an myriad of interwoven lines and forms.

"Oh, my god, Carter. It's…I don't even have words." I looked at him, my eyes wet. "How long have you been working on that?"

He shrugged. "Couple months. I was hiking with Tommy at the start of the summer-–—before I met you-–—and I saw this tree. Two trunks, two individual trees growing side by side, but they'd grown together until they were one. It made me think even then that it'd make a great sculpture. So when I met you and heard your story, I knew I had to make this for you. It's you and Ever."

"Did you use the actual tree?" I asked.

"Oh, no way. It was a huge tree. Like, forty feet tall, three feet in diameter for each trunk. That's why it was so amazing. The tree, I mean. You see trees like that every once in a while, but they're usually small, kind of stunted. This was literally two full-grown trees, just twined together."

I didn't know what to say. I'd once felt that way about Ever and myself. As one. Totally joined, almost sharing a brain at times. Yeah, I had some petty jealousy issues, but she was my twin. Absolutely a part of me. I wasn't sure what would remain, once the pieces of the wreck I'd caused were finally out in the open.

"So you carved this from scratch?"

He nodded. "Yep. It's what I do, babe." *He called me babe again.* It made something inside me churn; I wasn't sure if it was nerves or desire or happiness, but it was intense, hearing that one word drop from his full, expressive lips.

He held me, just held me. Threaded his fingers through my hair, smoothed his hands on my back in circles. I inhaled his scent. "Thank you, Carter. It's perfect."

When I moved away, he didn't let me go. Instead, he looked at me, meaningfully. "I did one other thing while I was here grabbing your cello."

I didn't want to look up. I had a feeling I'd know what I'd see. "Oh, yeah?"

"Yeah." He smirked at me. "Look up, Eden."

"No." I shook my head against his chest. "You're making me want things I can't have."

"Who said you can't?"

"I did."

He breathed out, a long, slow, sad sound. "The only way you'll ever really take your life back is to forgive yourself."

"I don't know how."

"You fucked up. Everyone fucks up, Eden. You know my story, what I did." He put his palm to my cheek, turned my face up to his. "It doesn't have to define who you are, or determine the rest of your life. It doesn't mean you have to live a life relegated to misery."

"What if she doesn't forgive me?"

"You won't know till you ask her to."

"What if I ruined their marriage?"

He pushed my hair behind my ear. "That's between them. He messed up, too. That's not up to you." Carter touched my chin with his index finger, tipping my face up. "*Look*, Eden."

I looked. He'd hung mistletoe from the lintel of my door. My heart stuttered, maybe even stopped for a split second, and then resumed beating with a thundering frenzy. His face was suddenly closer, his eyes palest blue and fiery, intent on mine.

"Just once." His voice was a whisper, a plea.

God*damn*, I did want to kiss him. But the question was, could I kiss him just once? Or would I feel his kiss and crave it again, and again?

He was waiting for me to say yes. He wouldn't kiss me if I didn't want to. He held my face in both hands, thumbs brushing my cheekbones.

"Once," I agreed.

He took a deep breath, and I watched his tongue slide out to run over his lips. My hands were trapped between us, my palms against his chest, and I could feel his heart beating beneath my right hand. Hammering, hard and loud, just like mine. That--—the thunder of his heart—that gave me courage. He was scared, too. Nervous. Maybe he was also if he could kiss me just once.

And then thoughts were banished. His lips closed in on mine, his eyes open. And then he stopped, his lips just barely brushing mine. "You're supposed to close your eyes," he said.

I breathed a laugh. "But yours are open, too."

"Because yours are."

"So let's both close our eyes at the same time," I suggested.

He chuckled, a low rumble. "Okay. But for the record, I don't think you're supposed to laugh before a first kiss."

"Oh, yeah?" I wondered if I'd messed it up somehow. I fell back on sarcasm. "And you read this in which rule book?"

"Good point."

As quickly as it had come, the humor was gone, and the air between us crackled. Sizzled. Taut as a tightrope, fraught with all the electricity of a lightning storm. I slid my hands up, snaked them over his shoulders, clutched his neck and the back of his head. Applied the gentlest amount of pressure, a subtle encouragement. It was all he needed. His lips descended to mine, touched, shifted and moved, a whisper of mouth against mouth. My eyes were closed, and all my senses were afire. He smelled like Carter, sawdust faintly, cologne, a hint of coffee. His body was hard, filling my space, his hair soft and his chest moving against mine with each breath, his hands on my face so gentle and far too tender, and his breath was warm and his lips were warm and moist and perfect. His thighs brushed mine, his toes touched mine.

Slow and questing, the kiss grew like ivy on a wall, strong and sure.

I fell into the kiss, felt myself drowning, felt my heart opening, blooming like a rose seeking the sunlight.

We might've kissed for only a moment, or for hours. I didn't know, and didn't care.

A part of me was torn away when Carter broke the kiss. I was left on my tiptoes, eyes closed, waiting for another kiss, for more. "Once." Carter breathed the word, a reminder of his promise.

"Damn you." I went flat-footed, fisted my hands in his shirt, and rested my forehead on his chest, inhaling his scent. "You say once, and then you kiss me like that. Not fucking fair." I stepped away, forcing my feet to take me backward, deeper into the living room, farther away from him. As if to remind me of the reason why I couldn't keep kissing Carter, the baby kicked me so hard I gasped and flattened my hands on my belly. "Shit, that hurt."

Carter had me in his arms in a blink. "Are you okay?" Concern filled his voice and his eyes.

I nodded, moved away from him and took his hand in mine, placed it on my belly where the baby was kicking me. "Feel that?"

A moment of hesitation, and then Carter molded his hand to my belly, closed his eyes as the fluttering and batting of tiny feet slid against the skin of my womb. "Holy shit." He laughed, a sound of amazement and disbelief. The baby kicked *hard*, and I winced. "Damn, that must really hurt, huh?"

"Yeah, sometimes. If she kicks me in certain places, it can really hurt. Other times, it's just... fluttering."

His eyes held his awe. "I've never felt that before. It really makes it seem...I don't know—"

"Reminds you that I really do have a baby inside me," I finished for him.

"Yeah. Exactly." He took my hands, wove our fingers together, and held them up between us, chest height. "Promise me one thing?"

"If I can."

"When it's time, call me." He squeezed my hands. "False alarms, three in the morning, I don't care. Call me."

"Carter…"

He dipped down to look into my eyes. "*Promise me.*"

"I promise."

"Okay. Good." He let go of my hands and backed toward the door. "I'll see you later."

"'Bye." And then he was gone, and I was alone.

Silence had never seemed so loud.

childbirth

It started with a slight ache in my womb. No big deal. Every once in a while over the past few weeks I'd get a couple of hard pains, contractions, but they were never regular or consistent. My doctor told me that if I ever felt contractions to time them. When they were evenly spaced and regular, and got closer together and stronger, then I should go to the hospital. If there were just one or two, or if they came sporadically for a few minutes, they were false contractions. Not because they hurt any less, she was quick to add, but because they were my body practicing, basically.

So, the ache. A long, slow ache, and then it faded. Another one, half an hour later. A third, after another twenty-five minutes, slightly more painful.

Shit. Shitshitshit. Three contractions almost exactly thirty minutes apart. It was three in the afternoon, Sunday. *Maybe it's just a coincidence*, I told myself. Give it more time. So I waited another two hours. And yep, every half an hour, a tightening in my belly had me hissing. Then, at the beginning of the third hour, they got a little closer together, coming every twenty-five minutes. And then those fuckers started hurting. By seven that evening they were so painful they stole my breath. I set down the PB-and-J sandwich I'd been eating to calm my nerves. I dug my phone out, rifled through my purse until I found Carter's business card, and called him between contractions.

I ignored the red icon on my phone signaling that I had voicemails—thirty-seven of them, to be exact.

The line rang twice. "Carter."

"It's time."

"Be right there."

He was at my door in ten minutes, by which time I had a bag packed with everything I'd need. He took my bag from me, wrapped his arm around my waist. "We'll be at the hospital in about forty minutes." His eyes searched me, concerned and compassionate. "Should I call an ambulance?"

I shook my head. "No. They're still more than fifteen minutes apart, but it's for real. I've been timing them since three."

He glared at me. "Since *three?* Why didn't you call me sooner?"

He had the passenger door open and handed me in, slammed his door closed as he slid in, and the truck jerked forward as he peeled out. "We're not in a hurry, Carter. I'm not gonna have the baby in your truck." *I hope.* I clicked the seatbelt in place. "I wanted to be sure before I called you. And, anyway, from what I've read, once you're in the hospital it's just a lot of waiting and sitting through contractions, and I can do that more comfortably at home. But they're getting really painful now, and...." I trailed off, clutching my belly and hissing as a contraction speared through me, gripping me in a vise. I tried to breathe through it, and eventually it passed. "God, it's really happening. I'm gonna have this baby. I don't even know what I'm going to name her. I don't— holy shit."

Carter took my hand. "One step at a time. Let's get you to the hospital. Worry about names later."

A few minutes passed, during which my brain began to spew out all sorts of worst-case scenarios. What if there was something wrong with the baby? What if I'd had too much caffeine? Or ate the wrong food? What if...what if something went wrong during the birth and I died? What if the baby died? What if they had to do a C-section?

Another contraction gripped my body, and I clutched the door handle with one hand and Carter's hand with the other, gritting my teeth and trying to breathe through it: *one—two—three—four—five—six....*

"You've got it," Carter said, glancing at me briefly. "Breathe through it, babe. That's it."

When it passed, I gasped for breath and wiped at my forehead. "Oh, my fucking god. Those are starting to hurt." I looked at Carter, my eyes wide. "I'm scared, Carter."

"I'll be with you the whole time, Eden." We were stopped at the Garfield/M-37 intersection, and he turned to brush my sweat-damp hair away from my cheek, offering me a reassuring smile. "I promise. Okay? I won't leave your side. You're not alone."

"You're amazing."

He shook his head, focusing on the road as the light turned. "Not really."

Another few minutes of driving brought us to the Munson Medical Center. Carter parked and circled the truck, grabbed my bag from off the floorboard, and held my hand to help me down. His arm wrapped around my waist and guided me through the melting slush and swirling snow to the entrance. As we passed through the doors, a wave of pain seized me, the strongest one yet, doubling me over. I stumbled, and Carter caught me, holding on. I gripped his bicep with both hands and hung on, teeth clenched, trying not to cry.

They tell you childbirth is the some of the worst pain a human being can experience. Sounds scary enough. But I was finding out with every contraction that nothing can prepare you for the reality of childbirth contractions. There are no words to explain it, no comparisons that do it justice. And these were the just the start. When it passed, I gasped for breath and blinked away the mist in my eyes. A nurse had seen me doubled over during the contraction and brought a wheelchair over, helped me sit down. I sighed in relief. I was brought to triage first, where monitor leads were attached to my belly before I'd even changed into a hospital gown. A different nurse appeared with a laptop on a rolling cart, and started processing me for admittance. Partway through the questioning, a contraction tore through me, and I was too out of breath to answer.

The nurse, naturally enough, turned to Carter. "Has she ever had any kind of surgical procedure?"

Carter's mouth flapped. "I—um. I don't know. Not that she told me."

I sucked in a breath. "No. No surgery," I grated through clenched teeth.

"Is she allergic to any kind of medication?" She addressed the question to Carter again, who watched me. I shook my head slightly, all the motion I could manage.

"No allergies."

"Is this her first birth?"

"Yes," he said, glancing at me for confirmation. I could only incline my head slightly as I struggle to breathe through the vise-grip of the contraction.

"Any history of illness in the family?"

"I—I don't know."

The nurse seemed irritated. "You don't know."

The contraction had passed, and I slumped back against the triage bed. "He's not the father, okay? He wouldn't know any of this stuff." I wiped at my forehead. "No conditions in my family that I'm aware of. The father's…I'm not sure. I know his mother died of breast cancer, but I never heard about any other family illnesses."

The nurse was tactful enough to stick to the questionnaire, but I could sense her disapproval. I didn't know much about the father, who wasn't the same person as the man at my side. Skanky indeed. When all of the information she needed had been entered to her satisfaction, she gave me a cursory glance. "We'll get you to an L and D room in a few minutes. Just hang tight." And then she was gone in a bustle of efficiency.

"I'm sorry, I should have thought to find out—" Carter started.

I interrupted him. "Don't. Please don't apologize. You have no reason to know any of that."

I was already aware of the difference between a hospital's notion of "a few minutes" and reality, but I soon learned that when you're giving birth, the discrepancy is even more pronounced. In my case, a few minutes turned into more than an hour before someone showed up to transfer me to a labor and delivery room. The nurse gave me a gown and asked me to change into it. I stepped into the bathroom and managed to get changed before another contraction hit. I felt bare, exposed. Nobody likes hospital gowns, obviously, but when I stepped out of the bathroom wearing it, clutching it closed at my backside, I felt ugly and frumpy and awkward and naked. My hair was a sweat-tangled mess already, I was red-faced, and all my bits were on full display, and not in a sexy or attractive way.

Nothing to kill a budding romance like giving birth, right?

Carter had only ever seen me at my worst. Except for the first few weeks before I started showing, he'd only seen me gain pound after pound, retaining water and getting increasingly awkward. I couldn't imagine he'd still feel even a shred of desire for me once this birth was done. I'd seen and read enough to know it was going to be messy. Bloody. Nasty. There might possibly be poop.

That thought struck me like a lightning bolt. I crawled clumsily onto the delivery bed, covered my lower half with the thin white blanket. Carter watched me, hands in his pockets, looking slightly nervous. I felt like I should probably warn him.

"So, Carter." I pulled my hair free from the pony-tail holder, combed my fingers through it. "This is going to be messy. Just FYI."

He nodded. "Yep."

"No, I'm not sure you understand. There'll be blood. I could possibly shit myself. There might be boobage, and not in a hot and sexy Mardi Gras sort of way." I tried to sound casual, funny. "You might very well be scarred for life."

Carter laughed and moved to stand beside me. He took my hand in his. "Eden. You're not going to scare me away."

"Okay, well, I'm scaring myself off, here."

He gave me a steady smile. "You'll be fine. You'll get through it. And I'll be here the whole time. No matter what."

"Even if I poop myself?"

He laughed. "Yes, Eden. Even then."

"Why? Why would you volunteer for something like this? I can't ever repay you for everything you've done for me." Damn tears, making my eyes burn. Damn Carter, being so fucking perfect and selfless.

He brushed a tear away from my cheek with his thumb. "Eden. You still don't get it, do you?"

I shook my head. "Nope."

"I'm not offering you my services, Eden. I'm not here with you for any kind of repayment. It's not a favor, or pity, or charity. This is me spending my time with someone whose company I enjoy."

I snorted. "You like pregnant, moody, sarcastic skanks, then?"

His expression lost all traces of humor. "Don't you dare knock yourself like that, Eden Eliot. You're worth more than that. You're not a skank."

I couldn't meet his eyes. "You don't know me that well, Carter. The thing I had with Caden was the most serious relationship I've ever had. My boyfriends up until then were all…they were only about one thing. And once they got that from me and got tired of it, they moved on. You should know this about me. I have horrible taste in men, and even worse judgment."

"Because you doubt your own worth."

"Yes! I do!" Deep breaths, in and out. Don't lose it. "I always have."

"Has no one ever told you how beautiful you are?" His middle finger brushed across my temple, his eyes soft and warm and sincere. "No one has ever made you feel special and perfect for being exactly who you are?"

I shrugged. "Maybe my mom, when I was a little girl."

He sighed. "That's a sin. Seriously. You're—"

I held up my hands, feeling a contraction coming on. "STOP, CARTER! I can't—I can't handle your sweetness right now. I can't—I just can't deal with that. You're not going to fix a lifetime of low self-esteem with a few pat compliments."

Carter ducked his head. "I know. I'm not trying to fix you—"

"Yes, you are. And—oh, Jesus, oh, shit…" Pressure like a thousand tons of bricks crushed me, a giant's fist inside me squeezing.

His hands clutched mine, and I squeezed so hard it had to have hurt. "Breathe, babe. In through your nose, out through your mouth. One, two, three, four, five…." He counted calmly as the contraction wrung every ounce of strength from me, and I tried to focus on his voice.

Yet another nurse came in at that moment and introduced herself as Vicki, the night shift nurse. She attached leads to me, wrapped a strap around my belly, and plugged a cord into a circular disk on the strap. With a tap of a few buttons, the sound of a steady heartbeat filled the room.

"And there's Baby," Vicki announced. "Nice and steady. Very good. Now, you just relax and try to breathe through the contractions. Dr. Nasri will be in to check your progress in a while."

It passed, and Carter pulled up a chair to sit beside me, held my hand, and moved the conversation to other things. He told me stories of his childhood—running amok on his parents' acreage with his brothers, climbing trees and jumping dirt bikes, breaking arms and getting into fights and catching fish, adventures that got more dangerous as he and his brothers got older. He told me how they'd put all their money together when they were teenagers and bought a classic Mustang, spent two years restoring it so they could drag-race it. Kirk wrecked it the second time they raced it, rolling it a dozen times and almost getting himself killed in the process.

He passed the hours with stories, and even got me to tell him stories of my own childhood, my fights with Ever. I cracked him up with the story of the one time, when we were ten, that Ever and I did the whole *Parent Trap* thing and dressed identically to make our parents doubt their own sanity. We kept up the ruse for almost a month, answering to each other's name, one of us vanishing and the other taking over. We did it at school, too. I attended her classes and she mine, and we finished each other's sentences and spoke in tandem, playing the identical-twin card to the max. Eventually even we got sick of it.

The on-call OB, Dr. Nasri, came by around mid-night to check my progress, and said I was doing lovely, and it shouldn't be too long now. Which, in doctor-speak, meant sometime next week, I assumed. I was dilated to a five, and fifty-percent effaced, he said, which meant I was about halfway there. If I kept up the same pace, he predicted I'd deliver sometime the following afternoon.

"Has anyone asked you about drugs?" he asked. Dr. Nasri was a portly young Arabic man with a thin goatee and thick-framed glasses.

I shook my head, clenching my teeth and gripping the bed rail as a contraction rippled through me. "Drugs? What kind of drugs?"

"An epidural."

"Will it…make it stop hurting?"

He nodded. "Sure will. You'll still feel pressure, but it'll take off the lion's share of the pain."

"Drugs. Please drugs."

As the hours had passed, the contractions became stronger and stronger until each one left me panting and limp. I wasn't sure how much more I could take. Yet, I didn't have a choice. The only way out was through. If there were drugs that would make it easier, I was all for it.

The OB chuckled. "I'll send the anesthesiologist in, then. He's with another patient right now, but he'll be along as soon as possible. Keep up the good work, Miss Eliot."

"Keep up the good work?" I asked, when he was gone. "I'm not doing anything. My body is doing this all on its own."

Carter stifled a laugh. "You're dealing with it, and that's work enough."

"I'm going crazy, is what I'm doing. So if you want to call losing my shit dealing with it, then yes."

The drugs-man came by nearly two hours later. He was a short older man with a graying goatee covered by a surgical mask. He glanced at Carter. "If you're squeamish, you might want to wait out in the hall."

Carter shook his head. "I'll be fine."

The anesthesiologist helped me sit up with my legs off the edge of the bed, my gown parted to allow him access to my spine. "Bow your spine out to me, please. Good. Stare at your toes for me. Perfect. Now, deep breath. You could hold her hands if you wanted, Dad. This is a pretty big needle."

"I wish you hadn't said that," I muttered. I didn't like needles all that much. It wasn't a phobia, but they made me nervous.

Carter sat in a chair facing me, both of my hands in his. My fingers were swallowed by his huge, rough hands. "Don't think about it," he told me. "Just look at me."

I focused on Carter, on how small my hands were in his, how blue his eyes were, on the stubble shadowing his jaw. His eyes widened slightly, which I assumed meant the needle really *was* that big. He turned his eyes to me, and neither of us looked away as the needle went in. Which felt, roughly speaking, as if a giant sword had been shoved between my spine and my skin. Not awesome.

And then, once he attached the line and started the drip...bliss. A contraction had just started, and it faded away, as the OB had said, to a dull pressure.

"Oh, that's nice," I said.

"Then it's doing its job," the anesthesiologist said. "The only drawback is, you can't eat until it comes out. It has a tendency to make you a bit nauseous."

"If I'd known that, I would've eaten something better than a peanut butter sandwich for my last meal," I said.

"I'll get you whatever you want when they let you eat," Carter promised.

With a wish for good luck, the doctor took his cart of drugs away and left Carter and me alone. It was almost three in the morning by this point, and poor Carter looked exhausted.

"Why don't you go home and sleep?" I suggested. "Nothing is going to happen until tomorrow anyway."

He gave me a *yeah, right* look and drew up the visitor's lounge chair, then rocked the seat back until he was nearly horizontal, his feet propped up on the edge of the bed near my knees. "This is good." He shifted until he found a comfortable position. "You should try to sleep."

And so, on the eve of the most important day of my life, fear pounding in my veins along with my blood, I managed to sleep. The room was darkened, the only sound the muted *whump-whir-whump-whir* of the baby's heartbeat. Carter was close by, snoring gently.

I wished, as I drifted into an uneasy sleep, that I could see my sister, just once.

Seven the next evening, and I was a hundred-percent effaced, and dilated to a ten. Even with the epidural, the pressure of the contractions was dizzying and almost painful. The doctor had been paged.

It was time.

One second, it was just me and Carter and a single nurse, and then the next moment the small room was a bustle of chaos. Dr. Nasri came in, looking exhausted, accompanied by another doctor—an anesthesiologist, I was told, to take out the epidural—and a team of nurses.

Carter stood at the head of my bed, clutching my hand, watching the scurry of activity. He looked nervous, tired, and excited. "Are you ready, babe?"

I shook my head. "No. Not even close." I tried to smile at him, but couldn't. "But it's happening whether I'm ready or not, right?"

The anesthesiologist helped me sit up, and then he shut off the drip, using a key attached to his scrubs to do so. As soon as the drip stopped, feeling in my legs returned and with it a hellish wave of raw agony. Suddenly, the distant but ever increasing pressure was a roaring inferno, a crushing vise clamped on my womb and my core, a storm of fire and lightning and pressure.

The contractions were nonstop, one after another. I had to suck in a shuddering breath and grabbed at Carter's hands, tears streaming freely down my face as I gritted my teeth and tried not to scream.

"Don't push yet, Eden," Dr. Nasri told me. "Not yet. Hold on for me, okay? You're almost there. Not yet."

I had to push. Everything inside me told me to *push*, to get this thing out of me. Push. I had to push. But I couldn't. They'd said not yet.

Carter was talking, but I couldn't hear him. I watched his mouth moving. He had a beautiful mouth. It was an odd thought, stolen from the shreds of my lucidity. Lights shone on me from the ceiling, blindingly bright. The bed was transformed: a piece removed from the end of the bed so the stirrups could keep my legs apart, my upper torso angled up slightly. Dr. Nasri had a clear plastic facemask on, like something an arc welder would wear, and a nurse tugged a pair of sterilized gloves onto his hands. I saw snatches of activity, nurses preparing a little bed-incubator thing. A tray of instruments, all looking like liquid silver in the lights, medieval torture devices, it seemed. Dr. Nasri settled on a stool between my knees.

My gown had shifted, tugged down as I'd scooted up to a sitting position for the delivery. My entire left breast was exposed, but the pain was lancing through me so hard I couldn't even breathe, much less worry about it. Carter saw it, though, and pulled the edge of the gown up to cover me. I wanted to thank him, but words were impossible. My teeth ached from clenching them, my throat hurt, my eyes burned.

"Okay, Eden. On three, push for me, okay? Dad, you count for her. Count to ten, slowly." Dr. Nasri bent forward, glanced at me from between my knees. "Okay, ready? One…two…three…and *push!*"

I bore down with every muscle in my body. I heard Carter's voice from a million miles away— *one—two—three*—calm and steady, a thread of familiarity in a universe of unimaginable pain and terror. I pushed. I pushed. I grabbed the railing in a white-knuckle hold and pulled myself down as I forced every ounce of myself into the instinct to *push*.

And then I heard Carter reach ten, and Dr. Nasri told me to take a breath. "You're doing good," he said. "Just great. Okay, now push! Another good push!"

I screamed then, unable to stop it. I felt something shift between my legs, pressure splitting me apart, as if an entire world was trying to emerge from within me. Carter was counting again, and I seized on his voice. When Dr. Nasri told me to take a breath, all I could do was sob. Carter leaned down over me, both of my hands in his somehow, his eyes wide and frightened yet calm and reassuring all at once. So blue, his eyes. Pale and beautiful.

He pressed a trembling kiss to my forehead. "You're doing so good, Edie. You're doing perfect. One more for me, okay? I just saw her head. She's coming, babe."

I nodded, gripping his hands more tightly with my sweaty fingers, and prepared. I took a deep breath and bore down as hard as I could.

And then I felt something slippery happen between my thighs, accompanied by a fiery ribbon of agony slicing me, and then a sensation of emptiness. I heard Carter choke and laugh, amazed, awed.

"She's here, Edie. You did it, you did it." He whispered in my ear, and I'd never needed anyone so much as I needed him in that moment. "I'm so proud of you, babe. She's beautiful, just like you."

I wrapped my arms around his neck, clung and wept. "I did it? She's out? Is she—is she okay?" I hadn't heard her cry.

And then I did. There was a squalling, tiny and tremulous and soul-piercing.

"You have a healthy baby girl, Eden!" Dr. Nasri said, wrapping a gray and red and bloody and slimy thing in a blue papery blanket, resting her on my chest.

I sobbed as I took the bundle. A thatch of black hair. Skin and bones and blood, the umbilical cord, trailing down between my legs. Screaming and wailing, fists clenched and shaking. A pause for breath, and a peek at dark eyes that I knew would be amber.

I stared down the human being that had just been inside me. A little person, now totally dependent on me. Caden's daughter. My daughter.

Maybe it was the trauma of it all or maybe it was just exhaustion, but, strangely, I felt nothing. I felt empty. Relieved that the birth was over, but…nothing else. Exhausted, limp, torn.

But this tiny baby girl? Shouldn't I feel a sudden rush of love? An instant connection, or something? I'd read a thousand posts on various online chat lines, and all those women had written about how the instant they'd seen their baby, they'd been taken over. Love so powerful it could move mountains. Immediate and life-changing.

I felt none of that. What was wrong with me?

Dr. Nasri fixed two sets of clamps on the umbilical cord, offered a pair of medical scissors to Carter. "Daddy? Would you care to do the honors?"

Carter froze then, and I saw a million emotions rifle through him. "I—I'm not—"

I smiled at him as best I could, squeezed his arm with one weak hand. "Cut the cord for me, Carter. Please. It should be you."

The doctors and nurses surely all felt something huge and tense unfolding in that instant of hesitation, and then Carter accepted the scissors. His eyes stayed on mine, hot and roiling blue. And then he cut the cord, and I thought he might cry for a moment.

I couldn't help breaking down then. The nurses took the baby, who still had no name, and cleaned and weighed and measured her, then took her away for various tests and immunizations.

And just like that, Carter and I were alone.

I couldn't think, couldn't speak, couldn't feel. I was wrung completely dry, empty. "I'm so tired, Carter." I wanted to cry more, but I didn't even have tears. I didn't feel like a mommy. I felt like I'd been battered and bruised and broken. "Can you lie up here beside me? I just…I need you to hold me. Please."

I'd never felt more empty and vulnerable in all my life.

Carter edge a hip onto the bed, and I shifted aside, weak and sore and on the verge of passing out. I was starving suddenly, but even that was too much. I felt my eyes sliding shut, and felt Carter beside me, his arm over my shoulders, holding one of my hands.

I fell asleep trying to think of a name for the baby. And hating myself for thinking "the baby" instead of "*my* baby."

childbirth

It started with a slight ache in my womb. No big deal. Every once in a while over the past few weeks I'd get a couple of hard pains, contractions, but they were never regular or consistent. My doctor told me that if I ever felt contractions to time them. When they were evenly spaced and regular, and got closer together and stronger, then I should go to the hospital. If there were just one or two, or if they came sporadically for a few minutes, they were false contractions. Not because they hurt any less, she was quick to add, but because they were my body practicing, basically.

So, the ache. A long, slow ache, and then it faded. Another one, half an hour later. A third, after another twenty-five minutes, slightly more painful.

Shit. Shitshitshit. Three contractions almost exactly thirty minutes apart. It was three in the afternoon, Sunday. *Maybe it's just a coincidence*, I told myself. Give it more time. So I waited another two hours. And yep, every half an hour, a tightening in my belly had me hissing. Then, at the beginning of the third hour, they got a little closer together, coming every twenty-five minutes. And then those fuckers started hurting. By seven that evening they were so painful they stole my breath. I set down the PB-and-J sandwich I'd been eating to calm my nerves. I dug my phone out, rifled through my purse until I found Carter's business card, and called him between contractions.

I ignored the red icon on my phone signaling that I had voicemails—thirty-seven of them, to be exact.

The line rang twice. "Carter."

"It's time."

"Be right there."

He was at my door in ten minutes, by which time I had a bag packed with everything I'd need. He took my bag from me, wrapped his arm around my waist. "We'll be at the hospital in about forty minutes." His eyes searched me, concerned and compassionate. "Should I call an ambulance?"

I shook my head. "No. They're still more than fifteen minutes apart, but it's for real. I've been timing them since three."

He glared at me. "Since *three?* Why didn't you call me sooner?"

He had the passenger door open and handed me in, slammed his door closed as he slid in, and the truck jerked forward as he peeled out. "We're not in a hurry, Carter. I'm not gonna have the baby in your truck." *I hope.* I clicked the seatbelt in place. "I wanted to be sure before I called you. And, anyway, from what I've read, once you're in the hospital it's just a lot of waiting and sitting through contractions, and I can do that more comfortably at home. But they're getting really painful now, and…." I trailed off, clutching my belly and hissing as a contraction speared through me, gripping me in a vise. I tried to breathe through it, and eventually it passed. "God, it's really happening. I'm gonna have this baby. I don't even know what I'm going to name her. I don't— holy shit."

Carter took my hand. "One step at a time. Let's get you to the hospital. Worry about names later."

A few minutes passed, during which my brain began to spew out all sorts of worst-case scenarios. What if there was something wrong with the baby? What if I'd had too much caffeine? Or ate the wrong food? What if…what if something went wrong during the birth and I died? What if the baby died? What if they had to do a C-section?

Another contraction gripped my body, and I clutched the door handle with one hand and Carter's hand with the other, gritting my teeth and trying to breathe through it: *one—two—three—four—five—six....*

"You've got it," Carter said, glancing at me briefly. "Breathe through it, babe. That's it."

When it passed, I gasped for breath and wiped at my forehead. "Oh, my fucking god. Those are starting to hurt." I looked at Carter, my eyes wide. "I'm scared, Carter."

"I'll be with you the whole time, Eden." We were stopped at the Garfield/M-37 intersection, and he turned to brush my sweat-damp hair away from my cheek, offering me a reassuring smile. "I promise. Okay? I won't leave your side. You're not alone."

"You're amazing."

He shook his head, focusing on the road as the light turned. "Not really."

Another few minutes of driving brought us to the Munson Medical Center. Carter parked and circled the truck, grabbed my bag from off the floorboard, and held my hand to help me down. His arm wrapped around my waist and guided me through the melting slush and swirling snow to the entrance. As we passed through the doors, a wave of pain seized me, the strongest one yet, doubling me over. I stumbled, and Carter caught me, holding on. I gripped his bicep with both hands and hung on, teeth clenched, trying not to cry.

They tell you childbirth is the some of the worst pain a human being can experience. Sounds scary enough. But I was finding out with every contraction that nothing can prepare you for the reality of childbirth contractions. There are no words to explain it, no comparisons that do it justice. And these were the just the start. When it passed, I gasped for breath and blinked away the mist in my eyes. A nurse had seen me doubled over during the contraction and brought a wheelchair over, helped me sit down. I sighed in relief. I was brought to triage first, where monitor leads were attached to my belly before I'd even changed into a hospital gown. A different nurse appeared with a laptop on a rolling cart, and started processing me for admittance. Partway through the questioning, a contraction tore through me, and I was too out of breath to answer.

The nurse, naturally enough, turned to Carter. "Has she ever had any kind of surgical procedure?"

Carter's mouth flapped. "I—um. I don't know. Not that she told me."

I sucked in a breath. "No. No surgery," I grated through clenched teeth.

"Is she allergic to any kind of medication?" She addressed the question to Carter again, who watched me. I shook my head slightly, all the motion I could manage.

"No allergies."

"Is this her first birth?"

"Yes," he said, glancing at me for confirmation. I could only incline my head slightly as I struggle to breathe through the vise-grip of the contraction.

"Any history of illness in the family?"

"I—I don't know."

The nurse seemed irritated. "You don't know."

The contraction had passed, and I slumped back against the triage bed. "He's not the father, okay? He wouldn't know any of this stuff." I wiped at my forehead. "No conditions in my family that I'm aware of. The father's…I'm not sure. I know his mother died of breast cancer, but I never heard about any other family illnesses."

The nurse was tactful enough to stick to the questionnaire, but I could sense her disapproval. I didn't know much about the father, who wasn't the same person as the man at my side. Skanky indeed. When all of the information she needed had been entered to her satisfaction, she gave me a cursory glance. "We'll get you to an L and D room in a few minutes. Just hang tight." And then she was gone in a bustle of efficiency.

"I'm sorry, I should have thought to find out—" Carter started.

I interrupted him. "Don't. Please don't apologize. You have no reason to know any of that."

I was already aware of the difference between a hospital's notion of "a few minutes" and reality, but I soon learned that when you're giving birth, the discrepancy is even more pronounced. In my case, a few minutes turned into more than an hour before someone showed up to transfer me to a labor and delivery room. The nurse gave me a gown and asked me to change into it. I stepped into the bathroom and managed to get changed before another contraction hit. I felt bare, exposed. Nobody likes hospital gowns, obviously, but when I stepped out of the bathroom wearing it, clutching it closed at my backside, I felt ugly and frumpy and awkward and naked. My hair was a sweat-tangled mess already, I was red-faced, and all my bits were on full display, and not in a sexy or attractive way.

Nothing to kill a budding romance like giving birth, right?

Carter had only ever seen me at my worst. Except for the first few weeks before I started showing, he'd only seen me gain pound after pound, retaining water and getting increasingly awkward. I couldn't imagine he'd still feel even a shred of desire for me once this birth was done. I'd seen and read enough to know it was going to be messy. Bloody. Nasty. There might possibly be poop.

That thought struck me like a lightning bolt. I crawled clumsily onto the delivery bed, covered my lower half with the thin white blanket. Carter watched me, hands in his pockets, looking slightly nervous. I felt like I should probably warn him.

"So, Carter." I pulled my hair free from the pony-tail holder, combed my fingers through it. "This is going to be messy. Just FYI."

He nodded. "Yep."

"No, I'm not sure you understand. There'll be blood. I could possibly shit myself. There might be boobage, and not in a hot and sexy Mardi Gras sort of way." I tried to sound casual, funny. "You might very well be scarred for life."

Carter laughed and moved to stand beside me. He took my hand in his. "Eden. You're not going to scare me away."

"Okay, well, I'm scaring myself off, here."

He gave me a steady smile. "You'll be fine. You'll get through it. And I'll be here the whole time. No matter what."

"Even if I poop myself?"

He laughed. "Yes, Eden. Even then."

"Why? Why would you volunteer for something like this? I can't ever repay you for everything you've done for me." Damn tears, making my eyes burn. Damn Carter, being so fucking perfect and selfless.

He brushed a tear away from my cheek with his thumb. "Eden. You still don't get it, do you?"

I shook my head. "Nope."

"I'm not offering you my services, Eden. I'm not here with you for any kind of repayment. It's not a favor, or pity, or charity. This is me spending my time with someone whose company I enjoy."

I snorted. "You like pregnant, moody, sarcastic skanks, then?"

His expression lost all traces of humor. "Don't you dare knock yourself like that, Eden Eliot. You're worth more than that. You're not a skank."

I couldn't meet his eyes. "You don't know me that well, Carter. The thing I had with Caden was the most serious relationship I've ever had. My boyfriends up until then were all…they were only about one thing. And once they got that from me and got tired of it, they moved on. You should know this about me. I have horrible taste in men, and even worse judgment."

"Because you doubt your own worth."

"Yes! I do!" Deep breaths, in and out. Don't lose it. "I always have."

"Has no one ever told you how beautiful you are?" His middle finger brushed across my temple, his eyes soft and warm and sincere. "No one has ever made you feel special and perfect for being exactly who you are?"

I shrugged. "Maybe my mom, when I was a little girl."

He sighed. "That's a sin. Seriously. You're—"

I held up my hands, feeling a contraction coming on. "STOP, CARTER! I can't—I can't handle your sweetness right now. I can't—I just can't deal with that. You're not going to fix a lifetime of low self-esteem with a few pat compliments."

Carter ducked his head. "I know. I'm not trying to fix you—"

"Yes, you are. And—oh, Jesus, oh, shit…" Pressure like a thousand tons of bricks crushed me, a giant's fist inside me squeezing.

His hands clutched mine, and I squeezed so hard it had to have hurt. "Breathe, babe. In through your nose, out through your mouth. One, two, three, four, five…." He counted calmly as the contraction wrung every ounce of strength from me, and I tried to focus on his voice.

Yet another nurse came in at that moment and introduced herself as Vicki, the night shift nurse. She attached leads to me, wrapped a strap around my belly, and plugged a cord into a circular disk on the strap. With a tap of a few buttons, the sound of a steady heartbeat filled the room.

"And there's Baby," Vicki announced. "Nice and steady. Very good. Now, you just relax and try to breathe through the contractions. Dr. Nasri will be in to check your progress in a while."

It passed, and Carter pulled up a chair to sit beside me, held my hand, and moved the conversation to other things. He told me stories of his childhood—running amok on his parents' acreage with his brothers, climbing trees and jumping dirt bikes, breaking arms and getting into fights and catching fish, adventures that got more dangerous as he and his brothers got older. He told me how they'd put all their money together when they were teenagers and bought a classic Mustang, spent two years restoring it so they could drag-race it. Kirk wrecked it the second time they raced it, rolling it a dozen times and almost getting himself killed in the process.

He passed the hours with stories, and even got me to tell him stories of my own childhood, my fights with Ever. I cracked him up with the story of the one time, when we were ten, that Ever and I did the whole *Parent Trap* thing and dressed identically to make our parents doubt their own sanity. We kept up the ruse for almost a month, answering to each other's name, one of us vanishing and the other taking over. We did it at school, too. I attended her classes and she mine, and we finished each other's sentences and spoke in tandem, playing the identical-twin card to the max. Eventually even we got sick of it.

The on-call OB, Dr. Nasri, came by around midnight to check my progress, and said I was doing lovely, and it shouldn't be too long now. Which, in doctor-speak, meant sometime next week, I assumed. I was dilated to a five, and fifty-percent effaced, he said, which meant I was about halfway there. If I kept up the same pace, he predicted I'd deliver sometime the following afternoon.

"Has anyone asked you about drugs?" he asked. Dr. Nasri was a portly young Arabic man with a thin goatee and thick-framed glasses.

I shook my head, clenching my teeth and gripping the bed rail as a contraction rippled through me. "Drugs? What kind of drugs?"

"An epidural."

"Will it...make it stop hurting?"

He nodded. "Sure will. You'll still feel pressure, but it'll take off the lion's share of the pain."

"Drugs. Please drugs."

As the hours had passed, the contractions became stronger and stronger until each one left me panting and limp. I wasn't sure how much more I could take. Yet, I didn't have a choice. The only way out was through. If there were drugs that would make it easier, I was all for it.

The OB chuckled. "I'll send the anesthesiologist in, then. He's with another patient right now, but he'll be along as soon as possible. Keep up the good work, Miss Eliot."

"Keep up the good work?" I asked, when he was gone. "I'm not doing anything. My body is doing this all on its own."

Carter stifled a laugh. "You're dealing with it, and that's work enough."

"I'm going crazy, is what I'm doing. So if you want to call losing my shit dealing with it, then yes."

The drugs-man came by nearly two hours later. He was a short older man with a graying goatee covered by a surgical mask. He glanced at Carter. "If you're squeamish, you might want to wait out in the hall."

Carter shook his head. "I'll be fine."

The anesthesiologist helped me sit up with my legs off the edge of the bed, my gown parted to allow him access to my spine. "Bow your spine out to me, please. Good. Stare at your toes for me. Perfect. Now, deep breath. You could hold her hands if you wanted, Dad. This is a pretty big needle."

"I wish you hadn't said that," I muttered. I didn't like needles all that much. It wasn't a phobia, but they made me nervous.

Carter sat in a chair facing me, both of my hands in his. My fingers were swallowed by his huge, rough hands. "Don't think about it," he told me. "Just look at me."

I focused on Carter, on how small my hands were in his, how blue his eyes were, on the stubble shadowing his jaw. His eyes widened slightly, which I assumed meant the needle really *was* that big. He turned his eyes to me, and neither of us looked away as the needle went in. Which felt, roughly speaking, as if a giant sword had been shoved between my spine and my skin. Not awesome.

And then, once he attached the line and started the drip…bliss. A contraction had just started, and it faded away, as the OB had said, to a dull pressure.

"Oh, that's nice," I said.

"Then it's doing its job," the anesthesiologist said. "The only drawback is, you can't eat until it comes out. It has a tendency to make you a bit nauseous."

"If I'd known that, I would've eaten something better than a peanut butter sandwich for my last meal," I said.

"I'll get you whatever you want when they let you eat," Carter promised.

With a wish for good luck, the doctor took his cart of drugs away and left Carter and me alone. It was almost three in the morning by this point, and poor Carter looked exhausted.

"Why don't you go home and sleep?" I suggested. "Nothing is going to happen until tomorrow anyway."

He gave me a *yeah, right* look and drew up the visitor's lounge chair, then rocked the seat back until he was nearly horizontal, his feet propped up on the edge of the bed near my knees. "This is good." He shifted until he found a comfortable position. "You should try to sleep."

And so, on the eve of the most important day of my life, fear pounding in my veins along with my blood, I managed to sleep. The room was darkened, the only sound the muted *whump-whir-whump-whir* of the baby's heartbeat. Carter was close by, snoring gently.

I wished, as I drifted into an uneasy sleep, that I could see my sister, just once.

Seven the next evening, and I was a hundred-percent effaced, and dilated to a ten. Even with the epidural, the pressure of the contractions was dizzying and almost painful. The doctor had been paged.

It was time.

One second, it was just me and Carter and a single nurse, and then the next moment the small room was a bustle of chaos. Dr. Nasri came in, looking exhausted, accompanied by another doctor—an anesthesiologist, I was told, to take out the epidural—and a team of nurses.

Carter stood at the head of my bed, clutching my hand, watching the scurry of activity. He looked nervous, tired, and excited. "Are you ready, babe?"

I shook my head. "No. Not even close." I tried to smile at him, but couldn't. "But it's happening whether I'm ready or not, right?"

The anesthesiologist helped me sit up, and then he shut off the drip, using a key attached to his scrubs to do so. As soon as the drip stopped, feeling in my legs returned and with it a hellish wave of raw agony. Suddenly, the distant but ever increasing pressure was a roaring inferno, a crushing vise clamped on my womb and my core, a storm of fire and lightning and pressure.

The contractions were nonstop, one after another. I had to suck in a shuddering breath and grabbed at Carter's hands, tears streaming freely down my face as I gritted my teeth and tried not to scream.

"Don't push yet, Eden," Dr. Nasri told me. "Not yet. Hold on for me, okay? You're almost there. Not yet."

I had to push. Everything inside me told me to *push*, to get this thing out of me. Push. I had to push. But I couldn't. They'd said not yet.

Carter was talking, but I couldn't hear him. I watched his mouth moving. He had a beautiful mouth. It was an odd thought, stolen from the shreds of my lucidity. Lights shone on me from the ceiling, blindingly bright. The bed was transformed: a piece removed from the end of the bed so the stirrups could keep my legs apart, my upper torso angled up slightly. Dr. Nasri had a clear plastic facemask on, like something an arc welder would wear, and a nurse tugged a pair of sterilized gloves onto his hands. I saw snatches of activity, nurses preparing a little bed-in-cubator thing. A tray of instruments, all looking like liquid silver in the lights, medieval torture devices, it seemed. Dr. Nasri settled on a stool between my knees.

My gown had shifted, tugged down as I'd scooted up to a sitting position for the delivery. My entire left breast was exposed, but the pain was lancing through me so hard I couldn't even breathe, much less worry about it. Carter saw it, though, and pulled the edge of the gown up to cover me. I wanted to thank him, but words were impossible. My teeth ached from clenching them, my throat hurt, my eyes burned.

"Okay, Eden. On three, push for me, okay? Dad, you count for her. Count to ten, slowly." Dr. Nasri bent forward, glanced at me from between my knees. "Okay, ready? One…two…three…and *push!*"

I bore down with every muscle in my body. I heard Carter's voice from a million miles away—*one—two—three*—calm and steady, a thread of familiarity in a universe of unimaginable pain and terror. I pushed. I pushed. I grabbed the railing in a white-knuckle hold and pulled myself down as I forced every ounce of myself into the instinct to *push.*

And then I heard Carter reach ten, and Dr. Nasri told me to take a breath. "You're doing good," he said. "Just great. Okay, now push! Another good push!"

I screamed then, unable to stop it. I felt something shift between my legs, pressure splitting me apart, as if an entire world was trying to emerge from within me. Carter was counting again, and I seized on his voice. When Dr. Nasri told me to take a breath, all I could do was sob. Carter leaned down over me, both of my hands in his somehow, his eyes wide and frightened yet calm and reassuring all at once. So blue, his eyes. Pale and beautiful.

He pressed a trembling kiss to my forehead. "You're doing so good, Edie. You're doing perfect. One more for me, okay? I just saw her head. She's coming, babe."

I nodded, gripping his hands more tightly with my sweaty fingers, and prepared. I took a deep breath and bore down as hard as I could.

And then I felt something slippery happen between my thighs, accompanied by a fiery ribbon of agony slicing me, and then a sensation of emptiness. I heard Carter choke and laugh, amazed, awed.

"She's here, Edie. You did it, you did it." He whispered in my ear, and I'd never needed anyone so much as I needed him in that moment. "I'm so proud of you, babe. She's beautiful, just like you."

I wrapped my arms around his neck, clung and wept. "I did it? She's out? Is she—is she okay?" I hadn't heard her cry.

And then I did. There was a squalling, tiny and tremulous and soul-piercing.

"You have a healthy baby girl, Eden!" Dr. Nasri said, wrapping a gray and red and bloody and slimy thing in a blue papery blanket, resting her on my chest.

I sobbed as I took the bundle. A thatch of black hair. Skin and bones and blood, the umbilical cord, trailing down between my legs. Screaming and wailing, fists clenched and shaking. A pause for breath, and a peek at dark eyes that I knew would be amber.

I stared down the human being that had just been inside me. A little person, now totally dependent on me. Caden's daughter. My daughter.

Maybe it was the trauma of it all or maybe it was just exhaustion, but, strangely, I felt nothing. I felt empty. Relieved that the birth was over, but…nothing else. Exhausted, limp, torn.

But this tiny baby girl? Shouldn't I feel a sudden rush of love? An instant connection, or something? I'd read a thousand posts on various online chat lines, and all those women had written about how the instant they'd seen their baby, they'd been taken over. Love so powerful it could move mountains. Immediate and life-changing.

I felt none of that. What was wrong with me?

Dr. Nasri fixed two sets of clamps on the umbilical cord, offered a pair of medical scissors to Carter. "Daddy? Would you care to do the honors?"

Carter froze then, and I saw a million emotions rifle through him. "I—I'm not—"

I smiled at him as best I could, squeezed his arm with one weak hand. "Cut the cord for me, Carter. Please. It should be you."

The doctors and nurses surely all felt something huge and tense unfolding in that instant of hesitation, and then Carter accepted the scissors. His eyes stayed on mine, hot and roiling blue. And then he cut the cord, and I thought he might cry for a moment.

I couldn't help breaking down then. The nurses took the baby, who still had no name, and cleaned and weighed and measured her, then took her away for various tests and immunizations.

And just like that, Carter and I were alone.

I couldn't think, couldn't speak, couldn't feel. I was wrung completely dry, empty. "I'm so tired, Carter." I wanted to cry more, but I didn't even have tears. I didn't feel like a mommy. I felt like I'd been battered and bruised and broken. "Can you lie up here beside me? I just…I need you to hold me. Please."

I'd never felt more empty and vulnerable in all my life.

Carter edge a hip onto the bed, and I shifted aside, weak and sore and on the verge of passing out. I was starving suddenly, but even that was too much. I felt my eyes sliding shut, and felt Carter beside me, his arm over my shoulders, holding one of my hands.

I fell asleep trying to think of a name for the baby. And hating myself for thinking "the baby" instead of "*my* baby."

ruins

Caden

"Turn right," Ever told me, pointing at a narrow dirt road, lined with skeleton-finger trees.

I turned, and the road wound around a corner, past a tiny post office and an abandoned old clapboard house with a crumbled lean-to of a front porch, overgrown with ivy and saplings and knee-high grass, and then the bay was visible, glinting through trees. Beside me, Ever was a ball of nerves. With every mile that brought us farther north, the more tense she got.

And then, without warning, we were there. A small yellow house facing the bay. In the driveway, Eden's VW Passat.

"She's here," Ever said, her voice catching. "That's her car. She's here." She was out of the car before I even had it stopped completely, running up the short sidewalk to the front door, pounding on the new-looking storm door. "EDEN!"

There was no answer. Was she hiding? I couldn't picture Eden sitting in a room, ignoring the pounding of a fist on her door and her twin sister's voice.

There was no room in the road for me to park, and the driveway was taken, so I had to go down a ways and park in the beach lot. Ever tried the door, found it unlocked, and went in. I followed at a distance, fear making my heart hammer. By the time I got to the door, Ever was emerging, breathless and confused.

"She's not here," Ever said, slumping down to sit on the top step, heedless of the damp on her jeans. "Her stuff is here. Apollo is there, books, food. There's a crust of a sandwich on the table, like she just—just stepped out. But she's gone."

"Maybe she's on a run?" I suggested.

Ever shook her head. "No. I saw her iPod and running shoes in her room. She wouldn't go running without that stuff."

"She might've just…gone somewhere. She'll be right back. She wouldn't leave her house open like this for long. Not with Apollo right out in the open." I couldn't make any more sense of it than Ever could, and I hated that a part of me was relieved to put off the truth a little longer.

"Yeah," Ever agreed. "Let's just wait here for a minute. See if she comes back."

We sat in silence on the steps for half an hour, and then my nerves took over. "Let's go down to the beach. We'll stay where we can see her when she comes back," I said, standing up and offering Ever my hand.

We walked on the beach, keeping an eye on the little yellow house. Hand in hand, despite the fact that mine were shaking ever so subtly, despite the fact that, when Eden showed up, everything would change.

An hour passed and the sun descended on the bay, casting long shadows and shedding golden light over everything. I was about to suggest we leave and come back the next day, and then I felt a clenching in my chest, a knowledge. I shaded my eyes with my hand, watching the road. A faint rumbling of an engine, and then a classic '60s pickup truck rolled into view, stopping in her driveway.

Ever had followed my gaze, standing frozen in place. "Eden."

A lean, dark-haired man hurried around the hood and opened the passenger door, and Eden stepped out of the truck, moving gingerly, as if sore or injured. And then she reached back into the truck and lifted out a baby carrier.

My blood turned to ice. Stopped in my veins.

"What?" I heard Ever whisper beside me.

Eden stood in the driveway, holding the baby carrier with both hands, staring over at us. The man took the carrier, and Eden stumbled, sagged against him. His gaze looked up and he saw us, too. Eden said something to the man, and he nodded, then took the carrier into the house. Eden approached us, each step careful and slow.

Ever came unstuck, rushing sobbing, to her sister. She slammed into her, wrapped her arms around Eden's neck, crying. "Eden—Eden. God, it's really you."

Eden physically flinched at the contact, and I saw her wince in pain, and then her arms went hesitantly around Ever. "You're here."

Ever let go, stepped back. "I have so many questions. But…did I just see a—a *baby?*"

Eden ducked her head, and her hands went to her belly and then dropped away, as if she'd started to perform a familiar gesture and then stopped. "You should come inside." She looked up at me. "Both of you."

In that moment, I knew. I knew why she'd run. My throat was thick, my heart no longer pounding but rather stuttering in a staccato rhythm.

We followed Eden across the road and into the house.

Ever stopped just in the doorway, hand over her mouth. "It looks so different than I remember."

"Carter remodeled it. The place was falling down around me when I first got here." Eden gestured to the man who'd driven the truck. He was a few inches taller than I, but leaner. He had black hair and pale blue eyes, and he was watching Eden carefully.

He stepped forward, held out his hand to me. "I'm Carter Haven. You must be Caden." He shook my hand, and then held out his hand to Ever. "And you're Ever."

Ever and I exchanged a bewildered glance. "Nice to meet you, Carter," Ever said.

"You're the sculptor," I said, because my mouth was running on its own, spitting out inanities to put off the inevitable. "We saw your woodworking sculptures downtown.

Carter nodded. "Yeah, that'd be me. I have a few pieces displayed in a gallery there."

Eden sat down on the couch, lowering herself slowly, a hand on the armrest to support her weight. "Are we seriously talking about Carter's sculptures right now?"

As if to emphasize Eden's point, the urgent wail of a newborn baby filled the living room. Every eye fixed on the carrier. Carter was the first to move, kneeling on the floor to unbuckle the baby and lift it out, wrapping it in a swaddling blanket. He held the baby in his arms, staring from the baby to Eden, and then to me and Ever. He knew.

We didn't even know, but this guy knew.

I had no right to be angry about that, but I was. But then, I did have a right to be angry, didn't I? My emotions churned, spiraling out of control from angry to panicked to devastated to confused.

Ever stared at the bundle in Carter's arms. Stepped forward. Reached, glancing at Eden. She took the little baby in her arms, her expression too turbulent to read. "You had a *baby?*"

I moved to stand beside her, and looked down at the tiny face. I saw my own eyes staring back at me, and my knees went weak. Buckled.

Ever wasn't breathing. Just staring. I saw the moment when understanding fully penetrated. Her shoulders shook, and she curled over the baby in her arms. Her head seemed suddenly too heavy to be supported by her neck. I wrapped my arm around her shoulders to keep her upright, and she jerked away as if burned.

"*DON'T!*" she hissed. "You—you get away from me."

A tear started down my cheek at the viper venom in her voice. I wiped it away quickly, harshly. "Ever,

I—" I didn't even know what I was going to say, but she cut me off.

"Shut up. Just shut—shut up." She stepped away, toward the kitchen, the baby clutched in her arms, turning to face us all. Her face was a rictus of agony. "Eden…how—how *could* you?"

Eden didn't respond. Just sat with her hands folded on her lap, shoulders hunched.

"It's his, isn't it?"

"She. It's—it's a girl," Eden whispered.

"A girl." Ever looked back down at the baby, who had gone quiet. "What's…what's her name?"

"She doesn't have one yet. I didn't know what—" Eden's voice faltered, gave out.

"She's his, isn't she? Caden's?" Ever glanced at me, and then away. She seemed to not even recognize me. "Of course she is. Who else's could she be? Why else would you vanish like you did? You've been gone for seven months, so she can't be *his*." Ever jerked her head at Carter, who had sat down beside Eden.

"Yes," Eden whispered, barely audible. "She's Caden's."

I should say something, but I didn't know what. I could only stare at Ever, at the baby. At my *daughter*.

Ever shuffled forward, stopped in front of Carter and Eden. Held out the baby. Carter stood up, took her, and sat back down. He offered her to Eden, who shook her head, choking on sobs. "I—can't. I can't right now."

Ever turned away, her arms wrapped around her middle, head hanging. "I don't have a uterus," she whispered. Then she turned around to face Eden. "Did you know that? That I had been pregnant, and I lost it? They had to cut my womb out of my body. Did you know that? Did you know they took my uterus from me? Did you know I'll never have a baby?"

Eden nodded. "Yes. I know."

I was frozen in place, silent, immobilized. Numb.

"You were pregnant," Ever said. "With my *husband's* baby. And you ran. You didn't tell us. We thought—I thought you were dead. I didn't know where you were. Or what had happened. Why did you abandon me when I needed you most?"

"How could I tell you?" Eden asked, standing up. "You'd just come out of a coma. I'd just found out I was pregnant. You—you could barely *talk*. You couldn't walk, or even go to the bathroom on your own. How was I supposed to tell you that I was... that I'd—"

"That you'd *fucked* my husband?"

Eden flinched as if struck. Tears sluiced down her face. "I didn't know how to tell you. I was *scared*, Ever! I've been terrified for nine fucking months!"

"You dropped off the face of the planet. You vanished without a backward glance. Without a word."

"I said goodbye," Eden mumbled.

"You left me! You abandoned me! I needed you, and you—you—" Ever couldn't finish. She was crying too hard.

I wanted to comfort her, but I couldn't.

No one spoke for a long time.

Eventually, finally, Ever turned her eyes to me. "Did you know?"

I shook my head, barely able to do even that. "N—" My voice cracked, broke, and I started over. "No. I didn't know."

"You fucked my twin sister. While I was in a coma." Ever took a step toward me, and I'd never seen such hate in her eyes, such violence. "You slept with *MY SISTER!*" She slammed both fists into my chest, knocking me backward; she followed me, striking me again. I took the blows, accepted them silently.

"I'm sorry." I stood and let her smash her fists on my chest a third time. "I'm sorry, Ever. I was…fucked up. So messed up. I know there's—I know there's no explanation, no excuse, but—you don't know what it was like for me. While you were—"

"In a *coma!*" Ever straightened and stepped away from me, gasping for breath, grasping for composure. She looked from me, to Eden, to the baby in

Carter's arms. "I have to go. I have to get out of here. I can't—I can't even look at you. At any of you." She turned away, fists clenched and shaking.

Eden hobbled slowly to the dining room table, where her purse sat beside her overnight bag. She dug through her purse until she found her keys. She shuffled over to stand beside her sister, holding out the keys to her car. "I understand if you—if you don't come back. I just—please know that—that I'm sorry. That I love you. You're my sister. My only family, and I never—I never wanted to hurt you. Or betray you. And—and I'm sorry. I'm so sorry."

Ever stood completely still, not looking at her twin or at me. A long, tense moment passed, and then Ever snatched the keys, jerked the door open violently, stepped through it, letting it slam behind her and then she was gone. Not a single look back. An engine roared, and then gravel spat under spinning tires.

She was gone.

I couldn't breathe. My heart wasn't beating. My mind was an empty chasm. My legs carried me to the door, and outside. Into the cold.

I heard a shuffle behind me, and then Carter's voice. "Let him go, Eden."

My feet carried me at a dead run across the road, down the beach, and onto a dock jutting out into the water. The sun was low, its bottom edge resting on the water. The wind blew, knife-edge cold. My boots echoed on the metal dock, and I tripped, fell to my knees on the frigid metal. I choked, gasped, and then broke apart.

Eden had my baby. *My baby.* My daughter. I sobbed, coughing, wracked with pain. She'd run off because she was pregnant. And now Ever was gone, and I'd never see her again. I opened my eyes and looked down into the dark, rippling water. Maybe I could just fall forward into the cold blue and never come up. That'd be easier. Nothing mattered, not without Ever. She was all I had, all I would ever have, and she was gone. She hadn't even looked at me.

Slow footsteps rattled the dock. I turned around, saw Eden approaching me, a thick coat on, the hood drawn, hands in the pockets. She stopped several feet from me. "I'm sorry, Caden. I didn't know what else to do. I panicked, and then…days turned into weeks, and I just didn't know how to tell you. How to tell her. And then it felt like it was too late to just—show up. I should've told you, but I couldn't. You had to take care of Ever, and she'd just—and she was so frag-ile—and…" She trailed off, staring out at the water.

I forced myself to my feet. "I don't even know what to say. What to think." I turned to look at the road down which Ever had disappeared, as if I could conjure her from where I was. "Think she'll ever come back?"

Eden shrugged, a tiny, defeated motion. "I don't know."

"What do we do now?" I asked.

"I don't know." She tipped her head back, shuddering. "*Fuck*, I don't *know!* I don't know who I am anymore. I don't know what to do. Where to go. How I'm going to—to make it. How I'm going to survive this. I don't know how to be a *mother*, Caden! I don't know anything. Not anything at all."

"You've had nine *god*damned months to get used to the idea that you're gonna be a mother!" I shouted. "I just found out five fucking minutes ago! How am I supposed to suddenly be a father? How am I—how am I supposed to do anything without her?"

An icy wind blew, and Eden shivered.

"You shouldn't be out here," I said.

Back inside, Eden shed her coat, and accepted the crying baby from a frazzled-looking Carter.

"I think she's hungry," he said, visibly relieved that she was back.

Eden dug with one hand through the overnight bag on the table, found a four-pack of tiny little bottles of tan liquid, as well as a bottle. Carter took the bottle and opened it, fixed the nipple to it, handed it back to Eden, who sat down on the couch with the baby in her arms. The baby mewled and whimpered, cried out, and then settled in to sucking as Eden tickled her mouth with the bottle.

I watched in misery, confusion, and amazement. That teeny little thing in Eden's arms was a part of me. It felt surreal. I moved to sit on the opposite end of the couch and reached out. "Let me." I didn't know what prompted me, but it felt right.

Eden stared at me for a moment and then leaned toward me, settling the baby carefully in the cradle of my arms. I hadn't thought I would know how to hold her, but as soon as the warm bundle touched my arms, I knew. Her little head fit perfectly into the crook of my arm, and my forearm nestled beneath her, supporting her. She was so light, so small. She felt like nothing at all in my arms, but she changed everything. I held the bottle with my free hand, watching her mouth move as she drank, her eyes closed.

She opened her eyes, just a little, and I saw amber.

acknowledgment of paternity

There was an inn down the street from Eden's cabin. It was really truly an inn, rather than a hotel or motel or B-and-B. I retreated there, sat on the old white metal-frame bed with the fifty-year-old quilt, and I sketched. Feverishly, obsessively. I drew Ever, again and again. I drew the baby, who did not have a name as yet.

Days passed. I didn't leave the inn, except briefly to find food at a gas station a few miles south. I called Ever, but she answered the phone and hung up without a word. It was her way of letting me know she was alive without talking to me. I wasn't sure if she would ever talk to me again.

I got a text from her, at three-thirty in the morning, three days after she left: **Don't call me again. I need time.**

Okay. Im at a little inn not far from the cabin. I hit "send" and waited for a response. There was so much else I wanted to say, but I knew I couldn't, not via text.

My phone vibrated with her single-letter response: **K.**

Nothing else after that, for two more days.

And then, at eleven at night: **Do you love me.**

I'd been asleep, too distraught and numb and afraid and mixed up to function. I was barely eating, barely sleeping, floating through the days, hoping against hope that she'd come back, or call me, or anything.

I answered immediately. **Yes.**

You do?

Yes. Forever and always. I don't deserve your love back, and I don't expect you to forgive me. But I'll always love you. I sent it, wishing I could pack more into the message as it sped through the ether.

Don't, Cade. Just don't. I'm not ready yet. I might never be.

The next morning, a knock on my door woke me up. I opened it, wearing a pair of gym shorts and nothing else. Eden was standing there, looking uncomfortable.

"I won't be long. I just—" She glanced up, then quickly away. She had a piece of paper in her hands.

"I wanted to give you this. It's an acknowledgment of paternity form."

I took it, stared at it. "I don't have a pen."

She shook her head. "No, you don't understand. I'm not…making any sense." She blew out a shaky breath. "You don't have to sign it. I've thought a lot about this, and—god, I'm so nervous. I don't expect anything from you, Cade. If you…you can go. You can…do whatever you want."

I shuffled backward, confused and needing time to regroup. "Come in. Let me grab a shirt." I slipped a T-shirt on over my head and sat on the edge of the bed. Eden took a chair in the corner, by the window. "I don't understand what you're saying, Eden."

She didn't look at me. "I'm giving you the option of—of walking away."

I was angry. "Walk away? What kind of man do you take me for? She's my *daughter*. My child. I had my parents taken away from me, and you think I'd— I'd just—fucking walk away? Leave her with one parent?"

Eden shrank away from me. "I just wanted to give you the option. Let you know that I don't—I don't expect you to—"

I cut her off. "I don't know how this will work, but I'll never just walk away. There's no us, there will never be an us," I gestured between the two of us, "but she's my daughter, and I'll always be a part of her life. I don't know how, but I will."

Eden sniffed. "You're a good man, Cade. I didn't think you'd walk away, but I had to tell you. You deserved the option, at least."

"Give me a pen." She dug in her purse, handed me a slim gray ballpoint pen. I signed my name to the form without hesitation. "Have you named her yet?"

Eden shook her head. "I'm…trying, but…nothing seems right. And I'm—I'm fucked up, in my head."

"Me, too. God. Me, too." I glanced at her, saw the guilt etched on her face. "This is my fault," I said. "I let this happen."

"We both did." She stood up. "You should be the one to name her."

I nodded. "I'll give it some thought."

She paused in the doorway. "Have you heard from her?"

"A couple of texts. She's alive, and needs time. That's about all I know."

Eden nodded, and then left.

I was officially a father, legally. I'd claimed a baby as my own.

The next day—after a week away—just past eight in the morning, Ever came back.

it's not for you

I was sleeping, and I dreamed she was there with me. Watching me, sadness in her eyes. Anger in her posture. I dreamed she watched me, crying silently.

And then I woke up, and realized the dream wasn't a dream. It was reality.

She was in the same clothes she'd been wearing when she left, a pair of tight, dark-washed jeans, a white V-neck T-shirt, and a black hooded North Face fleece. Her hair was tangled, tied back in a messy bun, unwashed and greasy. Her eyes were dark-rimmed with exhaustion, and held a thousand-yard stare of resigned bitterness.

I was still in bed, my hair sleep-matted, naked from the waist up. "Ever." I kicked the blankets off, lurched out of bed.

"Stay—stay over there." She pointed at the bed.

I sat back down. "Ev, babe—"

"No, Cade, you don't get to call me that. Not now." The venom was quiet, but it sliced like razors.

I slumped, rested my forehead on the heels of my palms, knowing what was coming. "This is goodbye." I glanced up at her, my eyes burning already. "Isn't it?"

She pulled her legs up onto the chair, folding them beneath her. She shook her head, the bun containing her black hair wobbling. "Just listen."

"Okay." I felt a sliver of hope.

She glanced over her shoulder at the small bathroom, and sighed. "You know what, I feel nasty. I haven't showered in I don't even know how long. I don't even know what day it is."

"It's Thursday. You've been gone a week."

"A week. Jesus." She stood up and moved toward the bathroom, then paused and glanced at me. "Is there a toothbrush?"

I pointed at the small suitcase in the corner, zipped closed, untouched. "That's all your stuff. I brought it in from the car. You should have all your toiletries."

She knelt by the bag, opened it, pulled out her toiletries case. "Thanks." I just nodded, and she closed the bathroom door behind her.

Half an hour later, she emerged wrapped in a towel, another turbaned around her hair. She tossed her brush on the bed and sat down beside it, shaking the turban loose. She bent over at the waist, squeezing her hair dry and then brushing it. I watched her from the other side of the bed. I'd dressed, and took a moment while she was brushing her hair to brush my teeth. It was an odd moment, strange yet comfortably domestic, familiar but poisoned with tension. When her hair was straight and shining, she turned around on the bed, facing me while sitting cross-legged, still wearing nothing but the towel.

Her jade eyes were rife with a myriad of emotions, too many to name, to list, to understand. She just stared at me for a very long time, as if trying to sort out what she was going to say. I could only wait.

Finally, she took a deep breath and let it out. "Cade, I don't even know where to start. This is all... so much. I guess I can understand why you were so closed off after I woke up. Why you seemed to be pulling away."

I forced myself to meet her eyes. "Because I couldn't bear knowing what the truth would do to you."

Quietly: "You don't know what it's done to me."

"Then tell me. Tell me everything."

She shook her head, and then jabbed her index finger at me. "*You* tell me everything." She squeezed her eyes shut. "I'm not sure I *want* to know, really, but I *have* to know. So tell me."

"What do you want to know?"

"Everything! Why? How—how long—how many times?" A long, agonized pause, tears in her eyes. "Who else?"

"No one. No one else. I swear. Not that it makes it any better, but—there was no one else." I wiped my face with both hands, groaning. "As for the rest? How, why? How long? God, it was…it didn't start right away—you'd been in a coma for a year—"

"'Didn't *start*,'" Ever repeated. "Meaning it was more than once."

I could only nod and try to breathe. When I could speak again, it was in a rasped whisper. "Yes. It was more than once. You'd been—gone. I don't even know how to talk about it, Ever. You were gone. But you weren't dead. I could *see* you, I could visit your body, watch you breathe and watch the heart monitor spike. I could touch your hand. But I couldn't touch *you*. I couldn't grieve, or mourn, or move on, because you weren't dead. And I didn't want you to be. Please, you have to know that. I never stopped loving you. I never lied to you. There was only you. But…I was so fucked up, Ev. I'd lost *everyone*. Mom. Dad. Grams. Gramps. And then you. I had *no one*. I was completely alone. And I was hurt. Physically. I'm not sure I've ever really told you what it was like for me, when I first came to in the hospital. I'd shattered my left leg, basically. Broke it in three or four places. I've got pins and rods holding it together. And my arm...it was sliced to fucking meat by a piece of the car. I'd cracked my head open. I wasn't—I wasn't as hurt as you, obviously, but I was pretty fucked up. I couldn't walk. Couldn't dress myself, could barely feed myself."

Ever's eyes were pained, compassionate. "God, Cade, I had no idea. Why didn't you ever tell me?"

"Because it didn't matter. I'm fine now. My leg aches when it's super cold, and sometimes before a thunderstorm. But I'm fine. All that mattered—all that *matters*—is you." I scraped my thumbnail along the seam of my jeans, on the outside of my leg, unable to look at her.

"I had to go through a shitload of physical therapy before I could really function. And the only person who could take me there, after I'd been released, was Eden. She was the only person in my life. Period. She was the *only* person who knew me, or who knew anything about me, or who knew you. Your dad took me home from the hospital, but he vanished again after that. And Eden was just...she was all I had. My only friend. And she was hurting, too. She'd lost you, too. Her twin, her other half. It tore her up like it did me. She took me to visit you until I was out of the cast and could drive. And after that it was just...

someone to talk to. For a year and a half, that's all it was. Someone who understood."

A thick silence, and then Ever sighed. "And then?"

"And then it got to be too much. A year of... emptiness. Missing you, and visiting you. Talking to you. Writing you letters—"

"I read them. All of them, the letters you wrote."

I nodded. "I had to keep going, knowing you were technically alive. But, according to the doctors, you would almost definitely never wake up, and, if you ever did, there was a huge possibility that you'd be severely brain-damaged. They talked to me about—about donating your organs. Letting you die. It'd be more merciful to everyone, they told me."

"Did you want to do that?" She whispered the question. "Did you consider it?"

"I almost knocked the doctor's teeth down his throat when he suggested it. It was...right around Christmas. Around the one-year anniversary. He seriously called me into his office during fucking Christmas and suggested I let you die so they could harvest your fucking organs. Eden had to push me out of the office before I fucked him up."

"So, no," Ever deadpanned.

I laughed. "No. I didn't think about it for a goddamned second. You were my wife, my one true love. And if there was a chance—a *chance*—I'd take it." I had to pause to breathe, to gather my courage. "You can't...you simply *cannot* fathom the pain. How much I missed you. How much I needed you, and you weren't there. But you *were*, yet I couldn't have you."

"I read your letters," she said, "I think I have some idea of what you were going through."

I snorted. "Ev, babe. Those are *words*. And...there aren't words for what it was like. Those letters were as close to how fucking completely shredded and empty I was as the flame from a lighter is like the goddamned sun."

"Oh." Her voice was tiny.

"Yeah. Oh." I sucked in a long breath. "And then there was Eden. And she was—she was *you*. But not you. I could never mistake her for you, physically, emotionally, anything. So it wasn't that. Like she could replace you. Nothing, no one could ever replace you. But she was like...god, how do I even put it? She was like a mirror image of you. A reflection of you. Part of you—enough to remind me of what I was missing, what I'd lost. But hadn't lost enough to be able to heal from it. It was like someone had gouged out my heart, and every time I saw you it was like having acid poured into the open wound. Every day. And it never healed. Never closed, never hurt any less. Not for a moment. And Eden being around was a reminder of what it had been like to be whole."

Ever shuddered a sigh. "Holy shit, Cade."

"Yeah. So that's how it happened. I was so lonely, Ev. So alone. And she was *there*. The tiniest bit of… not pleasure, but—what? How do I even say it?" I scrubbed my hand through my hair. "A split second, a minute or two of…of not-pain. A chance to feel *anything* but the fucking endless pain."

"How long? How many times?"

I shrugged. "I don't even remember. I stopped keeping track. I never counted." I looked into her eyes, let her see into me. "It wasn't just once, but… that's all that matters. There's no way in hell I'll tell you details. I just want to forget it ever happened, in some ways. But in other ways? It was all that kept me sane, Ever. That doesn't make it okay. That doesn't make it any less of a betrayal. And I know that. I know there's no forgiving or forgetting. I regret that I hurt you, and it's fucking breaking me knowing it's destroyed what we had. But, in a way, that thing with Eden was all that kept me from…I don't know. Self-destructing. Just dying, like Dad did after…after Mom died. So you can get as mad as you want, but I'm not going to tell you anything else, other than that it lasted…a couple of months, at most."

She nodded, sniffing. "I don't want to know any more."

I swallowed hard, preparing. "I'm sorry, Ever. I love you. Please know that. Now, then, always. I've never stopped loving you. I never will."

I stood up and zipped my duffel bag shut.

"Where are you going?"

I shrugged. "I don't know."

"Well, hold on a second, Cade. That was your turn to talk. Now it's *my* turn." I never heard her move, but she was there behind me, the tips of her fingers touching my arm. "Don't you want to know what I have to say?"

I nodded wearily. "Yeah."

"Then sit down, and don't think you know what I'm going to say, because I'm pretty sure you don't." She took several deep breaths as I sat back down on the bed beside her.

"Okay, first. I get why it happened. It doesn't make it hurt any less, but I get it. As much as I can, I understand. You've been through so much in your life, Cade, and the accident, me in a coma...I know I can't imagine what you went through. What Eden went through. You both needed comfort and you found it, really, in the only place it existed. So I get it. That was the easy part. Honestly. Mentally understanding *why* it happened, *how* it happened was the easy part of what I've been working through the past week."

"Where did you go?"

She shrugged. "I don't know. I just drove. I drove until I couldn't see straight, and I stopped to sleep and eat, and then kept driving. I ended up in... Illinois, I guess? In the middle of some field, out in the middle of nowhere. Thank god Eden's car had GPS, 'cause I wasn't paying any attention to where I was going. I just drove. At first, I just tried to stop crying. That took most of the first day. I stopped in that field because I was crying so hard I couldn't see the road. I almost wrecked, actually, so I pulled over and cried. And then I kept driving. I sat in some little diner just off the freeway for probably eighteen hours, drinking coffee and trying to figure out what I was even thinking. What I was going to do. How I felt. If I was even going to come back." She glanced up at me, honesty in her eyes. "I almost didn't, Cade. I almost just kept going. Florida sounded nice. But... in the end, I had to come back."

"Why?"

"Because even with as bad as it hurt, as angry as I was, I *missed* you. The past week was the hardest, longest, and loneliest of my life. Not just because I couldn't sleep or eat, but, but because I—I fucking missed you, Cade." Ever rarely swore in normal conversation, so when she did, it was a little shocking. "And I realized...I just *knew* that I couldn't go on without you. You're a part of me, Caden. Just as much as Eden is, if not more. I *need* you. Which is why

I'm still so—so *angry*. But I also can't help knowing that—I can't say that you didn't have a choice, really. But I know that you were in so much pain, after having gone through so much already."

The towel tucked just above her breasts was loosening, and she untucked it, pulled it taut across her back, and re-fastened it.

She sighed. "And the fact that it was Eden…that was harder for me to come to terms with. My *twin*. My sister. My only family. I'll never be able to look at her without knowing that you *fucked* her." She choked, her head hanging. "But it wasn't as empty as fucking, was it? I can't make it make any sense in my head. I tried to put myself in your shoes, her shoes. If you were in a coma, not dead but not alive? What would I do? Like I said, I understand why. But the fact that it was Eden? That's harder. It makes it better in some ways, honestly. It's strange, but…it would hurt *more* if it had been some random girl, someone who meant nothing to you. I don't know, maybe that's messed up a little, but it's my truth. It makes it harder, too, of course, because she's my sister and, like I said, I'll always know. She's my only family, all I have left. I think she thinks she can just run away or hide from me, but she can't. I haven't talked to her yet, but I will. It's not that easy for her. She can't just run away from this. From me."

"I don't think it was easy for her. I think she didn't know what else to do."

Ever's eyes blazed. "You let *me* worry about what happens between Eden and me, okay?" She ran her fingers through her hair, her eyes distant. Then, "She's part of me. No one knows her like I do."

"I know."

"What it comes down to, Cade, is that I forgive you."

Shock hit me like a tidal wave. "You what?"

"It's not for you. It's not about you. I'm doing it for *me*. Because I can't picture life without you. I love you. And I couldn't live knowing I'd walked away from the best thing that ever happened to me, if I just gave up on you. On us." She took my hands, and I dared to meet her eyes, hope blooming inside me like a flower of sunlight in a bottomless pit. "I love you, Cade. I'm angry. I'm hurt. I don't know if things will be quite the same, and it'll take time for me to…feel okay about us. But the funny thing is, I still trust you. You didn't cheat on me—not in the traditional sense. You weren't sneaking around behind my back because I wasn't enough for you or something. And I know you love me. I think in some ways, how things happened, you not telling me for so long…that was a good thing. I don't know if I would've been *able* to forgive you if I'd known any sooner."

I felt my eyes burning again, felt joy and confusion and a million other emotions warring inside me. A tear trickled down my face, unheeded. "I do love you. I don't know how you can forgive me, honestly. I really don't. And I don't know how things will work. How we can be...*us* again, after all this."

She seemed confused. "You're not...you're not still leaving, are you?"

I shook my head. "No, of course not. I'm just... confused. I was...for the past eight, nine months, ever since you woke up, I've been dreading this day. I've been dreading this conversation because I expected it to be the end."

"But it's not." Ever shivered and stood up, turned away from me and let the towel fall, then knelt in front of her suitcase and dug out an outfit. She spoke while she dressed, sliding on panties and fastening a bra, stepping into jeans. "I guess I thought you'd be...happier. I thought knowing I'm forgiving you, that—"

"I *am* happy, Ever. I am. But there's more than just the knowledge that you're forgiving me." I hesitated. "There's the baby."

She hung her head. "Shit. I'd almost forgotten." She wiped at her eyes. "I was so focused on *us.*"

"You have to go talk to Eden."

She nodded. "Yeah."

"You should know…I signed to accept paternity. I don't know what to do, how this will work, but I can't—I can't just…do nothing."

Ever sighed. "I know. I wouldn't expect anything less from you." She tilted her head back, staring at the ceiling. "Fuck, this is so complicated."

"So, so very insanely complicated."

Ever slumped into the chair and put on her shoes, her coat, and then glanced up at me. "Come on. I've got to go talk to my sister."

I stomped my feet into my boots, shrugged on my coat, and followed her out the door. The future was still clouded by a fog of uncertainty, but Ever still loved me.

There was hope.

part three

the courage to forgive

Carter

Things were…tense. By which I mean—*fuck*. Eden was a disaster. The baby still didn't have a name after a week, and she was loud and constantly unhappy. Eden refused to breastfeed, for reasons I didn't dare ask about, which meant I'd been down the peninsula three times over the last week to get more formula, since Baby seemed to be hungrier than Eden expected. Eventually, I stopped a woman in the infant aisle at Meijer and asked her what kind of formula was best for a newborn, and how much to get. I returned from that trip with a tub of Enfamil that she told me would last a month, at least. Eden was in pain. I mean, she'd just had a baby, but not breastfeeding was causing her pain as well.

She wasn't talking to me—not with any serious-ness. Not about things that mattered.

All this was made more difficult and awkward by the fact that Eden and I weren't actually a couple, and I had my own life to tend to. I had clients who needed attention, employees working on the tasting room who needed supervision. And I had my own home, which I hadn't been to in a week and a half. I'd spent nearly four days at the hospital with Eden, sleeping in a chair, and then the rest of the time at her house, sleeping on the couch. My back was pro-testing. I was exhausted to the point of collapse, and I needed five seconds alone.

But Eden needed me. The baby overwhelmed her, my presence overwhelmed her, and the fact that Ever and Caden were still around made her tense. Yet Ever had vanished, with Eden's car, and hadn't returned. Eden had spoken briefly to Cade, who had acknowledged paternity. She'd returned from that visit shaking with shredded nerves. I'd held her as she cried, although I hadn't quite understood the full extent of the reason for her emotional outburst.

Maybe it was just him, I thought. A reminder of her mistake.

I was about to tell Eden that I had to go home for a while. I had to sleep. I had to get new clothes. I'd been wearing the same two pairs of jeans, the same two T-shirts, the same pair of boxers, the same socks. I'd showered once in almost a week.

And then, at eleven in the morning a week after Ever had run off, there was a knock at the door. Eden was on the couch, feeding Baby a bottle, so I answered the door. Ever and Caden stood waiting. They'd obviously come to some sort of understanding, but there was still enough tension between them to cut with a knife.

I stood aside. "Come in."

Ever halted abruptly in the middle of the room, staring at Eden. Good lord, Eden was a mess. A beautiful, tortured mess. Her hair was like straw, greasy and unwashed and loose around her shoulders. The black roots showed a full three inches from her scalp. I don't know if she'd changed her clothes in as long as I had. She looked as if she hadn't slept in days.

When the knock came, she looked up at the door, and when she saw Ever, I could see the journey of her emotions. Happiness at seeing her sister, then sorrow, then fear. Then, finally, resignation.

"Hey, Ev." Eden spoke in a whisper, although the baby was wide awake, staring up at Eden.

"Hi, Edie." Ever took a hesitant step forward, glanced at Caden, and then at me, and then back to Eden. "Can you guys give us a few minutes?"

Caden nodded and left without a word.

I glanced at Eden. "You need anything?"

"My Diet?" She pointed at a silver can of Diet Coke on the table. She'd been indulging since giving birth, although she hadn't had any alcohol yet. I think that was coming, at some point.

I gave it to her, then shrugged into my coat. "Text me when you're…done. Whenever."

I headed out to the beach, found Caden standing with his hands shoved into his hip pockets, staring out at the bay. I stopped at the water's edge next to him, stuck my hands into the pockets of my pea coat.

After a few seconds of silence, he spoke without looking at me. "You and Eden. What's up there?"

I shrugged. "Friends." I figured he deserved truth. "For now."

He nodded. "She's a good person. Deserves… she deserves good things. She deserves to be taken care of." He finally looked at me. The baby had his eyes, piercing amber. "Looks like you've been there for her."

I chewed on my lip. This was supremely awkward. "I've done my best. She is a good person. What happened was…there was no easy answer."

"She told you what happened?"

I nodded. "Yeah." I kicked at the sand. "You and Ever. You work things out?"

"Sort of."

"How sort of?" I glanced at him. I didn't know him, but I recognized a man at war with himself when I saw one.

He pivoted slightly, assessing me. I met his gaze evenly. "She came back. She forgave me. I don't—I don't know how the fuck she can do that. After—after what I did to her."

"Sounds like she's pretty amazing. Eden talked about her a lot."

He nodded, ducking his head and sniffing. "Yeah." He turned away from me, took a step closer to the water, knuckling his eye socket. "Shit. Sorry."

I stayed where I was. "No apologies, man. Shit's intense." I hesitated, wishing I knew what to say, how to draw him out. He clearly needed to talk. "So, she forgave you?"

He nodded while staring at the ripples of lake water. "That's what she said. She did it for herself, not for me. She couldn't live with herself if she gave up on us."

"Makes sense to me."

Caden's head jerked up. "It does?"

I didn't understand his confusion. "Yeah. Sure it does. Woman loves you, bro. She's willing to *make the choice* to forgive you. Jump at it, man. I don't know what your fucking hang-up is, but you need to *jump* at that shit when it's offered."

He looked up to the sky, laughing somewhat hysterically, and spun in a stumbling circle. "My hang-up? My hang-up is what if she's just *saying* she forgives me, because she feels like she doesn't have a choice? Eden's got the baby, their dad isn't worth shit except for a goddamn check in the mail. She's…she hasn't finished her degree. She's worked one job in her entire life—answering phones. She's an incredible artist, but…that's hard as hell to turn into income. What if…what if she's just hanging on to what she thinks we had? What if…what if she's trying to forgive me, and she can't?" He sniffed again, wiped angrily at his face. "What if she can't?"

I stepped in front of him. "I don't know you, Caden. I only know the little bit that Eden told me, which wasn't much. But I know you've been through a lot. You were put in a shitty situation, and you made a choice. That choice had consequences. You gotta live with that, move on. If your wife is saying she forgives you, then you have to take that at face value." I pushed at his shoulder to get his attention. "Do you even understand how much courage it took to come back here and forgive you? How much strength it took?"

"What? What do you mean?"

"Think about from her side, dude. She was in a coma. She lost a year and a half of her life. She woke up, and she was trapped in a body that wouldn't do what she wanted it to do. She had to relearn everything. And then she finds out that you had an affair while she was in a coma? And now you have a kid with her sister?"

Caden stumbled, dropped to his knees in the cold wet sand, his shoulders shaking.

I kept talking. "The easy thing would have been to keep running. Start over. She'd get over things eventually. Or she wouldn't, and she'd just be miserable the rest of her life. No way to know. But she didn't. She came back, and she told you, flat out, she's making a choice, for *herself*, to forgive you. Not many men in your shoes get that chance. Who the fuck are you to turn that down?"

He looked up at me, his eyes red.

I met his gaze, letting my words sink in. "Caden, listen. Don't think I'm judging you. It was a fucked-up situation with no easy way out. I don't know what I would have done in your shoes. But I know if the woman I loved was offering me a lifeline, I'd take it. And I'd spend every single goddamn minute of my life proving to her that I loved her. That I cherished her, treasured her. I wouldn't let a single *second* go by where she didn't know in her bones that I was totally and completely hers."

Caden fell back onto his butt. "Shit."

"Just think about it, man." I extended my hand to him. He took it, and I tugged him to his feet.

"You're right. I don't have to think about it. You're right." He wiped at his jeans, and we walked along the beach. After a moment, he glanced at me. "How's the baby?"

"In need of a name," I said, laughing. "I don't know anything about babies, but she's eating a lot, and pooping a lot, and sleeping a lot. And crying a lot."

"So, being a baby, I guess."

I nodded. "Basically."

"Does Eden have any plans?"

I didn't really want to talk about Eden. I was worried for her. I just shrugged. "Not that I know of."

"She's just gonna stay up here?"

"I really don't know. If she has a plan, she's not telling me."

Caden seemed to sense my tension. "Well, she's smart. She'll figure something out."

Right then I got a text from Eden: **You can come back now.**

"We can go inside," I said.

When we entered the house, Ever was holding the baby on her lap, sitting cross-legged on the couch with the baby's head cradled in the crook of her crossed ankles. She was tickling Baby's little toes, her tummy, tugging her fingers, cooing and making the kind of indecipherable noises women make to babies. Cade watched, seeming drawn, fascinated. I bumped him with my shoulder, and he glanced at me. I nodded at Ever. He knelt on the floor beside Ever, reached up and touched a lock of Baby's black hair. A smile crossed his face.

Ever lifted the newborn and handed her, somewhat reluctantly, to Eden. "We'll come back tomorrow?"

Eden nodded. "Yeah. I'll see you tomorrow."

When they were gone, Eden held the baby and watched as she looked around the room with avid interest. Eden seemed lost in thought. I sat beside her, reached over, and smiled as a tiny hand clutched my finger. "How'd it go?"

"Intense. She's forgiving Cade. They're staying together."

"How do you feel about that?"

She lifted a shoulder in a shrug. "It's good. I'm glad for them. For both of them. I never wanted to be a home-wrecker."

"No one thinks that was what you wanted." She didn't respond. "What about you and Ever? Where do you two stand?"

"I don't know. The baby throws a wrench in everything. If not for this little lady," Eden touched a little button nose, "it might be less complicated. But...here she is. So, here we are. Status unknown."

"What do you want to have happen?" I took the baby and laid her on my legs.

Eden stood up, flipping the bun of her hair. "I don't know. I want us to have a relationship. I want Cade and Ever to be happy. I want…I want to know what I'm supposed to do with my life."

"Maybe start with a shower and clean clothes?"

She turned on me and laughed. "Are you saying I stink?"

I shrugged, chuckling. "I'm just saying…a shower sometimes helps clarify things."

"Nicely avoided." She sniffed at her armpit, and backed away with a cough. "Maybe that's a good idea."

"I have my moments," I said.

Baby fell asleep while I was holding her, so I set her gently into the bassinet beside Eden's bed. When I came out, Eden had a towel clutched to her chest. She was still dripping wet, hair sopping. She was crying. When she saw me, she sobbed and flew at me. I caught her, held her. Wet hair soaked my shirt, and the scent of clean woman and shampoo filled my nostrils.

"What's wrong?"

She buried her face into my chest. "Everything," she said, her voice muffled.

I touched her cheek. "Tell me."

"I don't know what to do. I don't know how to be a mother. I feel like I'm doing everything wrong. And I—I—I feel like sometimes I don't love her.

Like I should. Like a mother." She trailed off, shaking and shuddering. "And I'm afraid. I'm terrified of every day. And I feel like the two times that Ever has been around the baby, she's been better with her than I am. It should be Ever. *She*—" Eden gestured at the door, meaning the infant in the crib, "should be Ever's. Not mine."

I just held on to Eden, letting her cry, letting her get it out.

"I'm so terrible."

"No. No. God, Eden. No." I squeezed her shoulders, then took her face in my hands and lifted it so she could see me. "Eden, babe. You're not terrible. It's a hard situation, and you're doing your best."

"I just want…." She trailed off.

"What?" I prompted.

"You." Her voice was a thread, barely even a sound. But I heard it.

"I'm here." I brushed a tendril of wet hair aside. "We'll figure things out. One step at a time, okay?"

Eden nodded in my hands. "Okay." She hesitated, and then looked up at me. "That thing we did, when you dropped me off here, on Christmas?"

I smirked at her. "Kissed?"

Eden nodded. "Yeah." Her eyes were soft and green and searching mine. "One more?"

I didn't bother with words. I bent down, her cheeks warm on my palms. She lifted up on her toes to meet me. Her lips explored mine gingerly at first, softly, questioningly. I let her lead the kiss, opened my lips when her tongue slid along the seam of my lips. She pressed up against me, lifting higher on her toes, her arms wrapping around my neck, forgetting the towel.

For a moment, I lost myself in the kiss.

And then I broke away, smiling down at her. "One."

Her eyes seemed to darken. "Two." She lifted up, kissed me, demanding.

I responded because I couldn't help it. I felt heat building inside me, need and desire. So many thoughts whirled in my head: excuses, justifications. Whispers of need. But I knew right then wasn't the best moment for what was happening.

I pulled away again, settling her to her feet. I was careful to push the ends of the towel around her sides. "We should…slow down."

Eden breathed a sigh. "God. Yeah. I'm sorry, I—"

I stopped her with a finger to her lips. "Slow down, because I'm getting carried away. And I think we need to focus on the situation at hand. You need to sort things out with your sister. You need to make some decisions about your life. Hiding away up here won't last forever. You need to make some plans. Start living."

Eden nodded. "I know. You're right. God. I'm all over the place, huh?"

I traced her jawline with one finger. "I'm keeping up just fine."

"I don't know how."

I just smiled at her. "Why don't you get dressed? Let's get out of the house, go get some food. If you're up to it."

Eden ducked her head. "I'm not sure. I'm still a bit...tender. I'd like to go out with you. But...maybe not yet." Something in her body language spoke of avoidance.

"What else?"

She frowned at me. "What else what?"

"Why else don't you want to go out?"

She sighed. "How do you always know?" She turned away from me, tucking the towel tightly in place. "I just had a baby. I don't feel...ready. I need to work out." She whispered the last sentence.

And then I understood. I moved in front of her. Sat on the couch, and tugged her by the hand toward me. She fell sideways onto my lap, her legs hanging over the side of mine. "Eden. You're beautiful. You don't need to go to the gym. You don't need to work out. You don't need to lose weight." She flinched at that. I kept going. "You need to be happy. You need to find peace with yourself and with your sister. What you *don't* need is to think you have to suddenly drop every pound of pregnancy weight. You're beautiful. More than beautiful. So much more."

She licked her lips, shifted, uncomfortable. "Yes, I do. I gained, like, fifty pounds. I've never been this big. I feel…shit. I feel like even though I had the baby, I'm still carrying her around." She ducked her head, sniffing. "I know I want something with you, at some point. And I want to be beautiful for you. As beautiful as I can be, at least. I'll never look like Ever, but—"

I cut her off with a laugh. "You're *identical twins,* Edie."

She frowned at me. "That doesn't mean we're the same. I've always been a little heavier than her."

I slid my hand around her to cup her hip through the wet towel. "What if I like you this way? What if I think you're beautiful, and sexy, right *now?*"

"I've got stretch marks. Loose skin. My roots are taking over my whole head. I'm, like…thirty-five pounds overweight."

"God, Eden. You're not overweight."

She groaned. "I *know!* But it's how I feel, okay?"

I sighed. "I get it, as much as a guy can, all right? I do. But…I want you to believe in yourself. And I want you to know I like you, *a lot,* just the way you are."

Eden sagged against me. "I'm sorry I'm a mess."

I laughed, smoothing her damp hair away from my mouth. "You're allowed. I was a mess for a long time. I still have my moments. And being a mess isn't going to scare me away. I watched you give birth, Eden. I'm not going anywhere."

"You did, didn't you?" She laughed, sniffling. "Did I poop myself?"

I barked a laugh. "I don't know, I didn't see. I don't think so. I was kinda busy holding your hands."

"Getting your hands crushed, you mean."

"You do have a pretty strong grip."

She sighed. "Thank you, Carter. I feel like I'm going to be thanking you for a long time."

"Don't thank me. Just…be you. Be happy." I ran my hand along her back, across her shoulders, ignoring temptation. "Why don't you play your cello?"

An hour later Baby was awake, sitting on my lap and watching Eden play her cello. With every note, Eden seemed to strengthen, to find calm, to find center. After an hour of playing, she let the instrument go silent, the bow hanging near her foot, the strings still humming.

She looked up at me, and I saw determination in her eyes. "I know what I have to do."

saving forever

Ever

I dreamed of Eden's baby. Eden and Caden's baby. The baby I'd never have. I never knew how much I'd wanted that with Caden until the potential was taken away. Until I saw the visual evidence of what we could have had.

I woke up crying. The room was dark and silent, a hint of silver moonlight shining through a gap in the curtains. Cade was beside me, curled at the edge of the bed. Far away from me, emotionally and physically. I didn't understand why he still seemed so distant. I thought he would be relieved. Happy— at least a little—knowing things weren't over between us.

On the way back up here I'd stopped by our condo, on a whim, to get the boxes of letters. There were four shoeboxes full of envelopes. While Cade slept, I sneaked down to Eden's car and retrieved the boxes, sat on the bed, and read through them again.

Something woke Cade, and he rolled over to look at me, blinking sleep from his eyes. "What'cha doing?" Instead of an answer, I showed him the letter. "Why're you reading those?" he asked.

And I realized maybe he'd forgotten what we had. Things since I'd woken up had been so difficult, so strained and strange and dark. He needed to remember what we had once been like. Happy together. Free.

A deep breath, and then I started reading out loud the letter in my hands.

"Ever,

I finally got the insurance company to pay for a new truck. A Jeep Grand Cherokee. Brand new. You'd like it. It's green. Almost the color of your eyes, but a little darker. I wish I'd had you there to help me decide what to get. I wanted to pick something you'd love, but I just...I didn't know what. I almost picked another F-150, but I've had enough of those. I needed something different.

Your hair is getting long, you know that? They had to shave it all off when they did the surgeries on you. And now it's almost to your chin. I think it's actually a little darker black somehow. I think I remember reading that when you shaved your head, sometimes the hair would change a little. But then I read somewhere else that that wasn't actually true, it was just the ends of the hair being different or something.

I miss you so much, Ever. I miss talking to you. I miss waking up next to you. I miss the way you'd smile at me first thing in the morning. Sleepy, sexy, hair messy, like seeing me was the best way to wake up. I miss watching you put on your lotion. The way it made our bedroom smell like vanilla. I miss sleeping next to you. Jesus, I miss, most of all, the way you sounded when we made love. Your voice. How dirty you'd talk to me.

I'm going nuts, baby. Six months without you. Six months without touching you or kissing you. Six months, and I don't know what to do. About how horny I am. How I ache. For you. I wake up at night sometimes, and I've dreamed of you. Sex dreams of you. And I'll be on the verge of coming, just from the dream, but I always wake up, and then I remember that you're gone and I can't get the dream back, can't get the feeling back."

I had to stop and breathe, hold back the emotions. After a moment, I started again.

"I miss your skin. Soft, smooth, warm.

I miss you so much sometimes that I could cry. But I can't. Don't. Won't. It's stupid, maybe, but if I don't mourn you, don't cry for you, then part of me thinks maybe you'll come back. And I won't have to.

Come back to me, my love. Please. Come back to me, and make love to me.

Forever yours, and yours beyond forever,
Caden

"That was us," I said. I set the letter down on the bed. "Do you remember? You and I? Before?"

He shifted to a sitting position. "It's hard to, honestly. The coma, and the last several months have sort of…taken over."

"We can't move on if you're still stuck in what happened. I feel like maybe you're trapped in what was. In how things were. Me in a coma, and then afraid of all *this*." I gestured vaguely toward the outside, toward Eden's house. Meaning everything that was going on. "I *love* you, Cade. I want *us* back. That's all I want. Us. The happiness we had."

"Sometimes I think it's gone," Cade whispered. "I destroyed it."

I pressed my lips together, feeling a hopelessness. It wasn't just what had happened between him and

Eden that had me so upset. It was how…broken Cade seemed. I sorted through the pile of envelopes on my lap. Picked one.

"I don't know who I am anymore, Ever. I'm a castaway. Lost. Drowning. I love you. That's the only true thing I know, and it's all I have to hold on to. I love you. I'll love you forever. Until the day I die, and I'll love you in whatever world comes after this one." I looked at him, holding the letter up. "Is this still true? Or did you let go?"

"Part of it is true. I still don't know who I am. I still feel lost and drowning."

I swiveled on my backside to face him. "I'm right here, Cade. Don't you see? The only thing that matters is now. The future. Us. Everything else, what happened, it's done. Hold on to me, Cade. Let go of all that, and hold on to me. I'm here, and I love you."

"How can we get us back? How can you just… forget?" He closed his eyes. "What I did?"

"Not easily. But I can. I'm not saying it'll all suddenly be great and fine and wonderful. But…this? You, acting like life is over? I can't handle it. I just can't. It's worse than anything else. I feel like I can't reach you. Like you're gone. Like you're not you."

I shuffled envelopes and letters, Cade sitting still and watching. I could sense his thoughts, feel him parsing through things.

I chose another letter and read it. When I got to the end, I hesitated, and then read the last line again. "No matter what, I love you. I'll never stop loving you. I don't know if you'll love me when you wake up. If you'll be able to. But even if you don't, I'll love you. Forever, and after forever. Even if I don't deserve your love back." I pushed the letters aside, moved to my knees on the bed in front of him, took his hands in mine. "What you deserve is up to me, not you. Me loving you back? It's never been a question. The only question was, can I forgive you? Can I understand what happened and still be with you? I've never stopped being your wife. You needed comfort, Cade, and you found it in someone else—"

"Because it felt like you were dead!" he yelled.

"I *WAS* dead!" I shouted back. "I was dead, Cade. That's how it feels to me. There's almost two years of my life that are just gone. And…there are two me's. Before, and after. Two you's. Two us's. I was dead. My body may have been technically alive, but…that which made me *me*, that was gone. Dead. For me, and for you. For Eden. That's how I can accept what happened and still love you. Some people may say you cheated on me. They may not understand how I can take you back. But…there's no *back*. I was dead, and I came back to life. You were in hell, and you needed comfort. You needed something to keep you from going crazy. And as much as it hurts to know that it wasn't me who gave it to you, I'm…in a way, I'm glad you found it. And I'm glad you found it with someone who understood what you were going through. Who knew me. Who knew us. And I don't care what other people think, Cade. I don't. All I care about is that you and I find each other again, and that Eden and I find each other again. Because right now, I feel like we're all lost."

I fished out the letters he'd kept from our teen-age years, the ones I'd written to him before we were together. I flipped through envelopes, skimming letters until I found the one I wanted. I unfolded it, and winced at the childish, girly handwriting, the scented stationery, the younger me. I skimmed until I found the part I wanted to read: "Regarding your feelings for me, god, that really complicates things. I felt the same way. You were so different from everyone I'd ever met, ever seen. You're handsome, but that's not the right word. It's not enough. You're…god, rugged is the only word I can think of. Is that stupid? It's better than cute, which just doesn't apply, in a good sort of way. And I really did have a crush on you. When you came out to the dock right at the end of camp, the way you put your arm around me and just held me, I've never felt so comforted in all my life. I know I said I wouldn't talk about Will, but he's a part of this discussion. He and I are dating. It's just a fact. But then I have this relationship with you. I feel like I know you, like we're connected in some way, like our souls are cut from the same cloth. Does that make sense? So it almost feels like cheating to have this with you, but it's not. We're pen pals. Maybe that's all we'll ever be. I don't know. If we met IRL (in real life, in case you're not familiar with the term) what would happen? What would we be? And just FYI, the term you used, a literary love? It was beautiful. So beautiful. That term means something, between us now. We are literary loves. Lovers? I do love you, in some strange way. Knowing about you, in these letters, knowing your hurt and your joys, it means something so important to me that I just can't describe." I looked up at him. "Remember? Literary lovers?"

"God, every time you talked about Will, I wanted to puke. I was so jealous, but I knew I didn't have any right to be."

I set the letter aside and scooted closer to Cade. He shifted backward toward the headboard and drew his knees up, let them fall apart. I moved between his knees, hugged my arms around his legs. "But you did have a reason to be jealous. I think we were meant to always be together, even then. I think we're made for each other. The years between camp and when we met again, that was…time to grow up. Time to learn to value what we have together."

Slowly, as if clawing toward the surface from a drowning deep, Cade reached for me. His hands slid over my shoulders, his fingers dug into my flesh and muscle, and his eyes fixed on me. I watched a light spark in the depths of his amber gaze.

"While you were talking to Ever, Carter told me something." He scratched my back with his fingers. "He said…he said that it took a lot of courage and strength for you forgive me, and who the fuck was I to refuse what you were offering."

"Sounds like a smart man."

He nodded. "Yeah." Caden paused, and then started again, slowly. "You have other choices. You know that, right? You can do anything, go anywhere, be with anyone. You don't *have* to be here with me."

He still doubted. "Yes. I know. But I *want* to be here. I *want* to be with you. I want to forget the past two years. I want to pretend there's only ever been you and me." I moved closer still, as close as I could get to him while still sitting on my knees between his legs. "I want *us*, Cade. I'm *choosing* you, intentionally."

"Why?" His eyes slid closed, pained. "I'm such a fucking mess. I'm…broken. I'm lost. I'm…god, I'm just fucked up."

I pulled him to me, my hand around the back of his head. "I know you are. But I knew you when you weren't. I've known you since we were fourteen."

"Fifteen," he mumbled.

I laughed. "Okay, fine. Fifteen. Almost ten years, regardless. I've seen all of you. I know your talent, I know your strength. I know your sweetness. I know your humor. I know your faults and I know your brokenness. I love it all." I held his face against my chest. He shifted forward, and we moved together so I was sitting with my back to the bed and he was lying with his head in my lap. "I didn't vow to love you only when things were great. I vowed to love you through everything."

"So did I."

"Do you feel like you broke those vows?"

He shrugged. "Sometimes. And sometimes I think maybe I didn't, really."

"I'm the same way." I ran my palm on the stubble of his cheek. "And I'm making a choice, right here, right now, to say that it doesn't matter. Not anymore. No more blame. No more guilt. Let's just try to move forward, as us. As Ever and Cade. We had forever, and it was taken from us." He spun around, and his eyes met mine. I smiled at him, putting every hint, every last shred of love and forgiveness into my gaze and my smile. "Let's save our forever, Cade. Please. Let's take it back."

His eyes held mine, searching, I suppose, for any hint of doubt. I let him see that I had none. Nothing came easy. I knew that. There would be pain still, and arguments, and late-night fears and doubts. But then, in that moment, there was none of that. Only us.

Cade's hand slid up my neck, cupped my nape, held on. He tugged me down to him. His lips were cool and chapped, and I leaned into him, bent over him, kissed him slowly and tentatively, seeking to know the emotions of this kiss. And I realized, as his mouth moved gently but hungrily against mine, that he had been giving in, all those months.

He'd been giving me a part of himself each time he kissed me. Giving me something he didn't think he deserved to get back, giving what I needed, what I wanted, all with the knowledge that it would be gone eventually. That's when I found out. I'd be gone, and he would be alone. It took a strange kind of self-lessness to do that, I thought. He was a guy, and guys lived for sex. So some people may have thought that he was taking something he didn't deserve. But even if that was true, to give me the pretense of happiness when he was consumed by guilt? I couldn't have gone through therapy without him, wouldn't have had the determination and strength to get better and to reclaim my life if I hadn't had him, if I hadn't had his love and the illusion of happiness. Maybe that's fucked up. Maybe I was only justifying what he did so I could keep him in my life. But I was okay with that. Cade was my best friend and my husband and my lover, and I needed him. More than needed, I *wanted* him. Need was in my body and my blood and my soul. Wanting was in my head and my heart. The choice to forgive him and put the past behind us belonged to me alone, and no one could dare judge me for that. No one could make the choice for me, or tell me it was wrong. I loved him and that's all that mattered.

I opened up then, as these realizations rocked through me. I opened my mouth and kissed him harder, curled my hand under his head and rested my other hand on his chest, slid it up his shoulder to his throat, his jaw, cupped his cheek. I pulled him to me, and he pulled me to him. We met, and our hunger expanded.

I shifted my legs out from beneath him, letting his head fall to the bed. Threw one thigh over his stomach and straddled him, cradled his face in both hands and crushed my chest to his and kissed him breathless. Kissed us both dizzy. Kissed us both frantic with need and burgeoning fires of passion. He let his hands wrap around my waist as we lay horizontally across the bed, our feet hanging off the side. My T-shirt rucked up as I moved on him with the rhythm of our kiss, and his fingers sought my flesh. Found it, warm and waiting. Up my spine, caressing in slow circles. I sighed into his mouth as he palmed my shoulder blades.

I backed away from the kiss, stared down at him. "Don't give, this time. *Take.*"

I knew he was finding his way back, because he nodded as if he knew exactly what I meant.

He lifted up to capture my lips, and his hands descended my spine, slid between denim and satin to cup my ass. I rocked my core against him, leaning down once more to bury myself in his kiss, and I felt my heart blossoming and exploding with need so fierce it hurt. He withdrew his palms from my backside and slid them back up my torso, pushing my shirt with it. I broke the kiss long enough to let him tug the shirt off my head and then attacked his mouth once more, devouring his lips, sucking his tongue into my mouth. As his fingers fumbled with the clasps of my bra, I pushed his shirt up and away, frantic, smoothed my hands over his bare torso, his firm muscles, his hard warm flesh. A lift of my torso, and my bra was gone, and then in a matter of seconds both of us had helped each other shed our pants and underwear. Naked together, I moaned into his mouth, savoring the sweep of his tongue against my lips and gums, against my teeth and tangling with my tongue. I slid my core against his erection, gasping at the hot silky steel of him brushing my sensitive flesh.

He took.

I felt my hips lifted in his hands, felt him nudging, searching for my entrance. I planted my palms on his chest and gathered my knees beneath my hips, leaned over and reached between our bodies to grasp his cock in my hands, lined the broad soft head up to my damp nether lips, sat poised thus, waiting.

His eyes burned into mine, heated, hooded amber, his mouth parted to pant for breath, his pulse throbbing in his throat, his chest expanding. The tips of my breasts brushed his chest, my thick, erect nipples scraping the dusting of hair on his chest and sending slow bolts of heat through me.

"I love you, Cade," I whispered.

He smiled up at me, released one of my hips and brushed his palm up my ribs, cupped my breast and slid his touch over it, his rough hand scratching my nipple, eliciting a sharp inhalation from me. Up to my face, holding my cheek. "I love you, Ever."

"Forever and always?" I said, not caring how desperate I sounded, how completely I was begging him.

"For forever, and after forever."

When I heard the words I'd been waiting to hear, I sank down on him. We both moaned, and our foreheads touched as bliss shot through us. When hipbones met, his length sheathed totally within me, I leaned onto him and wrapped my arms beneath his neck, every inch of our bodies pressed together, flesh merged, breath joined, souls spiraling up and out to weave together, meeting once more, broken parts matched, jagged edges smoothed.

And then he gripped my hips in his and lifted me, pulling himself out of me, and then, after slight hesitation, drove up into me, bringing my hips down at the same moment. I cried out as his hot hardness filled me, as his body completed mine.

His lips brushed the shell of my ear. "Talk to me, Ev. Dirty. The way you used to."

I was weak from the overwhelming bliss of his driving hips as he set a slow, gentle rhythm, but I lifted up onto my hands, my fists in the comforter on either side of his head. I held still and let him move, let him do the work, let the force of our joining make my tits sway, and remembered how much he loved that, how much he loved watching my tits bounce. Soon I'd sit up and give him that, but not yet. First, I had to draw him out. He was still holding back.

I let my eyes fall closed as his cock slid in and out of my wet folds, slipping and sliding slow and smooth. "You want me to talk dirty?"

"Uh-huh," he murmured.

"You like that, don't you?" I demanded.

"So much. I love the things you say. Hearing how much you like what I'm doing."

"Well, I need more, Cade. If you want me to talk dirty, you have to fuck me harder. It's been so long since we've made love like this, and I need it so bad. I need more. I need you to fuck me like you've never fucked me, baby."

He sighed and his hands clawed into my hips. "God, yes. You want me to fuck you harder?"

I nodded, unable to hold back from meeting his rhythm with my own counter-thrusts now. "Yeah, Cade. I need it harder. I need to feel your cock slamming into me. Take me, Cade. Take me however you want me. Fuck me any way you want me. I can ride you just like this, if you want. Or I can go onto my hands and knees, and you can fuck me doggy-style. I know you like that. Looking at my ass as you fuck me." I curled backward, grinding my core against him. "I just need to know how much you want it."

"I don't want it," Cade gasped. "I *need* it. Sit up for me, Ev. Let me see your tits bounce. Ride me until you come."

I sat up and balanced on my shins, sitting back so his cock was stretched away, and he had to lift up off the bed to get deep into me. I rocked on him, lifting up and sliding down, my hands on my thighs.

His fingers danced up my stomach to my ribs, and I leaned forward slightly so he could reach me, gasping as he found my nipple and tweaked it, rolled it. His thrusts grew harder, our bodies merging with a jarring clash, and my boobs shook and swayed, and I watched his gaze follow their motion.

I felt a burgeoning heat inside me, made hotter by every powerful thrust of Cade's huge hot cock. I moved with him, leaned forward with my hands on his chest, and rolled my hips to meet his strokes. My tits swayed and swayed, and I couldn't look away from Cade, watching the passion take over, the pleasure hood his eyes.

Words poured and tumbled from my lips, no longer calculated to inflame but merely drawn from me by the perfection of our union. "Oh, god, Cade...oh, god. Oh, fuck. You feel so good, baby. I can feel you inside me. You're so big, so hard. So thick and perfect." I fell forward and bit his lip, whispered against his face. "I love the way you fuck me. I've missed this so much. You don't even know how much I've missed this with you. It hasn't been the same, but now it's what I need. I'm getting close, Cade. I'm gonna come soon, and I'm gonna come hard."

"Please, Ev. Come for me. Let me watch you come." He held my hips and shoved me down into his thrusts, smashing deep and striking every nerve, pushing me toward the edge. "Come for me, baby."

The "baby" thing was new for us, but I liked it. I felt myself nearing the edge, felt the heat billowing through me, felt the pressure expanding and the need deepening. I rocked with him, gasping and unable to speak except to swear and cry his name.

So that's what I did.

And then he brought my tit to his mouth and sucked my nipple so hard it sent a twinge of almost-pain and all pleasure through me, pushing me over the edge.

I came with a hoarse scream. "Fuck, Cade! I'm coming…oh, shit, I'm coming. God, yes, fuck me, god, don't stop…don't stop."

"I'll never stop. Never stop." He spoke around my skin, and the heat of his breath made me whimper.

I exploded and my muscles contracted and I clung to him, grinding my core against his hard length.

And then he slowed, and stopped. I was shivering, wracked with post-orgasm tremors. "Why'd you stop?" I gasped.

He grinned at me. "My turn."

My eyes widened as he sat up with me, moving me off him, and then rolled me to my stomach. He gently guided my hips back to him, so I had to shift my knees beneath me. He'd held back. I groaned deep in my throat as I felt him take my ass in his hands and caress it, his length nestled between my cheeks, thick and iron-hard. I breathed and waited, watching over my shoulder as he smoothed my skin under his hands, and then pulled me back, spread me apart, gripped his cock in his hands, and probed my soft wet entrance.

I twitched forward as he penetrated my core, sliding deep into me. Shoved back against him, my ass to his hipbones. "Now fuck me, Cade. Fuck me until you come."

He pulled back, his eyes on mine, and then he grinned. "Hard?"

"So hard."

He slammed home, and I whimpered. Pulling out, poised with just the thick head inside my pussy, he hesitated again, watching me. And then drove in hard, deep. I shrieked at the fullness, the perfection of his stroking cock sliding deep where it belonged. I'd already come, but he'd make me come again, I knew. Not until he'd come, though.

He withdrew and thrust hard again, and I rocked back to meet him. He groaned, a rumble in his chest, and his hands held my hips in a crushing grip, jerking me back against him. Hard, and hard, and hard, he fucked me. And I loved every single driving slide, let my voice go loud and fill the small room, encouraging him to fuck me harder, fuck me harder. And harder he did, our flesh slapping together as he began to lose himself, his moans coming nonstop now as he neared his release.

Except, he faltered, and then stopped. Pulled me backward until I felt the bed sliding up beneath my body, felt the carpet touch my toes. I groaned, needing friction and needing him to start again, needing to feel him come, needing the second climax I felt approaching.

Now he was standing up behind me, driving up and in so deep and so hard I felt him through every inch of my body, and I loved him for bringing me to this position. And then, when he leaned forward and put his lips to my ear, I loved him even more. I pushed up to rest my weight on my hand, bending at the waist to keep the delicious angle.

He was moving hard and fast now, his face sliding near mine, his breath coming in gasps, his cock filling me. I felt him thicken and harden more, if that was possible, and I felt his rhythm stutter.

"Oh, god, Ev. I'm coming…"

"That's it," I gasped. "Come inside me. Let me have it all. I'm close, too, baby, so don't stop after you come. Keep fucking me until I come again."

He slammed deep, once, and then thrust his hips flush against my ass and ground against me, growling and thrusting desperately. I felt him release inside me, felt him fill me with a gush of liquid heat, and I felt my core clench. His hand reached between my body and the bed, cupped my boob and squeezed it, then found my nipple as he started to move again, his throbbing cock moving inside me slow and deep. He was softening, but was still hard, and I moved against him, milking him for all I could, feeling my inside tense and coil.

He took both of my tits in his hands and pinched my nipples hard enough to make me gasp, twisting them until I writhed, and he moved with me, groaning and whispering my name.

"Ev. Ev. God, baby, come again for me. Let me feel it, right now."

As if his words were a command, I exploded on him, crushing back against him. He released my nipples as I shrieked my orgasm, flicking them with his fingertips, and I felt everything inside me come apart, detonate, implode.

"Yes, Ev. Yes. Just like that. God, you're so beautiful when you come. I love hearing the sounds you make." He kept moving in me, with me, until I shuddered and went still. "I love you so much, Ev. So fucking much."

He pulled out of me, and then helped me climb onto the bed. He pulled me into the nook of his arm, and kissed my temple. I turned my face to catch his lips, pressed a long, slow kiss. "*That* was what I needed. Just you. Us, just like that."

"Me, too."

I crashed then, weak and limp and deliriously happy, if only temporarily.

I was awakened sometime around mid-afternoon by a text alert. Eden: **Can you and Caden come over? I have something to talk to you about.**

I sighed, not wanting to let go of the illusion of perfect peace Caden and I had created. We'd made love twice more, sleeping in between and enjoying the kind of bare, unfiltered pillow talk that only comes during the afterglow of intense sex.

Sure. Be there soon. I sent the text and then showed it to Cade, who'd been watching me with my phone.

He sighed deeply. "Okay, let's go. Probably should shower, though."

I giggled. "Yeah, probably. We both stink like sex."

He grabbed me by the waist and pulled me on top of him. "It's a good stink, though. I love the way you smell after we've been fucking all day."

I breathed in his scent. "I love it, too." I rested my head on his chest. "I don't want to get up. I want to stay here. Get you hard again."

He growled. "Don't tempt me."

I shifted my hips to brush my core against him. I felt him hardening against me. "Too late."

He rolled us over until he was on top of me. "Now you're gonna get it."

"Oh, good," I breathed. "I was hoping I would."

He pushed into me, slick and hard. "How is it this feels better every time? No matter how many times I do it, sliding into you never ceases to feel exponentially better than the time before."

"That's called true love, I think." I held onto his ass as he moved, slowly and gently and rhythmically. "Just like this, yeah. Slow and gentle."

We came almost right away that time. Silently, breathing each other's breath, eating gasps and swallowing sighs, we clung together and shook.

When the shuddering after-quakes subsided, we climbed out of bed and took turns showering.

Twenty minutes later, we were sitting on the floor of Eden's house, playing with the baby, laughing as she kicked her little legs and pawed the air with her little hands. Eden sat in the corner of the couch, watching us, Carter perched on the arm of the couch. They were holding hands, her palm resting on his thigh, his fingers tangled in hers.

With a deep breath, Eden spoke. "I've been thinking a lot. About everything." She closed her eyes briefly, as if summoning courage. "And I've come to a decision. Please—please don't say anything until I'm done, because this is really hard for me to say."

Cade and I exchanged worried glances. "We're listening," I said. "And—whatever it is you've decided, I love you, Edie. No matter what. Okay?"

Eden nodded. "I know. And I love you. That's why I think this is…best. For all of us." Her eyes went to the baby, who, as far as I knew, didn't have a name yet. "It's about her. I think—I think—"

She cut herself off with one sharp hyperventilating breath. Carter squeezed her hand, and then moved his palm in circles on her back, brushing her hair out of the way.

Eden started again. She spoke without taking her eyes off the baby cooing on the floor. "I think you and Caden should adopt her."

Nothing could have surprised me more. My eyes misted, and tears fell. "*What?* You want—Eden, why?"

Eden was fighting tears, too. "Be—because she should have been yours. If not for the accident, you'd probably have a baby by now. And…and—Jesus, I didn't think this would be this hard." She tipped her head back and wiped at her eyes. Leveled a look at me that spoke of renewed determination. "She should be yours. Yours to name. To raise."

"Eden," I said, searching for any kind of words, "I—are you sure? I mean, she's—she's your daughter."

Eden shook her head. "No, that's just it. It doesn't feel…I don't feel like she belongs to me." A sob shook her. "I haven't felt like she's mine, not from the very beginning. And not now. It's tearing me up inside, Ev. You don't even know. I—I can't raise her. She's yours. Yours and—and Caden's." Her eyes went, for the first time, to Caden. "It's the only…the only way."

Cade's voice rumbled as if from the bottom of a well. "You want us to raise her, or to adopt her legally?"

"Both."

"That's a huge decision, Eden." Cade looked down at the baby. "For you. For us. And most of all, for her."

"I know. But I think it's right. For all of us." She looked up at Carter, as if for courage. "I'm not ready for this. For parenthood. And you'll never be able to—to have this. You could adopt, or foster. But…it won't be the same. This is your blood, Ever."

"She'll have so many questions," Cade said. "I don't know if I could ever answer them."

"We'll all handle that when the time comes," I said. "Regardless of whether we do this or not, she'd have questions as she got older. She looks so much like you, Cade, that no one could ever mistake her for anything but your daughter. She looks like us, too," I gestured at Eden and me, "and that eventually would lead to questions. We don't have to have the answers now, though. She's just a baby."

Caden glanced at Carter. "What do you think about all this?"

Carter didn't answer for a long time. "It's not my decision, not in any way. I'll say what I said to Eden when she told me her idea: a child deserves the best possible chance at life. Eden believes that's with you two. This isn't an easy situation, not for anyone involved. But you have to think about what's best for her," he nodded at the baby, "before anything else."

"We need to think about this, talk about it," Cade answered for both of us.

"Obviously." Eden shifted forward off the couch and sat by me, watching as the baby wiggled and kicked. "I just want her to be happy. To have the best possible life. Two parents who love her. And—if I'm going to be brutally honest—I'm not sure I can be that. I don't know why. I don't know what's wrong with me, but...I need to do the best thing for her. And it seems like this is it."

I leaned in to hug Eden, and she fell against me, wrapped her arms around me. "I love you so much, Eden. I missed you. I wondered every single day where you were. Why you'd left. I understand now, and—and I can't lose you again." I pulled back to look at her. "Tell me honestly, and think about it hard: if we adopted her, could you look at us, and her, and not...wish? Wonder? Resent us, maybe? You know us, and you know we'd always be around each other. Our families would be together all the time. You'd see her, and—"

"And I'd know I gave her the best thing I could. You and Cade." She took my hand in hers. "I probably will wonder, sometimes. If I did the right thing. But...I know, right now, in my gut, that this is right."

I glanced over at Caden, who was bouncing the baby on his knee, one hand splayed at her neck to support her head. He nodded at me. "Let us think about it. Okay?"

Eden nodded. "Of course."

I stood up, and Carter rose to his feet, the baby in his arms. He gave her to Eden, who sat down on the couch once more with her. "We'll see you soon, okay?"

"'Bye." Eden watched us go, looking relieved, yet still filled with turmoil.

Instead of driving back to the Old Mission Inn, we walked along the beach, ending up almost a mile from Eden's house, staring out at the sun as it lowered toward the bay.

I stood at the water's edge, my heart and mind whirling.

Caden stood beside me, took my hand, and looked at me. "What are you thinking?"

I shrugged. "Too much." I laughed. "It's kind of chaotic in my head right now."

"Mine, too."

"Let's boil it down to o-ne word answers, based on initial reaction." He turned to face me, taking both of my hands in his. "We'll think about, talk about it, sleep on it. But right now, what are you thinking? Yes, or no?"

I met his amber gaze with mine. "Yes. First thought? Yes." I watched his reaction. "You?"

He nodded, looked out at the rippling golden water. "Me, too. Yes."

"Are we crazy?"

He laughed. "Probably. But…have our lives ever made sense?"

I shook my head, laughing with him. "No. Not really."

"So this would just be one more chapter. And… god, this might sound even crazier, but the first moment I walked into that house and held that little baby, I—" Cade ducked his head, sucked in a breath. "I loved her. I didn't want to let go of her. I wanted to—watch her. Just keep watching her."

"It's not crazy," I told him. "I felt the same way. Immediately, just—something clicked."

We walked slowly back to the car in silence, each of us lost in our own thoughts.

We didn't discuss it again until after we'd gone to the Peninsula Grill for dinner and then returned to the inn. I'd been turning things over and over in my head all day, almost obsessively, trying to picture Cade and me as parents. Imagining taking that little bundle of warm baby home with us. Changing diapers. Feeding. Waking up at all hours of the night. First days of school. Backpacks and lunches, little friends coming over to play. A million things.

And I *could* envision it. So easily.

Every time I thought of her—of our lives with her—a name floated through my mind. Cade and I sat on our bed, him leaning against the headboard, me in front of him, resting back on his chest, between his knees. The TV was on, tuned to some prime time, basic cable feature film. Neither of us was really paying attention, though.

I twisted back to look at Cade. "I know what her name is," I said.

Cade shut off the TV and met my eyes. "Yeah? What?"

"Cadence."

He sighed, a long, slow breath. "Cadence." His eyes slid closed and then opened. "It's perfect."

We both knew, by giving her a name, that we'd decided.

going home

Eden

They sat on my couch, holding hands, decision in their eyes. I couldn't bear to sit, to be still. I paced, and paced, until Ever stood up and caught me, grabbing my hands.

She smiled. "Yes."

I laughed, but it was almost a sob. "Yes?" Sick of crying, I choked it back.

"Yes." Ever reached up and wiped a middle finger under my eye, brushing away a tear. "As long as you're absolutely sure."

"I am." I breathed in, blinking hard. "It's not easy, but it's right."

Carter spoke up. "What's right is rarely easy."

Caden moved to stand beside Ever, curling an arm around her waist. "We've got a name for her."

"You do?" I looked from one to the other. "What?"

Ever spoke. "Cadence."

I pulled away, fighting emotions. Of course, I instinctively found Carter, and found his arms waiting to hold me. "Cadence." I rested my face on his chest, looking over at the Pack-N-Play in the corner of the living room where the newly named Cadence lay sleeping. I watched her sleep, and I asked myself if I was really doing the right thing. I only found affirmation within. "It's perfect for her."

Cadence stirred at that moment, giving a peep of waking-up displeasure, which turned to a full-throated wail. Ever left Caden's side in a rush, bent over the rail, and lifted her up, settling Cadence's face on her shoulder, bouncing and shushing and patting. Within seconds, Cadence had quieted, sleeping once more. The only way I ever got her to calm down was to feed her, and Ever had her quiet just by picking her up.

I closed my eyes and turned my face into Carter's thick flannel shirt. He rubbed my shoulder blades with both hands, and I wondered if he understood the strange and chaotic mix of emotions running through me. I was happy, sad, relieved, sick at myself for being relieved, amazed and glad that Cadence had responded so perfectly to Ever. A little hurt by that same response—over everything, really—hoping I was making the right decision for the baby, and for myself.

Carter's voice surprised me. "My dad's friend is a lawyer. I asked him about the legal side of things." He glanced down at me, assessing my reaction to his proactive action. I only smiled at him, grateful. "He called me this morning, and as soon as we give him the word, he can start the paperwork."

I took a deep breath, held it, and then let it out. "Tell him to go ahead."

"Are you sure?" Carter asked me.

I nodded. "Yes. As sure as I can be."

I watched Ever and Caden as Cadence nuzzled into Caden's chest when Ever passed her over to Cade...to her daddy. The love and awe shining in Ever's eyes as she gazed at her husband and... and daughter, made my decision worth everything. Giving her up was hard. I knew it was for the best— for me, for Cadence, for Caden and Ever, but it was hard all the same. I'd carried her for nine months, gave birth to her, and I'd taken care of her for the last week and a half. I'd gotten used to the sounds of her crying in the middle of the night, used to the feel of her in the bed with me. As much as I didn't feel as if she really belonged to me, I was still...attached to her.

It wasn't about whether I loved her or not—because I did, deeply. But…for me, she belonged to them. She was meant to be with them. They were her parents.

I was making the right choice.

It took two weeks and an emotional court appearance, and then Cadence Irene Monroe officially belonged to Ever and Caden. Over the past two weeks Ever stayed with me, basically taking over the care of Cadence. Cade, meanwhile, had returned to Royal Oak to get their condo ready for the homecoming. They'd picked out a crib, changing table, and dresser from a store in downtown Traverse, and the pieces were being shipped south. Ever had told him to turn her art studio into a bedroom, which I knew was a sacrifice for her, but she'd done it happily.

"I can figure out somewhere else to paint. Or I can start working with watercolors, something that doesn't need so much ventilation and prep work." She'd shrugged. "It doesn't matter. Only this little girl matters." She nuzzled Cadence with her nose, cooing and babbling, so sweet and so happy it made my chest ache and my stomach flip.

By the time the court hearing came around, Cade had the condo ready and had returned to Traverse City. Carter came with me to the hearing.

I stood before the judge and acknowledged that I was giving up all parental rights, that I was doing so under my own free will. I signed a paper, and Ever and Caden signed as well. I watched Ever's pen swirl across the document, my heart swelling with both joy and sadness.

And then the judge banged his gavel, and it was done.

Outside the courtroom, Ever and Cade stood side by side. It was spring, late afternoon, the air cool but holding hints of warmth. Birds chirped, squirrels chattered, and a long cold breeze blew off the lake. Cadence was in her carrier, sleeping.

I knelt in front of her, kissed her nose, blinking away tears. "Goodbye, sweetheart." I blinked harder, but salt burned and liquid trickled down my cheeks anyway. There was so much I wished I could say, but nothing else came out. "I love you." It was the first time I'd said it to her.

I stood up, wiping at my face.

Ever grabbed me and held me in a long hug. "God, Edie. Are you okay?"

I nodded. "Yeah." I breathed out, forcing a smile. "It's hard, but it's right. For you, and for her, most of all. It is. I know it is. Doesn't mean it's not hard."

"Are you coming back to Royal Oak?" I knew the question had been on her lips for weeks.

"Not yet. Maybe at some point. I need—I need some time for me now." I kissed her cheek. "But I'll visit."

"*We'll* visit," Carter corrected, putting a hand on my back.

I glanced over my shoulder at him, smiling shyly. "We'll visit."

Ever looked between Carter and me. She hugged me close again, putting her lips to my ear. "*He's hot,*" she whispered.

I giggled, sniffing. "I know."

"Does he make you happy?" She asked it out loud, shooting a meaningful glance at Carter.

"He will. When I give him the chance." I laughed, grinning at him. "He's been…perfect. For real. I don't know what I would have done without him."

Carter seemed uncomfortable. "I'll make her happy, if she'll let me."

I slid away from Ever, toward Carter, happily accepting his arm around my waist, leaning into him. "And I'll let him."

"Good." Ever faked a tough glare at Carter. "You'd better."

Another goodbye hug to Ever, and an awkward, short embrace between Caden and me, and a shake of hands between Carter and both of them, and then they got into their green Jeep Cherokee. They drove away, with Cadence buckled firmly in place.

I watched them go, and when they were out of sight, I sagged against Carter. "That was hard—harder than I'd ever imagined."

He turned so I was buried in his chest, his arms around me, tight and safe and warm. "I know." He breathed a sigh. "Now let's go home."

I nodded. "That sounds good."

He hesitated. "I mean my home. My island."

I'd never been there. I think it was significant that he'd phrased it as he had. "Home?"

Carter tipped my chin up. "If you want."

I only hesitated for a minute. "Yeah. I do. I need some of my stuff, though." When we got to my house—the cabin, which had been home for so long—I realized I only had a very few things. Some clothes, some other sundries for day-to-day life, books, and my cello. I turned to Carter, stopping in the act of stuffing a handful of underwear into my suitcase. "For how long?"

He only smiled. "As long as you want?"

I ducked my head. "I don't have much to bring."

Carter chuckled, stepping up to me, gazing down at me. "So bring it all."

"Everything?"

He nodded, his eyes serious. "Everything." We weren't talking about my things anymore.

"If you're sure you want me there."

He tipped my chin up with a finger. "I've been waiting to bring you to my house for a very long time, Eden Eliot."

I blinked at that. "I can't—I mean, we can't do anything. Together. Yet." I swallowed hard. "Six weeks, which is another three weeks away."

Carter only dipped down and kissed me, ever so gently. "I've waited this long. I can wait a bit longer." He kissed me again, a nudge and a peck on the corner of my mouth. "It's not about that, anyway. It's about you."

I peeked up at him. "It's not about that at *all?*"

He laughed. "Maybe it is, a little." His voice went serious again. "Listen, Eden. When you're ready, not before. I only want you, as you are. Good, bad, beautiful, and messed up."

"Then let's go home."

It took a very short amount of time to pack the rest of my things into a suitcase, and to sort out a few boxes and storage containers. It all got piled into Carter's truck and strapped down. The hardest piece to get there was the sculpture Carter had given me for Christmas. He wrapped it in a couple of blankets and secured it in the truck bed. But before we closed up the cabin, I stopped in the living room, staring at everything. I wouldn't miss it that much, I realized. I associated the cabin with Carter, and all my memories of the cabin included him, and I was going with him. Home. With him.

Oh, god.

I finally admitted to myself that I wanted that. I wanted him. All of him. Very, very much. More than I'd really dared to think about.

I locked the door behind me, tucked the key into my purse, and slid into the passenger seat of the truck. Carter closed the door behind me, as he always did. The drive to the marina where his boat was docked took less than ten minutes. He had a forty-foot cruiser—a big, beautiful, expensive-looking thing. I stood on the dock, admiring her. And then I saw the name across the bow.

Carter followed my gaze. "Does that bother you?"

I read it again. *Britt*. I shook my head. "She's part of you. Part of who you are."

He breathed a sigh of relief. "Good." He tossed the line onto the dock, then handed me across into the boat. "She was a gift from Dad. For my twenty-sixth birthday. He gave it to me after I'd bought the island. He knew what I'd name it, and he had it painted on her before he gave it to me."

"She's beautiful." I sat in the seat beside the captain's chair, excitement thrilling through me as he backed out of the slip.

"That she is. Ironic thing is, Britt hated boats, hated the water. Got seasick. She wouldn't have set foot on this thing. And here she has a boat named after her."

I reached out and rested my hand on his forearm. There wasn't much to say to that, so I didn't say anything. The trip only took about ten minutes, and then an island came into view. It was small, dominated by the house. There was a sward of bright green grass ringing the house and a cluster of pine trees on one end. A boathouse sat beside a long dock, a path of white rocks leading away from the dock toward the house. A white gazebo, overlooking the water, was located midway between the dock and the house.

The house itself was breathtaking. Pale blue with white trim, huge amounts of glass. It had a tower with a copper roof and floor-to-ceiling windows and a small balcony. A wraparound deck circled most of the house, and white stone pathways led from the deck off the walk-out basement to the dock. It wasn't a huge mansion of a house, but it was glorious and perfect. Carter cut the engines and let the boat drift to a gently bumping stop in front of the boathouse. He stepped out onto the deck surrounding the boat slip, extended a hand to me, and helped me cross from boat to him. He then went back down to the boat and handed my small pile of belongings onto the deck. I carried my suitcase, rolling it behind me, while he carried a storage container and two boxes of books, leading me up the path through the gazebo and up to the house, to what I'd thought was the walk-out basement.

But, as I pulled open the wide french doors, I discovered the entrance to the basement was actually the main entrance to the house, leading to the kitchen.

Carter saw my confusion. "There was no reason to have a traditional front or back to the house, no reason to have an actual 'front door,' per se, you know?" He made air quotes around the phrase. "So I designed the house to capture the most light, and to be accessible from all parts of the island. I always come in from the boathouse, obviously, so I figured this was the most obvious place for a main entrance. But I didn't want to compromise the architectural design with a stupid door."

He set the boxes down in a corner of the kitchen, took my suitcase and put it aside, and then led me back out to the gazebo, where he pointed at the house while he explained. "See, up there, what you thought was the back of the house, with the deck? That's the main living room, the den, whatever you want to call it. The kitchen is on the bottom level, accessible from the boat dock, since I have to bring in groceries and didn't want to hike up the stairs. I like to sit out here in the gazebo and eat. I wanted the living room to have a ton of natural light and the best view of the bay, since that's where I relax.

And then up there, that turret?" He pointed at the copper-roofed structure that had first captured my eye. "That's the main bedroom. There's another, smaller bedroom on the upper floor, and a third on the kitchen level, and a bathroom on each floor. Plus there's my woodworking shop off the kitchen, which you can't really see since it's largely underground."

"You built this place?" I asked, awed.

He shrugged. "Yeah. It was first owned by some wealthy bigwig—meant to be a vacation home, I guess. They bought the island and laid down the plumbing, electrical and all that, running it out to the mainland. At *huge* expense, I might add. It's almost three miles from here to the peninsula, and to lay down all that piping and wiring? Jesus. I don't even want to know what it cost, what kind of permits they had to pull for that. Then they started the foundation, laying out the groundwork and such. At some point, though, they ran out of money and had to sell. I think whoever it was that started the project must've gone bankrupt, because the price I got the island for was just plain ludicrous. So the hardest part was done—plumbing and wiring an island for modern life. I just built the house on top. And, yes, I designed and built it myself." He stared at the house, clearly proud.

As well he should be. "It's incredible, Carter."

"Thanks. Let's grab the rest of your stuff and get dinner going. I'm hungry." He grinned at me and tugged me back to the boathouse.

I carried Apollo, and he took the rest of what was left, putting it in the kitchen. The sculpture he put in the living room upstairs, in a corner between windows. He kicked off his boots and toed his socks off, wiggling his bare toes against the floor. And just like that, I was moved into Carter's island home.

It was just him and me.

Nerves shot through me, and I wondered if I knew what I'd just gotten myself into. I'd never lived with a guy before. Never done more than stay the night, and even that was unusual. Usually I'd leave that night, or early in the morning. I was an expert at the walk of shame.

Granted, it had been a long time since I'd done that walk, but until my…thing…with Cade, it was what I knew. I'd grown to expect that once a guy had gotten his fill of me, I'd be sent packing. If not right away, then in a day or two. At most a couple of weeks. So I started bolting before the awkwardness of "so yeah, it's been fun, but I've got…plans" could begin. Would that happen here? How long before Carter got tired of me? How long before I was piling my shit back onto his boat?

Of course, as I leaned against the granite counter of his kitchen, Carter seemed to sense my sudden onset of nerves. He dug into his front pocket and withdrew a five-dollar bill, set it on the counter beside me. "Five for your thoughts?" His voice was quiet, his eyes knowing.

Damn the man for always sussing out my insecurities.

I shrugged. "Just…I've never lived with anyone before. Except dorm roommates, I mean. I just— don't know what to expect."

Carter shook his head with a small smile. "Nope, that's not it. Not entirely. That's not enough for the dark look you just had."

I sighed, examining my fingernails so I didn't have to look at him. "No one's ever—there's never been a reason to stay. Not for more than a night or two, at most." I found myself unloading the most painful truth possible, bluntly. "No one ever wanted me to. There'd be a tumble or two. Maybe a month's worth of interest. Then? Buh-bye. See ya. Don't let the door hit your ass on the way out. Even Cade, he was torn up about what we were doing. You know? I mean how could he not be? I was torn up, too, but… it was worse for him. It was his condo, his and Ever's. *Their* place. *Their* bed. I never stayed long, even with him. And it was…intense with him." I blew out a pained breath. "Shit, I know you probably don't want to hear about this. Sorry."

He leaned against the counter beside me. "No. I want to know everything about you. I told you: the good, the bad, the ugly and the beautiful, the perfect and the broken."

I shook my head. "Shut up with your stupid poetry. There's mainly just the bad, the ugly, and the broken. Sorry to disappoint." I sniffed. "He was always very up front about the fact that I was only getting the leftovers, you know? That even if Ever never woke up, if he had to take her off life support, he'd never be able to love me. I was too much like her, but I wasn't *her*. And whether it was me or not, someone else, someone random, he'd never love them. Not the way he loved her. So I was just getting what he had left. And I *still* got attached. See, I always get attached. Even when I intellectually, mentally *know* they're just gonna hump-and-dump me, I get attached. And, with Cade, it fucking—it *meant* something. We were two hurting, broken, fucked-up people. We were the only ones who understood what the other was going through—losing someone who wasn't totally gone. It doesn't make it okay, and I'll never try to excuse it, or justify it—"

"You don't have to. Not to me, not to anyone."

I sighed and shook my head. "Yeah, I do. But regardless, my point is, *this*," I gestured at the kitchen, at my pile of things, "this is totally outside my comfort zone, outside my realm of expertise. If you want me to be gone in the morning before you wake up, I can do that. Well, it might be more difficult, since we're on an island and I can't drive a boat *or* swim three miles. But under normal circumstances, I could do that. I can dump you right when you're thinking of dumping me. I can tell you we don't have to worry about expectations or complicated things like emotions."

Carter's face was taking on an expression that I could only describe as tragic. Pitying. It made me angry, and a little scared.

I swallowed hard. "But…this? Whatever this is with you and me? I don't know how to do it. I don't know what you want from me. What I'm supposed to do, or…or anything. So. So maybe you should just take me back. Before things get even more fucked up."

Carter frowned. "Do you want me to take you back?"

I shrugged. "I don't know. I like it here. Your home is the most gorgeous place I've ever been."

"But?"

He always knew. "But…I don't know what we are, or how to be what you want."

He let out a long breath. "You're complicating things, babe." He turned to face me, but I stayed as I was, so he was looking at my profile. He didn't allow that, though. He touched the side of my jaw and turned my face to his. "It's easy, Edie. Just be."

I glared at him in confusion. "What the fuck does that mean? Is that some Zen bullshit?"

He laughed, hard. "God, you're making this so difficult when it doesn't have to be. And it's so cute."

I was pissed now. I backed away from him, walking toward the door. "Cute? It's *cute?* I don't like being made fun of, Carter, and that's what this feels like."

He went serious then. His face hardened, his eyes blazed, and he stalked toward me. I wasn't afraid of him, but his demeanor made me nervous. "Eden. I'm not making fun of you. You seem to be under the misapprehension that I have some set of expectations. That there's some list of rules that you don't know about. There's not." He grabbed me by the shoulders and turned me around, seemingly oblivious to the fact that I was resisting him. He wanted me to move, so he moved me. And here I thought I was strong. "Have I ever put any kind of expectations on you?"

I didn't answer.

"*Have* I?"

Tiny, minuscule, embarrassed voice. Unable to look at him. "No."

"You're in my home because I want you to be." He brushed my hair away from my face, the way he always did. "I'll tell you a secret: Not even my brothers have been here. Only one person on the entire planet has ever been inside my house after it was finished." He let me go, but I stayed close to him, looking up into his blue eyes.

I was curious now. "Who?"

He grinned at me playfully. "My momma. That's who."

I smiled. "That makes sense. You seem kinda like a momma's boy."

He nodded seriously. "Absolutely. I accept that label with complete and total confidence in my manhood."

Is there anything more attractive than a confident, sexy man who loves his mother? I'm not sure there is. Except maybe that same man barefoot in blue jeans. Something that's also mysteriously and unfathomably sexy.

I blinked at the enormity of what he'd just said. "Why not your brothers? You seem close to them. Or your dad? He did give you the boat, after all."

He only shrugged. "I'm a private person. You're also the only person, and this time I mean the *only* person, who knows everything about the night Britt died. I never told anyone, obviously, because I never spoke after that night."

"Until you met me."

"Until I met you."

"Why me? I don't get it. I didn't do anything. More than one person has asked what I did, how I got you to talk. And I just don't know."

Carter sighed. "I don't know any more than you do. I just—I saw you on the beach, and that was the first time I even wanted to talk to someone. I wanted to say hi. And then that time I accidentally kicked sand at you? I wanted to apologize. But I couldn't. And for the first time, being silent seemed like a burden. So then, when you wouldn't let me drive you home, even though it was so hot and you nearly passed out, I just *had* to talk to you. So I did. And after that, it was easy to just go back to being me." He ran his big toe along the seam of the tile underfoot, tracking the line of the grout. "It wasn't like I just flicked a switch, or anything. Like I was suddenly okay with what happened to Britt. But I'd had a year up to that point to come to grips. I still feel guilty about it. I know I should've done things differently. But the not talking wasn't about my guilt. It was about…the trauma of it, I guess. I don't know. I tried seeing shrinks, but they don't do much good when you don't talk."

"So where are you, in terms of…guilt, and trauma, and everything? Are you over it?"

He frowned. "I'm not sure you're *ever* okay, or *over* things like that. I loved Britt. I was at least partially responsible for her death. That will always be a part of me. But…I can't change what happened. And I can't keep living in the past. I want to be *alive*. I want to be happy. I want to have a future. If I'm

this silent shadow just floating through life living
in a pattern, not really participating in my life, then
what's the point? Why don't I just become a shut-in?
Just give up. You didn't intentionally do anything.
You didn't fix me. One person can't fix another. I'm
not trying to fix you. What you did was provide me
with a reminder that there's life out there. That I have
something to say. I have desires. I have pet peeves
and fetishes. Maybe not *fetishes*, that may not be the
right word. I'm not into, like, feathers or whips and
chains and hot wax. I just meant I like certain things
and not others. My point is, you were a reminder
that even though I'd lost someone I loved—still love,
really, because that kind of love never goes away—
I'm still alive, and I deserve to live my life. I have
the guilt still, because that also never goes away. You
make a mistake, do something wrong—it doesn't just
go away. You have to come to terms with it, Eden.
Accept the guilt, acknowledge your fault. Then live.
Learn from it, and keep going. You don't forget, you
don't block it or bury it. You just…live. Don't let
guilt define you."

I laughed bitterly. "You make it sound so simple."

"It is simple. It's just not *easy*." Carter stepped
away from me, moving into the kitchen and rummaging through cupboards. "Is what happened with
Cade the only thing about you that I need to know?
Is it the totality of *you?*"

"No, but—"

"Is having had a baby and giving it up for adoption to your sister and brother-in-law all of what makes Eden Eliot a person?"

"No, but—"

He set two wine glasses on the counter, rummaged in the fridge and pulled out a bottle of Chateau Chantal Riesling, twisted the top off and poured a big glass for each of us. Handed me one, and sipped at his before he continued. "Then who are you? What makes you, *you?*"

I stared into the pale gold liquid. Except for the tiny half-glass on Christmas, I hadn't had a drop to drink for over nine months. I thought about the question. "How do you define yourself in a few words? I'm a cellist. I'm a twin. I'm a musician, a composer. I like to read romance books. The smutty, steamy, bodice-ripper kind. I like car-chase movies like *Gone in 60 Seconds* or *Fast and Furious*. I also like end-of-the-world movies, like *Armageddon* or *Day After Tomorrow*." I sipped at my wine, closing my eyes and savoring the sweet, cold taste. I thought, and let whatever came to mind about myself emerge from my mouth. "I really, really like sex. I like it hard and fast, and slow and gentle. A little rough, but I don't like pain. I like to be the instigator, and I like it even more when control is taken from me. But that rarely happens. I like wine, mostly white, and a few kinds of red. I hate light beer, and I like reds, like Killian's. I hate whiskey. I love gin. I'm a gin snob. Don't bother if it's not Sapphire. I can't sew, knit, crochet, or anything like that. I suck at cooking. I can burn water and chronically undercook chicken, overcook red meat, and I can't ever seem to time my dishes to be done at the same time. Recipes confuse me, but I don't have the instinct for improvisation. I love food. I'm a foodie. It's why I work out so much. Dieting makes me angry, so I work out like a madwoman instead, so I can eat what I want. I was on a diet from the time I was thirteen till I was twenty, and then one day I just said 'fuck it.' I'm gonna eat what I want, when I want, and if I gain weight because of it, I'll just work it off. But yet I still try to eat healthy, just not a diet. I had a baby, but I don't identify myself as a mother."

Carter's eyes were watching my mouth as I spoke, but I knew he was cataloguing everything I said. He sipped his wine, his hooded eyes piercing sky blue over the rim of his glass, hot on me.

"I've never done anal, and I've always secretly wanted to." I had no idea I was going to say that. It just popped out.

Carter sputtered and coughed, choking on his wine. "Jesus, wasn't expecting that. Okay."

I blushed. "Sorry. I—I'm not sure why I said that. TMI, probably."

He chewed on his lip, and then shook his head. "No. Nothing is TMI. I've never done that, either. With Britt, it—we weren't like that. I'm not gonna go into details, but…it wasn't like that."

"You don't have to say anything, tell me anything, but just…you *can*. You can talk about her, if you want. Talking about exes is usually a no-no, but that's different, I think. For me, at least."

He didn't answer right away. "We were eighteen when we met. We weren't each other's firsts, but almost. After your first, you're sort of…you feel—I don't know. Adult? Like you know what you're doing? But you don't, not really. That was us. It was always just…simple. Nothing adventurous or crazy. I think the craziest thing we ever did was sex outside, on a picnic. A blanket on the grass, under a tree." He laughed self-consciously. "It was *so* uncomfortable. There was a root under the blanket, and the tree kept shedding those little helicopter things, you know? The seed things? They kept hitting me in the head. Landing on us. And ants had found our food and were freaking Britt out. But…for us, it was just… easy. Simple. Us together was all we needed. I don't think we ever even thought about…I don't know, trying stuff, I guess."

I could see that about Carter. "There's nothing wrong with that." I set my glass down. "I'm not into anything weird, okay? Don't get the wrong idea.

I've never told anyone that before. About wanting to try…that. It was a sudden confession, I guess you could call it."

Carter reached out and took my hand. "Since we're talking about sex, I want to make something clear. I sort of said it earlier, but I want to say it again. I don't have any expectations, Eden. None. I want you. I'll be honest. Yes, I want that, with you. When it's right for you. You've been through a lot, and I don't want you to feel any pressure. You're not physically ready yet anyway, but even after you are, I didn't bring you here for that. Not for that alone, at least. I brought you here because I enjoy your company. I want to be around you all the time." He pulled me against him. His heartbeat was a steady, comforting rhythm on my cheek. "I've gotten addicted to being around you. Especially over the past few weeks. You've become a part of my everyday. And I don't want to give that up. I don't see why I should, either. Our relationship may not fit into any easy boxes or categories, and I don't care. Are we dating? I don't know. Are we a couple? I don't know. We've been together every single day for months, but we've never done more than share a couple of kisses. I've slept beside you more than once. I held your hand while you gave birth. You know all my secrets, and I know yours. But *what* are we? I don't know. And I don't think it matters. We are what we are. I want us to do what's comfortable and right for *us*, regardless of whether it has a label or box or pigeonhole." He touched my chin, a soft and tender smile on his lips. "That's all I meant when I said 'just be.' It doesn't have to be complicated. Just be you. Be yourself, in my home. Be yourself, in my life. That's it."

I felt an ache in my chest, a swelling of hope, the germinated seed of happiness sending a tendril up toward the sun that was Carter. "I can do that. I think."

He smiled. "Good. That's all I'm asking. Be you. Be open and honest and exactly who you are. Don't hide your fears, don't hide your insecurities. Don't push me away because you're afraid. I'm a little scared of this, too, okay? I haven't been with anyone since Britt, either, and that's scary. She was the last person I was with in any sense. So I've got my own set of nerves and fears. And I'm perfectly willing to share those with you." He lifted his glass up for a toast. "To us, whatever the hell we are."

I laughed and clinked my glass against his. "To us, whatever the hell we are."

We sipped our wine, and Carter began taking food out of the fridge, assembling the makings for a meal. "Lucky for you," he told me as he put pork chops into the oven, "I can cook. I'm no gourmet, but I can put some good food on the table. Mom made sure all of us boys could make real food for ourselves by the time we graduated high school. You wouldn't think it, but Tommy is the best cook in the family. *He* can whip up some gourmet shit, lemme tell you."

Carter made a salad of fresh spinach, walnuts, fresh strawberries, and gorgonzola cheese, as well as hand-mashed potatoes and broccoli with rice. I helped peel the potatoes and mash them—according to his instructions—and we sat in the hand-carved chairs on the small porch outside the kitchen. While waiting for the food to cook, we sipped our wine and talked of lighter things, the kind of casual, random conversation you can only have through mutual vulnerability, the familiarity of shared secrets.

Carter plated the food and carried it out to the gazebo, where we ate and watched the sun set, going through a second bottle of wine. I was loose and warm inside, comfortable and easy around Carter as always, but now there was a subtext of desire, the knowledge that eventually, someday, sometime, we'd act on the sexual tension that was building between us.

The air was chilly still, and on the island there was a constant wind, but Carter kept blankets and extra fleece jackets in a hidden cabinet in the gazebo. I wore one of his old jackets, a faded, well-worn rust-orange Columbia that was several sizes too big, perfect for burrowing into, my hands tucked inside the sleeves. It smelled of him, of his natural scent, and it was deliciously warm and soft. When we finished eating, I curled up against him, his arm around me. I nuzzled into his chest, my wine glass nearly empty, full of good food and full of hope for the future.

For the first time since Ever's accident, perhaps for the first time ever in my life, I felt totally at peace.

He'd made it clear that I could choose where I slept. There were spare bedrooms, but I didn't see the point. I slept with Carter, in his bed. He was a perfect gentlemen, offering me privacy to change, making sure I had my space in the bed if I needed it. I didn't. I stayed modestly covered, wearing a T-shirt and boy boxers to bed, but when we slid into the blankets, I cuddled against him and enjoyed the feeling of being held.

He gave good cuddle. The bed was huge and soft, the blankets warm, and he was a solid, strong, safe presence. The knowledge that there were no expectations for sex made it easy. He just held me. I'd never been just held. Never. So at first, I was anxious, uncomfortable.

That first night, tipsy and nervous, I was tense in his arms. Eventually, his voice, sleep-muzzy, said, "Relax, Edie. Just sleep."

So I let myself relax, I turned away from him and curled up as I would if I was alone. And, wonder of wonders, he let me sleep however I wanted. Yet, unexpectedly, I woke up in the middle of the night cold and feeling alone, and so I turned into him and his arm slid around me automatically and pulled me tight and held me close, and I fell asleep right away, tucked against his heartbeat and his soft warm skin and hard muscles. And I slept perfectly, dreamlessly, deeply.

We developed a domestic routine. He'd wake up at the ass-crack of dawn and work out, which I envied. I wasn't allowed to do anything strenuous yet, and I desperately wanted to get back in shape. I'd taken up yoga, which wasn't nearly as satisfying as a tough workout, but it was something to do with him while he lifted weights.

Those weeks were idyllic. Slow, peaceful, contented, calm. He taught me to cook; it turned out I was simply untaught rather than incapable. I watched him carve and build cabinets and rocking chairs and bookshelves for clients, sculpt blocks of wood into mammoths and succubae and lynx and marten and twisting spires of abstract beauty. I played, improvising merely for the delirious joy of playing Apollo. The dulcet golden notes from Apollo's aged belly scattered across the bay, and I imagined someone on the distant shores catching faint strains of cello music from somewhere unknown.

We didn't kiss, by unspoken agreement. We both knew if we kissed, if we touched, it would spark a fire that couldn't be doused, once lit. So he held me and I burrowed and nuzzled into his warm embrace, and I held his hands, and it felt like being fourteen all over again with my first boyfriend, strolling the echoing marble halls of Somerset Mall, watching movies in my basement and cuddling and wondering when he'd kiss me.

I'd woken up next to enough men in my life to know what happened to them early in the morning, and I knew that was part of the reason Carter always woke up and got out of bed before me. I'd felt it, once in a while, as I drowsed in the pre-dawn gray, the hard thickness pressing against me. And then he'd stir, take a deep breath and yawn and stretch, and then he'd start gently. Slip out of bed, tug on a tank top, and hit the weight bench adjacent to the workshop. I'd get out of bed more leisurely, put on a sports bra and join him in the exercise room, put my mat down and stretch out. Basic stretches first, toe touches and lunges and palms planted on the floor between my wide-spread feet. Then I'd go into Downward-facing Dog, and hold it, pushing until I felt the burn in my muscles. I'd slide from one pose to another, and I always felt his eyes on me, especially if the pose required bending over. I liked his eyes on me, and I wasn't shy about watching him, either.

As the weather got warmer, Carter began testing the water. He'd dangle his feet off the dock, and then he'd wade out to waist-high, coming in shivering and laughing. A week before my six-week appointment, he went for his first actual swim, a slow circuit of the island. I sat on the gazebo with a cup of coffee, the sun a half-circle on the water, and watched him do an easy crawl stroke, graceful and powerful. He emerged dripping on the dock, shaking, his lips blue, a triumphant grin on his face.

"First swim of the season! Brisk, baby!" He shook his head like a dog, water spraying on me, so I laughed and shielded myself with my hands. "You gonna swim with me?"

"Maybe when it's warmer?" I said, wiping my face with my sleeve.

"It's not that bad. I'll have to spend a few weeks getting into condition before I make the whole distance to the mainland. If you start swimming with me now, you'll probably be able to keep pace with me. You're pretty badass. That run south from the lighthouse? You remember that? I thought I'd die trying to keep up with you." He sat down on the bench next to me, stretched his arm out behind me, and stole my coffee from me to take a sip.

I laughed. "God, that was crazy. I was so pissed off that you wouldn't talk to me, but I would be damned before I let you show me up. By the time I got back home, I could barely walk. I had to literally crawl into the house." And then what he'd said about me penetrated. "You think I'm badass?"

He lifted an eyebrow. "Um, yeah."

I blushed. "Thanks, I guess. I don't feel badass right now. I feel fat and sloppy and slow and soft. I used to be…fit. You could bounce a quarter off my ass. I could run a mile in six minutes and almost lift my own body weight. I was actually thinking about doing the Tough Mudder at some point. That was before, though. Now? Probably not. I'd be lucky to be able to run a mile at all, let alone in any kind of time."

Carter frowned. "You're really hard on yourself, physically, aren't you?"

I nodded. "Yeah. I struggled with my weight all my life. I was never actually overweight, and I know it. But I always compared myself to Ever. She'd always been effortlessly slim. She can eat whatever she wants and not have to worry about it. If she'd been the one to get pregnant, she would've been back to her initial weight already. I'm still twenty pounds over my pre-pregnancy weight, and I'm super out of shape. I just…it's part of me now. The need to exercise. Work out. Stay fit. Run off what I eat. I work out when I'm upset. If I'm super pissed off, I'll work my legs until I can't move. If I'm depressed, I'll work a heavy bag until it goes away."

Carter's eyebrows went up. "You box?"

"Kickbox. Used to. Haven't in a long time, though."

"I'd like to see that," he said. "It'd be hot."

I laughed, blushing. "You have a heavy bag?"

He shrugged. "Not yet. But I'll get one now." He rested his hand on my waist. "You're beautiful the way you are, right now. I want you to feel good about yourself, so if there's any exercise equipment you need, let me know. But you don't need it. You're gorgeous, okay?"

I shook my head. "You're sweet, Carter. Thank you."

"But you don't believe me?"

I sighed. "Yes, and no. I know you believe that, and I know your feelings are genuine. But that doesn't change how I feel. It doesn't change the fact that I need to work out to feel okay about myself. I'm not as worried about my weight as I used to be. I'm not panicked or comparing myself to Ever, or watching my pants size. I just have to feel in shape."

He bobbled his head side to side. "I get that. I feel the same way."

"The other thing is, I'm getting bored. I need to find work." I glanced at Carter to make sure he didn't misunderstand. "I love being here, and I love your house and I love how things are, but I need to be busy."

Carter took my coffee again and sipped it. "I need more coffee. I've drunk most of yours." He stood up and held out his hand for me. We walked hand in hand up to the house, and he made us both coffee. "So, give music lessons. It's something. There's always kids around here, and I bet you'd get some pretty steady clientele with only a little advertising."

It turned out he was right. I used Carter's massive iMac to make a flyer: *Private cello lessons with Eden Eliot, Cranbrook Academy educated, first chair cellist. To inquire, call 248-555-3456.* I included a close-up photograph of Apollo's bridge, and my official headshot in the ad, printed out a few, and the next time we ventured downtown for dinner I posted them in a few places, leaving them in restaurants and bars and music stores.

Within a week I had my first client, a little eight-year-old girl named Annie. I developed a relationship with the proprietors of the music gear stores, so I could refer my clients to a rental facility. I taught out of the cabin three days a week, and I made a hundred and fifty dollars a week. It wasn't much—not enough to sustain me on my own, but it was something. It was my own thing, and it kept me busy while Carter tended to the vineyard and the tasting room and delivered art pieces to clients.

Weeks passed in that slow-fast taffy way time has. Carter took me to the doctor for my six-week, post-natal checkup. He stayed in the waiting room for the actual vaginal exam, thankfully. I wasn't quite ready to include him in that kind of thing yet. I wanted to be, though.

The doctor tugged off his rubber gloves, tossed them in the trash, and washed his hands, then turned to address me. "You're in perfect health, Miss Eliot. You're clear to resume exercise, sexual activity, what-have-you. If you feel any unusual discomfort or bleeding, however, please call the office immediately. Otherwise, you're good to go." He leaned back against the counter. "Will you be going on any form of birth control?"

I nodded. I'd thought about that. "I think I'd like to go with an IUD, actually."

A few minutes later, I was on birth control, with a clean bill of health, and ready to go. I thanked him and left with Carter, feeling relieved, excited, and more than a little nervous. As we drove back to the marina, Carter clearly wanted to ask how it went, but didn't seem to know how. I decided to spare him.

"Everything's fine," I said. "I can go back to working out, and…whatever."

"Good. I'm glad you're healthy," Carter said.

To celebrate, he took me to The Boathouse, a beautiful, upscale restaurant overlooking the West Arm. We ate rich, delicious food and drank expensive wine, and talked about anything and everything except what my all-clear meant for us.

I was thinking about it, though. I was thinking about how it would happen. Would he wait for me to start something? Should we ease into it the way teenagers did, gradually? No, that wouldn't work. We were both adults and totally aware of what came after kissing. I didn't want to be the one to start things between us; I wanted him to. I wanted to feel pursued by him. He'd been a perfect gentleman for months—now it was time for him to show me his dirty side. His passionate and loving and voracious side. It was time for me to show him *mine*. It had been buried for so long, suppressed and ignored and pushed away, that it felt like a distant memory—like an old me, somehow. But I realized I'd changed. I wasn't the same woman I'd been before Ever's accident. That single event had changed all of us, each of us in different ways.

I wanted to think I was smarter, wiser, and more mature now.

Maybe not. All I could think of was getting Carter home and finding out what he'd do. How he'd handle this all-clear. Would he shy away? Want to wait? Would he pounce on me as soon as we hit the kitchen? Or maybe even sooner. Maybe he'd be so overcome by need for me that he'd ravish me on the boat.

I almost laughed. Not likely. He'd be waiting for some kind of signal from me, I knew.

He paid the tab, and led me by the hand to his boat docked at the marina connected to The Boathouse. He climbed aboard and started the engine while I untied us, a routine now familiar to us both. He'd taught me the proper knots, and I tied us up when he pulled into the slip, and untied us when we pulled out.

The ride across the rolling waves, lit orange and pink by the setting sun, was quiet and tense. Carter seemed uncomfortable, at loose ends. As if he didn't know what to say, how to act. I knew he wanted me. I'd felt his gaze, felt the heat in his eyes, felt his hands on my waist, going lower until he chickened out. He'd told me he wanted me. But he was too aware of my past to push it on me.

I was different, though. So different. I'd approached sex casually throughout the end of high school and most of college. I'd always wanted more from it, wanting it to be special and meaningful. It just hadn't happened yet. It had meant *something* with Cade, just not what I wanted, and not what he wanted. Now, after nearly a year of abstinence, I was nervous. Anxious. Carter and I had been skirting this issue for so long that it was now a big deal. We'd been so clear about the boundaries of our relationship that crossing that line would be a big step. And for me, that step had to be into something meaningful. I couldn't go back to doing the walk of shame. I couldn't go back to one-night stands with frat boys and two-day benders with art majors. I'd been through too much to treat myself and my life and my body so casually.

And *we'd* been through too much to treat my relationship with Carter so casually. If we crossed that line, it would mean something. A very, very important something.

He'd been there for me through everything. He'd taken care of me, done a hundred-thousand-dollar remodel for free, because he liked me. He'd held my hand as I'd delivered a baby. He'd taken me to his parents' house for Christmas. He'd brought me to his home, which I'd realized was a very sacred place to him. It was his private place, his lair. And he'd brought me here. He'd slept next to me night after night for a month and a half, and never once tried anything, nor had he made me feel bad or uncomfortable about it.

With the island just coming into view, the sun a huge orange ball to our left, I realized something: Carter loved me. He wouldn't have done everything he'd done if he didn't. He'd never asked me for anything in return. Not once. Such selflessness only came from a place of love.

Did I love him back?

I asked myself the question, addressed the deepest part of my heart. I asked my mind, my soul. I asked my body. *Do I love Carter Haven?*

The answer was immediate: Yes.

I slid off my chair, reached across him, and pulled the throttle back to a stop. Carter let me do it, an interested expression on his face. The boat rocked forward as our momentum slowed, and the wind of our passage faded to a slow, warm breeze. I turned Carter's captain chair to face me, pushed between his knees. He knew something significant was happening but, in true Carter fashion, he didn't ask any questions; he simply wrapped his arms around my waist, lower than he'd ever dared hold me before, his forearms resting on the bell of my hips, and stared up at me. His ice-blue eyes were hot and intent, burning like pale fire.

I leaned into him, pressing my breasts to his chest. Curled my hands around the back of his head, cupped his nape, dipped in to kiss him.

"I just had an epiphany." I spoke with my lips brushing his.

"Oh, yeah? What's that?" His hands played on my back, on my waist, on my hips.

"You're in love with me."

His chest swelled, and his head tipped back to assess me. "Yes. I am."

I brushed my fingers through his hair, the way he did to me. The wind had tousled his thick beautiful black hair until it was a mess across his brow. I smoothed it aside with my middle fingers, the way he did to me. I brushed my thumb across his cheekbone. Caressed his jaw with my palm. Leaned in and kissed the corner of his mouth. His lips, quickly. The opposite corner. His cheekbone. His eyes, each in turn, which closed as he sighed, and then I kissed his forehead, slow and softly and with great meaning. Then, at last, I pulled back, met his eyes.

"I love you." I said it evenly, smoothly, although my heart was hammering.

Carter's fingers tightened on my hips. "I've loved you since Christmas. Seeing you with my family? That was what told me it was for real, forever. I'd been fighting it before that, falling for you." His mouth moved on my lips, his breath a hot whisper. "But seeing you with my family, how absolutely perfect you fit in with us all, that was the day I knew."

"You never let on."

He shook his head. "I couldn't. You had to love me for yourself, not because I'd...been your friend. Because I'd been there. If I'd let on, I was afraid I'd scare you away. I was afraid you'd feel pressured to do something you weren't sure about."

I nodded. "Probably smart." I sat on his lap. "I just want you to know this isn't directly about the appointment. About what that means. I was just thinking, you know, about us. About myself, and how much I've changed since I came up here. Since I met you. And I thought about everything you've done for me without ever asking for anything in return, and I realized you could only have done all that if you loved me. And it made me ask myself if I felt the same. And I do. With all my heart." I took his hand and turned his palm to touch the left side of my chest. "And I'm terrified. What if…what if I don't know how to love you? I've never been in love before. And I feel like telling you this is putting…god, everything I am, everything I want, in your hands. Like I'm totally trusting you. I'm opening up and showing you part of me that I've never even seen myself."

Carter left his hand where it was to feel my heartbeat, and took my hand to place my palm so I could feel the mirrored hammering in his chest. "You feel that way because that's exactly what love is. Giving yourself, with all your faults and vulnerabilities, to someone else, trusting that they'll treasure what you're giving them." He let those words sink in. "I'm telling you right now, Eden, that I treasure it. I can't…I don't have enough words to tell you what your love and your trust means to me. I'll just have to take all the time in the world to show you."

I sniffed back tears of roiling emotions. "God, Carter. Could you be any more perfect?"

He laughed. "Yes, I could. I'm not perfect."

"You seem that way to me."

"I hope to stay that way, for you." His brow furrowed, and his eyes narrowed. "But I won't. For example, I'm going crazy right now. I want to kiss you so badly, but I don't dare because if I do, it'll end up with us on the floor of this boat. And you deserve better than that."

I breathed in his breath. Curled my fingers into his shirt. "See, here's the thing, Carter. That *is* perfect. That's what I want. On the floor of this boat. On the counter in the kitchen. On the couch. In your bed, with candles and roses. In the gazebo, as the sun sets. At dawn, on your weight bench. Anywhere, every-where. All the time. So, if that's what you're tempted to do, then do it. Give in to temptation. Because now, it's perfect. It's what I've always wanted, but I finally feel like it's okay to have it."

Carter sucked in a breath, and then his eyes closed slowly, as if summoning reserves of resistance. "Babe, I promise you, someday, I'll take you on the floor of this boat. But not this day. I've waited for you for months. When I make love to you for the first time, it's going to be perfect and beautiful, and it's going to last all night. It's not going to be a quick tumble on the floor of my Bayliner."

I was pleased by his answer. I didn't want our first time to quick and rough either. I wanted that with him, but not for our first time. "Then get us home."

He held me on his lap, shoved the throttle forward so the boat tipped back and the engine roared. He held me around the waist with one arm, as if afraid I would try to escape, piloting with the other hand. I leaned into him and held onto his neck, inhaling his scent, breathing in the essence of Carter, loving the excitement that thrilled through my blood, the anticipation boiling low in my gut, loving the feel of his hand sliding possessively now over my hip and brushing low to caress the upper bell of my ass. I loved the easy way he guided the boat through the water, cutting the engine at the perfect moment so momentum brought us to a soft bump at the boat-house. I loved the powerful way he lifted me to the dock and the impatience in the way he led me in to the kitchen.

I really, *really* loved the way he closed the kitchen door behind us and then halted, his hand on the glass, the other on my hip, pressing me back against the door, hot hunger in his eyes. I thrilled with need when his hips pinned me to the door, and I gasped with my own fierce heat when I felt the thick ridge between our bodies. I lifted up into his kiss, clung to him and shook as he kissed the breath from me. His hand curved around to cup my ass, and I gloried in that touch.

I palmed his spine, under his shirt, pushing the cotton up and over his head, off. He stopped me there, though. "Not yet," he whispered. "I want—I want to get a few things ready."

"I *am* ready," I protested.

He laughed. "I know. But I want to…god, just trust me, okay? I want to do this right. Just give me a few minutes."

I let go of him with a sigh. "I trust you. Do what you gotta do, but don't be long."

"I won't."

"Should I do anything to help?"

He shook his head. "Just be you. Just be sexy, perfect you."

I blew a raspberry. "Sexy, perfect me might need a few minutes to *get* sexy."

He shook his head at me, frowning. "Eden, baby. You're a fucking siren right now, right this minute. The only thing you have to do to get sexy is to breathe."

I pushed at him. "Thanks, babe. Now go do your mysterious mission."

I'd never used a term of endearment before. Words like *honey*, or *sweetie*, or *babe* usually made me wince. But now I understood. Carter started away and darted back to steal a kiss, and then was gone, heading up to the turret bedroom. I had a brush and makeup in my purse, and packed away in one of my boxes was my collection of "depressed Eden needs to feel sexy" lingerie that I hadn't worn since Ever was in a coma. Maybe it was time to see if I could fit into that. It would probably suck if I couldn't, but it was worth a try.

I dug through the boxes that were still piled in a closet off the kitchen, and eventually found what I was looking for. I chose a set of black lace Victoria's Secret bikini-cut panties and a front-clasp push-up. I ducked into the ground-level bathroom, shed my clothes, and pulled on the underwear. A little tight, but doable. Not pinching off my circulation, and I didn't look like I'd stuffed myself into them. Good. The bra would probably make him hyperventilate. It was already a push-up, and my still-bigger-than-normal tits overflowed the confines of the lace. I stared at myself in the mirror. I looked good. Still a bit heavier than I'd like. I still had some stretch marks and extra skin, but it would either go away on its own, or not. Nothing I could do about it. If he loved me, he'd love me despite those things. I brushed out my hair, teased it out a bit, leaving it loose. The roots were awful. I'd have to re-dye my hair soon, as I'd neglected it for too long. Yet…for the first time since I was a preteen, I didn't want to. Maybe instead of platinum blonde, I'd go back to black. I put on some makeup, just some light blush and lip stain and eyeliner.

Hanging between my breasts was the pendant Karen had given me. *Courage* was facing out, *Trust* pressing against my chest. Rather fitting, really.

I took a deep breath, and left the bathroom. All the lights had been turned off while I was in the bathroom. A single candle burned on the kitchen counter. There was a torn scrap of paper with Carter's handwriting: *follow the light*.

I glanced at the stairway, noticed another candle burning on the bottom step. I left the candle burning on the counter and picked up the one on the stairs and ascended to the living room. Another candle burned on the coffee table, with another note: *maybe some music to set the mood*. There was a remote for a Bose iPod dock. I hit the power button, and then "play." Acoustic guitar floated up, accompanied by a single male voice, breathy and soulful, joined after a few beats by a woman's voice. The song was "Cripple Me" by Elenowen. I listened for a few moments, and then focused on yet another candle flickering in the darkening gloom of lowering night. It sat on the bottom step of the stair leading up to the turret. I took that candle in my other hand, carried them both up the spiral staircase to the bedroom.

I loved his bedroom. It was circular, with huge windows letting in the starry light and silver moon glow. Soft off-white plush carpeting sank under my feet, the walls painted a pale pastel green that was still somehow masculine. The furniture was dark and heavy and sleek, setting off the color of the walls. The music was faintly audible, the romantic and haunting melody floating gently up from below us. Several more candles burned in the otherwise darkened room, on the bureau and the nightstands. Carter stood in the center of the room, lighting another candle. He was still shirtless, clad in nothing but faded blue jeans. I felt my core heat up and tighten as I watched him light the candle, the muscles in his broad back rippling as he set the candle on the counter in the bathroom.

God, he was gorgeous. Muscled, but not bulky. Lean, hard, and powerful, but graceful and quick. Thick black hair that needed cutting in the most adorable way. Pale blue eyes shining out from sun-dark skin, sharp and beautiful features, strong hands.

And he was here with me. Mine.

He turned to look at me, and I realized he'd known I was there the whole time. His nostrils flared, and his eyes raked over me. "I hope this is okay," he said. "I wanted to…give you what you deserve."

I melted. "It's…more than perfect. It's overwhelmingly perfect." I smoothed my hands over my stomach, feeling self-conscious, wondering if I'd pushed it coming up in lingerie.

"You're overwhelmingly perfect," he said, his voice a husky murmur. He tossed the lighter on the bureau and moved toward me in a predatory stalk. "So perfect. So beautiful. God, Eden. I'm dying here."

I stood where I was and let him approach me, my hands splayed over my belly. I knew I was doing it to cover the residual stretch marks, and I knew I should stand with confidence and pride and all that, but I just couldn't. I'd never worn lingerie for anyone before. It had always been unnecessary. My knees were shaking and my palms were sweating, and I was afraid he'd suddenly change his mind, and keeping my hands over my stomach was simply something I couldn't fight, not with all the other nerves shooting through me.

Carter tilted his head, listening to the music. "'Save me,'" he said, "I love the lyrics to this song."

He was inches away from me, not touching me, and I wanted, needed, his touch, but I listened to the song anyway. *Promise, promise to never leave...*god. So poignant.

I tilted my face up to look into his eyes. "I wanted to do something for you. I knew you were doing something ridiculously romantic, and I couldn't just show up in jeans and T-shirt, no makeup, hair a mess. I wanted to look at least a little sexy for you."

Carter literally growled. His hands floated over my ribs, just beneath my bra. Slid down my sides. Around to my back, up over my shoulders, down my arms, exploring my skin. Down to my hips, over the lace to my ass. He cupped my backside, pulled me to him. "'A little sexy.'" He repeated my words

as if reciting something absurd. "Eden, baby. You…
you take my breath away. From the first time I saw
you on the beach, you've taken my breath away. Like
this? In that fucking amazing lingerie, with your hair
like that and your eyes all smoky? Jesus, Eden. I could
die now a happy man, just having gotten to see you
like this."

"Don't die yet, though," I said, unable to stop the
smile of flattered pleasure from curving my lips. "I
have plans for you."

He murmured a rumble of interest. "Oh, yeah?
What's that?"

I lifted up on my toes and just barely, oh-so-softly
touched my lips to his. Tasted him, and spoke with
our lips touching. "It starts with this."

He pushed down to deepen the kiss, and then
wrapped his palm around my nape and simply and
purely ravished my mouth with his. I moaned as he
kissed the breath from me, kissed the sense from me.

I summoned my thoughts, my intentions, the
strength in my knees, and reached between us, flicked
open the snap of his jeans. "It also includes this," I
whispered.

"I like where this is going," he said. "What else?"

The zipper fell away easily, and he stepped out of
the jeans. I didn't even notice what he was wearing
under them, other than that they were black and soft
and tight. I couldn't help stealing a roaming caress

of his firm ass, and then ran my finger under the elastic of his underwear. "This." I kissed him, pulled away. "And this." I stroked him over the fabric of his underwear, and inhaled at the size of him.

"Jesus, Eden. Too much of that, and I'll embarrass myself."

I stroked him again, unable to resist. "It wouldn't be an embarrassment. It'd be beautiful. And perfect. Anything we do will be."

"True. But I want to feel you around me when that happens." He pulled away from me, just slightly. "I need to see you. All of you. Feel you. Touch you. Kiss you all over. Show you what real love feels like."

I felt my throat go thick and tight and hot at those words. "I need that, too. Please?"

He nuzzled his nose against my throat, and his hands traced the lace of my underwear. "Then let's get rid of these, as sexy as they are. I want what's beneath them."

He pressed his fingers to my flesh and slid the lace away with a long, slow caress down the sides of my legs, dipping at his knees to kiss down my chest. My head fell back as his lips found the swell of my breasts, and I could only hold onto his shoulders as he let my underwear fall to the floor. His hand lifted my foot, and I stepped free of them, kicking them aside. Never in my life had I felt so vulnerable being naked with a man, so bare. I let my hands fall to my sides as he searched the strap of my bra for the clasps.

"Front…" I murmured.

His eyes went from mine to my boobs, fixed on the front-clasp. His hands trembled as he freed the hook from the eye. I shut my eyes briefly as he brushed the straps off, and tried to swallow past the nerves as the undergarment fell away, into his hands. He set it aside, gently tossing it the floor. I fought the urge to cross my arms over my breasts, and failed.

He didn't say anything, though. He threaded his fingers through mine, brought my hands to his waist. The feel of his warm skin under my hands lit a fire inside me, a gentle flame that burned away some of my nerves. I was hot and cold, I knew, and I had to be confusing him. One second I was talking boldly and touching him, the next I was covering myself and acting like a fainting virgin.

"I'm sorry I'm so nervous all of a sudden," I said. "This just…it feels different."

"For me, too." He held up his hand between us so I could see the faint tremor. "See?"

I took his hand and kissed his palm, nudged into his touch. His eyes closed as I kissed his hand again, and then leaned in to taste his mouth. The kiss blossomed, swiftly turning to hungry devouring starvation. It was exactly what I needed, to forget my nerves at being naked with him. I wanted to be bare with him, to feel him. My nerves were over silly things, things I knew he didn't care about. I was being silly, and I knew it.

The kiss unfurled, and this time neither of us would stop it. I felt his hand slide down my bare back, and I felt him groan in his chest as he caressed my ass, cupping and kneading, exploring both cheeks and my thighs just below, up to my back and to my hips, touching me all over, kissing me until I was lost in the taste of his mouth and the stroke of his tongue against mine.

I sought his skin with my hands, tracing the muscles of his shoulders, the strong straight line of his spine, and I didn't deny myself the pleasure of tugging his underwear over his erection and letting it fall to the ground. I didn't take him in my hand yet, though, no, not yet. I pressed our bodies together, murmuring a moan as the hard hot thickness of his cock pressed against my torso. Instead, I lifted up on my toes to bring the kiss to him, cupping the cool firmness of his taut backside, exploring and caressing. At that moment, he was mine.

God, god, the way our bodies fit together was magic, pure fantasy. And we were still standing up together, as yet unconnected in that most intimate way.

Now, finally, I slid my palm between our tight-pressed bodies. Carter widened the space between us, allowed me room. The kiss ended, and he stared down at me as I slowly curled my fist around his cock. He sighed and groaned as my fingers sheathed his thick length.

I pulled my eyes from his to look at him. "God, Carter." I glanced back up at him, my heart pattering. I slid my fist down, and back up. "God*damn.*"

He was actually blushing. "What?"

I stroked him again, slowly, an intentional gesture. "All this." I smiled up at him, bit my lip. "Take to me bed. Please?"

He bent and took me in his arms, my head on his shoulder and my legs draping down over his arm. He set me on the side of the bed, leaned down and kissed me, and then stepped away.

"Let me look at you first. Can I?"

I summoned all my courage, all my desire to please him. I shifted to the center of the bed, drew up one knee, laid one arm over my head, on the pillows, the other resting on my hip. I turned slightly toward him, letting him see me. All of me. Stretch marks and all.

My own eyes weren't idle while he perused my body. He was glorious. There was no other word. In swim trunks he was sexy and handsome. Naked? Stunning. His muscles were cut into his body as if by a sculptor's blade, and his cock stood huge and long and straight against his belly, straining, bobbing as he breathed. I lay still for him, my breath coming hard and deep.

"Eden, god. Do you know what you look like?"

I shook my head. "Just…like me?"

"Like…" He shook his head, rested his knee on the bed beside me. "I don't have the words. I can't even make sense. That's how gorgeous you are. So sexy you've taken my words and my ability to think straight."

"Keep talking like that, I might just eventually believe you." I reached up to touch his cheek. "Especially when you look at me like that."

He smiled at me, nudging into my hand. I loved how he did that, as if my touch was the sweetest thing.

Carter eased onto the bed beside me, my palm on his face, and he leaned into me, slowly, kissed me as he had the very first time, with tenderness and exquisite thoroughness. I heard harmony in the distance, music soft and faint and providing a touch of mood. His body was long and lean beside me, his flesh hot, his hands rough-callused and roaming my body. He touched my ribs, my hips, my thighs. I sighed into his kiss as his hand moved up to cup my breast. Our foreheads touched as he watched his hand caress my breasts with reverence. One, and then the other. Exploring their fullness, thumb brushing across my nipple, tracing the undersides.

"God, Ever. You have the most perfect tits I've ever seen."

I could only grin. "I'm glad you like them."

"I want—"

"Don't tell me," I cut him off, "Show me."

He cupped one of my boobs and slid down to kiss the sloped mound of skin, his lips nearing my areolae. "I love this." He traced a finger around the dark circle. "And I really love this." He took my thick, erect, sensitive nipple between his finger and thumb. "I've spent more time than I'd like to admit wanting to do this. Wondering what your tits looked like bare for me."

"Do they live up to the expectation?"

"More. *Fuck,* so much more." He flicked a nipple with his tongue.

"So much more," I said, reaching down to grasp his thick cock in my fist. "That's exactly how I feel. You might have to go slow at first. I'm not sure I can take all this." I stroked his length as emphasis... and just because I loved stroking him. Feeling the ridges and ripples of his veins, feeling the soft springiness of the broad head, the rough curl of hair at the base. I delicately cupped his balls, explored them as well, and then back up. "I could touch you for hours and not get enough."

He huffed a laugh. "I'd be fine with that."

"But not tonight. I need to feel you inside me."

Carter's lips left my boobs, and he gazed at me. "I'm not done looking at you yet."

I frowned. "You've seen all there is to see, I'm pretty sure."

"Not quite yet." He traced his fingers down my thigh to my knee, pressed my knee to one side.

Oh. He wanted to see *all* of me. Even that? I couldn't be that pretty, I didn't think. I'd done stretches and muscle flexes and all the things I could think of to get my girly bits tight again, but I wasn't too sure I'd been as successful as I'd like. God. Oh, god. I couldn't deny him, wouldn't. So I let my leg fall aside, slid my heel away. Parted my legs for him, so he could see what there was to see.

I opened my mouth to say I wasn't sure what, but he shook his head. "I know you're going to say something about how you don't look how you used to, or how you'd like to. Save it, sweetness. I know you're self-conscious. And I know how much courage it took to let me look at you like this. So…thank you. Now just let me show you how beautiful you are to me."

He kissed my thigh, farther in. I grabbed his head, threaded my fingers into his hair. "Please, Carter. Not yet. Not that, not yet." I was close to tears. "I'm sorry. I'm sorry, I just…not yet."

He slid up my body and cupped my face, kissed me until I forgot what I was upset about. His hand caressed my ribs, my tits, brought the fire of need burning hot with gentle, insistent thrumming of my nipples. Heat built between my legs, pressure building in my core as his mouth plundered mine and his hands paid homage to my breasts.

I threaded my fingers through his and dragged our hands together down my body, between my thighs, and I delved our joined fingers into my cleft. He gasped into the kiss and leaned away to watch. His fingers curled into me, and I withdrew my hand, lifted my hips up into his touch in a silent urging. I wanted him, needed him. Needed this. His touch. Him, inside me. I needed to feel him explode in me. Needed to come apart around him. But it all started with his touch, there, on my aching clit.

He didn't hesitate. He circled my erect, sensitive nub, gave it slight and gentle flicks with his finger, delved in deep to search inside me, two fingers sweeping in, curling, finding that place that made me arch and ache and whimper, and he rubbed his fingertip along it. Retreated, coated my clit with my own juices and rubbed me in slow circles. I moaned, lifted off the bed, into his hand.

"God…Jesus fuck, Carter. You touch me perfectly. God, five seconds and I'm…oh, *shit*…I'm already close."

"Good," he murmured. "I've been close since the moment you took my pants off and touched me."

I gripped him, matching the slow circles of my clit with long plunging strokes of his cock. He quickened his circles as I began to push into his touch, urging him, needing more. And he gave me more. So much more. He brought me there, never hurrying, never touching too hard. Just right. Exactly what I needed, how I needed it.

I was on the edge, aching. But I stopped him. "You. I…I need you. I don't want to come without you."

He hovered over me. "Before we…before we do this." He leaned on his elbow, his face inches from mine. His eyes were sky-blue and impassioned. "I love you, Eden. I don't want you to hear it from me after, or during. In the moment. I want you to hear it now."

"You always know what I need to hear." I held onto his ass, just because I liked the way it felt. "How do you always know?"

"I don't. I just say what *I* need you to hear. So you know me."

"I know you." I kissed him quickly, a swift peck, a flick of tongue. "I know you, and I love you."

He smiled, and bent down to kiss me, not as I had kissed him, quickly, but deeply, with ravening hunger. His knees went between mine, and I pulled him toward me by his butt. Dug my fingers into the muscle, my eyes closed, my mouth locked to his.

But again, moments before I had him where I needed him, he paused. "Are you—"

I interrupted him. "Yes. I'm protected."

"But we should use one anyway."

I groaned. "Yes. I don't want to, though. I want to feel you bare."

"Me, too. But…"

I nodded. "Yeah."

He slid off me, went into the bathroom, and rummaged in a cabinet under the sink. Brought out an unopened box of condoms. I watched him rip open a packet, and then took the rubber from him, met his eyes as I rolled it down around him. His jaw clenched, and his muscles tensed at my touch.

I lay back on the pillows, reached for him. He settled over me, about to say something. I shushed him with two fingers over his mouth. "No more talking. Put your cock in me. Please, Carter. I need to feel you inside me. I'll go crazy if I don't get that right now."

One hand a fist beside my ear, the other cupping my hip, he slid against me. I reached between us, gripped his cock in my hand and brought his tip to the entrance of my pussy. Our eyes met, and I licked my lips, and then he shifted forward at the same time that I lifted up.

Slowly, perfectly, he penetrated me. He slid deep. He filled me. I arched up and cried out, a wordless sound of raw pleasure. He buried his face in my tits and moaned, back arched and flattening as he glided into me until I was full of him and panting at the aching burn of the way he stretched me.

I held him in place, needing a moment to get used to him. He waited, flush to me, breathing hard, muscles tensed. I had a feeling he needed a moment as much as I did.

I held his head against my breast, pushed him slightly to the side, lifted my tit to his mouth. He gave me what I wanted, the wet pressure of his mouth, suckling hard. When the tugging heat was too much, I clawed my hand on his ass and pulled at him, wrapped my legs around him, and pulled.

"Move with me, Carter."

He lifted up to meet my eyes. He pulled back and thrust deep, and I had to force my eyes open, needing to see his expression as he moved inside me. It wasn't a rhythm we set, then, it was a mutual heartbeat. It was union. He thrust, and I met him, he pulled away, and I crushed against him. We gasped and we cried out each other's names.

He leaned in to kiss me, breathed. "Come with me, Eden. Come with me, love."

I clutched his shoulders with all my strength and whimpered. "Now. Now. Yes, Carter, now. Please come now."

Together, we shattered.

The End

epilogue: the cadence of life

Caden

Ever,

It's been over three years since I've written you a letter. Three years. So much has happened in those years. The art gallery, Cadence turning two, Eden and Carter's wedding. A thousand day-to-day memories. You, putting on that lotion. Cadence taking her first steps. Laughing as I swing her over my head. You and me, in our bed, in the starlight.

I've drawn you so many times. You don't even know. Someday I'll show you my stash of 2 a.m. sketchpads. There's a dozen of them, all full of you, naked in our bed. You have this thing you do. After we've made love and we fall asleep, you get hot. You kick off the blanket, and you put one leg under the sheet, the other above it. You lie on your stomach, one arm beneath the pillow, the other curled beside your cheek. I wake up to pee, and there you are. Like that, so, so beautiful. And I just have to draw you.

It's been three years, and I hope I've proved that I love you, and only you. But I need to keep proving it. I need the rest of our lives to prove it. To make sure, absolutely sure, that you know. Maybe by the time we're ninety you'll really understand how deeply and madly I love you. How thankful to whatever there is, or isn't, out there that you came back to me.

You came back, Ever. I thought I'd lost you, twice. And you came back.

I'll never be able to pay that debt. It is a debt, you know. I owe you my very soul. And I'll spend every moment of my existence loving you to repay that debt.

Yours,

Forever and always and after forever,

Cade

I read the letter out loud, with the surf crashing beside us. It was an hour before sunset on a beach on St. John. Ever was dressed in a simple, elegant knee-length dress, strapless, white. Her black hair fluttered in the wind.

At her side stood Cadence, two and a half, her amber eyes wide, going from me to Ever and back. "Mommy?" She only had once voice: loud. "Daddy crying? Daddy sad?"

Ever knelt and kissed Cadence's cheek. "He's happy, baby." She whispered in her ear, a loud stage-whisper. "But I bet if you gave him a hug, it would make him even happier."

Cadence trotted over to me, jumped at me with the kind of complete abandon only a child is capable of. I lifted her, clutched her to me. Her little arms went around my neck. A sloppy kiss made my cheek wet, and my eyes wetter. I choked back the emotion as I held my little girl. My wife stood in front of me. She held a piece of paper, and she read from it.

"Cade. My Cade. I think I loved you from the first time I saw you standing there at Interlochen. You were so tall, and so handsome, and I wanted you to like me. But life brought us other people, and other places, and I learned then how much I would love you, when you finally found me. I remember our first kiss like it was yesterday. I was painting."

Cadence wiggled, and I let her down. She scampered off, getting her toes wet and the hem of her dress. I watched her, and I listened to Ever.

"You knocked on my door, and you kissed me. Lady Antebellum was playing. You kissed me, and I knew then that I'd never love anyone more. I never could, and I never will." She stopped, breathed. "Cade, baby. My love. My one true love. You and I have been through so much together. We faced death together, and we came through it. We both learned to walk and use our hands all over again. We even had to learn to love each other, and to forgive each other, and to forgive ourselves. We've learned how to be parents, and how to be lovers while being parents. And that's quite a trick, let me tell you. And through it all, you've been so devoted to me, and to Cadence. You've spent every moment trying to prove yourself." She paused, took my hand, and recited the rest from memory. "And now, Caden, you have to listen to me. You have to know. I don't doubt you. I've never, ever, doubted you. Not for a moment. You don't have anything to prove. You're mine, and I'm yours, and that's all there is."

I took her hands as she folded the letter and handed it off. "I love you, Ever. You and only you. Forever."

She leaned in, kissed me, and backed away. "I love you, Cade. Forever, and after forever."

There weren't many people on the beach with us. Eden and Carter. Ever's and my business partners in the art gallery in Birmingham, Lance and Irena. Carter's brothers and parents. They all clapped as Ever and I kissed again. It was a kind of vow renewal, a second wedding. The first had been so small, with just Eden there. Now we had so people in our lives--—friends, family. Loved ones. A life. And we wanted to make public our commitment to each other. Also, it was a good excuse to go to the Caribbean on the honeymoon we'd never had.

I noticed Eden watching Cadence as the ceremony ended and the party began. Eden had cut her hair to chin length, and let it go back to black. It made her look totally different, in a good way. She was happy, I knew. That was all that mattered. Carter's family vineyard was quickly becoming one of the most successful wineries on the Michigan peninsula, and was gaining recognition on a national level. Eden had finished her degree and taught private lessons while she finished her master's in education. Her plan was to teach at Interlochen. She'd also recorded her solo suite and was selling it independently on iTunes and other avenues, including a music video she'd made and put up on YouTube.

She seemed happy but more than that, at peace. As I was. Ever and I had made friends with another artist couple, and together we'd opened a gallery, displaying our own artwork and that of other local talents, scouted by all four of us. It gave us all an outlet for our art, and a chance to interact with artists, as well as providing a surprising amount of income.

None of us had forgotten what had happened. It was a couple of months before Ever and I saw Eden again, but with time we all grew close once more. There was always awkwardness between Eden and me, but it was bearable. The important thing, really, was that Ever and Eden were close. They talked on the phone all the time, and Skyped every once in a while. And of course, Ever, Cadence, and I spent a week or two during the summer up in Traverse City.

It took time for Ever to totally trust me, and for me to accept that it was okay to move on, to be happy. And I knew Carter and Eden had had their own difficulties. The decision to have children or not, mainly. They'd gotten married a year ago, in a quiet ceremony on the beach where they'd met.

My presence at that wedding had been odd, and slightly tense, but we'd gotten through it. We'd all faced the discomfort, pushed through it.

That was really the lesson in it all, though, wasn't it? Sometimes, all you can do is push through. Make mistakes and accept them. You can't always make the right decision. Sometimes there isn't one. Sometimes there's just everything getting all fucked up, and the only thing you can do is go through it and pick up the pieces on the other side.

Forgiveness is a choice, and so is love.

Learning all this, learning to choose and to live and to love, messing up and being forgiven and trying again, it's a rhythm. Getting up and living your life, despite hurting and despite mistakes, it's a pattern. It's the cadence of life.

Cadence. God, what a handful. She's every bit of both her mothers, her biological mother, and her mommy. To Cadence they are Mommy and Aunt Edie. She's wild and funny and spirited, showing a talent for art, if her finger painting is any indication. And her musical ear, the way she sings her favorite TV show songs, shows musical talent. But I might be prejudiced.

She's me, too. Her eyes, the way she sees things. She looks at you, and you know she's seeing *you*. That's a uniquely Cadence thing, that perceptiveness. She looks *into* you. She climbs up on your lap and she listens, and you know she's not just hearing, but really *listening*. And then she'll hop down and run off and try to feed her blocks to our very long-suffering Yorkie.

I never thought I'd be a parent. And I never thought I'd enjoy it. Having kids had never crossed my mind,. It was a "maybe someday" idea. But now, I'm all in. Totally sold out to that little girl.

And, of course, to her mommy.

author's note

All the Traverse City descriptions are accurate. If something is labeled by name, it's real. The only liberty I took was the island. Carter's mysterious island home is a fiction, sadly. I might move there myself, if it was real.

playlist

"Run For Your Life" by The Fray

"What Was I Thinkin'" by Dierks Bentley

"Misery Loves Company" by Three Days Grace

"One Day You Will" by Lady Antebellum

"Cripple Me" by Elenowen

"Save Me" by Elenowen

about the author

New York Times and USA Today bestselling author Jasinda Wilder is a Michigan native with a penchant for titillating tales about sexy men and strong women. When she's not writing, she's probably shopping, baking, or reading. She loves to travel, and some of her favorite vacations spots are Las Vegas, New York City, and Toledo, Ohio. You can often find Jasinda drinking sweet red wine with frozen berries.

To find out more about Jasinda and her other titles, visit her website: www.JasindaWilder.com.